"Non-stop action, pulse-elevating romance and a fast pace keep this book flowing smoothly. Damschroder definitely knows how to write one sexy, saucy, exhilarating tale."
—*RT Book Reviews,* 4 stars

"This is a *really* good story. Yes, the sex is hot, but the plot is even better. For all romance collections."
—*Library Journal*

"The action was incredible, the medical science was fun, and the forbidden romance was absolutely delicious."
—*The Romanceaholic,* 4 stars

"[I'd] never read this author, but I was so excited about how good this book was. The action is non-stop with some great suspense. There is the romance story line between Jason and Lark with some sizzling scenes between them (one of his side effects is extra nerves which makes him super-sensitive to touch...wowza!) but there is also a romantic story line between Matt and Jason's doctor which I enjoyed almost as much as the main one. All the main characters in this were extremely likable and I enjoyed reading their stories. Really just a fabulous book. I am going to have to look up more from this author!"
—*Smitten with Reading*

Also available from Natalie J. Damschroder and Carina Press

Fight or Flight
Behind the Scenes

Natalie J. Damschroder

ACCEPTABLE RISKS

carina press®

carina press®

ISBN-13: 978-0-373-00239-9

ACCEPTABLE RISKS

This edition published by arrangement with Harlequin Books S.A.

www.CarinaPress.com

Printed in U.S.A.

Dear Reader,

Several years ago, I wrote a superhero book that currently remains unpublished. In that book, when the heroine seeks help hiding (temporarily, of course) from the shadowy bad guys, she gets it from an equally shadowy character: Jason Templeton, her sister's boyfriend, who says he works for Hummingbird. That heroine's response was "*Whoa.* Hummingbird was a security company so large, successful and secret that everyone knew about them."

That line, contradictory and maybe even hokey as it is, sent a sizzle up my spine. I copied it into a new document and let my brain explore Jason and Hummingbird while I wrote other stuff. I usually write heroines who could have starred in *The Terminator,* so I wanted Lark Madrassa to be a little softer. Not weak by any means, but maybe out of her element. I found her when the scene with the gun cartridge (you'll know when I get there) popped into my head. Despite her father's career, she's not part of the world Jason inhabits. That's part of what he likes about her. Of course, her being his boss's daughter puts a damper on things, but only for a little while....

This book was more ambitious for me, with a secondary romance that grabbed me in the heart almost more than the main one did. I think in some ways I identify with Gabby more than any other character I've written. I hope you love her—and Matthew and Jason and Lark—as much as I do.

Thank you!

Natalie J. Damschroder

This book is dedicated to Margaret Henry—
Nanny—who embodied every admirable trait
I bestow in my heroines.

ACCEPTABLE RISKS

ONE

"SECTOR ONE, ALL CLEAR."

"Sector two, all clear."

"We've got an unidentified hotel employee in sector three," the third voice said.

Jason Templeton tapped the keyboard of his laptop to bring up the cameras for that sector. "Detain him."

"Already on it."

Jason watched Allison, his mission leader for sector three, and one of her agents close around the young man who'd just come out of one of the conference rooms. Allison hadn't activated her com, so he couldn't hear the exchange, but all three stayed relaxed as the guy showed his ID card, nodded, and removed his wallet from his back pocket. He slipped out another card—probably his driver's license—and handed it over. A few seconds later, he went on his way and Allison and the agent moved back to position.

"All clear, JT, he was on the list. He cut his hair yesterday and shaved his goatee. Looks a decade younger." She sounded amused.

"Thanks, Allie. I'm coming down with Matt and the client in a few minutes. Sweep the hallways and station two agents in the Madrid room."

"You got it."

"I'm clicking off. Buzz if you need me." Jason

turned to his boss and best friend as he came out of the bathroom in their top-floor hotel suite.

"Everything in place?" Matt rubbed his dark, silvered hair with a towel and automatically scanned the laptops lined up on the antique sideboard. "No flags?"

"So far, so good."

"Good." Matt turned away from the computers and leaned back against the desk. "For being a paranoid businessman, Kolanko isn't very logical."

"I know. But I couldn't convince him to hold this meeting in his offices." Hotels weren't easy to secure, even hotels used to hosting the world's leaders and other at-risk guests. But Hummingbird's job was to take the highest-risk locations and eliminate those risks. In fifteen years, they hadn't been compromised. Now their reputation was as much of a deterrent as their presence.

Normally, Jason ran a job like this one on his own. But Kolanko was one of their biggest clients, a weapons manufacturer with three dozen government contracts, most with the U.S. but some with countries the U.S. currently found less than friendly. He'd insisted on meeting military officials in a neutral location, despite Jason's advice to avoid public access. He'd also requested Matt oversee the meeting personally. Jason originally thought the guy just wanted to show off, but overseas tensions had risen lately, generating resentment between competing governments that both bought from Kolanko.

"Ready?" Matt checked his now smoothly combed hair in the mirror and straightened his suit jacket.

"As ever." Jason tapped his com onto open frequency. “Allie, we’re heading to the principle’s suite. We’ll be down in five.”

“Got it. We’re ready.”

As they walked down the plushly carpeted hall toward the elevators, Matt’s phone beeped. He pulled it from his inside jacket pocket and checked the display. “Dammit, I forgot to call Lark. She says she’s coming home next week.”

“Her fellowship is over?” Jason hadn’t seen Matt’s daughter in years, not since she left for college and a career that took her all over the world.

“Apparently.”

Jason shook his head. “You don’t know?”

Matt shrugged as he tapped out a reply to Lark’s text. Jason knocked on the door of Kolanko’s suite and one of their operatives opened it. He nodded at Jason and signaled to someone inside the room.

“Lark does her own thing,” Matt said. “Checks in once a week, tells me when she’ll be around. You know.”

Jason knew Matt wasn’t as cavalier as he sounded. When Lark’s mother had died a decade ago, Hummingbird—the company she’d named, claiming the incongruity would feed their mystique—demanded all of Matt’s attention. He could have pawned his daughter off on caregivers and private schools, but he’d helped her with her homework, chaperoned school dances, and tried to teach her the business. Though she’d become a botanist instead, they’d stayed close.

Something Jason tried not to envy. He hadn’t chosen to be alone, though many in his position did. A family had always been one of his goals. It hadn’t worked out so far, but he was only thirty-six. There was time.

Matt pocketed his phone and straightened as Kolanko and two gigantic bodyguards—not Hummingbird issue—came into the hall. Jason schooled his features. He disapproved of massive bodyguards. Sure, bulk meant strength. But it also meant losing flexibility, and their size, especially compared to the always-smaller protectee, screamed, "Target this!"

"We are ready?" Kolanko asked.

Jason checked in with Allison, who confirmed status quo. He started down the hall, Kolanko and Matt side by side behind him, followed by the bodyguards. Jason pressed the elevator button and scanned the foyer, making eye contact with his agent positioned in front of the window. Reassured that everything was fine, he turned back to the elevator as the door opened.

Kolanko started forward, but Jason flung out his arm, stopping him. The hair on the back of his neck prickled. "Wait." He drew his pistol and held it ready, barrel at the floor, while he studied the empty elevator.

"What is it?" Matt came up on his left and saw what Jason had seen. He drew his own weapon. The elevator floor was about an inch lower than the hallway floor. It hadn't been that way yesterday.

"Back to the room." Jason reached inside and yanked the stop button to hold the elevator, then radioed his explosives guy to investigate. By the time he reached the room with the others, everyone was on high alert.

"I do not have time for such shenanigans over such a trivial thing," Kolanko blustered as Jason holstered his gun and shut the door to the business suite. "This is an old hotel. Perfection is not anticipated."

"Maybe not from elevator cars," Matt responded implacably, "but it is expected from my people. If Jason thinks someone tampered with the elevator, someone probably tampered with the elevator."

"Are you the elevator repair guy?"

Jason could not remember the last time something had taken him by surprise. The small, high voice, coupled with a tug on his pants leg, made him jerk to the side and spin, his hand back on his weapon, before he realized it was a little girl.

Holy fuck.

He managed to keep the words inside his head. "Who are you?"

"I am Adrina. That's my daddy." She pointed at Kolanko. "If you're the elevator repair guy, how come you're in here?"

"I'm not the…never mind. Matt." He raised his voice over Kolanko's. Matt lifted a hand to stop the client's rant and turned his head, his eyebrows rising when he saw Adrina.

"Who's this?"

"She is my daughter. Ignore her."

"I'm afraid that's not possible, Mr. Kolanko." Matt's tone didn't change, but the temperature in the room dropped a few degrees. "Her presence compromises your security."

"How? She is no threat to any—"

"She's a variable. An unaccounted-for variable. You know better," he finished quietly, and the posturing, self-important businessman sagged.

"I had to bring her," he explained to Matt. "Her

mother will not allow her to be away from me, and this meeting—"

"Who else is here we didn't know about?" Matt demanded.

"My assistant, Bella." He motioned to a woman in a suit who stood near the windows, hands folded. "She was to remain in the suite with my daughter during the meeting."

Jason sighed. "Come on, Adrina." He held his hand down, and she reached up and took it. "Show me your room." It would be better if she didn't hear the rest of this conversation, and he doubted she'd remain in her room alone with all the excitement out here.

While the five-year-old chattered about her age, the ages of all her stuffed animals, and her mother, who was on a shopping spree in Prague, Jason quietly checked in with his team. Everything was normal in the conference corridor and the main lobby. Their expert was descending into the elevator shaft now.

"How old are you?" Adrina settled at a small table and resumed coloring a half-finished picture of what appeared to be a knight on a white horse.

"I'm thirty-six," he told her automatically. This room of the suite was an interior bedroom, no windows, one door. A secure trap.

"And the other man? The shiny one?"

Jason's mouth twitched. "You mean the guy with silver in his hair?"

She nodded. "It shines. So do his teeth. Not his suit, though. It is a good suit." She said this last solemnly, and Jason figured her mother was training her to be a professional shopper.

"Mr. Madrassa is forty-six."

"Does he have any children?"

"A daughter." Jason fidgeted.

"How old is she?"

"I don't know, twenty-five, maybe, twenty-six." Older than his image of her, he realized, which was barely out of her teens.

"Does she have any children?" She colored hard and fast, turning her sky purple behind the dark gray knight and white horse.

"No."

Allison's voice came over his com. "JT, they found something."

"Report."

"No explosives, but cables were cut. The weight of you big brawny men would have sent it plummeting."

He eased out a breath. "Were the brakes or fail-safes tampered with?"

"They're bringing in engineers. You'll be stuck up there for a while."

His neck prickled again. "No. Send me six men up the stairwell. We'll meet them on the way down. Have the rest clear the way to the parking garage." He moved away from the wall. "Adrina, honey, come with me."

She obeyed without question, taking his hand again until he passed her off to her father. Jason beckoned Matt to the side. He wasn't trying to keep anything from Kolanko, but he didn't want to frighten the little girl.

"Someone's trying to trap us up here." He told Matt about Allison's report. "We need to go downstairs, now."

Matt didn't question him. They hustled the others

out into the hall, Adrina taking Jason's hand again despite her father's presence. He let her, amazed at her calm acceptance. What had Kolanko exposed the poor kid to?

The hallway was empty. Jason led the way to the end opposite the elevator, shifting Adrina to his left to free his weapon hand and angling his body to block her as they neared the stairwell door. She let go and backed toward Matt and her father as Jason carefully opened the door and checked the landing.

"All clear."

They followed him into the cement-and-metal stairwell. Footsteps echoed up and down the rectangular shaft, the direction unclear. Jason kept his gaze up the last short flight to the roof, knowing an attack would come from that direction, to take them by surprise.

Allison came over the com. "They're almost to your floor, JT."

"They see anything?"

"Negative."

"Okay. Thanks. Matt, start down, take point. Bodyguards, flank your boss and the girl. Our men are coming up from below, so be alert but hold your fire. Actually, hold your fire no matter what," he added. "Ricochet." The bodyguards nodded and holstered their weapons. Jason held on to his, reluctant to give up the threat it presented to enemies, even if he wasn't willing to fire it in here.

The group started down, moving more slowly than Jason liked. He backed down the steps, tensing with each second that ticked by. He was missing something. He paused, listening hard over the clatter of dress shoes on concrete.

There was a faint, felt-rather-than-heard *whump.* The door on the landing they'd just left vibrated. Jason registered the explosion on some level other than his brain, and panic sped through him.

"Go! Go! Go!" he shouted, shoving his gun into its holster and racing down the steps. He hauled Adrina into his arms and followed Matt and Kolanko, letting the bodyguards take the rear.

The roar wasn't as loud as he expected, but the heat was intense. He ducked instinctively and grabbed the rail so he didn't stumble. Matt, one turn below him, looked up, his shocked face orange in the glow from above.

The heat receded, the noise abated, and they kept running. No one asked the obvious questions. Adrina clung to him, her face damp against his neck. He paused for a second to check her for injury, but she seemed unharmed, only scared.

He didn't blame her.

Chatter from his operatives, reacting to the blast and reporting in from their sectors, buzzed in his ear, only half processed. Someone shouted from below. He did a quick glance over the rail, keeping Adrina back. His men ran toward them, a few floors below.

"Here." Jason handed Adrina to her father. She tightened her hold for half a second before letting go.

He faced back up the stairs, waiting. He knew the blast wasn't the end of it. Thank God they had the floor to themselves, with orders to keep even housekeeping away unless summoned. There should have been no casualties. He tried not to think about the guys in the elevator shaft. Depending on where the explosives were on the floor…

There. A scrape of sound, maybe two flights up. Hard to tell, with his ears ringing and all the noise from below. But then he heard it again—just before a figure hurtled over the railing above, landing on the steps in front of him, already slamming a flat palm in his face.

Jason managed to deflect the blow, and the next one, and settled into a classic rhythm of block and strike. But his opponent had the advantage, backing him down the stairs, and was more skilled. Jason tried to sweep the man's legs and missed. Then they reached the landing, and his superior height allowed him to actually land a punch on the guy's cheek. The attacker's dark eyes gleamed as he fell back. He obviously hadn't expected street tactics. Jason allowed a grim smile. But he knew his opponent would adjust.

And he did. His foot kicked up at Jason's crotch. He dodged, off balance, and saw stars as the man shoved his head into the wall. Jason rebounded toward the rail and the abyss on the other side, but recovered and snapped a punch into the guy's nose.

And then, suddenly, there were three more. Jason fought fiercely, knocking out two opponents but knowing he wasn't going to win. His goal was simply to allow time for the others to get to safety. A blow landed on his temple, blurring his vision. He used his stagger to land a shoulder in the second guy's gut and was rewarded with a grunt, but a fist in his kidney banished his satisfaction. He gasped, trying to keep his feet, arms up to protect his face from the final strike.

But then Matt was there, at his back, turning him so they each faced one opponent. New energy infused him, and in short order both opponents were on the ground.

Jason panted, his hands clenched, waiting. Listening. These people were too determined to let it end here. But long minutes passed with nothing coming.

"Thanks for coming back."

"Thanks for staying." Matt didn't sound nearly as out of breath as Jason did. Unfair. Of course, he'd only fought one guy.

Without discussion, they started searching the men sprawled all over the stairs. Jason radioed down for pickup and for the police, who were already on site.

"No IDs," he said.

"Didn't expect any," Matt replied. "Kolanko and the girl are in—"

The only warning they had was a chip of concrete block hitting Matt in the cheek. Instinct had Jason in motion before the blood welled on his friend's face. He leapt up the two steps between him and Matt, shoving him back against the wall, out of the line of fire. Something hot pierced Jason's shoulder. He jerked, tripped over the legs of the attacker at his feet, and lost his balance.

He had only a moment to register the shock and horror on Matt's face before tipping backward over the railing.

TWO

LARK STOOD NEXT to her father at Jason's graveside, while the reverend said a few final words and the casket was lowered into the ground. All around them people wept, but aside from a moment in the church, while he gave the eulogy, her father hadn't broken. Yet to anyone who knew him well, which included Lark and probably half the agents here, he looked ravaged. It didn't help that her mother was buried here, a few feet away. He hadn't so much as glanced at Kelly Madrassa's grave. Simply because the memory compounded his pain? Or was it more complicated than that?

Her mother's death hadn't had the suddenness of Jason's. They'd seen it coming, the awareness that she'd be gone from their lives pressing down until the grief crushed them. But this loss had shredded her father, ripped something out of him. She'd never doubted his strength ten years ago. Now...now, she was less sure.

She accepted condolences as the service ended and everyone moved off toward the cars lining the cemetery road. Minutes ticked past and her father didn't move. Finally, chilled by the early-December air, she stepped closer and slid her hand into his.

"Daddy."

The quiet word seemed to snap Matthew back into himself. "I'm sorry, Lark. We can go." He folded his other hand over hers, but didn't tear his eyes away from the grave.

"Take as long as you need."

But he shook his head slightly and finally started walking.

"I don't think I can face the crowd at the house," he admitted, scanning the sea of dark clothing ahead of them. "Would it be too much to ask you to step in?"

"Not at all." She hesitated. "I didn't see Jason's parents."

"No. They didn't come."

Lark recognized by his tone that it would do no good to ask why. "All right. Anything I need to know? If people ask about his…fall?"

He flinched, but shook his head.

He was silent as the limo glided through the streets of suburban Virginia back to his house. The heavy car seemed to cocoon them from the world, but it offered no comfort. Instead, it held in the broody darkness. Lark held her father's hand, her gaze at the window, but not really seeing the world outside it.

She hadn't known Jason that well. Once she left for college, their paths didn't cross much. But she understood how important he was to her father. As important, in a different way, as her mother had been. Lark didn't have anyone who meant that much to her, except her father.

When the car pulled into the circular drive, the house was already full. Her father's assistant, Caitlyn, had arranged for the caterer and arrived early to let everyone in.

"Please pull around to the back of the house," Matthew instructed the driver, who followed the narrow drive to the space in front of the garage. The driver got out and opened the door for them, accepting Matthew's tip with a somber nod. Lark followed her father through the kitchen door into the tiny mudroom at the base of the back stairs.

"Thank you, sweetheart." He kissed Lark's cheek.

"Can I bring you anything?" she asked. "A plate of food, or a drink?"

"No, I'm fine. Just dealing with this—" he indicated the clusters of people in the kitchen and dining room, "—is more than enough." He disappeared up the stairs.

He wasn't even close to fine. Lark blew out a breath and braced herself to circulate.

Over the next two hours, she accepted so many hugs her back ached, and no drink alleviated her dry mouth. Finally, everyone had left except the clean-up staff and Caitlyn. The assistant took a stack of plates out of Lark's hands and set them back on the oak coffee table in the large living room. "Leave this stuff. That's why we hired people. You should go rest."

Lark rubbed her hand across her forehead, trying to ease the tightness that forecasted a headache. "*You* should. You were closer to Jason than I was." She'd been so focused on her father, she hadn't thought about that before. "You've done so much. I shouldn't—"

Caitlyn waved her down, her smile wan. "The distraction helped. I'm a doer. That's why I have this job in the first place." She looked around at the now-clean living room. The cleaning staff had been discreet but quick, wiping down surfaces and whisking away debris. Sounds of swishing water and clinking glassware drifted out from the kitchen. "They should be done soon. Are you staying long?"

"Just another couple of days. I can't miss more work than that, not right now." Ralph, Lark's boss, hadn't even wanted to give her that much, but her fellowship trip to Indonesia had brought Botanical Medicality enough promising new source material to keep them in R&D funding for years. That gave her a little clout. But Ralph suspected she was working on some things on her own, they'd fought about it, and he hadn't been in the mood to be generous when she requested time off. Her compound was developed from plants she'd obtained before going to work for BotMed, which fell outside the terms of her contract. She'd also sold it and wasn't officially working on it now. Bottom line, though, was that she couldn't afford to take extra time.

She looked up as her father entered, his shirt untucked and tie missing, hair mussed and the lines around his eyes strained. Guilt twisted her insides. He needed her. How could she leave him?

"I'm sorry, I didn't realize anyone else was still here. Caitlyn, thank you for everything."

"It's nothing. The least I could do." She looked dissatisfied by the clichéd words.

"It's a lot. And appreciated." He looked at his watch. "You go on home. We'll finish up here, and I'll see you in the office on Monday." As he walked her out, Lark thought maybe the time alone had helped him. His step seemed lighter, more natural. She started to follow, but held back when her phone rang. She checked the display—it was Carl.

"Hey, babe," he said when she answered. "How you holding up?"

She sank onto the soft brown suede sofa, her legs and back aching. "All right. Better than my father." Her feet had swelled inside the heels she rarely wore, and rejoiced when she toed them off. She barely held back a groan of pleasure.

"I'm sorry I couldn't come down with you."

"It's really okay." She'd never expected him to even offer. They'd only been dating a few months, and their relationship wasn't that deep. "I wouldn't have had much time for you, anyway. There were so many people." They talked for a couple of minutes about the funeral and the work that had kept Carl from flying down from Boston with her. Lark quickly wrapped up the conversation when her father came back into the room.

Whatever lightness she'd thought she'd seen had disappeared, replaced by murky despair. He settled into one of the matching armchairs as if uncertain he'd be able to rise again. "I'm sorry I left you to deal with everyone," he said.

"It's all right." She pushed to her feet and went to sit on the arm of the chair. "Do you want anything to eat? There's still plenty of food." She smoothed his hair and frowned when he felt warm to the touch. "Maybe some fruit, at least?"

"Not right now."

She bit her tongue. Nagging wouldn't force him to take care of himself. She'd have to be sneaky about it. But even then, she couldn't force him to eat or sleep, and she was only going to be here a couple more days. Maybe she could talk him into coming up to visit her in Boston. A change of scene had to be good, and being away might make it easier for him to pull out of himself.

"Who was that on the phone?" he asked.

Lark chewed her lip, taken off guard. "Just a guy from my building."

For the first time all day, her father looked straight at her. "Oh, yeah?" His mouth curved slightly. "Just a guy, huh?"

Lark couldn't help smiling back. "So far. Oh, stop," she said when he raised his eyebrows. "It's not serious, and probably won't be. Don't start with the whole 'you need a partner' thing." The words reverberated in the room and struck her in the chest, bringing immediate regret. He'd lost both people in his life that he'd considered partners. "I'm sorry, I didn't—"

"I know." He rested his hand reassuringly on her knee, but his gaze was troubled. "Lark, I hope you understand I wouldn't trade it for anything. Our friendship was worth enduring this, and so was my life with your mother."

"Of course I understand." She was grateful for the sixteen years she'd had with her mother, too. But she'd never had a best friend or anyone else she loved as much as she loved her father. Chances were good she'd lose him someday—a thought that left her cold to the bone.

He lapsed into silence again, staring as hard at the floor as he'd stared at the coffin. His fingers plucked at the piping around the edge of the chair arm. Lark's heart ached. Jason had been his best friend for ten years, and especially after her mother died, he'd been his rock. Now the only one he had to help him through was her. She was afraid she wasn't up to the task.

"Is he good to you?"

Lark started. "What?"

He looked up, his head turned to face her. "That guy on the phone. He a good guy?"

She shrugged and smoothed down the skirt of her black silk dress, thinking longingly of the comfy clothes in her suitcase upstairs. "He treats me fine."

"Would you tell me if he didn't?"

"No," she said without hesitation, and he laughed. "I can take care of myself, Dad, and you don't need to worry about me."

His eyes narrowed at her for a minute, then he nodded. "Okay. I guess I have to accept that."

"So you're going to run a background check."

He gave her a "well, duh" look. But again, the light moment didn't last. Lark watched the cloud settle over him again, and her eyes prickled. With nothing else she could think to do, she opened her mouth to offer to fix him a dinner plate, but he spoke first.

"If you're okay here for a few hours, I'm going to go to the office for a while."

"But you shut down today," she said, "for the funeral. You've got to be exhausted."

He shook his head and pushed to his feet. "Not nearly enough. I need to keep my mind busy. Plus, there are things..."

She hugged him, understanding. Fallout from the explosion had been swift, with canceled contracts and long-time clients questioning Hummingbird's effectiveness. If anyone could hold the business together and salvage his powerful reputation, it was her father. But the man who'd helped him build both was gone, and she was worried he would never recover.

"Dad, it's okay to take some time off. One day won't—"

"Yes, it will." He kissed the top of her head. "Don't wait up, I might be late."

She watched him go, an awful foreboding sinking into her.

The next two days were no different. Lark struggled to find ways to help him. She made his favorite foods, brought meals to the office, tried to get him to talk to her by opening up herself. Nothing seemed to work. He grew more despondent, until she got Caitlyn to cancel a meeting, trying to force her father to come home early. When he realized what she'd done, however, he just put on a mask and pretended he was fine.

The only reason Lark left was because Ralph refused to let her take any more time off. She was in the middle of too many promising projects that BotMed claimed ownership of, or she'd have considered quitting and moving back to DC. So she went home and launched into plan B. Which, of course, was just as unsuccessful as plan A. Weeks went by, and her father refused every request to come visit. After a few months, he'd stopped returning her calls. He left messages on her home machine when she was at work, false-cheery updates that didn't fool her. And he knew it, or he wouldn't be afraid to talk to her directly.

Lark talked to Caitlyn, his assistant, a lot. She gave Lark all the details her father left out of his messages. He was fighting hard to hold on to the business, and things were getting worse, with competitors circling Hummingbird like wolves. Lark hadn't felt so helpless since she watched her mother getting sicker every day.

On the six-month anniversary of Jason's death,

Caitlyn tricked Matthew into taking Lark's call. Lark didn't like the subterfuge, but she wanted to hear her father's unguarded voice for herself. She made the call right before she left work for the day.

"Madrassa," he answered. His tone was brisk, almost impatient.

"I'm told your company is the best. I'd like to give you a chance to prove it."

Silence. Then, "What are you doing, Lark?"

She sighed. "Finally. You're talking to me. Don't even try to deny it," she added when he started to lie. "I'm coming down there if you can't convince me you don't need me."

"Don't ever doubt that I need you, Lark."

She had to choke back a sob of relief. "Then why all the avoidance? The stupid voice mails where you pat me on the head and tell me not to worry?"

He chuckled. "That's why. I knew you'd see through me. I can't hide anything from you."

"So it's been bad." Her throat tightened, and she decided she had to fly back down there.

"Yeah, it has been. But it's getting easier. We picked up a few new contracts, and a couple of clients have come back." Papers rustled in the background, followed by the clack of keyboard keys. "If you knew all the details of this stuff, you'd worry, but you can't do anything about it. Why put you through that?"

"How about because I love you?"

"Good. So you see my point."

Lark had to laugh now, and the fact that he could joke made her feel a lot better. "I miss you, Dad. Stop hiding from me."

"I promise." The noise on his end picked up. "I

have to go, I have a meeting. We'll talk this weekend, okay?"

Lark let him go and locked up her office before heading out, finally relieved that he might be pulling out of the funk. A little while later, she walked in the front door of her apartment building.

"Evening, Miss Madrassa." The guard at the desk in the lobby tipped his hat to her, but barely glanced away from the monitors on his desk.

"Hi, Bill." She leaned over the counter a little, curious about his uncharacteristic focus. "Problem?"

"Nope."

She shook her head. He wouldn't tell her the truth. He'd met her father the day he helped her move in and assured him that Lark couldn't live in a safer building. In his mind, that meant making sure she felt safe, too.

"Then you must be watching the game," she teased. He snorted his response, but still didn't look away.

"You have a good night," he called after her as she headed for the elevator bank.

"You, too." She used her key card to activate the car, whose doors opened immediately.

"Hang on! Hold the elevator!"

Lark rolled her eyes and reluctantly hit the "door open" button as it glided closed. A hand slid between the panels, and Carl grinned at her as he squeezed through. He wore a suit and carried a briefcase, apparently coming home from working late.

"Thanks."

"No problem." She pressed the button for her floor and spared him a smile. He beamed back. Surprised and a little disconcerted, she pressed twelve for his floor. "You look happy."

"I'm always glad to see you."

"O-kay..." They'd broken up three months ago by mutual agreement, and the few times they'd run into each other since, Carl had been coolly polite.

"I've missed you." He shifted to face her, raising his arm to brace it on the wall. He obviously thought it showed off his body better. It did, but the calculation killed the effect.

"Carl—"

"No, wait. I think we made a mistake. I mean, I think about you all the time. We have so much in common. How about I come up and we can talk about it?"

She stared at him, willing the elevator to climb faster. "No, I'm sorry. You can't come up to talk about it. There was no mistake. We're wrong for each other. We agreed."

"We had chemistry." He eased closer and stroked the backs of his fingers down her cheek. "That doesn't disappear with logic, you know."

"You've got to be kidding me." She laughed and nudged him back. "We don't have any chemistry."

Carl frowned and tucked his dress shirt more securely into his suit pants. "Then maybe we can be friends. I miss talking to you about stuff."

Lark shook her head as he rambled on about being more interested in her work and sharing more important things than sex. They had no more to offer each other as friends than they had as lovers. She had no idea what was going on with him, but hoped it was temporary. He'd never made her want to call him an idiot before, but he sure did now.

"Goodbye, Carl." She shook her head when he

looked perplexed at the open doors. "This is your floor," she prompted.

"Oh, right. Okay, then I'll call you."

The doors closed, and she sagged against the back wall. "That was weird."

She shook it off and went through her evening routine, her mind back on her conversation with her father. She slept better than she had in a while and woke feeling rested and determined, and actually positive for once.

The feeling lasted until she was in the shower. Then hair on the back of her neck started to prickle—or the wet approximation of a prickle—and she found herself peering around the curtain to make sure no one was in her bathroom. Which was ridiculous, given all the security in the building. And the alarm system and locks her father had had installed when she moved in.

The bathroom had no window anyone could look through. The door was closed, and the steam lay heavy on the air, undisturbed. Still, she couldn't shake the feeling, and she rushed through the rest of her shower and got out of the bathroom as soon as she could.

Once she did, the feeling faded. She didn't brush it off—she put more stock in her instincts than that—but she didn't fret over it, either. She'd ask the guys down front to review their guest sheets and the video footage in her hall for anything suspicious, and she'd take extra care when she was alone in the apartment.

She did allow herself to be a few minutes late for work, though, to check her tiny greenhouse on the roof. Very few people knew she kept any of her work at home, but all it took was one wrong person. Everything was intact and untouched, but she set up a few disturbance detectors along the lines of the tape-across-the-door trick, and double-checked the alarm.

And hoped it was all unnecessary.

THREE

JASON DIDN'T ATTEND his funeral.

In fact, he didn't even know about it. Six months after he'd tumbled eight floors, shattering bones and bursting internal organs, someone finally mentioned the solemn, well-attended service.

He should have been there, of course, and not alive. When he watched the DVD he imagined himself, rather than a hundred and eighty-five pounds of rocks, inside the satin-lined mahogany. Thinking about the fabric made his skin crawl. That brought on claustrophobia, so he shut off the DVD player and ran ten miles on the treadmill to banish the feeling.

Sarah, his old girlfriend, had attended the funeral. He hadn't seen her in nearly two years, since the day she'd told him that as happy as he made her, she didn't love him. She'd wept when they lowered the coffin.

He punched the speed up another couple of increments and increased the incline, but it didn't help. Allison, the lead agent on the Kolanko job, had cried, too, and she was their toughest agent. Matthew had given the eulogy, and when he choked up, so did Jason. A decade of friendship, wrapped up in five minutes. Agent after agent filed past the closed casket, some touching it, others moving quickly past. Mourning someone who wasn't gone. His parents hadn't been there. He wondered what people thought about that.

For damn sure not the truth—that his mother stayed away because she couldn't act worth shit.

"Slow it down, Jason."

Awareness clicked in and the sterile, glass-and-high-tech-plastic interior of the lab came into focus. He realized his finger was mashing down the speed button and his legs burned. He backed it down until it was slow enough to walk and accepted the towel Gabby handed him. "Thanks."

"How do you feel?"

"Head clear, no chest pain, resps high but in range, heart rate…" He put his hands on the grips and waited for the machine to register. "One sixty. No nausea. Sweating like a horse, though." He mopped his face. "What brings you to the lab, Dr. Berwell?"

She didn't look up from her clipboard. "It's not a lab, Jase."

"Looks like one." He snorted. "I mean, could this whole situation be any more of a cliché?" He stopped the treadmill and grabbed a water bottle off the table next to it. "Bionic man comes back from his fake death, engineered to be better, stronger—"

"Stop it."

Her sharp tone halted him mid-stride. She never lost her composure. "Stop what?"

"That's copyrighted material."

He stared at her, then laughed, the anger he hadn't labeled finally fading.

"Seriously, Jason, you're not bionic. And I know you hate being cooped up in here, but you won't talk to anyone."

"I talk to you. And Matt." When Matt bothered to

come down, into the bowels of Hummingbird's headquarters on the outskirts of Washington, DC.

But that wasn't fair. In the aftermath of Hummingbird's greatest failure, his friend had had his hands full. Kolanko and the kid were fine, and none of the Hummingbird team had been injured except Jason, but his own death had been spectacular enough without the explosion to compound it.

He sat on one of the hard benches and rested his elbows on his knees. "I'm okay, Gabby. I just feel a little cooped up."

"I know. And I know telling you it's not forever doesn't help, but I have something that might."

He raised his eyebrows. "My final test results?"

"Your final test results."

"All of them?"

Her red-lipsticked mouth curved. Huh. He hadn't noticed her lipstick before. She looked good with it on.

"So tell me." He was intimately familiar with the list of original damage. His spleen had taken the worst internally, and they'd removed it, which was part of the reason for his forced isolation. They'd repaired all his damaged bones with a gluelike compound that not only held them together to heal properly, but made them stronger. Enough of his two-hundred-six bones had been broken to make him wonder how much of his skeleton was now fake, but after three months floating in a special harness, it was solid enough to support his weight and the weight of the building besides.

Okay, maybe not that strong.

"Imaging shows that with one exception, your skeleton has fully solidified. Your white blood cell count is in a normal range, so the marrow is operational.

Which, frankly," she added, "we weren't sure would happen."

"I know." It was one thing he appreciated. They'd been completely open with him about his chances from the first day he was awake. He'd insisted on hearing every detail of what had been done to him and what the results were expected to be. Death had been a constant possibility. "What's the exception?"

"There's a point in your sternum that's not going to seal completely."

"I have a hole in my chest?" He rubbed the spot in question, but couldn't feel anything.

"Not a hole. Just a…thin spot, I guess you could say. It won't interfere in anything day-to-day."

"But."

"But the original impact traumatized your heart, and it's more sensitive to additional trauma. Another hit to the sternum, besides the possibility of splinters piercing your lung—unlikely, but possible—would induce ventricular tachycardia. Without immediate response you'd die."

Jason shrugged. "I'll wear a vest to my next prize-fight."

Gabby frowned at his attitude. "You need to take this seriously. The impact would only need to be less than half of what it would normally take to do damage."

"Is that a scientific calculation?" He waited a moment but she only glared at him. "Okay, sorry. Go on."

"If you go into arrhythmia, you'd need a defibrillator to shock the heart back into normal rhythm."

"All right."

Gabby consulted her clipboard again. "The muscles have developed beyond our expectations." They'd used a compound that bonded to muscle cells to knit his shredded tissue back together. Healing had been a sonofabitch. Jason still cringed at the remembered agony. But he could bench press twice his former maximum. He wasn't bulkier than he used to be, but his definition still made him stare at himself in the mirror, flexing like a seventeen-year-old.

Not that he'd admit it.

"What about the skin issues?" he forced himself to ask.

Gabby adjusted her dark-framed glasses and peered at her clipboard instead of at him. Damn. He wasn't going to like this answer.

"Unfortunately, there's nothing remarkable about your skin tissue. However, the regeneration therapy we gave you has continued to exert an influence, even though we tapered it off weeks ago. Which means more nerve growth."

"Which means increased sensitivity."

She nodded. "I'm sorry."

Jason shrugged again but doubted he fooled her. Everything inside him was stronger, but his skin was ultrasensitive. Light touch had the effect of fine wires poking his skin, while heavy touch or stroke felt too good. He'd tried to explain without coming right out and saying a massage set him off like a rocket. After an excruciating number of days "shopping" for clothes he could tolerate, he'd found enough to develop a wardrobe. One he hadn't worn yet, since he didn't see enough people to matter. Gabby and her team of specialists and the technicians who did the drudge work didn't care if he wore bike shorts and shirts twenty-four/seven.

"What about the important stuff? You said the white cells..."

"Yes, they're within normal limits. But the risk of overwhelming post-splenectomy infection is high. We've vaccinated you against anything we possibly could, though for some you'll need additional shots. You can come back for those."

Jason perked up. "Come back?" No way. She had to mean eventually. Every time he'd asked when he could go home, both she and Matt had evaded the question.

Gabby lowered the clipboard and squared off with him. "Listen to me, Jason. You have to avoid illness. Wash your hands every chance you have. Stay away from sick people. Minimize touching surfaces in public, and keep hand sanitizer handy at all times." She jabbed her pen at him for emphasis. "If you have *any* increase in your temperature or any flulike symptoms, you must come in here for immediate treatment. Fatality rate for other OPSI cases is nearly fifty percent. And obviously, you're an exceptional case."

"Obviously." He couldn't keep the wryness from his voice and, to prevent her from bringing up his mental condition again, he asked, "So when am I getting out of here?"

She pursed her lips. "I wanted it to be two weeks. But it doesn't seem we have that luxury."

"Why not?"

"I need you." Matt walked into the room, looking haggard and wearing jeans and a wrinkled T-shirt. Jason hadn't seen him dressed that casually at work in—ever. The flash of concern drowned under a rush of adrenaline. He wasn't just getting out. He was getting a mission.

He refused to show eagerness. "Need me for what?"

Matt flinched at the hardness in his voice. Jason knew it was unfair to treat Matt that way, but feeling rarely had anything to do with knowing.

"Thank you, Dr. Berwell," Matt said, dismissing her.

Gabby flushed and backed out of the room. "I'll have a few more things to go over, Jase, before you go. But we're pretty close to done here."

"Thanks, Gabby."

Matt waited until the door closed, then clicked the lock and crossed the room to sit on a table opposite Jason. "I'm sorry I haven't been down in a while."

"It's fine."

"It's not, and I know it." His eyes looked bleak, and he rubbed the spot between his eyebrows with his thumb. "We've got a lot to talk about."

Jason snorted at the understatement. Matt had wanted him to concentrate on his recovery, not whatever was happening outside the lab for the last six months. "Like why everyone thinks I'm dead?"

"Not everyone."

True. Jason's parents knew he was alive. He didn't think Matt had given them much detail, though. He had talked to them on the phone, but they didn't seem to have any clue about the extensiveness of the damage or how close to death he'd been. His mother had described the "nice funeral" as if it had been a graduation party. But then, she'd only seen the video, herself.

"Close enough." Jason stood, his butt sore from the hard plastic. "Where'd you get the decorator for this place, anyway? Secret Experiments R Us?"

"I don't know, it was here when we moved into the building." Matt's voice was weary, and a shard of pity stabbed through Jason's frustration.

"Why don't you just start with the accident and go from there," he said.

Matt drew a deep breath and blew it out. "You saved my life. The bullet that hit your shoulder would have gone right through my heart."

For the first time, Jason had an inkling of what Matt had gone through, watching him fall, thinking him dead. He couldn't imagine life without Matt in it. They'd been friends, members of the same health club, before they'd been boss and employee. Jason was only twenty-one when they met, but he'd known since high school what he wanted to do. After a criminology degree, three summer internships with the FBI, and jobs running security at various businesses during the school year, he'd convinced Matt to make him one of his operatives. Within five years, he'd worked his way up through each level in the company until he'd become Matt's right-hand man at the office, as well as his sounding board, weightlifting spotter, and designated receiver during pickup football games in the park. Since Kelly, Matt's wife, died, Jason often felt that all they had was each other.

"I'm glad you weren't hit," was all he could think of to say. He folded his arms and leaned against the treadmill.

"I'm not. Well, I wasn't. I watched you trip over that guy's legs—"

"Yeah, can we not mention that part anymore?" Jason cut in. "Kinda ruins the whole hero thing."

Matt's eyes crinkled but he didn't seem to have enough energy to smile. "I saw you go over. Heard your body bouncing from rail to rail. Watched you hit the steps eight floors down. I didn't think there was any way you could be alive."

Jason knew the rest. How he somehow hadn't hit his head, at least not hard enough for brain trauma. He'd ruptured his spleen, lacerated his liver, and damaged enough intestine to require a resection and a temporary colostomy (thank God he'd been asleep until after they reversed *that*). Plus all the shredded muscle-shattered bone stuff.

They didn't need to dwell on the how. Jason said, "No one seems to know if you found out what it was about. Who attacked us and why."

"Hummingbird wouldn't still be here if we hadn't." Matt slumped over and rubbed his hands together, slowly, between his knees. "Kolanko's ex-wife—not Adrina's mother—found out he hadn't updated his will. I don't know how."

"Probably boinking the lawyer."

"Probably. Anyway, the guys in the stairwell talked. They were hired guns, no loyalty to who hired them. They're in jail on reduced sentences. The ex has been extradited from Italy and is awaiting trial. The will's been changed."

Jason pushed away from the treadmill and started pacing. *Stupid fucking reason to be killed.* He was glad he wasn't really dead.

"And the aftermath?" He had a feeling this would

be worse. When you hired a company to protect you, you expected a low number of explosions. Like none.

"It hit immediately," Matt admitted. "Half our ongoing private sector clients have fired us. The government hasn't managed to find a way out of the stuff we do for them already, but they haven't given us anything new. The media frenzy has died down, of course, it always does, but in the industry there's still a furor. Some say our failure on the Kolanko job has damaged relations all over the industry."

"That's bullshit."

"Doesn't matter if it's true or not, if people believe it."

And Jason had been down here running on a fucking treadmill, listening to Harry Potter audiobooks for the last three months. "I should have been—"

"No, you shouldn't. It was hard enough losing you the first time." Matt stopped. Swallowed. "The risk of infection was too great for you to be out."

Jason nodded. It didn't help his guilt, but it was reality and couldn't be changed. "I appreciate what you've done, Matt. But—"

"There's a reason I had you declared dead." Matt rose and came closer to him, visibly steeling himself for whatever he was going to say. "The technology we used to fix you is a big deal. It can mean saving a lot of lives. But none of it is approved for use in humans yet. We didn't know if it would work, and there wasn't time… I had to make a quick decision."

Jason bit back his response. He knew he was an experiment, and didn't blame his friend or the doctors who, except for Gabby, treated him like a lab specimen. So he couldn't yell at Matt for that. It wasn't what he was really angry about, anyway.

"There was no way you should have survived the fall," Matt continued. "If anyone had known you did, we wouldn't have been able to save you."

Jason nodded. It wasn't that he wasn't grateful or anything. But resentment burned in his gut for the implications of the lie.

"Plus, I knew if anyone found out about the technology, found out it had worked, we'd have enemies after all of us, from worldwide."

"Why won't we when I go topside, anyway?" Matt didn't respond right away, and the resentment swelled. "Because they won't know, right?" This time, he didn't wait for a response. "Fuck that, Matthew. I'm not changing my identity." It was one thing to use dangerous technology to save his life, and to use him to test dangerous technology. It was another to strip Jason of everything he'd done and been for thirty-six years. Every experience, every success and failure.

"You won't have to," Matt said, derailing the head of steam Jason was building.

He scowled. "How do you figure that? I'm dead." He didn't *want* to change his identity, but Matt's decision six months ago had left them little choice. His intentions had been good, and Jason understood he'd been protecting both him and the company. So for Matt to now say he didn't have to change his identity… His brain chewed on that for only a few seconds before he understood.

"Crap."

"Yeah." Matthew shoved his hand through his hair. "We can do some damage control. Since you left your assets to me—"

"Back up." He pushed away from the treadmill and faced his best friend. "You're not going to keep hiding me." Matt didn't move, didn't change expression, but Jason knew he was right. "You'll let them find out I'm alive. Why?"

"I'll get to that." Matt's voice was strained. "As I was saying, since you left your assets to me—"

"Actually, I left my assets to my parents, under your guidance as trust manager." Security at Hummingbird's level was lucrative, and Jason had built what his mother called "quite the nest egg." Not wanting his parents to face the repercussions of suddenly having a huge sum of money, he'd set it up to take care of them for life without causing a burden.

"Exactly," Matt acknowledged. "They're getting their allowance, and having a lot of fun with it, you'll be glad to know. But I created a pocket fund for you. It's been paying your ongoing expenses, including your property taxes and housekeeper."

Jason raised his eyebrows. "My home is still there?"

"Yeah."

"My neighbors—"

"Moved out, a month ago. Place is still vacant."

What a coincidence. He only had one family living close enough to notice his presence, and they were gone? Matt had been busy.

"How come I didn't know about this stuff?" He motioned around the lab. "Before, I mean. It had to be long-term research."

Matthew winced. "Yeah, I kinda hoped you'd be mad enough about the rest to not mention that." He rubbed the back of his neck and left his hand there. "It's a separate company, not part of Hummingbird. And what they were doing was so sensitive, so advanced—"

"You didn't trust me."

"That's not true."

"Then why didn't you tell me?"

Matt didn't talk for several seconds. Finally, he admitted quietly, "It was so sensitive and advanced, even before we used it on you, it skirted moral if not legal channels. I didn't think you'd approve."

Jason watched him straighten and turn away. An unfamiliar warmth soothed the burning. He'd been wallowing down here for months, thinking one thing, and the opposite was the truth.

He cleared his throat and snatched at the towel hanging over the treadmill, just for distraction. "Okay, so." The words stuck, and he cleared his throat again. "So. The risk of someone wanting the technology and coming after either me or the company."

Matt turned around again, his face tightening. "I figured it would be acceptable to you."

It was. "Except—"

"Except I underestimated our enemies."

"Someone already knows."

"Suspects."

"Any idea who?" Jason's mind clicked into work mode and started considering possibilities.

"Someone who knows me. Knows us, and what would hurt us most."

His brain halted on one name. "Kemmerling."

"I think so. I don't know for sure."

Isaac Kemmerling was a former employee. Slightly younger than Jason, he'd been an excellent agent for Hummingbird until two years ago, when he was promoted to mission leader, got cocky and risked all his agents' lives on a job, and was censured. He didn't take well to that and left the company. Since then, he'd done his best—unsuccessfully—to discredit Hummingbird and "take down" Matthew and Jason, as he'd threatened in a taped interview with a small-town Maryland reporter. It made sense he'd try to capitalize on the misfortune following the Kolanko incident.

"Who else could it be?" he asked, his mind searching for possibilities and not coming up with any.

Matt shrugged. "No one we've pinpointed. No one who has the knowledge, contacts, and especially motive to come after me. I could be wrong. But it's the best place to start."

Jason nodded. "So that's what you need me for." He looked around for a pad and pen. "To investigate Kemmerling without anyone knowing."

"Not exactly."

Matt's voice had tightened even further, and Jason stilled, his heart thudding even though he had no idea what was coming.

"I got intel today that leads me to think Kemmerling is going after Lark," Matt said.

Jason swallowed. "What kind of intel?"

Matthew pulled a folded piece of paper from his back pocket. It was a single sheet with a printed photo. Lark—*whoa,* had she grown up!—stood in the shower, her hair slicked back, eyes closed. Luckily for Matt's sanity, Jason thought, she had her arms in front of her.

Jason didn't think that helped much, though, considering the red laser sight in the center of her forehead.

FOUR

"HANG ON, I'M LOOKING."

Lark startled at the strange voice in what was supposed to be an empty, secure greenhouse. Wrist-deep in soil, she squinted through the leaves of the plant she was repotting, trying to see the person who'd spoken. He definitely wasn't any of the BotMed scientists who had access.

The figure moved toward her from a few aisles away, but with an odd gliding step that seemed to indicate stealth.

She followed her instincts and warily shook dirt off her hands, sidestepping between the tables in the opposite direction of the person at the other end. He didn't speak again, but she could see flashes of white between green leaves and purple and blue flowers as he kept coming her way. She shifted to stay out of sight, not frightened so much as suspicious and annoyed.

Fishing her cell phone from the pocket of her khakis, she kept moving, keeping some distance between them but not heading toward the door. Her father would freak if he knew she wasn't fleeing, but she was *not* leaving sensitive, top-secret work at the mercy of this...whoever.

The call she speed-dialed went through and Phil's

voice said, "Security." Lark ducked below the edge of a table and whispered her situation.

"Don't hang up," Phil told her. "People are on their way."

She rose, trying to spot the guy. He could be innocent, a visitor or new employee Ralph had forgotten to tell her about. But the unease she'd felt in the shower the other day returned, and she wondered if this was connected. She had to get a look at him without getting in his way. The wooden tables supporting the plants had cross braces that made it impossible to crawl under them. She crouched low and settled for running along the end of the rows until she saw movement again, then got down on her hands and knees and eased forward.

Man, would she feel stupid if he was legit and caught her doing this.

The man was moving away from her down the aisle, his head turning back and forth as he checked the tags on the plants. The light on his Bluetooth earpiece pulsed, signaling an open call.

"I don't see her. Not yet. Look, the tags aren't in English. It's not going to be easy—" He tilted his head back, an exasperated move. "Well, which do you want, the paperwork or the plants? I'll try, boss, but if she doesn't show up… Okay, fine. Girl, papers, plants. In that order. Yeah, I got it. I said, I've got it. No, you don't have to—hey. Crap." He ended the call and pulled a pistol from a shoulder holster under his preppy jacket, muttering something under his breath.

Fury and fear bubbled through her, making it difficult to hold her position. Fury won the short skirmish. This guy was after her work. Which study? His tag checking didn't give a clue. Why would he want any of it? Her research was always preliminary. Development occurred in other departments.

His motives didn't matter. She'd ferret them out later, after she saved the data.

She eased back on her haunches. She needed a weapon. Most of the stuff here heavy enough to do damage was also too heavy for her to lift. Or too short to use without moving within the guy's reach, which would be stupid. She had basic self-defense and kept up with training, but there was no point in putting it to the test if she could avoid it. She watched him turn the corner into the main aisle, and then inspiration struck. She wound through the greenhouse to the room in the back. Her speed meant she wasn't very silent, and her keys rattled when she opened the door, but she had one advantage. This was her place.

The man's footsteps echoed as he hurried in her direction. Adrenaline spiked. Lark grabbed one of the transfer buckets and a hose and braced herself. When the man pushed open the door to the storeroom, she flung the contents of the bucket—dry fertilizer—in his face. The bucket clattered to the floor and she raised the hose, spraying the sputtering, spitting man with water. He yelled as the mix ran into his eyes.

"That's got to burn." She strode forward as he backed away, keeping the spray on his face so he couldn't recover and come after her, or run away. He smacked into a stand of pots, knocking them over, and staggered as they tumbled around his feet.

Lark dropped the hose and picked up a clay pot, swinging it at his head.

"That's enough."

Startled at the voice behind her, Lark pulled her swing and spun.

The man was young, only a couple of years older than her, and good looking in a sparkly-blue-eyes, pale-blond-hair, tennis-muscles kind of way. But the glee on his face almost made him look ugly.

"What the hell is going on here?" she demanded, still angry. "How do you people keep getting in?"

"Yeah, we're gonna tell you." The blond eyed the other man, who whimpered and rubbed at his face. "Did you blind him?"

"Probably."

He tsked. "That doesn't make me happy."

Lark didn't say anything. If these guys knew anything about her, they weren't surprised by her response to their attempt to steal her work. And her, apparently.

"Oh, well. Come on, Donald."

The man tried to follow the command. The tennis blond reached for Lark's wrist. She attempted to jerk away, but hc was ready for her and held on.

"Ah-ah!" He held up a finger. "Your father taught me well. And unlike you, I've used what he taught me for years."

Lark frowned at him. "You—what?" Her mind raced as she leaned away from him, her arm stretched out. Pieces came together, clicking quickly into place. Her father's business might be struggling, but he had few true enemies. Her heart sank. "You're Isaac Kemmerling." *Shit.*

He smiled. "Daddy talks shop at home. Great, that saves us the whole getting-acquainted period." He laughed and tugged on her arm. "Come quietly and no one gets hurt." He turned to leave.

A man Lark hadn't seen creeping up on them slammed his fist into Isaac's face. He crumpled without a sound, his slack fingers sliding off Lark's wrist.

She gaped at the new guy. He was blond, too, but a darker color that would bleach into streaks in the sun. His skin tone was "computer geek" but his body was—well.

Then he looked up, and all the edges of her vision went fuzzy and dark. She swayed and blinked fast to bring it back. A hard, warm arm wrapped around her back, grounding her, and she stared up into the green-gold eyes of a dead man.

"Jason," she breathed.

He grinned. "I guess Matt didn't tell you."

Before she could respond, blue-uniformed security men flooded the building, fanning out and scampering up aisles, peering under tables.

"They're over here!" she called.

"We have to go," Jason said, his arm tightening around her.

"I can't, I have to—"

"We have to go *now*."

Lark didn't argue. She should stay with company security, talk to the police, make sure the two men on the floor—one still, one writhing—were taken into custody. But this man was her father's best friend, and though she hadn't seen him for years before he died, she trusted him.

It didn't keep her from casting a reluctant look over her shoulder at her rare, delicate plants as she and Jason trotted behind a row of cabinets and around to the main door, now stupidly unsecured. Jason gave her a significant look as he pushed through, and she nodded. Whatever was going on, there was a distinct lack of safety here at the moment.

Jason led her to a navy sedan she recognized as Hummingbird issue. He'd obviously driven here from DC.

"Is my father okay?" she asked as he opened the passenger door for her.

"He's fine."

"Where is he?" She tried to look at his face for assurance, but he firmly guided her into the car and she only caught a glimpse of determination.

"I don't know. I last saw him at the company." He closed the door behind her and jogged around the front of the car, sliding in and starting the ignition with a surprising economy of motion, given what his condition should be.

"That had to be hours ago, at least," she argued. "Can I call him?"

Jason handed her a slim cell phone. "Press and hold one."

She did, watching "Matt" appear on the display, then lifting the phone to her ear with a sudden surge of fear. Jason died six months ago. This guy couldn't be Jason. She'd been stupid to get into the car with him. She had no proof her father sent him, or that she was even calling her father. She put her hand on the armrest, near the handle, ready to dive out when the car slowed, holding her breath while the line rang.

The third ring cut off abruptly. "Did you get her?"

"Dad?"

"Lark." His relief made her ear tingle. "You're okay?"

"When I was six, I built a sand castle. I was very

proud of it and angry when the waves came up and destroyed it. What did I say?"

Her father chuckled. "Good girl. You said 'piss-flaps.'"

Tension released, her muscles weakening. Jason glanced at her from the corner of his eye before turning the car onto the main road to the entrance gate. She thought she saw approval before he looked back at the road, and warmth suffused her. Her brow wrinkled, but she concentrated on the phone.

"Dad, what's going on? I'm with Jason, but he's—"

"Dead, I know. I tried to call you to tell you he was on his way but you didn't answer."

"I turned my phone to vibrate while I was working. I didn't feel it." Her father didn't have to say what she knew he was thinking: *Typical.* "Dad, how—" But understanding hit her in a wave of shocked euphoria. "Oh, my God, it worked. You did it." Without thinking, she grabbed Jason's forearm. He hissed in a breath and she let go, quickly. "You used the regeneration therapy." *It had worked.* Suddenly, Isaac and his goon trying to get her and her work made more sense.

Now Jason looked at her full on, his slightly parted lips the only expression of his surprise.

"We did," her father admitted. "Among other things. Look, Lark, I'm in the middle of something—"

"Important, I'm sure. And Jason will tell me everything. Yada yada. I know the drill."

"Yeah," he said softly. "I love you, Larkling."

She winced and was glad he couldn't see it. "I love you, too, Dad."

"I'll see you soon. Let me talk to Jason for a second."

She handed the phone over and listened to Jason give her father a shorthand version of what had happened. They were done in less than a minute, and Jason laid the closed phone in the console between them.

"Where are we going?" she asked.

"To a safe house on the other side of the city. Tomorrow we'll go to your apartment and get whatever you need for a short trip. We'll meet your father back at Hummingbird."

"And when we get to the safe house you'll tell me what's going on."

"Yep."

"All of it."

"Yep."

"No 'protect the little lady, the delicate daughter of the big boss, from the things that go bump in the night'?"

Jason snorted. "No. I think Matt knows better than to try that now. And I definitely do."

Lark smiled, remembering the incident he was referring to. "Perry was the team captain."

"I understand."

He smiled back at her, and something zinged Lark, deep under her breastbone. Her breath caught. *Oh, boy.*

She faced front again. "Dad should never have told me not to worry my pretty little head."

"He was joking."

"But he meant it. And all I wanted was to go to a high school dance."

"And he knew a threat had been made against the school."

"It was kids!" She subsided immediately, remembering other schools, threats that had been real. "Okay, I get it now, but he should have explained it instead of expecting me to just do as he told me. I was seventeen."

"I know, Lark. He knows. No one's patting you on the head. You have to know what the threat is to be safe from it. And we need your help."

Well, that was a new one.

"My curiosity level just went to red. But we have to go to my apartment first."

"Lark—"

"Jason."

Jason closed his mouth. Part of her gaped in amazement that he was here. That she was talking to him. Questions raced through her head, dragging so many emotions there wasn't time to feel them before the next one crowded in. But prioritizing them was easy.

"My work is there. The plant that led to the compound that led to the regeneration therapy that's partly responsible for you being alive and whole. And all the data supporting it."

Jason immediately turned the car around, and Lark sank into her seat. He didn't say anything, but she didn't need him to. He'd just confirmed the reason Isaac had been after her. Despite the cauldron of questions and emotions, she appreciated the silence the rest of the way to her apartment. She needed a few minutes to absorb what was happening.

Since her father didn't exactly participate in Take Your Daughter to Work Day, Lark had never seen Jason in action. Not that she actually saw him this time, either. He left her in the car outside her apartment house and in five minutes, figured out where the Kemmerling spies were and identified their blind spots. Then he got her inside, slipping past the guard at the desk, who didn't look up.

Lark waited until they were in the elevator before asking, "What did you do?"

Jason quirked an eyebrow in question.

"The guard ignored us. They don't do that here, even the ones I don't know very well."

"Your father knows them all. It didn't take much to convince him not to see us come in. Now he doesn't have to lie if Isaac or his guys try to get information from him."

Lark winced. "I hope they won't hurt him to get it."

"Isaac is smarter than that."

"Yay." Smart wasn't a good thing in an enemy.

Jason insisted on entering the apartment first. As soon as he'd cleared the entryway, he pulled her in and made her wait by the door. The alarm was armed and undisturbed, but Lark waited patiently while he searched the rest of the apartment.

"Okay, where first?" He holstered the gun he'd strapped on in the car, hidden under a snug jacket he now wore over his super-tight long-sleeved T-shirt. Clothes that showed off in delicious detail how fit he was. Lark wondered again how that was possible. The regeneration therapy could only do so much.

"Roof. Greenhouse." Since she had the top-floor apartment of the small building, she had the only access to the roof. Still, she breathed a sigh of relief when she found her low-tech precautions intact. Isaac must have assumed all her work would be at BotMed. But since she'd developed the compound before she went to work there, both the data and the remaining plants were all here.

She strode to the rear of the greenhouse but then stood, fists on her hips, staring at the four plants sitting on their table.

"What's the matter?" Jason asked.

"I don't know what to do with them. We can't cart them all over the place. And I can't hide them in a safe or something. They need light and air."

Jason picked up two and carried them to another table. "Mix them in with the rest. Then pull all the labels."

She stared at him, openmouthed. "Pull all the labels?"

"He won't be able to tell which ones are the right ones."

"Neither will I!"

Jason gave her a look and came back for the other two.

"Okay, fine." But she hesitated, then pushed the tabs with all their important data down into the soil, instead, brushing it over the top so no one could tell they were there. Jason watched for a second, then nodded and helped her.

"He doesn't really want the plant, anyway," Lark tried to convince herself. "He'll want the data. It won't help him much, though. The stuff at—wherever they treated you. That's what he really wants."

"He can't get to it. This is the next best thing." He pushed the last one down and covered it. "Come on, we're running out of time."

Lark didn't need further urging. She grabbed her files from the spare bedroom, which were extensive but still fit in a lockable case Jason could carry. Then she threw a few things in a bag, checked her messages, watered her regular plants, and called work to take a leave of absence for "stress" after the afternoon's incident. Luckily, Ralph was still tied up with the break-in. Lark left a message with his assistant, brisk and straightforward and giving her no time to ask questions. Then Jason ghosted them out again.

Back in the car a few minutes later, she took a deep breath and blew it out slowly. "You've got some explaining to do."

"At the safe house."

She considered arguing, but she didn't want to split his attention. First, because it occurred to her he might not have driven for six months, and they'd both be safer if he could concentrate. Second, because she wanted it all. So she just said, "It better not be far."

"It's not."

"Good." She slid down on her spine and closed her eyes. "Wake me when we get there."

Jason waited until he had some open highway and was positive they weren't being tailed before he studied Lark. He knew she wasn't sleeping. She'd never been able to sleep while traveling. That could have changed, but her breathing stayed light, her body held taut, if not tensely.

He let out a breath. Shit, she'd grown into her potential. Matt had shown him pictures so he'd be sure to recognize her when she wasn't wet. The photos displayed plastic beauty. Perfect skin, brilliant teeth, smooth forehead, and glossy dark hair covering a hard shell and projecting little substance. In person, though, she was different. Her ancestry—as far as he knew, a mix of Middle Eastern, Native American, and Far Eastern origin—gave her exotically shaped dark eyes and dark hair that was almost a living color, it had so many variations. Her beauty appealed to him more than he'd have expected, and it took him off guard, even after he'd adjusted his mental image of her from coltish teenager to sophisticated woman.

Jason had watched Lark with Isaac, as he'd slipped up behind him in her greenhouse at work. She'd resisted but kept her head, didn't do anything foolish, and had shown no fear. She'd probably kept up some self-defense training; that gave confidence in a confrontation. Plus, Donald probably *was* blind, but she wasn't freaking out at what she'd done. The combination was a bigger turn-on than anything had been in a long time.

He glanced at her again. She had the glossy hair and the perfect skin the pictures displayed, but she also had dark dirt under her fingernails and streaking her pants. Her shirt was worn denim, and hid a body that had felt small but strong under his arm when he caught her earlier. He had a feeling she kept good care of herself out of practicality rather than vanity. She hadn't packed a lot of makeup and junk when they were at the apartment.

He stared at the road ahead, trying to ignore the feeling filling him now. He'd conditioned himself against adrenaline-fueled attraction once he hit the management track. He worked with—and was the boss of—too many women to risk indulging it, even as a quick rush. This wasn't like that, anyway. Not superficial excitement pumping through him, but something deeper, more complex. Fuck.

He's your best mate floated through his brain. Jason tried not to imagine Matt's reaction if he ever found out. He was ten years older than Lark, for one thing. Even though Matt was ten years older than Jason, he still saw them as peers. That would affect how he saw the age difference. Matt took pride in never interfering in his daughter's choices, but Jason knew a relationship with her would damage their friendship. Not worth it, especially now.

He rubbed a hand down his face, not quite believing his thoughts. He should be planning. Trying to get into Isaac's head. Figuring out his next move, so he could both keep Lark safe and stop the man from achieving his goal.

Not lusting after his best friend's daughter.

FIVE

CERTIFICATE OF ACHIEVEMENT awarded to Abigail Berwell, M.D., for outstanding contribution to the advancement of medical science.

The framed certificate hung at eye level over Gabby's desk, but even as her eyes traced over the familiar words, her mind dismissed them. Matt had given it to her when it became clear Jason was not only going to survive, but excel, and her work might never be recognized due to the issues surrounding what they'd done. She'd been practically giddy with pleasure then. Now, she was afraid she was sinking into a deep depression.

"Dr. Berwell, we have the samples prepared for storage."

Gabby forced a smile for the assistant who hovered in her office doorway. "Thanks, Mel. You guys can go home. I'll put them in the locker."

"Are you sure? I don't mind helping. There are a lot."

Gabby stood. "No, it's okay, it's getting late and I'm sure you have plans. I don't." She winced at how pathetic that sounded. "Go ahead, it's okay. I'll follow protocol and you can double-check me on Monday."

Mel laughed. No one would ever doubt Gabby's dedication to procedure, documentation, and evidence of integrity.

"On second thought, take next week off. You've

all earned a break. Let the others know." She wasn't going to be able to stand floating around here with nothing to do *and* a staff at loose ends.

"All right, Dr. B, thank you. Have a good weekend."

"You, too."

Mel was apparently the last one out, because when Gabby went into the lab—she hated calling it that, but face it, that's what it was, no matter how hard she tried to humanize their work—no one else was there. The trays of tissue, blood and other samples from Jason's treatment and recovery were on a cart by the center counter running the length of the room. Gabby spot-checked the labels, all written in a fine, meticulous hand, and nodded in satisfaction. With Jason's treatment complete, they had to move these from the smaller refrigerator here in the lab down the hall to the larger, more secure unit.

She hated to do it.

Her footsteps echoed on the tile floor, combining with the rattle of the cart's wheels to make her feel lonelier than ever. What the hell was she going to do now? They'd immorally, if not illegally, used untested medical treatments and technology on a live human being. There was no way their work could go forward, save for periodic checkups and tests they could do on Jason. Unless another agent got shot and knocked over a railing. Which she didn't want to happen, of course.

An image of Matthew tumbling down the middle of a stairwell flashed into her head, and she gasped.

"Don't think about it," she muttered furiously, shoving the cart faster and yanking it to a halt outside the refrigeration unit. It didn't matter that Matthew couldn't see past her white coat and status reports.

If anything happened to him, she'd be as crushed as if they were married. She keyed open the unit and pushed the cart inside, locking the hinge so the door wouldn't close, then started transferring the trays to an empty case in the corner.

"Get over it," she told herself. "You won't even be seeing him anymore, now that Jason's gone." She grunted under the weight of a laden tray and slid it onto the shelf with a rattle. "You'll probably be fired within a week, anyway."

"Fired? What are you talking about?"

Gabby shrieked and jumped a foot in the air, smacking an arm into a stand of glass tubes as she spun to face the open door. Where Matthew stood. Shit.

Feeling like an idiot, she pressed her hand to her chest and blew out a breath. "Sorry. I didn't hear you come down the hall."

His smile was a shadow of what it had been before Jason's accident, but it warmed her nonetheless. "I should have made more noise. What's this about being fired?"

"Nothing. Nothing." She checked the tubes to be sure she hadn't broken any and turned her back to slide them into the case. "I was just talking to myself. No one else to talk to, with Jason gone." *Idiot.* What a stupid thing to say. She had a staff, and it wasn't as if she'd sat around shooting the breeze with her patient, anyway.

"No one's getting fired, Dr. Berwell. There's still a lot to be done."

"Please, for the millionth time, call me Gabby." She transferred the last batch of samples and closed the case, locking it and printing the record of her access.

Matthew pulled the cart out into the hall and closed the door behind her, watching as she secured it, too.

"I'll try to remember."

They started walking down the hall, back toward the lab and her office.

"What are you…I mean, what can I help you with?" Gabby asked him.

Matthew shrugged and waited as she opened the door to the lab and stood back for him to push the cart through. "Everyone else has left for the weekend, mostly. There aren't any active jobs I can monitor tonight. Jason checked in, and Lark's okay. I don't know what to do with myself."

They went into Gabby's office and she motioned to the love seat in one corner. Matthew dropped tiredly onto it and rubbed his hands over his face. She sat in her desk chair, watching him.

"Was Lark in trouble?"

He froze, then let his hands drop. "In a way. It doesn't matter."

She thought it did matter, but he'd obviously not meant to bring up the subject. "Well, I'm glad she's okay." They sat in silence for a minute. Gabby felt awkward and had no idea what to say. "Um…probably not the best time to ask, but…since we're done actively testing the technology, what—what's going to happen now?"

Matthew stared at her for a moment. She could almost see his brain click over from whatever he'd been thinking about to her question.

"Don't worry, there's still plenty to do. We can't use what we learned from Jason's application, but we can continue the work we were doing before his accident."

That was the problem. Gabby hadn't been involved until Jason was almost killed. She'd been a consultant on the theoretical application of the science, but only came on board full time that night to be the overseer of the medical team. They didn't need her for that now. She wasn't a researcher, which the program required at the stage it had been six months ago.

She sighed and pushed ahead, even though she didn't want the answer. The uncertainty was much worse. "Given the way things have changed, though, do you really need me here?"

He frowned. "Have you had offers elsewhere?"

"No! And it's not—I mean, I'm happy—" She deliberately stopped and tightened her jaw. She *hated* being the babbling misfit, unable to communicate smoothly with her boss. "I don't want to go anywhere. But I can't see what role you want me to play now."

"Of course you have a role to play. The team is used to following you. They need you to guide them." He leaned forward, his elbows braced on his knees. "You know how vital it is that we go in the proper direction without taking shortcuts or revealing what we've done with Jason."

She noticed his voice changed when he said his friend's name. Not for the first time, she wondered if she was being blind. But she couldn't ask him if he was in love with his best friend, for God's sake.

"I thought you'd want Tompkins to take over again," she said, a bit reluctantly.

"No, you're a much better leader than he is," Matthew assured her, but in a practical, not pandering, tone. "You relate to people, get the best out of them."

She couldn't help the blush spreading over her entire body. "Thank you. He does have the research background, though. Maybe a co-leadership would be best?"

Matthew nodded. "Sure, that could work."

"Okay. Good." Tension soaked out of her, and she smiled, feeling more at ease than she ever had with him.

More silence, though she didn't think his attention went as far away this time. "Do you want to—I don't know, go get a drink? Or dinner?" came out of her mouth before she realized she was going to say it. Mortified, she stood and took off her lab coat, turning away to hang it on the rack in the corner so she couldn't see Matthew's face. So he couldn't see hers, suddenly flaming.

"It sounds great."

She could hear regret in his voice—the upcoming "but"—and didn't have the experience to know if it was real or fake. "It's okay," she said, "I'm sure you have plans with someone. I just thought, since you were at loose ends…" Though she'd turned back to face him, she kept her gaze on her desk while she retrieved her purse and glasses case.

"No, I definitely don't." This time he sounded amused, but he'd stood and begun moving toward the door. "I don't feel like going out anywhere, though. I'll just head back to the house and wait for Jase to check in again."

"Okay." She smiled nervously and followed him out of her office, locking it and the lab as they went out to the hall. She headed for the elevator but stopped when Matthew didn't join her. He walked a few paces in the other direction, toward the stairs.

"Have a good weekend, Dr. Berwell." Then he disappeared through the fire door at the end of the hall.

"It's Gabby," she whispered, letting go all hope he'd ever remember.

MATTHEW POUNDED UP the sixth flight of stairs, halfway from the sub-basement lab to his office on the top floor. Gabby hadn't asked, but if she had, he'd have told her it was part of his commitment to ongoing conditioning. Part of the job, more now than ever, with the flux the company was in.

It would have been a lie.

For the first two months after Jason tipped over that railing, Matthew hadn't been able to enter an office building stairwell. Weakness was unacceptable. As soon as he knew Jason would make it, Matthew forced himself to face his fear. The long runs up and down, to and from the lab on a regular basis, had kept him in the best shape of his life, but also gave him plenty of time to come to terms with his problem.

He wasn't into self-analysis in general, but he'd been through enough to understand its value. Growing up in gang territory, he'd seen things that had shaped him, carved him—even gouged him. Joining a non-military black ops organization hadn't been the escape he'd intended it to be. He'd only shared his past with two people: Jason and Kelly. She had taught him how to be happy, and when she died, he refused to disgrace her memory by turning his back on that happiness. Jason helped, probably more than he realized. Back then, understanding himself, his feelings, and his role in his daughter's life had been the key to staying out of the darkness.

Somehow, it wasn't working now.

He pushed harder around the eighth floor landing, his breath blowing out in short bursts. It didn't take a genius psychologist to tell him why he hated stairwells now. He didn't expect bullets to come flying down every flight, or dark shapes to attack him from under landings. No, it was that image, the horror of Jason's crashing fall, that made it so difficult.

Gabby thought he was gay. He slowed at the ninth floor and checked the door, making sure it was locked. Telling her he wasn't would have made things even more awkward between them. He wasn't too preoccupied to notice her crush. But he didn't have anything to give anyone right now, never mind a smart, sweet-natured, pit bull of a woman who deserved more than he could offer even before all this mess happened. So he let the question go unanswered, called her Dr. Berwell, and hoped things evened out over time.

No, he wasn't gay. But the pain when he lost Jason had rivaled the pain of losing Kelly. Lark had teased him once, back during some psych or sociology class she'd been taking in college, that he and Jason were platonic soulmates. He'd scoffed, but she was right. Matthew had never known another person—except Kelly—who understood him and supported him like Jason did. Jason wasn't afraid to tell him when he was being stupid, or an ass, or both. But he had Matthew's back, no matter what, and that was something you didn't let get away.

He stopped when he reached the top floor, walking in a circle and shaking out his burning legs while his breathing slowed. He wished Lark's call hadn't come while the Secretary of Defense was in his office. Now he had to wait until they arrived at the safe house and called him again. He couldn't believe how close Kemmerling had gotten. He'd hoped the shower photo was a ploy, meant to scare him, and hadn't expected them to actually make a move on Lark. But not only had Kemmerling made a move, he'd gained a valuable advantage—he knew Jason was alive.

Matthew wanted them both here, now, where no one would threaten their safety again.

Cursing, he punched in the access code on the pad next to the door and impatiently submitted to the biometric checks before it let him through. He almost forgot to wipe his print off the scanner and cursed again. If only he could have been the one to go get Lark, he'd have ripped Kemmerling to pieces.

He smoothed his scowl. Despite confirming his survival, it had been the right thing, sending Jason. Ripping Isaac, while satisfying, was definitely not what Hummingbird needed right now.

Matthew reached his office and eased into his chair, spinning to stare out the window at the empty parking lot, busy street, and sparkling Potomac in the distance. The sun had begun to sink on the other side of the building, and it lent a rosiness to the picture that would normally be soothing. He inhaled and let his breath out slowly. This was his first chance in weeks to sit calmly with nothing and no one demanding his attention. Inevitably, that thought led him to the pile of paperwork on his desk and a mental to-do list that had grown steadily while he took care of big-picture items.

He was just about to give in and do some work when the phone rang. Not his cell, so it probably wasn't Jason or Lark. He wasn't sure what traffic would be like up in Boston, and how long it would take them to get to the safe house. But there wasn't any reason for anyone to be calling him on the work line, either, with no agents on active duty tonight. He spun his chair and lifted the receiver.

"Madrassa."

"Matt? Matthew? You're there. Oh, I'm so glad." The woman, whose voice he didn't recognize, choked back what sounded like a sob.

"I'm sorry, who is this?"

"It's Ella. Ella Darron? I know, it's been years, but I just… I'm sorry, I'm going about this all wrong."

"Are you in danger, Ella?" He couldn't imagine why else his sister-in-law would call him. They'd lost touch years ago, before Lark even graduated from high school. Ella and Kelly had never been close. While Kelly was a mom first, hobbyist second, and quite content with not working a real job, Ella had been an odd combination of driven businessperson and wacky artist. She was…forty-two now?

"No, no, I'm not in danger. Not immediate danger. I mean, not in danger at all. That's not really what it is."

Matthew stifled a sigh of irritation. "Then take a breath, calm down, and tell me what's wrong."

She inhaled noisily and took a few seconds to exhale. "I can't tell you over the phone."

"My lines are secure," he said automatically.

"Mine's not. Can I see you? Meet with you?"

"I'm at the office now. Are you in DC?"

"Not yet. I'll be there in the morning, but I don't want to go to Hummingbird."

Scowling, Matthew said, "You can meet me at the house if you can make it early enough."

"Have an early tee time, Matthew?" The acerbic tone was much more the Ella he remembered, and he relaxed.

"No. But I will have to work."

"On Saturday."

"On most days."

She sighed. "Fine. The house in the morning. I'll try to be there by eight. Is that acceptable?"

"Of course. I hope I can help you, Ella."

"Me, too." She sounded scared and upset again. Something was off about her quick changes, but without being in the room with her, he couldn't tell what. He didn't have the time or mental capacity to take on someone else's problems, but she *was* Kelly's sister and Lark's aunt, and family was supposed to be there for family. More importantly, instinct told him to meet with her. And he always trusted his instincts.

SIX

LARK FELT THE weight of Jason's eyes on her and knew she wasn't fooling him by pretending to be asleep. That was okay. He wasn't going to tell her anything until they got to the safe house, and she didn't want to pepper him with questions. It would annoy both of them, and if her eyes were open, she wouldn't be able to help herself.

Not that she needed to open her eyes to look at him. She had a perfect mental image of his body up against hers, his face looking down on her like some big damn hero. He was as well defined as any Navy SEAL, the snug knit shirt and jeans he wore showing off his muscles to perfection. He'd moved fluidly, running with ease and comfort. Whole.

A frisson of excitement made her shiver. Based solely on the miracle, of course. Not on Jason's body and how he used it. Only on the fact that he was alive.

It had fucking worked. Excitement lifted her again. She'd tried not to pin too many hopes on her compound. Tried to make it enough that discovering the plant's properties could lead to bigger breakthroughs in medicine. It had qualified her for the fellowship, which brought new possibilities. But here in this car was proof she'd been right. And that she'd sold it to the right people, people who could develop it. Who *had* developed it.

A little bubble of sadness welled and popped, tempering her giddiness. It came from a pool that was always there, something she knew she'd never get rid of. Her mother hadn't needed such revolutionary technology when she fell from a horse. Whatever they'd used to put Jason back together wouldn't have prevented her mother's infections, or the complications, or the stream of surgeries that had left her vulnerable. She'd been one of those pure-of-heart, fragile-of-body women to begin with, and never recovered fully from the fall. She'd died of the flu, of all things, when Lark was sixteen.

So Lark couldn't play "what if." She couldn't imagine that her findings or the amazing things they led to could have ever saved her mother. But they could help, maybe save, other people. Maybe helped save Jason. And that validated *everything*. Her choice to say no thanks to her father's business, though he'd built it—and kept the silly name—as a testament to her mother. Her seemingly random venture into botany after a couple of science-related internships and summer jobs. Her focus on work and lack of social life, most of the time.

She couldn't wait to get her hands on Jason's medical records. His recovery was amazing. He didn't seem to have any stiffness or creaky joints or misshapen bone. She wondered if anything hurt, and if it had all healed right. If the regeneration therapy had been enough, and if not, what else they'd used on him.

We can rebuild him. God, it was *real.*

Okay, he wasn't bionic. She didn't think. No computer chips controlling his super movements or nanites boosting his senses. But he'd been *dead,* or almost.

Questions flooded her brain. Her eyes popped open and she quickly shut them again. *In time,* she whispered to herself. *He'll tell you in time.*

She'd make sure of it.

WHEN THEY ARRIVED at the safe house, Lark stayed right behind Jason as he searched the house and perimeter before declaring it all clear.

"I'm going to check in," he told her, securing the pistol he'd used to sweep the house. "Do what you need to do. You can talk to your father when I'm done, and then you and I will talk."

"And eat, I hope. I skipped lunch." It was well past dinnertime, and she was starving. She had a high metabolism and crashed when her blood sugar was low, but couldn't seem to remember that when she was working.

"Definitely. My stomach is eating a hole in itself." He started dialing his phone.

"Is that a side effect?" she asked without thinking, then held up a hand. "I know, it can wait."

Jason grinned and turned away, and that spark flared again inside Lark. She was going to have to make him stop smiling at her. A guy like him, who worked for her father and no doubt had a shitload of problems on his shoulders right now, would have zero interest in her. Even if he wasn't also her father's best friend, which placed her off limits. And even if his job didn't immediately eliminate him from her list of "safe" guys to date.

She headed for the bathroom, trying not to curse. She couldn't remember a man ever having an effect on her this strong. It figured the first guy who generated a spark was more off-limits than the work that had created him.

That thought sobered her. To her knowledge, there was no FDA approval to use the RT-24 on humans. She didn't care, but the company didn't need any more scrutiny, her father any more stress.

God, every thought she had generated a burst of questions. She quickly used the facilities, stifling a shriek when she caught sight of herself in the mirror. Dirt on her face and clothes, hair all tangled and ratty looking. The minimal makeup she'd put on this morning had disappeared. Why hadn't she brought her bag in with her? She shoved at her hair for a moment, then blew out a sigh. What was the point in making an effort? She'd looked like this for the last several hours already. A few more weren't going to make a difference.

Jason was still on the phone when she entered the kitchen. She opened the freezer and pulled out a large supreme pizza, set the oven to heat and readied the pizza to slide into it. She had her back to the doorway, but knew when Jason entered anyway. The pressure in the room changed, and now something fluttered in her lower belly.

"Here you go," he said, and the flutter became a vibration. Lark was glad she wasn't a guy, her reaction fully visible. She turned and accepted the phone he held out to her. Their eyes met, held, and heat crept up her face. The little lines around Jason's eyes deepened the tiniest bit, and she knew she didn't need different anatomy to display her reaction. Dammit.

"When the oven beeps, put the pizza in and set

the timer for fifteen minutes," she told him, just for something to say.

"I know how to make pizza." His lips curled.

She shook her head and lifted the phone to her ear, moving into the living room as she spoke. "Dad?"

"You two seem to be getting along fine." He sounded indulgently amused, and she rolled her eyes. She wasn't sixteen anymore. If he really knew what was going on, he'd react differently.

"Yeah, whatever," she said. "Dad…I don't even know where to start. He's alive."

"I know, sweetheart." He sounded regretful, and she frowned until he explained, "I'm sorry I didn't tell you."

Ah. He thought she would be upset at being kept in the dark. "It's okay. I can figure that out. But there's so much else I want to know!"

"Jason will fill you in, but I have to tell you a few things he won't, and I have a conference call in a few minutes, so I don't have much time."

Lark glanced at her watch, but the time didn't matter. The call was probably with someone in Asia. "Medical?" she guessed. What else would a macho guy keep to himself?

"He's still at high risk of infection," her father confirmed. "His immunization schedule isn't complete, and he had a splenectomy as well as all the bone breaks."

The hair on her skin stood on end, accompanied by a wave of dread. Just like her mother. "How bad was he, Dad?"

"He was nearly dead, Lark. Only a very powerful will kept him alive, I think."

He didn't say whose will.

She swallowed. "What do I need to do?"

"Watch him for symptoms. Fever, fatigue, anything that seems flu-ish, make him come back here."

She closed her eyes and tried not to think of her mother, to remember her last horrible days. Responsibility settled on her shoulders, a strangely familiar mantle. "I thought we are going there," she managed, forcing her mind on the here and now. Hummingbird would be the safest place for her, wouldn't it?

"You will, but probably not to stay. I don't know yet. I'm working on some things."

"Okay." She straightened, focused again. "What else?"

"He can't take a blow to the chest. His sternum is weak, and his heart suffered some trauma from the initial impact. Another hit, not even very strong, could send him into V-tach."

"I should carry an AED. Got it."

"I'm not joking around here, Lark."

"Neither am I, Dad." Not that she knew where to get an AED, or how practical it would be to carry one. But how likely was it that he'd get hit in the chest again? "Does he need meds or anything?"

"No, he's fine physically. More than fine. He was running sixteen miles an hour this morning."

She whistled. "You gave him super powers?"

"No, don't be silly. But the muscle fibers and the bone glue have made him stronger, more powerful, gave him more endurance. And we have no idea what else the regeneration therapy might have done."

"Besides grow nerve tissue?"

"Yeah." A phone rang in the background. Her father paused, probably checking who it was, then said, "I've got to go. But sweetie, we're not sure about his mental status. He hasn't really dealt with the reality of not dying, and everything that goes with it."

Lark kept her voice low. "What do you mean? Could he be unstable? Explode in anger or something?" She couldn't imagine it, but then, she hadn't seen him in years.

"I don't know. I trust him, Lark. He's there to take care of you. But he needs you to take care of him, too."

She couldn't help a smile. "You know I will, Dad."

"Thank you, sweetie. Love you."

"Love you, too."

"That's just so damned sweet," Jason said from the doorway. "Water or soda? They haven't stocked anything perishable."

"Water's fine." She went back into the kitchen and inhaled the spicy pizza scent. "God, I'm hungry."

"Here." He held out a bag of cashews, and she took a handful. "You wanna talk now or wait until we eat?"

"I'm bursting with desire…" She tossed a few nuts into her mouth and gave a little moan at the explosion of flavor. Jason's eyes darkened. "…to bombard you with questions," she finished. "But I can wait. Eating won't take long."

It didn't. They devoured all but two pieces of the pie, which Jason wrapped in plastic and stuck in the fridge. In silent agreement, they went onto the back deck with bottles of water and sat in the Adirondack chairs looking out over a wide, flat yard shadowed by the remnants of the mid-June sun. Lark realized she was tired. She'd had a big day, what with people trying to abduct her and coming back from the dead and all.

She covered a yawn and said, "Where do we start?"

"Where do you want to start?"

The coming-back-from-the-dead stuff was bigger, and less urgent. It should wait. "With Kemmerling."

"You know him, then."

"I know who he is." Anger put an edge in her voice. "He was an excellent agent who got too big for his britches and has been gunning for you guys ever since. I figure he wants to use the aftermath of the Kolanko job to tear down Hummingbird. Coming after me seems more personal, though. Unless..." She raised an eyebrow. "The RT-24?"

"Smart girl."

"Call me a girl again, you'll feel it." She brandished her bottle at him. "I'm not that much younger than you, you know."

He held up a hand. "Sorry. Figure of speech. But yeah, that's the start of it. We think he still has connections inside, because he somehow got wind of my miraculous recovery and figured out how it happened. Any ideas?"

Lark considered, picking at the label on her bottle. "I don't know much about the medical team. What do you have so far?"

Jason blew a small breath through his nose, not quite a snort. "I didn't even know there was a medical team before I woke up rebuilt. And I just found out about all this today. Matt didn't have time to give me a rundown. You were the priority, and I'm the only one he trusted to get you out of harm's way."

They sat in silence a moment while Lark let her mind whir back over years of interactions with the Hummingbird staff. There hadn't been much in the last few years, just the occasional holiday party and company picnic. Not that they were typical of corporate America. They'd had stealth and weapons competitions, and hand-to-hand—

"Nils!" she half yelled as a memory burst into her brain. "I bet you anything it's him."

"I don't know a Nils."

"You wouldn't. I mean, you should, but he's one of those guys people don't notice. The ones who get all resentful about it and go dark side."

"What does he do for Hummingbird? He can't be an agent."

"No, he was support. But he wanted to be in protection. He was really pissed when I beat him hand-to-hand at the company picnic one year."

Something dawned on Jason's face. "I remember hearing about that. I wasn't there, I was on a job. Redhead, right? More orange. Lots of freckles."

"That's him. Caitlyn told me he was a jack-of-all-trades at Hummingbird, efficient at whatever was asked of him." More came back to her the longer she thought about that particular picnic. "I think he hung out a lot with Isaac. They were the same age. And it's possible he was assigned to the lab at some point."

Jason frowned. "Probably not likely, but possible, sure. If he had a spotless background and was good at grunt work." He pulled his phone out of his pocket. "How long ago did you sell them your patent?"

"Nearly two years now. Right before I started working at BotMed. I never dreamed things would happen this fast. But they were probably working on the other stuff even before that, right? Dad said you had a lot of bone breaks, and the regeneration therapy wouldn't help those. Nils could have been assigned to the team before Isaac was censured. What are you doing?"

"I'm texting Matt to find and question Nils. Do you know his last name?"

"Fredlund."

He tapped at the keypad for a minute, waited for the phone to beep, and put it away. "Anyway, Kemmerling thought I was alive and thought he knew how. He sent a threatening photo to your father, who sent me to get you."

Lark grimaced. "I'm sorry."

He looked at her. "What? Why?"

"For dragging you away to babysit."

He barked a laugh. "You have no idea. Lark, this was my first day out of the basement."

"Oh!" She stared at him. "Really? You've been holed up the entire time?"

He shrugged. "Well, yeah. I haven't actually been conscious that long, and was rehabbing, and had to be under constant observation and all that. I just got released—reluctantly, I might add, on the doctor's part—and Matt sent me up here immediately. If I hadn't had a mission, I'd have stood in the parking lot all day, basking in the sun."

He grinned, but Lark could hear the underlying truth beneath the casualness. Still, "He should have sent someone else. Or just called me, for cripes sake. I mean, I can take care of myself."

Jason shook his head. "I'm sure you can, under routine circumstances. But he doesn't need another thing to worry about."

"You're right," she said, feeling guilty. She'd spent weeks wallowing in worry about him, and now this discovery had wiped it away as if it had never existed. "Still, he needs you. *Has* needed you." Except, he'd *had* him. The world tilted with the realization. All this time she'd thought her father was deep in despair over his loss, but it was a lie. Okay, granted, he didn't know if Jason would survive, and the company stresses were the same, and Jason couldn't work. But he'd been there to talk to, which maybe explained why he hadn't needed to talk to *her*. She looked down, blinking fast against the sudden, stupid burn of tears under her eyelids.

"Sure," Jason said, and out of the corner of her eye, she saw him swig from his bottle. "He needed me."

The sarcasm in his words banished her self-pity. There was definitely more there than she understood, more than she had a right to understand. She cleared her throat. "Um, anyway, I don't…quite…" She pressed her lips together and gave her head a quick shake of annoyance. "I don't know why Kemmerling has targeted me. I'm hardly involved with the technology at all. I can't help anyone recreate the compounds or anything."

"That's not the only reason you're a target," Jason pointed out.

"I guess." It had been a long time since she'd considered herself leverage, with the possibility growing more remote as she got older. But being an adult didn't make her less of a target, as Isaac and his goon had shown today. "How did you know I was in danger? Your timing today was awfully convenient."

Jason lifted his body to pull a folded piece of paper out of his back pocket. His abs tightened under the revealing shirt, and the muscles in his arms and legs flexed, making Lark hum way back in her throat. Then Jason handed her the paper, and she forgot all about muscles.

"What the hell? How did they do this?" She narrowed her eyes at the red dot in the middle of her forehead, the strange sensation from the other day in the shower again prickling over her, when she felt like she was being watched. "This is impossible. No one was there. And I don't have a window in the bathroom." She squinted at the printout. "Is it doctored?"

"No. Someone planted a camera in the vent over the tub. I found it when I searched the place, before you went in this afternoon. The camera had a light, not a real laser sight, but you can't tell from that." He flicked a finger at the paper. "They probably took a constant stream of images and picked the one that worked."

She shuddered. "If they could get that close, why not just attack me there? Why wait until I'm at work, where people would be around?"

Jason plucked the paper out of her hand and refolded it. She raised her eyebrows as he tucked it back into his pocket.

"Because the immediate goal wasn't to get to you, it was to threaten your father."

"Okay, I get that." Hated every part of it, but understood it. "But they came after me anyway. The first guy, Donald or whatever, he was on the phone, presumably with Kemmerling, and he said he was there to get the girl, the papers and the plants."

Lark took a deep breath, sensing herself getting shrill and probably annoying. But Jason answered with patience and not a hint of frustration.

"Something obviously changed between then and now. Or maybe we're wrong, and the threat wasn't the end goal. Maybe they wanted to flush me out."

"Oh, no." She stared at him. "If so, it worked. Isaac knows you're alive." Jason nodded, and she closed her eyes, fury turning metallic in her throat. That Isaac had won anything, even something as preliminary as this, made her want to take his head off. That Jason was now at risk, in more ways than one, turned fury into a protectiveness she'd never felt for anyone but her father.

"What's the plan?" she asked, hoping neither emotion had branded her voice.

He shrugged. "Just what I told you. Get your stuff and get back to Hummingbird where you can be safe until Kemmerling is brought in."

"Wait." She frowned. "When we left BotMed he was out cold. With security surrounding him. And police coming. Shouldn't we be safe?"

Jason's face went granite. "Did you see any police on our way out?"

She hadn't been paying attention, shaken as she was by everything. But now that he mentioned it, she didn't remember seeing the police. Only the security people leaving the door wide open. "No. Dammit. Those incompetent… He got away, didn't he? Dad told you that?"

"Yep. Donald's in the hospital, though. No word on his vision."

She nodded absently and returned to her original train of thought. "I assume this safe house was established post Kemmerling."

"Of course."

She watched dark shapes—bats, probably, out for their dinner—soar across the sky above the yard. They could barely be seen against the final remnants of reflected sunshine on the horizon. "Anything else I need to know about this problem at the moment?"

"Not that I have to tell. You have other questions?"

She turned sideways in the chair and pulled her legs up. "Boy, do I."

He laughed, his teeth flashing in the meager light. His shaggy hair flopped back as he lifted his face. Lark shivered.

"Stop doing that," she demanded.

He stopped laughing, but his eyes still gleamed. "Stop doing what?"

"Um." She couldn't tear her eyes from his, yet she was one hundred percent aware of the softness of his mouth. Guh. "Stop—never mind."

They looked at each other, silent, for a long moment. Then Lark shook off the sensual tension and stared past him into the dark. *You can't have this. So focus.*

"Okay. Questions." They surged back, as did her professional excitement. "Tell me about your recovery. How long did they suspend you? I mean, all that damage, you had to be suspended for the bones to knit. What did they use? A bone glue?"

"Yes, among other things." He shrugged. "I was out of it for about three months. I assume that's how long they had me in the chamber. I'm just glad I wasn't aware of it." His voice tightened.

"You're claustrophobic?"

"Not really."

"Just don't like being trapped."

He shook his head at her. "How do you figure a person out so easily? You didn't minor in psych, did you?" His tone made it clear what he thought of such a thing, and she laughed.

"No. It just made sense."

Jason cleared his throat. "I think they did most of the repair work while I was under. Once I was awake and weight bearing and could start rehab, they injected me with your stuff."

Again, she could read his voice. Her heart sank, tanking the excitement. Of course, the compound was still experimental. She couldn't expect it to work perfectly. That it had worked at all was still a miracle, even if… "You don't like it," she said.

"What?"

"The RT-24. The regeneration therapy. You don't like it."

"It's fine. I'm grateful for it." He paused, not looking at her. "Not the side effects so much."

"Did the regrowth hurt?"

He smiled a little. "Like a sonofabitch."

"I'm sorry." There was probably little to be done. Nerves were the pain centers, after all.

He shrugged. "Being dead would have hurt more, I suppose. Anyway, it wasn't constant."

But she knew how horrible it must have been. Pictured him screaming in the night, bowing upward on his bed, naked…

Jesus Christ on a stick.

"Does it hurt now?" She took a swig of warm water to ease away the huskiness in her voice.

"Occasionally."

She winced in sympathy. "When did they stop the therapy?"

"A few weeks ago."

Her mouth fell open. "And it's still working?"

"Apparently. We don't know what that means, besides 'don't touch me.'"

She remembered, remorsefully, grabbing his arm in the car. "I'm sorry I hurt you."

"No—it's—never mind. It's fine."

She didn't believe him, but he clearly didn't want to dwell on it. "You said they used bone glue and what else?"

"Something that bonds with muscle cells, helps them knit together stronger."

That was so cool. "Does it make *you* stronger?"

He grinned briefly and rose. "Watch." He went over to a large planter on the corner of the deck. It was about three feet across, round, and filled with dirt, maybe stones on the bottom for drainage. The plants were typical houseplants—geraniums, petunias, philodendron.

Jason not only lifted the pot with one hand, he lifted it above his head, not even requiring the use of his other hand to steady it. And he stood there, holding it at an angle, so the weight was not over the pole of his upraised arm, but to the side.

"Holy crap."

He set the planter down with a light thump. "They don't know."

"Why the hell not?"

Jason sat back in his chair and picked up his water. "I found out accidentally. And I already hated being studied and poked and prodded. I didn't want to become a show pony, too."

"Yet you performed for me. You told me."

"Imagine that." He drank.

As she watched his throat working, her own dried out. She sipped her water, but it didn't help.

Her gaze dropped to the curves of his biceps, clear through the snug shirt, and the flat plane of his abdomen. Her heart pounded, and she didn't know if it was because of the implications of their breakthroughs, or how incredibly hot his strength was. She tightened her grip on the bottle to keep herself from fanning her face or plucking at her shirt.

"Umm…" She struggled to remember what he'd just said. "You can also run faster, according to Dad."

He shrugged.

"You move so smoothly," she marveled. "Like there's nothing wrong with you. Like nothing has been wrong."

"Rehab. Keeps the joints oiled, the muscles supple." He rotated a shoulder.

"But it's more than that," she pressed. "Normally you'd be sore—"

"I'm not normal," he cut her off.

"No," she agreed after a moment. She didn't say he'd never *been* normal. Even though he wasn't actively part of her life, his presence, his influence on her father, had been. When she was young, her father had told her stories of Jason's honor and skill and bravery. Her minor hero worship faded as she matured and then built her own life, but she still recognized one thing.

Very few people could have accomplished what

Jason Templeton had after he died. Someday, maybe he'd understand it wasn't what had been done to him that made his recovery a success, but what he'd done with it.

SEVEN

ELLA ARRIVED AT Matthew's house at ten minutes to eight on Saturday morning. He went out to the front porch when her Chrysler Sebring convertible pulled up in the front circle. She didn't dally, but immediately pulled herself out of the car and crossed the uneven cobblestones with a brisk, even stride, despite her very high heels. Neither the shoes nor the short—and wrinkled—gray business skirt seemed to hinder her movements.

In the decade since Matthew had seen her last, she'd aged mostly well. Her tan hid the wrinkles it was responsible for, though as she climbed the porch steps he could see faint white lines in the corners of her eyes. She either squinted a lot, or laughed while she soaked up the rays.

"Thank you for seeing me." She held out both hands and lifted her cheek for a kiss he declined to give her. Instead he gave her hands a quick squeeze and motioned for her to precede him into the house.

"It's my pleasure," good manners forced him to say. "Can I get you anything?"

"Coffee would be lovely, if you have some made." She smoothed her hands down the front of her skirt, and he wondered if it was for the wrinkles or her obvious nervousness.

"I do. Why don't you go into the living room and I'll bring it to you."

"Oh, no, that's okay, the kitchen is fine." She started to follow him down the hallway.

"Living room is more comfortable," he pointed out.

"I don't want you to go to any trouble. And I know you're in a hurry."

He was. He didn't have any appointments today, but he wanted Gabby to get some things ready to run a couple of extra tests when Jason and Lark arrived. If he hurried, he could probably beat Gabby to the lab. He'd awoken with an energy he hadn't had in a long time, and he resented having to meet with Ella this morning. Suspicion and curiosity had kept him from canceling, but he wasn't going to let her linger.

"Okay, then," he said to Ella. "Let's talk." But she was silent while he got two mugs from the cupboard and filled them with coffee, placing them on the island where she'd claimed a stool, then retrieving cream and sugar. Even once he stood opposite her, stirring sugar into his own coffee, he had to prompt her to speak.

"What can I do for you?"

She winced. "It's not me. I mean, I shouldn't have said I hoped you could help me. That's not why I'm here. It's more…more that I hope I can help you." Her hand shook as she raised the coffee mug to her mouth, and Matthew forced himself to relax so he could try to help her do the same.

"It's okay. I have plenty of time," he lied. "Tell me what you're doing now. It was real estate back then, wasn't it?"

"Yes." She blinked at him, frowned slightly, but answered more thoroughly. "I did residential real estate for an agency for about five years, but opened my own commercial-focused agency with a friend."

"Do you still do that?"

"Yes, of course, but we've branched out a bit. Financial services, a boutique travel agency. More of a relocation service," she amended, getting into her topic. "But we've done some regular travel arrangements for clients."

"You seem to be doing well. Who's your partner?"

She waved a hand. "You don't know him. Or—okay, maybe you do. You know everyone." What little loosening her muscles had done over the two minutes she was distracted now tightened up again. She was going to end up with a full body cramp.

"His name is Seamus Kemmerling."

Matthew's body jolted. He contained it with difficulty, but Ella didn't seem to notice. "Seamus Kemmerling?" he repeated.

"Yes."

"K-E-M-M-E-R-L-I-N-G?"

"Yes."

"I've never heard of him." He drank some more coffee and kept his tone disinterested and his body language neutral. He wasn't lying. He'd never heard of Seamus, and that pissed him off. The pre-employment background checks on Isaac should have turned him up, assuming they were related.

"Well, it doesn't matter. I've known Seamus for nearly fifteen years. We went through our Realtor licensing program together. He went to work for a commercial company right away, though, while I got my feet wet in residential. Then we opened our own office together, and…" She trailed off and looked uncertain, as if she wasn't sure where she'd been going with that.

"Are you romantically involved?" Matthew tried.

"No."

"Do you know his family?"

Her face cleared. "Yes, and that's actually the point of this whole thing." She settled more completely onto the stool and wrapped her fingers around the handle of the coffee mug as if it would leap off the counter if she didn't hold it tightly enough.

"A couple of years ago, Seamus's cousin Isaac showed up needing a job."

Matthew frowned. "Where is your office?"

"Florida."

"And Isaac came down there looking for work?" If he had found it, it had been short-lived. He started his own security firm only a few weeks after he left Hummingbird.

"He did, but Seamus ended up giving him money to start a business instead."

"Were they close? I mean, did Seamus talk about Isaac a lot, did you meet him before that?"

"No, Seamus is a lot older. He was surprised when Isaac came to him. But neither one of them has other family. It made sense."

Matthew drained his mug and turned his back on Ella to refill it. But he could see her reflection in the toaster and the stainless steel blender base. She rubbed her hand across her forehead before she continued.

"Seamus gave him a substantial loan, out of our savings. It was meant to be used to pay the mortgage in case we had a slow month or two. Seamus told Isaac not to start paying us back until he'd been established for several months."

"And you were to hope the bottom didn't fall out of the market in the meantime?" He turned back but this time leaned against the counter instead of rejoining her at the island.

"Right. Well, of course, it had already, but we were doing okay, and it stayed that way. Isaac started making his payments right on time. He paid us every month for a couple of years until six months ago, when he stopped abruptly."

Six months ago. Interesting timing.

"What does abruptly mean?"

She sighed. "Without notice. He refused to answer our calls, so I drafted a certified letter. It came back marked refused—not unable to deliver. I got mad and came up here."

"Why you? He's Seamus's cousin."

"I know. The family connection makes it harder."

Matthew didn't disagree. "Did you meet with him?"

"Yes, and he apologized and wrote a check for all the late payments. It was a good check—I called the bank—and I was shocked. I couldn't believe he had the money and not some song and dance."

"What reason did he give?"

"That's why I'm here."

Finally.

She spun her mug on the countertop. "He didn't really give a reason, but I noticed something while I was at his office."

"What?" Matthew prompted when she didn't continue.

"He was obsessed with you. The post office must

have made a mistake with my certified letter, because it was pretty obvious he'd forgotten to pay us, that his mind had been on other things. I had to wait to see him, and people were charging around, talking about you."

She wasn't telling him anything he didn't already know, and he was getting tired of the drawn-out lead-in. He straightened away from the counter and set his mug down.

"Thanks, Ella. I appreciate—"

"I'm not finished," she barked at his deliberately dismissive tone.

"Okay." He resumed his position, folding his arms and watching her face as she visibly controlled her temper.

"His payments continued normally over the last few months. But he contacted me this week. I don't know why now. He asked a bunch of questions about my relationship with you, and—"

Matthew waited, but she didn't finish. "It's okay, Ella, I can probably guess what you're going to say."

Her brows crunched together and she fiddled with the edge of the placemat. "Why doesn't that surprise me?"

He smiled a little. "Because I'm good at what I do." She still didn't continue, so he said, "Isaac waited until now to approach you because he probably just learned of our connection. Kelly's been dead for a long time, and in-law relationships aren't easily picked up on when they're not active." He retrieved her mug and put it in the sink with his own, this time not turning his back on her. "I'm guessing Isaac hoped you could get close to me. Get access to my files, maybe, or my people. Find vulnerabilities."

Ella picked up her purse from the island next to her and rummaged in it a bit. "Yes, that's exactly what he was getting at."

"And since you haven't been in touch with me for years, you knew that wasn't going to happen."

She looked up, astonishment painted onto her face. "What?"

"You came up with this, instead. Pretend to warn me about Isaac's intentions. Be all flustered and worried, maybe tell me he threatened you, to fire my protective instincts." He eased away from the counter and moved to her side. She stilled, one hand inside her purse, the other hidden between her and the island.

"No, that's—"

Matthew gently caught her wrist as she pulled her hand, fast but not fast enough, out of her bag. She clutched an uncapped syringe. A drop of liquid fell from the tip onto the tile floor. Her mouth trembled and she twisted her wrist slightly, but he didn't let go.

"It's okay, Ella. Isaac wouldn't expect you to succeed." He kept talking in as soothing a tone as he could manage. Ella leaned toward him, collapsing against his chest, an obvious trick so she could get her free hand up. She swung the other syringe high, trying to stick him in the neck.

He let her.

THOUGH LARK SLEPT poorly and suspected Jason did, too, they got up at dawn and headed out, grabbing fast food breakfast on the way. A few hours later, they were back at Hummingbird.

But her father wasn't.

It was a Saturday, and the office staff wasn't present. But this wasn't a nine-to-five business. There were always agents on site, contacts for mission leaders on jobs, and the occasional tech on standby for IT support. Today, they saw almost no one as they made their way up to her father's office.

Which was open and empty. The combination forced a sliver of fear into her heart, though she didn't know why. She'd never been here when her father wasn't, and didn't know how it was supposed to be. Unlocked didn't seem right, no matter how she looked at it.

"Where's Caitlyn?" she asked, as if anyone could answer. She checked the assistant's desk. Her computer was in standby, pending central backup. Lark checked the logout time. Five-fifteen the day before.

She inhaled hard as the sliver swelled to panic, her heartbeat pounding in her ears, her pulse in her neck and wrists. She swiped a finger at the cold moisture on her upper lip. "Dad was supposed to be here to meet us, wasn't he?"

"Yes."

The office's front wall was glass, and they could see there was no one inside. Still, Jason motioned for her to stay in the reception area while he went in.

Like she could stand here and do nothing. She whipped out her cell phone and hit the number for the house. No answer. Tried his cell. Went straight to voice mail. Maybe he was in the shower or something. She pretended it wasn't ridiculous to think he'd gotten out in three seconds, and dialed again. Nothing.

She paced and studied the office through the window, calling up old training as she checked details Jason had already cataloged. There was no mess, no overturned furniture, no crack in the glass or skewing of the computer's placement. The computer's external drive was in place, and the safe where he kept important files was closed. She watched Jason check the computer and try the drawers of the desk. He shook his head and came out to her.

"Why isn't he answering his phone?" She fought to keep her voice steady. Jason rested his hand on the back of her neck, and the firm grip, the warmth and slight scrape of callus, seemed to draw tension right out of her. He wasn't pretending to be calm, he *was* calm, and that, more than anything else, dissolved the panic back to a sliver.

"You tried the house?" he asked her.

"Twice."

He released her to look at his watch. "It's still early." They'd left Boston at five-thirty, Jason driving at maniac speeds but with precision that had made it feel like a Sunday drive. It was only a little after noon now, slightly before her father had expected them. But he was *always* there long before he was supposed to be. *He could be anywhere here. Or maybe he had unexpected lunch plans. Or a meeting. Anything.* She pressed her fingertips hard against her forehead. If her father had changed plans, he'd have let them know.

"We need to go home." It came out as a demand and she half expected Jason to argue, to say her safety came first, but he only nodded.

"Can you handle a gun?"

She stood from where she'd been perched on the edge of Caitlyn's desk. "Of course."

Jason went back into the office and behind her father's desk. He opened a cabinet in the credenza and worked a combination, added a thumbprint and spoke his name. The safe opened, revealing carefully placed weapons. He removed a small semiautomatic pistol and a box of clips, then reversed the process and came back out to her.

"Show me." He handed her the weapon, butt first, and the box.

She set the box on the table. The gun already had a clip in it. She checked the safety and made sure to keep the barrel pointed away from Jason. Pulled back the slide to check the chamber, then carefully released it. Hit the clip release, checked the clip, and slammed it home.

Except she missed, and the clip clattered across the top of Caitlyn's empty desk.

She froze. Jason didn't move. She waited, willing the clip to come soaring back to her hand. "Uh…"

Jason cleared his throat. "Okay, you can handle a gun."

Lark glared at him, but his amusement stayed behind his Captain Action façade. Still, the moment dissipated her tension a fraction.

"Can you shoot one?" he asked.

"I have." Not memorably, but she could aim and fire.

He hesitated, and she expected him to take the weapon back. But his hand fell to his side and he said only, "All right. Let's go."

It was a fifteen-minute drive to her father's house, the house where she grew up. Where her mother had died. That wasn't something she thought about every time she came back, and she didn't want to consider why it came to mind now. There was no reason to think her father was dead. She'd called Caitlyn's cell phone, and Jason had tried a couple of people, but they mostly got voice mail and no one they reached had seen Matthew since he left the evening before.

Lark inhaled deeply, trying to remain calm as they pulled into the circular driveway in front of the house. Then she gasped and barely refrained from grabbing Jason's arm again.

"Jason."

"I see it." The front door was open. "Stay here."

Not even. She got out of the car and stopped. She didn't want to get in his way, but she wasn't sure how long she could suffer the swelling in her throat before she charged in shouting "Dad!" She counted the seconds, forcing herself to keep them slow, and ignoring the images flashing in her head. All the things Jason could find in there.

Amazingly, he appeared back on the porch way before she expected him, and waved her in. Relief made her stumble as she dashed across the macadam and up the steps to the front door. He wouldn't call her in if her father was dead in there.

"What?" she asked breathlessly.

"Come here."

Lark followed him to her father's home office, the relief already having run its course. He'd found something. He stayed close beside her, as if ready to support her. Or catch her.

But there was nothing in the office to explain his concern. No blood on the floor, smashed computer, or scattered papers. The desk and files were as tidy as they always were. The computer was off.

But Jason didn't follow her to the desk. He stood in the far corner, where there was a sofa and television, a remote in his hand. There was a sticky note on the table where the remote usually lay.

"Don't tell me." She circled back around the desk and stood next to him, folding her arms around herself.

He looked grim. "I won't." He aimed the remote at the DVD player and pressed a button.

Her father's image appeared on the screen. He wasn't battered or unkempt, but his eyes looked dull and he didn't blink as he spoke in a near monotone.

"Larkspur. JT. I know you'll find this. The situation has gotten dire and I have decided to remove myself from your proximity to keep you both safe. I'll contact you when I get to Mexico. JT, I completed the investigation into the employee you mentioned. He was the only insider feeding Kemmerling. I want you to return to Dr. Berwell and complete your testing and immunizations. We need the results as soon as possible. Nothing is more important. I love you both."

The last words rang with truth, a stark contrast to the rest of what he said.

"It's all bullshit," Lark said. She couldn't catch a breath. Her chest burned. "He doesn't call me Larkspur."

"And he never calls me JT. Only the agents do."

Concentrate on the facts. Forget possibilities. Things her father had taught her. Nausea surged and she swallowed it down. All these quick-change emotions were churning her up. She wouldn't be any good to her father if she lost it. "He hates Mexico," she pointed out. “It was where he and Mom went for their honeymoon.”

“They had a horrible time, he got sick and refused to go back,” Jason added.

“He’d never leave us to ‘keep us safe.’ He knows what a crock of shit it is.”

“Nils has to be a low-level connection. Someone else in the company is a traitor.”

She wanted to weep. Her father was so careful about who he trusted, and to get burned this badly… “It sounds like this Dr. Berwell—”

“It’s not Gabby.” Jason cut her off. “But it could be anyone else.”

“How do you know it’s not Gabby?”

He turned his head, his expression intense. “Because she’s in love with your father.”

“Oh.” She worried her bottom lip, letting the revelation join the cauldron of details. “But she could—”

“I’ve just spent three months in intensive contact with her. She’s not part of this,” Jason insisted.

Lark didn’t bother arguing. Men could be stupid, but Jason had to have good instincts to do the job he did. That didn’t mean she would take this Gabby/Dr. Berwell off the list. Jason was right, though. It could be anyone.

He rewound the DVD and replayed it. “He’s wearing a different shirt than the one he was wearing when I saw him yesterday,” he said. “Unless he spilled coffee on himself, this was probably done today. See the light behind him?” He twisted to check the windows. “It came from there, and came across.” He swept his arm past the wall that was behind her father in the recording. "Morning sun. Couldn't have been too long ago."

"He was drugged." Lark moved closer to the TV. "He could have been putting on the monotone and the stare, but he can't dilate his eyes at will. Especially with that much light."

"There are two coffee mugs in the kitchen. One has lipstick on it. The other is full."

"So someone was here. A woman." She carefully didn't reference Gabby again. "Any sign—"

"No struggle. I don't think whoever it was used his coffee to drug him, and he didn't fight them."

Lark listened to the end of the speech playing on the DVD. "He wouldn't send you back to the lab, either. I can't figure—"

"It's not a lab," he said in a low voice, as if considering.

"What?"

"Gabby gets annoyed when I call it a lab. It's a medical facility. Or something, she never really said."

Her brow wrinkled. "Okay, whatever. My point is, Dad saved your life for *you*. Not to test the technology. He wouldn't trap you again."

"Thanks." He squeezed her shoulder and let his hand stroke down her hair before focusing on the DVD player again. "Let's see if we can figure anything else out."

They sat down and watched the recording half a dozen more times, picking up tiny things that only reinforced what they'd already deduced. After the last time, they sat for a minute.

"What do we do now?"

Jason knew what Matt would have wanted him to

do, or at least half of it. "I should hide you someplace and go find your father."

"But you won't." There was no doubt in her voice.

"No."

"The question is, will you not hide me because you need me as bait, or as help?" It didn't seem to matter to her one way or the other.

Jason chuckled and shook his head. "I like you, Lark Madrassa."

Her mouth curved, but she didn't respond.

"Either or," he told her. "Except Matt would kill me if I used you as bait. And wouldn't bring me back this time."

"He wouldn't be very happy with using me as a partner, either," she pointed out.

"No. But I can't trust anyone else." That reality burned his gut more than ever. You couldn't work in this business and be an idealist. They always knew the risk of betrayal. But they hadn't actually encountered it before, and since they had no idea where the threat lay, they had to believe it was everywhere.

"You said Gabby is in love with Dad," Lark said. "That she wouldn't betray him."

"I believe that. It doesn't mean I can trust her."

"But she's our only lead, right? In that whole speech—" she waved at the TV, "—she's the only one he mentioned specifically. Do you think she's back at the facility?"

"Probably. She doesn't seem to ever go home. But we can't go down there."

"Because that's what he wants us to do."

"Who?" Jason blurted, disconcerted how closely she followed his train of thought. He wasn't used to anyone but Matt doing that. Not even Allison, the mission leader he'd worked with longest.

"Kemmerling, if we're assuming he's behind this. I don't know who else it would be, but you might."

"No, he's pretty much the Big Bad in this scenario." Matt had mentioned others who wanted to get their hands on the technology, and maybe on him, but he'd talked about them as if they were distant buyers, not anyone who would actively pursue the information.

"Should we call Gabby to come here?" Lark's knees bounced in agitation, and Jason could tell he wasn't going to be able to hold her back. He stood and went to Matt's desk to boot up the computer.

"Not exactly." Matt synced his contacts list to a computer file, so Jason should be able to access phone numbers he wouldn't normally have, like Gabby's home and cell phones. It took a moment to get through his layers of passwords—Jason had limited access to certain areas of the computer—so to speed things along, he just added Matt's file to his own, telling the program not to overwrite duplicates, and explaining to Lark what he was doing as he worked. The top-of-the-line system zipped through the download, and a minute later he scrolled through his phone book to double-check they were all there.

"Give me your number, too," Lark said, her phone ready. "And Gabby's. Just in case we get separated."

"We won't get separated." But he did it anyway, just in case. Then he scrolled through the call log on the desk phone, but there was nothing within the last twenty-four hours, and the calls before it weren't connected to this situation.

"So what's the plan?" Lark asked when he finished.

He shook his head. She looked annoyed, but closed her mouth until they were outside and in his car—in his own car now, not a company-issued one. Settling into the seat of the old Range Rover had made him feel more in control than he had since he woke up three months ago.

Lark clicked her seat belt, then folded her arms and looked straight out the windshield. Then she unfolded them and let her hands rest, as if pretending she wasn't still annoyed. Trouble was, she looked like a cockatoo with its feathers ruffled. Jason barely managed to stop himself from smoothing her hair again. It had been silky against his palm, one of the few areas of his body where light touch wasn't excruciating.

"You can ask now," he told her.

"Ask what?"

"What the plan is."

"I didn't think you were going to tell me."

"I wasn't going to tell you in *there,* where it might be bugged. There was no point in taking the time to sweep the room when we were leaving anyway."

"Oh." She bit her lip. "I suppose if someone could get in there to plant the disk—and record it, too—they could have planted bugs at the same time."

"Right." Jason started the Rover and pulled around the circle to head down the driveway. "Same reason I didn't take the company car again when we left Hummingbird."

"What makes this one safe?"

"I have an automatic detection system on it." He tapped a unit hanging from the key chain. "It's clean."

"Okay. Then, what's the plan?"

"You'll see."

He chuckled at her yelp. She was fun to play with. Now wasn't the time for playing, of course, with her father's life possibly hanging in the balance, but it did help with the tension. Jason wouldn't underestimate the value of reducing the stress, even for a few seconds at a time.

"They wouldn't hurt him, right?" She looked left and right as he pulled up to a stop sign. "No, that's not what I'm asking. They would hurt him, if they thought they needed to. I meant—they won't kill him. Right?"

Jason knew what she wanted him to say. Luckily, he could say it truthfully. "I don't think so. Why bother making the recording if they're getting rid of him?" He went straight and pressed down on the accelerator on the open stretch.

"If they didn't want us to look for his body—"

"Don't." He rested his hand on her thigh, intending it as comfort or reassurance. Her quads flexed under his fingers, as if she wanted to squirm. "Keep your imagination on a short leash, Lark."

"Yeah." She put her hand on top of his, and it had just the right amount of weight to it. Her touch yesterday had been stronger, sending a bolt of pleasure through him. He couldn't afford that kind of distraction, especially now. But now, it was just a touch. He let it linger, both taking comfort and giving it.

After a moment, he said, "They went to a lot of trouble to send us in a certain direction. They don't want him dead. Not yet, if at all. Kemmerling isn't a killer." At least, the Isaac Jason knew hadn't been a killer. He didn't know him now. Didn't know how corrupt he'd become. But he didn't think it was a factor, at least at the moment. Isaac wanted something specific, and had a plan to get it. If he killed Matt, all incentive for Jason and Lark to play along would disappear.

He hoped Isaac saw that logic.

EIGHT

MATTHEW WOKE IN a pit.

Not literally, or at least he didn't think so. It was hard to tell. The dirt walls had no windows or doors. The ceiling seemed to be wood, but was out of his reach. The only light came through slits in the ceiling. He guessed he was in some kind of earthen basement under a cabin or something similar.

He kept still and let his eyes adjust to the darkness. He lay on a scratchy blanket, probably wool. Several of them formed a pallet on the bare floor. He didn't rate a bed, apparently. Isaac wasn't following the "respect your opponent" school of thought.

Matthew stretched, wincing at the ache in his muscles. They hadn't handled him delicately while he was out. Jason would kill him when he found out Matthew had let himself be taken. But it had been a calculated risk. He couldn't get near Isaac any other way.

The sedative Ella injected him with contained an added chemical that was supposed to make him compliant. He'd fought it, and though he'd made the speech she told him to make, he managed to put clues in it that both Jason and Lark should pick up on. Well, Jason, anyway. Matthew wasn't sure how Lark would handle his abduction. She might be too emotional to examine his words. He felt a pang of regret for putting her through that, but if his choice made her less of a target, it was worth a little distress.

He bit back a groan as he pulled himself upright to study the room. A camping-style chemical toilet sat crookedly in one corner. An old-fashioned pitcher and basin rested on a stand against the wall between the toilet and the pallet. An intercom unit had been pressed into the dirt wall, cables leading up into the structure overhead.

Matthew ignored the intercom for now. In the dim, striped glow from above, he took inventory of his body, tensing and releasing muscles, shifting and prodding to make sure nothing was broken or torn, before rising and taking a couple of small steps. Muscles twinged, evidence of both his age and rough handling, but he didn't seem to have any true injuries. No dried blood or healing cuts, aside from the tender spot where Ella had inexpertly plunged the needle into his neck. He shivered, partly because of being underground, partly a side effect of the sedative. Movement would combat both.

He paced around the room, testing the walls and checking corners, squinting up at the floor above. He couldn't see any interruptions in the light that would indicate either people or furniture in the room above him, and there was no noise, human or electronic. He found the faint outline of a well-cut trapdoor dead center of the room. They'd cut it there purposefully, to keep him from climbing the walls and breaking out. Most of the gaps between floor planks were too narrow to wedge his fingers into. But he wasn't planning on escaping, anyway. Not yet. It would defeat his whole purpose for being here.

He checked his pockets. Cell phone, wallet, car and house keys, all gone. He'd known they would be. Before Ella arrived, he'd locked his Hummingbird pass card in his safe, and had only the front door and main car keys in his pocket. Nothing would be helpful to Isaac or whoever had him.

"You *planned* this? From the beginning?" he could imagine Lark's outraged demand. She'd be shocked, first, that he expected the worst from her aunt. But he'd trained Isaac, and Hummingbird was a successful company not because they threw up walls when someone tried to hurt their clients, but because they understood the minds of those they were up against.

"Think like the enemy" was almost a motto. So Matthew had been spending a lot of time thinking like Isaac Kemmerling. The man was obviously desperate to capitalize on Hummingbird's bad fortune—or screw-up, depending on how you looked at it—and he'd be looking for any and every in he could get. Now that Matthew knew about her connection to Isaac, Ella was a fairly obvious asset for his opponent.

His examination of the cellar exhausted, he approached the intercom stuck in the wall. It was the kind of unit you'd find on the outside of an old apartment building. Most of the buttons were missing, which made it obvious which one would signal his captors that he was awake. Or fry him, if it was rigged or malfunctioning. He crossed the dirt floor to the stand holding the pitcher and basin. The pitcher was half full of water. Matt emptied it into the basin and carried the pitcher back to the intercom, where he used the handle to depress the button. There was a faint hiss, but no evidence the unit had been wired to electrocute him. He returned the pitcher and crossed back to the speaker just as a voice crackled through it.

"What?"

Matthew used his thumbnail to press the button. "*You're* friendly."

No response.

"Just thought I'd let you know I'm awake."

"Fine. You're awake." The voice still sounded at peak grumpiness. Matthew wondered how sparse the accommodations upstairs were. He was betting there was no plasma-screen TV.

"Let's do whatever I'm here to do."

He swore the silence hissed with confusion, and suppressed a grin. "How about some food?" he suggested. "Maybe a soda? The water down here is gross."

Again no response, but a few moments later heavy boots thudded on the floor above him. Dust filtered down through the cracks. Matthew stayed where he was while metal scraped on metal, followed by a heavy thud before the trapdoor creaked open, the door tilting upward. Nothing else happened.

Then Grumpy said, "Come over here where I can see you."

Matthew nodded approvingly. Enemy or not, Isaac had been trained by Hummingbird, and he'd trained his men the same way. You didn't stick your head into a hole in the ground without being able to see what might be coming.

Of course, by the same token, you didn't expose yourself to attack from a shielded enemy, either. Matthew stepped forward just enough for Grumpy to see him.

And jolted slightly when he recognized his guard.

"Hello, John."

John grunted.

"I thought you quit Hummingbird to go live with your mother in California. How's she doing?" He tried to keep his voice mild. Anger wouldn't serve him well here in any capacity.

"I did," John grunted again, but with words, at least. "She died early this year."

"I'm sorry." He waited. The guy wasn't very talkative today. Tonight? He had no idea what time it was, how many hours or even days had passed. "Why didn't you come back to Hummingbird? We'd have been happy to have you."

"Kemmerling was newer. Figured he'd have more opportunities."

Matthew nodded. John was a good agent. He did what he was trained to do, but he wasn't leadership material by Hummingbird's standards. Standards he might not meet at all now. John had put on a significant number of pounds. The semiautomatic rifle in his hands balanced the equation, though.

"Okay, well, it's good to see you again anyway. Isaac around?"

"No."

"Will he be?"

"Probably."

"When?"

"Eventually."

Matthew fought back a sigh and kept his hands at his sides. "Okay, then, how about food?"

A plastic-wrapped sub, the kind you buy from neighborhood kids for school fundraisers, dropped to the floor at his feet. "Ah, thanks. Drink?"

A diet root beer landed beside the sub. Matthew hated root beer. He guessed Isaac was trying to send him a message. But he didn't care how much Isaac thought he knew about his former boss. He didn't know enough.

"What time is it?" He didn't bend to retrieve the food. It would wait until the door was closed.

"'Bout two."

"P.M.?"

"Yep."

"Saturday?"

"Yep."

Good. He hadn't been out too long. Jason and Lark had surely found his message by now. If they'd decoded it properly, they would have also acted to secure the data from any Hummingbird staff who could have been compromised. They were probably also working to find him. As he had no way to tell them to stop, to ferret out the traitors instead, he'd just have to work on his own plans.

"That all?" John asked.

"Yeah, for now. Thanks for the food. Let me know when Isaac gets here, will ya?"

John gave one final grunt and dropped the trapdoor into place. There was more metal scraping, then John's heavy footsteps retreating. Matthew held still and listened hard. The door that creaked open and clicked closed was probably wooden, hollow, typical of any old house. There was no additional sound of a lock being engaged. Isaac—or maybe just John—was pretty confident he had Matthew secure.

Good.

JASON HANDED HIS phone to Lark as they neared the coffee shop he had in mind. "Find Gabby's number for me, please, and then I'll call her."

Lark scrolled through and found it, then handed the phone back. "Want me to call?"

"No, she'll be expecting to hear from me." He put it up to his ear. Gabby answered almost immediately.

"Dr. Berwell." Her tension came through, even though she was clearly trying to sound normal, professional.

"Gabby, it's me."

"Jason, thank God. I can't reach Matthew. I—"

"I know. Don't say more. I need you to come to me." He pulled the truck over to the curb half a block from the coffee shop. Lark climbed out and stuck some quarters in the meter. Jason watched her, noting steady hands, no tears or sniffling, her movements purposeful but not exaggerated or sharp. His respect for her rose.

"Where are you?" Gabby's voice shook a little, but had calmed.

"You know the historic hotel downtown? The one with the great Brandy Alexanders?"

"Of course I know."

"I'll meet you there."

"Okay, give me half an hour. I need to make up a reason to leave here."

"How about it's Saturday, and you have plans?" he offered sarcastically.

She giggled. Good. She'd be safer, and less obvious, if she wasn't so tense. "Yeah, they'd believe that. I wouldn't even believe it."

He smiled a little. "Okay, then. Half an hour."

Lark leaned back through her open door. “I thought we were going to the coffee shop.”

“We are.” He climbed out of the truck and locked it, setting the alarm and detection unit. He let Lark go ahead, keeping her in sight while he scanned the small town square. Besides the hotel and café, there was an insurance agency, a pharmacy, a Laundromat, and a large boardinghouse. Residences lined the streets in three directions, and a bridge over the creek, leading out of town, was a few hundred yards down the fourth. Visibility was good, with all the cars parked in angled spaces on two sides of the square. The street was empty in the center except for a flower-covered median.

Jason didn’t notice anything bothersome and opened the door to the café, pleased to see Lark had chosen a table centered at the window. Not only could they see clearly in all directions, the large business name scrolled across much of the window would make it difficult for anyone peering in to recognize them.

Lark glanced at him as he came over. “Coffee?”

“Yeah. What do you want?” He reached for his wallet in his back pocket.

She stood. “I’ll get it.”

Jason gave her his order and sat, allowing himself a moment to watch her walk up to the counter. Her arms swayed, loose, her gait smooth. Their banter had taken the edge off. But as she stood waiting, it sharpened again. He could tell by the way she shifted her weight from foot to foot and nibbled on the cuticle of her thumb. When the steamer went off, she jumped, then made a “disgusted with herself” face. Jason turned to look out the window. Urgency churned in his gut.

The back of his hand brushed the edge of the tabletop, sending tiny bursts of electric shock across his skin. He gritted his teeth against the pain and held his breath until it subsided. He needed to get used to these little agonies. Otherwise, they'd tank his career, as well as his sex life. He smiled a little, equating an attacker's glee at discovering the vulnerability with a woman's exasperation over trying to deal with it.

Lark wouldn't get exasperated.

Now he scowled. How the hell did he know what her reaction would be long term? And why the hell was he thinking the words "long term," anyway?

He was grateful when Lark appeared with the coffee and resumed her seat. "You see anything?"

Jason kept his attention outside. "No movement on the square since we got here, except Mrs. Beagle's dog got out again. What did you see?"

Lark sipped her coffee. "Not much. The windows of the hotel have a glare. We'd never be able to see in until after dark, even with binocs."

"Binocs?" he queried, amused.

She ignored him. "The pharmacy has three cars in front of it. This is the kind of town with old people hanging out in one of the businesses, and since independent pharmacies are rare nowadays, I'm guessing that's what those are. Plus, they're old-people-big-car makes. Olds and Buick, about fifteen years old."

"And you know Fran and Dennis from when you worked there during high school," Jason noted wryly.

"Wow, you're good." Lark's impish grin didn't go away. "My observations are valid, though."

"Since you can fit them into what you already

know, sure. Stop trying to impress me and tell me what you really see."

For half a second she looked shocked and sheepish. Then she locked her gaze on the Laundromat. "There's no one in the Laundromat, but the dryers are going. Someone will probably be coming back soon."

"Not bad. Relevance?"

She sighed. "Come on, Jason, Dad does this to me every time I see him. Can't we just do the job?"

He relented. "Sure. I just want you to be prepared. You're not a field agent."

"I'm not an agent at all."

"Matt trained you to be."

Her jaw flexed briefly before she answered. "It was years ago. He stopped when I declared my major."

Jason grimaced. "That's comforting."

She didn't smile. "I'm not trying to comfort you now." Which meant she had been trying to earlier, in the car. His heart rolled. *Matt's your best mate,* he reminded himself sternly, *and missing to boot. Forget it.*

A silver sedan came down the road and pulled into a space in front of the hotel.

"She's here," he said.

NINE

JASON WATCHED GABBY open her car door and put her foot out, then pause as she gathered her things.

Lark ducked her head a little to peer between a letter and a flourish on the café's window. "That's Dr. Berwell?"

"Yes."

"She's young!"

"She's older than me." Jason shrugged. He didn't consider age an indicator of ability.

But that apparently wasn't what Lark was thinking about. "But younger than my dad," she pointed out.

Jason chuckled. "Can we talk to her about the mess we're in before you start interrogating her about her intentions?"

Lark thought a second. "Okay, but I don't like her."

He didn't believe her. Maybe she *thought* she shouldn't, to protect her father's tender heart. Or maybe she wanted a target, someone to go after for his abduction. Whatever—Jason didn't think Lark was the kind of woman to judge at first sight.

As Gabby entered the hotel, a man wearing a black leather jacket—in June—followed, glancing over his shoulder and scanning the street as he did. Jason tensed and focused, his eyes narrowing as he studied the man's gait and profile. He didn't know him.

"She was followed from work," Lark guessed, her nose practically pressed against the glass.

"Maybe. Or he could be with her. Or have nothing to do with any of us."

"What do we do?"

"One of us goes over and sees what's happening over there."

Lark's eyes widened at him. "One of us? Like maybe me?"

The last thing Jason wanted to do was send Lark out of his sight. But he needed her. They had to determine the situation before they moved forward. "Gabby would spot me immediately. I'm kind of big, in case you hadn't noticed."

Lark *had* noticed, of course. Since her father was about six-two and Jason stood taller, she figured him at six-four. His shoulders looked as wide as the table, and his chest the perfect resting place for her whole body. The snug clothes made him impossible to overlook. And his golden hair and chiseled features were pretty memorable, too.

Crap. *Think about Dad, think about the job, think about...anything but Jason and his big sexy body.*

She cleared her throat. "Okay, Gabby doesn't know me," she agreed, "but if that guy is with Isaac, he might. Wouldn't Isaac make sure he would?"

"Not if you disguise yourself."

"With what?" she scoffed. "A mustache and pork-pie hat?"

Jason got up and went to the counter. He spoke briefly to the barista and then lifted a green apron from a hook near the end of the counter. He handed it to Lark.

"That's it?"

"It's all you'll need. Go in and ask the bartender if he can spare a few napkins. He'll think you're nuts but no one else will look at you twice."

Lark shrugged and put the loop over her head and tied the apron in the back. "You don't have a com on ya, do you?"

Jason leaned back, the front legs of his chair lifting, and grinned a wide, cocky grin. "Just one. Keep it in my wallet."

She rolled her eyes and smacked him on the shoulder. His hiss of breath registered, but Lark was past him and at the door before she realized what it might mean. Making a note to ask him about it later, she pushed to the outside, inhaled deeply and strode purposefully across the street.

The inside of the hotel was very dim after the sunshine outside. She took a second to adjust, then found the entrance to the bar/restaurant to her right. She headed over, blinking hard, trying to banish the light spots in her vision.

She found the doctor immediately, her curly red hair noticeable even in the dimness. Gabby sat alone at a table in the middle of the room. Lark couldn't believe she worked for the country's top security firm. Jason would never sit with everything exposed. She should have taken a corner table, or at least one against the wall.

Amazing how training prevailed. Over the years, as life and career had made her visits with her father less frequent, his quizzing and training had taken a backseat. She'd always done self-defense maintenance, the kind any normal woman living on her own would do. But despite the eight years that had passed since her father gave up on Lark joining his business, his training had stuck. She'd automatically counted the doors in the room, pinpointed a few hiding places, cataloged the bartender's relevant stats. It was almost as if her father were here with her.

Get to work, then. She smiled at the bartender and moved closer to the gleaming oak bar. "Would you believe we ran out of napkins?" she said to him. "Teddy is going to get some, but I wondered if you could spare a handful to get us by until he gets back."

The bartender grunted and walked to the other end of the bar. Lark idly looked around, wondering where leather jacket guy was. Gabby was the only other person in the room.

"Here."

Lark smiled again and took the brown-paper-wrapped stack of napkins. "Thank you. You're a doll."

"Plan ahead next time."

"Sure." She indicated the room behind her. "Quiet today, huh?"

He shrugged.

"Us, too, mostly. We have a few people in now. Some guy came in with a leather jacket on. Can you believe that? In June?"

The bartender didn't say, "Hey, he came in here, too!" and he didn't seem to care what she was talking about. But the doctor swung her head toward Lark and made eye contact, her own widening behind oval-framed glasses. She looked around frantically before starting to rise. Lark shook her head subtly but sharply, smiled at the guy behind the bar one more time, and went back out to the lobby.

Gabby knew who the guy was. Or maybe she'd seen him enter the hotel behind her. Or, Lark supposed, she'd turned automatically at the sound of Lark's voice. But she hadn't looked until Lark mentioned the leather jacket guy. And she'd obviously recognized Lark. Probably from a picture on her father's desk. She wished Jason were over here to tell her what to do.

She had to figure out where the leather jacket guy was. They couldn't talk to Gabby until she was in the clear. Spotting a tall ferny plant in one corner of the lobby, she sidled over, dropped the napkins, and slipped behind the plant as she started picking them up.

A moment later Gabby hurried out of the restaurant. But instead of making a beeline for the front door, she veered right down a hallway lined with room doors. Lark had picked the right spot; she could see all the way to the exit door at the end.

No one followed Gabby. Lark wanted to, but she waited, her breathing shallow, every muscle poised to act. Several seconds after the doctor left the building, someone came down the wide staircase behind Lark with hurrying footsteps. She peered carefully upward, and sure enough, it was the leather jacket guy. But he went straight out the front door and got in a car parked outside. He hadn't even pulled away when a woman wearing a strapless spandex dress and six-inch clear platforms clumped down the stairs. Her platinum hair was a bird's nest, and she was tucking money into her cleavage.

Shit. They'd been fooled.

Leaving the napkins scattered on the floor, Lark

hustled down the hall Gabby had taken. But too much time had passed. When she got to the outside door, she couldn't see the redhead anywhere. Dammit! Her cell phone rang. She ignored it and shoved through the door to the outside, searching around the parked cars. Could Gabby be behind the Dumpster, or had she turned left and gone back to her car on the main street?

When the phone rang a third time, she flipped it open without checking the number, still focused on her search.

"Where are you?" demanded Jason.

"Outside the hotel," she answered automatically

"Where?"

"On the side. Did you see the doctor?"

"Yeah, I've got her."

Lark blew out a breath. Thank goodness.

"Head back to the alley," Jason continued, "we'll pick you up. Any sign of the leather jacket guy?"

"Yeah, he was getting a quickie upstairs." She wove between cars, head up, looking for the Range Rover. "A hooker came down right after he did, and he wasn't in the bar and didn't go after Gabby when she left."

"Figures. Okay, I see you." He disconnected and pulled up next to her a few seconds later. Gabby was in the front seat, her eyes huge, her hand wrapped in the strap hanging just in front of her side window.

Jealousy was a quick, surprising burn in Lark's gut, but she hesitated only a moment before yanking open the back door and bouncing onto the seat. "I'm in."

Jason took off. Lark put on her seat belt and leaned over the seat to address Gabby. "Why did you go out the side door when you came out of the restaurant?"

The doctor twisted to try to look at Lark, but didn't let go of her strap. "I heard you say something about a guy in a leather coat. I figured you saw someone follow me in, so I went out the other door and circled around to my car. I was going to call Jason from the road."

"You did the right thing," Jason assured her.

Lark shoved herself back into her seat, a little perturbed. If Gabby was being watched, a different exit from the same lobby wasn't going to throw them off. If Lark had been the one being followed, and used that evasive technique, Jason would lecture her, not praise her.

They rode in tension-drenched silence until Jason stopped a few miles away, in a small gravel lot on a hill, where a picnic table and a trash can both leaned under a tall maple tree. He got out and the women followed.

"We can see anyone coming from here, and they can't get a good angle on us." He sat on the top of the table, his booted feet braced on the bench. "Gabby, do you know Lark?"

The doctor awkwardly held out a hand, her face pinkening to clash with her dark red hair. "I know who you are, Ms. Madrassa. It's a pleasure to meet you, really."

"You, too." Lark's irritation faded under the doctor's sincerity. "I see you made my preliminary research into a real miracle." She nodded at Jason.

"Well, a lot of us worked together to make it happen. And Jason deserves all the credit for pulling through. Any patient can die if they give up, or live if they work hard enough at it. Well, within reason." She gave a faint laugh. "You know what I mean."

"Basically. When did you last talk to my father?"

Gabby's back was to Jason and she didn't see his beaming smile at Lark's "interrogation" tactic. But he also didn't see the doctor's startled look.

"In person was yesterday evening, shortly after the end of the work day. I had a message from him in the lab last night. I must have been in the bathroom when he called. He didn't seem to need a call back."

"When was that?"

"About eleven."

"What were you doing in the lab at eleven?" Jason asked.

Gabby shifted to talk to both of them. "Um…I'm always—I mean, usually—it's not a lab, Jason." Her flush deepened. "I'm often there very late. You know that."

"But I'm not there anymore to attend to."

"No. Actually, that's why I was there." She shoved her hands into the pockets of her dress. "I felt a little adrift and went back to start planning our next steps. With the research. We have to backtrack now, and—"

"What did his message say?" Lark interrupted.

"He asked me to give Jason a copy of all my research on his treatments, and his medical file, when he came in today."

Jason cursed.

"Did you?" Lark demanded.

"Lark, I didn't—" Jason started.

"Did you?" she repeated, stepping closer to Gabby, stretching the scant couple of inches she had over the doctor in height. "Did you give the information to

Jason or someone looking like him? Or did you in fact collude with—"

"That's enough, Lark."

She backed off, slightly ashamed at the devastated look on Gabby's face. "Too far, huh?"

"A little." Jason slid off the table. "The first part was good, though."

"What the hell is going on?" Gabby stiffened. No longer flushed, she fisted her hands on her hips and swiveled her head back and forth between them. "Of course I didn't give the information to Jason or anyone looking like him. I've been alone all morning, until you called and told me to come here."

"Where is the information now?" Jason asked her more gently.

"Here." She pulled a flash drive out of her tiny purse. "Since I was seeing you, I figured I should hand it over."

"Don't." Jason curled his hand over Gabby's. Lark's fingers twitched. She wanted to see the data, dive into the miracle her work had helped create. But there'd be time for that later. Her father, and the bigger mess his disappearance was tied to, came first.

"But Matthew said—"

"It wasn't him," Jason interrupted. "Or he was coerced. Keep it, and don't give it to *any*one. Understand me? In fact, it's probably best if you disappear for a few days."

But despite her security gaffes, Gabby was no dummy. "No one coerces Matthew," she asserted. "If he gave me instructions under duress, he's drugged, or worse." She pushed the flash drive deep into her bag again and frowned, as if thinking hard. A moment later, she shook her head. "I think it wasn't him. His speech patterns were off. The whole message seemed strange, but I decided it was just because I—" She blushed again, even darker than before. "I'm going back to the lab—I mean, the facility. Someone needs to guard it."

"Hummingbird has perfect security," Lark said, knowing there was no such thing. "Your work is safe."

"You think I care about my work?" She glared at Lark through her glasses. "I care about Jason. And about your father. If someone wants my research and it would save either man's life, they can have it."

"Gabby—"

"Chill, Jason, I'm not going to give it up. If someone tries to steal it, they'll get a corrupted file they won't be able to access for shit. The real risk is them getting their hands on information about your vulnerabilities. I have to go protect that stuff."

Jason nodded. "All right. We'll drive you back."

"To my car. Then you go find Matthew and stay far away from Hummingbird."

Lark had to admit she liked the woman, after all.

JASON FOLLOWED GABBY long enough to make sure she wasn't followed—easy enough to determine on these small-town streets—then headed for the highway. He'd have preferred going with Gabby back to the lab to help her secure the data, but they had more than one calculated risk to consider. Matt was in more immediate danger.

"What next?" Lark asked.

"Kemmerling's office."

She raised her eyebrows at him. “Isn’t that a little, oh, nuts?”

He glanced over his shoulder for traffic and merged onto the moderately busy highway. “We need information. We have no idea where to start looking for your father.”

“What about the woman who was at the house this morning?”

“I don’t think we’ll get a lead on her from the shade of lipstick on the mug.”

Lark sighed. “What I meant was, unless she showed up out of the blue, there’s got to be a record somewhere of her contacting Dad.”

Jason’s hands clenched and released on the wheel. “True. But we can’t go back to Hummingbird to check the call log on Matt’s phone. Gabby can’t get into the office. Caitlyn won’t be in until Monday. And his cell phone is probably gone. The lead is too vague to follow right now.”

“You think Isaac has information at his office? Or even Dad?”

Jason hated the hopefulness in her voice. “Not Matt, no.” Isaac wouldn’t be dumb enough to keep Matt someplace he could easily get out of. But Isaac was also unreasonably cocky, and would probably think his own ground couldn’t be penetrated. He might have something in his office Jason could use.

The problem was what to do with Lark. He couldn’t leave her vulnerable on the outside, and he didn’t want to take her inside with him.

“Where’s his office?” Lark asked.

“M Street in DC.”

“How are you getting in?”

"I don't know yet. I have to scope it out." A cramp shot across his shoulders, and he loosened his hold on the wheel. Lark wasn't bombarding him with questions to annoy him. She was worried. But understanding didn't make the interrogation less grating.

But then he glanced at her and forgot his irritation. She was gnawing her full lower lip. When it slid from between her teeth it was reddened, and for a second he imagined soothing it with his tongue. *Stop that.* He looked away from her mouth, but his gaze fell to her tightly folded arms plumping her chest into the V of her light blue T-shirt.

Damn. He tore his eyes away and back to the road.

"I wonder what happened to Nils," Lark mused.

Jason frowned and struggled to trace the conversation back. "I don't know what that means."

"Nils is the gopher I told you about. And you texted Dad about it?"

The memory popped. "Yeah."

"Dad said in his message that he was taken care of. But it had to be a lie, right? Something the kidnapper made him say."

"I forgot about him," Jason admitted.

Lark snorted, making his lips twitch. It must be catching.

"Not in top form, huh Templeton?"

Now, that was unfair. Especially since she was the reason. "Cut me some slack. I nearly died. I've been out of the field for six months."

"Oh, yeah. I forgot."

Now Jason snorted and Lark laughed, and pretty soon they were both a little beyond normal.

"Oh, Jason," Lark finished with a slight whimper. "I don't want…Dad…"

"I know." He put his hand on her leg again, and she put her hand on top of his, and it was starting to feel familiar.

TEN

KEMMERLING SECURITY TURNED out to be on the fourth floor of a building down the street from the National Geographic Society, whose museum was open. It was a good spot for Lark to wait. Public and random, and she wouldn't look out of place loitering over the exhibits.

Jason walked the two blocks back to Kemmerling Security. He gained entry into the building by signing in to visit the accountant on the second floor, and took the elevator to the third instead. As soon as the door opened he swung out and to his left, reaching for the stairwell door. He didn't even think about it until he'd walked through. Even then, he was up three steps toward the fourth floor before it hit him. The cement stairs, painted cinderblock walls and metal rail spun. He tipped and had to grab the rail to keep from falling over. Panic slammed into him and he threw himself against the wall, away from the rail. His breathing rasped, echoing around him, duetting with the churning pulse in his ears. For God knew how long he stood frozen, halfway between the third and fourth floor landings.

It's different, rationality told him. *There's a wall there, no hole. You can't fall.*

It didn't matter. He wasn't in control. At least, not

enough to stave off the panic attack and move his body. Only enough to argue with rationality.

You're stuck in the middle, jerk. You want to be here forever?

Stupid question. He wanted out of here more than he'd ever wanted anything in his life. He could race down the steps and through that door in seconds. But he flinched when his imagination supplied black-clad attackers coming through before he reached the door. He should go up. A few seconds, and he'd be out and where he needed to be. But he couldn't make himself move.

Asshole. Too much at stake for this. Go. Up. Now.

Still frozen.

Do I need to start parading the names of everyone counting on you?

He dragged his left foot up a step and pushed. This would go faster if he closed his eyes. Maybe. He tried it, turning to run up the steps, and his hand smacked into the doorknob on the landing. He grabbed it and twisted. Locked.

His back crawling about all the possible things that could be coming up behind him, he crouched to pick the lock. Normally it would only take him a couple of minutes, but his hands shook. A few forced deep breaths later, equally forced concentration to block out everything but the lock, and it snicked. He eased the door open and peered through the crack. As soon as he could see something other than stairwell, the panic eased.

A gray industrial-grade carpet lined a hallway with windows along one side and cubicle walls on the other.

No voices carried to him, and only one bank of overhead lights was on.

Kemmerling wasn't this much of an idiot.

Jason checked the inside of the doorway for evidence of an alarm, but saw nothing. His angle was bad to look for motion detectors, but at least one had to be aimed at this door. He counted on two things. First that Kemmerling, like many security services, saw little need to invest in big ticket systems for their own offices because no one would invade, expecting them to be impenetrable. Second, that he would also make the mistake of assuming an intruder would walk in like a normal person.

As Jason had said to Lark just yesterday, he wasn't normal.

Luckily the building was an older one, with a vent over the door. He removed the screwdriver from his pick kit and climbed on the handrail next to the stairs, balancing on his toes and using one hand to grip the top of the doorframe while he unscrewed the vent. He pulled it out into the stairwell and lowered it to the landing, then stuck the screwdriver in his back pocket to leave both hands free to pull himself through the space. Piece of cake.

He'd been right. One motion sensor was aimed at the base of the door. It was possible, but improbable given the state of the external security, that Isaac had infrared beams crisscrossing the cubicle farm filling the entire floor.

The metal frame of the opening cut into Jason's midriff. He gauged the distance between the door and the corner of the cubicle, but it was too far. He couldn't get the leverage to leap it. The motion sensor sat at the left of the corner of the cubicle, and the corridor ahead of him was clear. If he could pull himself through, flip over and fling his body forward, he might make it. Impossible seven months ago, but now…

It was ugly, but he did it. The new muscle tissue in his arms, abs and legs gave him more strength and control than a gymnast. He did a slow roll through the vent, holding his legs up above the field of the sensor and gripping the edge above him with hands screaming in pain. He tensed his abs, arched and tumbled the two feet he needed, landing in a heap on the rough rug. Man, he was glad Lark hadn't seen that. He must have looked like a cat tossed through the air, flailing and twisting.

Jason scrambled up and over the top of one of the cubicles to avoid any other sensors. Dropping into the rolling desk chair, he tapped the keyboard of the cube's computer, activating it. After a bit of searching the network, he found the controls for the security system.

Huh. Maybe he was wrong about Isaac's brains. He used software Hummingbird technicians had designed—and abandoned because it was too easy to compromise. Jason inserted a few commands to make the system think it was still on, then deactivated it. Now he could move around without Isaac being alerted.

"Hello?"

Unless, of course, there was someone else in the room. Damn, he was an idiot.

Jason froze, listening. There were no footsteps, no rustle of fabric or shoe leather on carpet. No one called out again. He waited. They waited. Finally, the guy sighed, muttered something about "stupid supernatural TV show," and closed a door.

Jason's mind raced. The closing door had to belong to an office. From his look around at ceiling height, he thought the only two offices were near the main entrance. The voice hadn't been Kemmerling's, so probably hadn't come from Kemmerling's office. Searching it while someone was in the room next door was stretching the definition of acceptable risk, but at this point, doing nothing was worse.

He didn't have many options. He could sit right here and hope the guy left soon. But he might not, and every minute Jason was here was a minute he left Lark alone. Other people might come in, including the occupant of this cubicle.

Maybe he could access what he needed from here. He dug into the network, finding the central server and plenty of client files protected by passwords, but nothing of Isaac's. It had been worth a try, but it stood to reason the boss would have a stand-alone unit not connected to the server or the outside world. Jason had to get into his office, and he had to do it now.

Keeping low, he hurried up the aisle on the far side of the room from the offices. The main entrance area held a reception desk and a few chairs and plants. A couple of landscape prints hung on the walls. The glass-fronted entryway gave view to the elevators across a narrow foyer. A red light blinked on an alarm box next to the door. The system thought it was on.

Jason couldn't see the offices from here. He belly-crawled as quietly as possible to the corner, balancing speed and stealth. The second door had a strip of light under it and a small placard with "Hector Ramirez, Vice President" on it. The first door was Isaac's. Good.

Jason lingered for a few minutes, listening and looking. He heard a few murmurs, and the click of a phone being hung up. Some papers rustling, then low music.

Isaac's door didn't appear to be wired, but he did have more than a standard office handle and keyed lock. The keypad above the handle wasn't too sophisticated, though. No fingerprint pad or retinal scanner. He probably had a two-code fail-safe. One to allow for typing error, and a cutoff after the second "mistake." Jason thought for a while, trying to remember Isaac's habits. Jason had access to all the agents' passwords and codes, but could hardly memorize all of them.

Still, Isaac had been a special case.

He took a deep breath, checked behind him and down the hall, readied his lock picks and moved.

One second to the door. Three seconds to key in Isaac's birthday in reverse plus the numbers corresponding to the first three letters of his first name. The red light flicked to green, and he started picking the lock. Thirty long seconds later, the tumblers fell. And the light turned red. Dammit.

"For God's sake, I'm coming home now!"

Jason jerked, adrenaline flooding him at the sudden loud voice in the office next door. The phone slammed down, and Hector muttered as he moved around his office. "Try…work…shrew…wonder why…" The light shining under the door went out.

Closing his mouth around another curse, Jason keyed the numbers again, as fast as he could without making a mistake. The light flashed green. He twisted the handle and eased the door open, cursing again when it creaked.

He barely got inside and eased the door closed before Hector's opened. Jason didn't want to click the latch and alert Hector. He held his breath, his heart pounding, and watched through the crack as the man stalked by.

Jason waited while Hector "disarmed" the alarm, opened the door with a *whoosh* of air, armed it again, and locked the door behind him. The alarm reset would have overridden the commands Jason put in, but at least he was inside the system now. He'd worry about getting out when the time came. He eased the door closed and turned to survey the room he stood in. He made out the shape of a desk in the center of the room, a tall shelf or something in one corner. Darkness hid the details.

The office had one window, but the metal blinds covering it kept out any light. Jason didn't want to turn on the light, because if someone came in they'd see it under the door. But opening the blinds would be obvious from the street to someone who knew they should be closed. He compromised by fiddling with a few of the slats on the bottom, letting in just enough light to see.

The desk held two computers, one a match to the kind on all the cubicle desks, and one a higher-end model, stand-alone, as he'd expected. Being careful what he touched—he hadn't had any gloves or the time to buy some—Jason sat and powered up the stand-alone. He kept his senses tuned to the silence outside the office and his focus on the hard drive.

After an hour and a half of hunting and pecking

with the very tips of his fingers, he still had nothing. He'd managed to partially break into the files, but they were all client based and had nothing to do with Matt, the RT-24, or Hummingbird in any way. There was a double-protected section Jason couldn't get into, no matter what he did. And he was afraid to try harder and get closed out of the system.

He cursed and shoved the chair back as he got to his feet and skimmed the room for files or safes. Isaac apparently didn't keep many paper files on the premises, if any. He had no filing cabinets or shelves, and the modern-style desk had no drawers. But there was a freestanding dry bar. Jason circled behind it. The top shelf held the usual glasses and liquor bottles as well as a pile of bar cloths. The second shelf was for swizzle sticks and napkins, but the base of the bar, from the second shelf down, was solid.

Jason crouched and started lifting piles of napkins and plastic-bagged packages. In the back right corner, under a large box of toothpicks, he found an indent in the resin the entire bar was made of. He pressed it, and a small cover popped up, exposing a keypad.

He sighed. More codes. He tried the one that had gotten him into the room, with no luck. He reversed it, then tried each part of it. Luckily, this keypad didn't have an attempt limit. Finally, using the numbers for all of the letters of Isaac's first name—919113—worked. The bottom of the bar clicked open. Jason lifted the cover off and set it aside. There was another lock, this one pickable, though it took long enough for sweat to bead on his upper lip. He worried about Lark being alone for too long at the museum.

The space filled the bottom of the bar. Isaac stored

the usual things in here—money, weapons, ID both real and fake. Some contracts, papers relating to the business loan that had gotten Kemmerling Security started and the property the company owned. And a flash drive.

"Bingo." Jason strode to the computer and connected the drive, clicking fast to access it. His phone buzzed in his pocket, so he straightened to pull it out and check the text from Lark.

Hurry.

What the fuck did that mean? Did he need to abandon what he was doing and rush recklessly to Lark's side? *Hurry* could mean she was bored, or in danger. Matt would kill him if he let anything happen to her, but there was a bigger picture. Jason could race up the street and still not get there fast enough, and then he'd have abandoned his only chance at a lead. He checked the computer screen. The flash drive contained one folder, labeled "untitled." They'd be better off if he could check it here and leave the drive where he'd found it, but if it was protected, it could take him a while to crack.

He backed out of the file and yanked the drive from the port, shutting down the computer and wiping away his prints as simultaneously as possible. He set the chair right and relocked the bar safe, putting everything back and cleaning up after himself. Then he deactivated the power saver on the other computer—the one connected to the network—accessed the alarm, shut it down, and set it to reactivate in one minute. That gave him enough time to get out of the office. He couldn't lock the door behind him, but hopefully Hector would think he'd forgotten in his rush.

Elevators had memory of what floors they went to when, but Jason couldn't handle the stairwell again. The guard didn't even notice him leaving.

He flipped his cell phone open as he walked as fast as he could toward Sixteenth Street. He speed-dialed Lark's phone, but she didn't answer it. And when he got to National Geographic, he saw why.

GABBY SAT IN her car in the Hummingbird garage for half an hour, trying to coach herself through what she had to do. She wasn't afraid she'd been followed. She was no Hummingbird agent, but it's easy to spot a tail on an empty road. Nor was she afraid someone would attack her in the lab. Hummingbird's security was as impenetrable as possible, especially for the lab almost no one in the company knew about.

No, she was nervous about her ability to act normal. She was high-strung at the best of times, and knowing Matthew was missing… Not that anyone had confirmed he *was* missing. She'd inferred it from their behavior and questions, but they hadn't come right out and said it. She supposed it was better she not have any information, then she couldn't inadvertently reveal it to anyone. Certainly they'd want to keep Matthew's disappearance a secret.

Her breath hitched at the thought. Things happened so fast. Options you thought you had could disappear in an instant. She could have made a move with him last night, let him know she liked him. Even if he'd rebuffed her, he'd have known he didn't have to be alone.

Maybe he wasn't, her freaking-out brain whispered. Maybe he hadn't wanted to go out because he was meeting someone. Maybe he'd been in bed with her when—

"Arrrgh!" She slammed the flat of her hand on the steering wheel. "You're such an idiot, Abigail." She yanked her keys out of the ignition and flung herself from the car. Her frustration and self-annoyance propelled her past the security desk and two politely smiling operatives she passed on her way to the special elevator that took her, with the swipe of her ID card and fingerprint, down into the lab. When the doors opened she wiped the print pad clean and stepped out into the corridor.

The doors soughed closed behind her, and the engine of the machine whirred as the car returned to the lobby. She waited, listening, feeling. But it was as quiet as it should be on a Saturday, and felt normal. Except it didn't, really. It was only in the last two days that "alonc" was normal. Jason had always been here, and a variable number of medical personnel. Now the quiet was sinister, frightening.

She moved toward her office, the tap of her shoes echoing softly. She wasn't stupid. She understood why Jason hadn't wanted to talk to her here, why it was so important to protect the data.

Hummingbird was compromised.

She wished now she'd asked more questions. How much Jason knew about Matthew's disappearance. Who might be the traitor within the company. It could be someone she worked with every day, trusted to keep Jason's secrets safe. The idea made her sick to her stomach.

She reached her office and stood in the doorway, looking for anything out of place. She'd only been gone an hour, maybe a little more, but now everything was different. Had she left that file drawer open an inch? The files on her desk were stacked neatly, but she could have done that. She just didn't remember.

She crossed to the file cabinet and pulled the open drawer out with one finger. The files appeared as usual. One stuck up slightly, but it was the last one she'd put in, and the drawer was pretty full. It would have taken extra effort to shove down all the way.

When she nudged her mouse, her dark computer screen flashed onto the document she'd been working on when Jason called her. It was an outline of a plan for continuing their research, but she hadn't yet included any details that would benefit anyone outside the team. The recent documents list didn't show anything it shouldn't, but she didn't know how to determine if anyone had accessed other files, such as downloading them to a flash drive without opening them or something. But then, there wasn't any reason for anyone to be here on a Saturday, and they'd have to log in…

"Idiot," she muttered. After a few strokes on the keyboard, the personnel system came up. She was a supervisor in this department and had access to every employee's time records. No one could come into the lab without swiping their card and being biometrically identified. She scanned the list, saw she was the only one to come in today, and finally relaxed.

Now she could get to work. The research data was vast and housed on secure servers separate from the rest of the company. As she'd told Jason, if anyone tried to download the data to any external device, it would corrupt. She took a few minutes to test it, satisfied when gobbledygook scrawled across her screen.

Jason's most recent test data and final report were here in her computer. It didn't contain any information about his treatment and therapy, but described the end results. Which meant anyone who accessed it would know about his immunity issues and the weakness in his sternum. If someone was trying to tell her to give the data to Jason, she assumed they had plans to go after him. If it were up to her, he'd be locked up down here where he was safe.

She exhaled heavily and propped her forehead on the heel of her hand. He wouldn't be any safer down here than anywhere else. The building was as unbreachable as possible, but nothing was perfect. As evidenced by Matthew's apparent abduction from his own home.

She wondered why Lark hadn't reported it to the police. But then, what would she have said? She could easily imagine an authoritative, skeptical officer blowing it off because Matthew hadn't been missing for twenty-four hours, there was no sign of a struggle, and his message, taken at face value, said he was leaving of his own volition.

She missed him.

"Ridiculous." But she did. Maybe it was a stupid, adolescent crush, but she always sensed his presence. Even when he was out of town, she knew when he'd be back, and he called her frequently to check on Jason's progress. Now she didn't know if she'd ever see or talk to him again, and it hurt.

All she could do was what she could do. She squared her shoulders and went back to work, sending the final report on Jason into the secure server and erasing it from her unit. She ran the flash drive through a secure delete utility to wipe it clean, then reformatted it.

And that was it. She sat back and stared at the empty screen and blinking cursor, wondering what the hell came next.

ELEVEN

LARK PACED BEHIND the barricade set up by the police half an hour ago. All the people who'd been in the museum at the time the fire alarm went off milled around her. There weren't many, but ten minutes ago they'd confiscated all their cell phones and electronic devices. Best she could tell, someone had pulled the fire alarm falsely, and the police were holding the people who'd been in the museum at the time so they could prosecute whoever did it. She'd barely gotten a text message off to Jason before the police took her phone and had no idea if he'd received it.

The firefighters did their own milling outside the barricaded area. The immediate threat was over—the tension had dissipated when someone came out of the building and shook his head. And *she* hadn't pulled the alarm, so she wasn't worried about that. But not only was the detention frustrating, the incident had drawn crowds and news teams, and Lark was afraid someone would see her face on the news and come after her. Being captured or actively on the run would kind of hinder her ability to save her father.

If she weren't so worried, the thought would be amusing. Her whole life he'd been a superhero to her, indestructible. When her mother died, he'd become her best friend. She didn't care that most girls that age were finding their parents totally flawed. That was how it had been.

Until she decided to be a botanist instead of a security expert. Her father had never made her feel his disappointment, but she knew it was there. It changed their relationship—it had to—but she'd never regretted it until now. Now, when she didn't have the skills she needed, or the knowledge or connections.

That's what Jason's for.

As she thought it, she spotted him on the far side of the crowd. He looked anxious. Lark pushed past an elderly couple quarreling about whose idea it was to come here instead of the Smithsonian and pressed against the sawhorse at the edge of the barricade.

Jason spotted her immediately, and the lines between his eyes smoothed away. He held up a finger, and she nodded. He was telling her to stay put. She agreed with him. The police had her name, and if she disappeared or tried to, they'd be after her, too.

She made her way to the back of the crowd, where Jason waited. Her heart rate picked up, and her skin prickled with awareness.

"Did you find anything?" she asked as soon as she reached him. He gave a weird, tiny nod-and-shake she took to mean he had, but they wouldn't talk about it here.

She moved a little closer. "Do you think this is coincidence?"

Jason shrugged. "It's got to be. No way they could have set this up. We didn't even know you'd be here."

"We could have been followed."

He gave her a look.

"Okay, okay, we weren't followed." She rubbed her

eyes with the heels of her hands, a scream building inside her. She couldn't stand here doing nothing when her father needed her.

Jason's warm hand landed on her shoulder and the scream subsided, as did the tension driving it.

"It's okay," Jason murmured into her ear. "We'll get to him."

Lark nodded, shivering a little when the movement made his lips caress her ear.

"I'll be in the truck trying to read what I found." He pulled back, and Lark opened her eyes to see he'd moved the truck to just outside the roped-off area. How he'd managed to get this close, she had no idea.

"I'll be there as soon as they let us go," she said.

When Jason retreated, he seemed to take any warmth with him.

JASON PROPPED HIS laptop on the center console and alternated his attention between the computer and the group of people around Lark. He could have pulled strings to get her out of there, but calling attention to either one of them was foolish at this point, and the situation wasn't dangerous as long as she kept her face averted from the cameras. The news teams were more intent on filming the firefighters and cops than the hapless museum-goers.

The computer beeped its readiness and he slid the flash drive into the USB port. It opened automatically, listing options for accessing the files. He clicked "open folder to view files" and dove in.

Half an hour later a uniformed cop led a teenager in an AC/DC shirt out of the crowd, and moments after that Lark climbed into the truck. Jason handed her the laptop and started the vehicle. Before he could pull into the steady but light stream of traffic, Lark passed him a bottle of hand sanitizer.

"What's this?" he asked, rather stupidly.

"Dad said you have to be careful of germs. They had some in the gift shop. The stuff is everywhere since the H1N1 scare."

She'd said it casually, not looking at him while she scrolled through the list of files on the flash drive, and she didn't notice Jason had a hard time swallowing all of a sudden. He wasn't used to people taking care of him. Not outside the lab, anyway.

He cleared his throat, rubbed the sanitizer over his hands until it evaporated, and pulled away from the curb to head for his house just across the river in Arlington.

"Did you find anything helpful?" Lark opened a file, frowning.

"Only Isaac's entire plan, written out."

"Yeah, right." She swirled her finger around the touchpad and selected another file. "Seriously."

"Seriously, I think it's all there. I just can't read it." Frustration burned under his skin so he had to keep an eye on the speed limit and his foot light on the gas pedal.

"It's encoded?"

He slowed for the turn onto the bridge. "Not in the traditional sense. He has his own means of hiding what the information really is. But I think we can figure it out if we work at it."

Lark shook her head and slapped the laptop closed. "You can, maybe. You know him. I can't make sense of any of it. Brown Bunny? Manderlay? Why are you laughing?"

Jason grinned at her. "I think that file was his favorite movie list." He grinned harder when she glowered at him. "You never heard of those movies? Lars von Trier? Vincent Gallo?"

"It disturbs me that you have." She turned to face front and flattened her hands on top of the computer. "Why would he have a movie list in these files?"

"I scanned through most of them briefly. A lot of it is personal stuff. A packing list, some letters, images."

"Porn?"

"That would be expected, wouldn't it? But no. I think it's camouflage, to hide the important stuff." He turned down the shady street his house was on and swallowed against the lump swelling in his throat. He hadn't been home since the accident. Until yesterday, he hadn't expected to be able to go home. He pulled into the driveway and sat, engine running, and tried to concentrate. Sentimentality was stupid at the best of times; it could be more than dangerous right now.

He was sure they hadn't been followed, but Kemmerling's men could have been scouting his place. Property records and other public information would have led Isaac here. Even if the man knew Jason hadn't been here in months, any trained tracker knew that everyone wanted to be home, even if it was the worst place to go.

Jason hoped counter logic would come into play here. Isaac knew Jason knew it was stupid to go home, therefore Jason wouldn't go home, therefore Isaac might not bother surveilling it. Which would make it a safe place to go.

A few cars were parked on the street, all apparently unoccupied. There was only one other house on the street's cul-de-sac, the house Matt had said was empty. That would make it a perfect site for surveillance, but Matt had probably taken care of that. In fact, Jason wouldn't put it past his friend to have purchased the house to ensure it stayed vacant and secure.

The housekeeper Matt had continued paying wouldn't be here on the weekend, which could have made it easier for one of Isaac's people to be inside. Except they wouldn't have prepared for what awaited them. If someone was inside, Jason would know.

"Stay in the truck. Actually, come over here." Jason opened the door and slid out, motioning for Lark to climb over into his place. He had to be absolutely certain everything was safe before he brought her inside. "Be ready. I'll be right back."

"Where are you going?"

"Checking things out." He motioned to the street, and Lark nodded, settling herself in the driver's seat. He waited until the door locks clicked, then started walking.

The end of the cul-de-sac was empty, as was the next-door driveway. The nearest car was a four-door Saab, with a crew cab pickup several yards behind it on the other side of the street. Jason stayed loose as he passed the Saab, peering into the empty interior and checking the trunk as he crossed behind the car. The crew cab was harder to be casual about, but there was no one inside it, either.

He made his way to the end of the street. No cars left. There were no blankets bunched up in back seats, or suspicious piles of junk on the floor of the front passenger side. If Isaac had assigned anyone to watch his house, they weren't doing it from a vehicle.

Returning to the cul-de-sac and circling both empty houses took a few more minutes. Every glimpse he got of Lark showed him more evidence of her waning patience. She bit her nails. Swiveled back and forth in her seat. Put the truck into gear, then back into park. Adjusted her seat belt and the position of her seat. As Jason approached her window, he could see she was cursing.

"Are you done yet?" she demanded before the window was halfway down.

"Almost. When I signal you, open the garage door." He pointed at the opener clipped to his visor. "I'll check it out inside and then you can pull in."

"Finally." She poised her thumb over the button. "Well? Go on. Get into position."

Jason smiled, but hesitated when her expression changed. "You okay?"

"I'm fine. I told you to stop—never mind."

That just made him smile more.

Lark held her breath, watching Jason carefully as he positioned himself to the left of the garage door and crouched, his pistol drawn and ready. He'd have a good view of the inside of the garage, plus the entry door into the house, from where he stood. He glanced at Lark and nodded once. She hit the button.

And then hit herself. Dammit, she *had* to stop having palpitations every time he smiled at her. Nothing. Was. Going. To. Happen. Period.

Jason disappeared into the garage. Lark waited, unnerved by the suburban stillness around them. The trees dappled the sunshine so every breeze made shadows flutter inside the truck and across the front of the house. Every time the branch over the driveway waved, Lark jumped and gunned the engine. But besides that, there were no people jogging or mowing lawns or heading out to boat on the river or anything else Saturday-ish. It creeped her out.

Or maybe it was just the situation.

Jason leaned out the door into the house and motioned for her to pull into the garage. She did, staying centered in the two-car space, afraid her vibrating arms would jerk the wheel and knock over the motorcycle sitting under a tarp on her left. This level of tension was going to destroy her.

She hit the button to close the door, shut off the truck and heaved a giant breath to settle herself. If Jason knew how tense she'd been, he'd be less likely to keep her involved, more likely to want to stash her somewhere and just watch over her while he let her father get himself out of whatever he'd gotten into. That was unacceptable.

She grabbed the laptop as she climbed out of the truck, and went around to the back to get her files. Jason met her there and carried the heavy box while she slung her overnight bag over her shoulder.

"Do you have somewhere safe we can stow those?" she asked. "I don't want to haul them around, it's too risky."

He shepherded her into the house. "I have a hidden safe."

"Is it hidden in the kind of place Isaac is also trained to hide things, and will therefore find it?" Damn if he didn't smile again. Pleasure squirmed inside her, and she stopped trying to fight it.

"No. Don't worry." He carried the box through the clean, cozy kitchen and up the stairs into a carpeted hallway. Lark followed him into the furthest bedroom. Instead of pulling out a painting or opening the closet, he slid out a dresser drawer and reached in to twist something. A click made her look up. The light fixture had come partway out of the ceiling. Jason set the box on the quilted double bed and climbed up next to it. When he pulled on the light, an uneven patch of ceiling—uneven because the edges matched the swirl pattern of the textured paint—came down. Jason heaved the box up into the space, shoved the ceiling closed and jumped down to the floor.

Lark was impressed, but hid it. "Clever, but not very secure," she accused. "Anyone can just twist that thing in there." She waggled a finger at the dresser, an ugly pressboard box. "What if they find the twister when they search the drawer?"

"Try it." Jason folded his arms and watched her, looking smug.

Obviously, she wasn't going to be able to open it. But she shrugged and tried anyway. Sure enough, though her fingers found the butterfly nut, no matter what she did, she couldn't get it to turn.

"Okay, fine. Good." She shoved the drawer closed and dusted off her hands. "Now what?"

"You hungry?"

"Famished."

"The housekeeper left some food, probably on Matt's instructions. Nothing fresh, but it's better than fast food junk."

Lark's stomach rumbled. It had been an eternity since she'd eaten. "Anything sounds good."

A few minutes later they danced around each other making peanut butter sandwiches with pickles and chips. They sat at the kitchen table to eat, neither talking much. There wasn't much to say at this point. Lark floundered, with no clue what to do next, and she didn't want to badger Jason, who was probably working it out.

When they were done eating, Jason pulled the laptop over to Lark and handed her the flash drive.

"Why don't you start cataloging what's in here. Maybe with a list we can decide where to start." He grimaced. "I'm starting to cramp from all the driving. I'm going to do some time on the treadmill."

Lark stood, worried. "You shouldn't be cramping from that little bit."

"Another side effect. I just have to keep the muscles loose and limber, and I haven't been able to for a couple of days. It's no big deal."

"I could give you a massage," she offered, her pulse skipping as she imagined rubbing her hands over his body.

"No!"

His vehemence popped her fantasy and she rocked back, her feelings bruised.

"No, thank you," he amended more quietly. "I'm fine. I'll be back down in about an hour."

"Is it okay if I make some phone calls?" She pulled her cell out of her pocket, using the motion to duck her head and hide her blush. "I don't want people to freak that I'm totally uncommunicative."

"What kind of people?"

Her boss and her ex-boyfriend had left messages

for her, but she felt awkward mentioning Carl, so she just said, “My boss.”

“Sure. Use the house phone, though, it’s secure.” And he hurried up the stairs two at a time.

Lark lifted the phone off the wall, shaking her head at the cord, and carried the whole thing to the table. Maybe it had to be a landline to be totally secure, but it still hindered her need to pace. She sat and grabbed the pad and pen Jason had left for her. If she couldn’t pace, doodling would have to do.

She was curious why Carl had tried to contact her. She’d cut him off pretty good the other night. But she dreaded calling Ralph, and decided it would be better to get that over with first.

“Botanical Medicality,” said the melodic voice of the weekend receptionist who Lark privately thought was a robot. Or at least a cyborg.

“Cindee, it’s Lark Madrassa. Ralph in?” It was nearly five on a Saturday, but she figured after the break-in yesterday he’d still be there.

“One moment please, Ms. Madrassa. I shall consult his availability.”

Lark rolled her eyes and tapped her fingers as she waited.

“Lark!” Ralph boomed a moment later. “Where the hell are you?”

“Why, Ralph? It’s a Saturday.”

“The police keep calling me about getting your statement about yesterday. That guy’s gonna be fine, you know. The one you tried to blind. What the fuck’s wrong with you?”

TWELVE

LARK'S JAW DROPPED a little. "Ralph, I—did you just say the F word?"

"Hell, yeah, I said the F word. I was supposed to be sailing today. Instead, I'm in here trying to re-secure our most important greenhouse, make sure there isn't anything proprietary missing, deal with the insurance company for this asshole's medical bills, and run down my missing botanist, the one who caused all this, who isn't here to do her job!"

Her heart sank. "What do you mean, the insurance company? He broke into the greenhouse."

"Hell he did. If you'd be here to give your statement, maybe this could be straightened out. But he signed in at the desk as your afternoon meeting, and the idiot receptionist sent him back to the greenhouse. He says the door was open. He went in and looked for you, called your name, and the next thing he knew, you were dumping stuff on him and spraying him with a hose."

Shit. She'd trusted Jason when he hurried her out of there, but she hadn't meant for this to happen. "I'm sorry, I had a family emergency. I'll contact the police to give my statement. But I'm in DC. It's my father." She hoped Ralph wouldn't pry, because she hated to make something up, and the fewer people who knew her father was missing, the better. At least right now.

But he was still harping on the unsecure greenhouse and the "client" who might sue them for medical damages. Lark let him rant. She should be angry about Donald's story, but she couldn't blame him for trying to get out of his own mess.

"Okay, Ralph, I'll take care of it. And I'll be in Monday to inventory the greenhouse, okay?" She hoped she would. But she doubted they'd be able to locate her father and rescue him in one day. Even if they did, she wouldn't want to leave his side. Let Bot-Med fire her. She'd deal with that later.

Ralph fed her the name and number of the cop in charge of the case, but she wouldn't call until she talked to Jason. She probably couldn't give her statement over the phone, anyway, which meant they'd have to wait until she got back up north.

Next up, Carl. He answered on the first ring.

"Lark, sweetheart, I just heard. Are you all right?"

"Heard what?"

"About the break-in at work."

"I'm fine. Thanks for asking."

"How about I come up and make you some *osso buco*?"

"No, thank you. I appreciate the offer. Talk to you later!" She reached for the switch hook, but manners had her hand hovering while Carl kept talking.

"It's no trouble. I have all the stuff here. And I know how upset you must be after you attacked that guy. I mean, because he broke in."

Lark pulled her hand back, frowning. How did he know about it, anyway? "I didn't attack anyone."

"I know. Self-defense, right? Anyway, I have some wine—"

"I'm fine, Carl, thank you," she repeated a little more forcefully. "And I'm not home."

"Oh?" His tone of voice changed dramatically. "Where are you?" Now instead of slightly buffoonish he sounded shrewd.

"Out of town. But thanks for your caring." She hung up before he could respond, then sat for a minute, thinking. She and Carl had broken up weeks ago. They hadn't spoken in all that time except the one night in the elevator when he came on to her. So why all the sudden concern, and the shrewdness when he asked where she was? How had he heard about the BotMed thing? Ralph hadn't given any indication it was on the news, and if it had been, he'd have been even more furious. But any possible reasons she came up with for Carl's concern seemed farfetched and paranoid.

Jason hadn't come back downstairs, so she booted up the computer to make lists of Isaac's files. After she'd gone through a dozen, she was able to start grouping them. Personal stuff that probably wouldn't be helpful. Spreadsheets of data, some that looked client oriented, some clearly connected to Hummingbird. She knew Jason would be able to figure out what was what. She recognized a few employees, a few clients, a few government contacts, and flagged those as higher priority. But nothing seemed consistent. Other files contained photos and videos, none of anything she could identify at a glance. Some documents appeared to be surveillance reports and quotes for service.

By the time she finished, two hours had gone by since Jason went upstairs. Sticky and worn out, Lark shut down the computer, gathered it up with her notes and the flash drive, and headed upstairs to take a shower. She could hear Jason running on the treadmill behind a closed door. She paused, a little worried. He'd only planned to be up here for an hour. His breathing sounded okay, not ragged, and his pace wasn't too fast, so she continued down the hall to the room where she'd left her bag. Maybe he had another phone and had made some calls, himself.

But after she showered and put on the tank and knit shorts she slept in, the pounding steps on the running machine were still going.

"Jason?" She knocked on the door but didn't hear him respond. Maybe he was listening to headphones. She cracked the door and gasped. "Jason!"

He ran steadily, his pace and form perfect, but his face tight with pain. His muscles all stood out in sharp relief, even under the tight running clothes he wore.

Lark hurried over to the machine and pressed the speed button to slow him down, her heart pounding. "What's wrong with you?"

"Cramps," he gritted out. "If I stop running, they tighten." He reached for the speed button again, but Lark yanked the safety cord to deactivate the machine. Jason groaned and started to collapse, reaching for his right calf. Lark caught his arm and slowed his descent.

"You should have called me." She forced him to lie back on the floor next to the machine and grabbed his ankle to push his leg up. "Flex your foot." She started digging her fingers into his calf, feeling the knots and working them out. "Holy crap, Jason." She couldn't imagine the pain he was in, and dug harder.

"I know." He groaned again. "Don't, Lark, I'll work it out."

"Shut up." She continued massaging, the sheen of

sweat on his skin lubricant for her fingers. Some of the tension ebbed, but he was now clutching the left, which he had bent at the knee. “Straighten that.” She laid his right leg out and straddled it to reach the left calf. “Where else?”

“Nowhere.”

“Liar.” Why didn’t he want her to know? “Tell me. The quads?”

He nodded shortly, his eyes closed, his jaw still very tight. As his calf loosened up, she laid his leg down and put a hand on each quadriceps to work them both at once.

Jason threw his arm over his eyes and worked hard to contain the yells building in his chest. There was nothing he could do about the other effects of Lark’s hands on his body, though. Even with the extreme pain, the pressure of her fingers sent waves of pleasure through him, more intense as the cramps eased. The balance shifted, pain morphing straight into desire, and he hardened with each stroke of her palms up his thighs, throbbed as her fingers dug in, loosening the muscles.

“How often does this happen?” he heard Lark ask through the buzzing in his ears.

“It hasn’t. I’ve been running every day.” It hadn’t occurred to him that the random cramps on occasional mornings had been harbingers of something worse. He always did the treadmill and other rehab exercise in the morning, and any mild cramping he had when he first woke up disappeared. Lark dug her thumb particularly deep into the groove of muscle close to his inner thigh and he gasped.

“I’m sorry, did I hurt—” She stopped, and he

guessed she'd spotted his raging erection. *Touch it.* He bit his tongue to keep from begging and peeked under his arm to see her focusing her gaze on his toes. "Did I hurt you?" she finished.

"No." His voice came out rough. "The opposite."

She swung her head quickly around to lock onto his face. "What do you mean?"

Jason covered his eyes again. He didn't want to tell her. It would sound like the lamest excuse to try to get a woman into bed. "Nothing."

"I can't help you if you don't tell me."

"Lark, drop it." He bent one knee, then the other, and the cramps didn't come back. He curled his torso to sit up. "Thank you. I'm fine now." But she laid her hand oh-so-gently on his forearm, and the shocks shooting up and down his arm made him want to scream. "Don't…touch me. Please."

The hurt that flickered across her face was impossible to miss. He growled out a curse and dragged himself to his feet. Lark glided up beside him, and he finally noticed what she was wearing. Gray tank top, no bra. Short knit shorts that hugged her ass so well he knew she must run regularly, too. And absolutely nothing else. She was bare skin from her fingertips to her shoulders, from her toes to the tops of her thighs. He slammed his eyes shut.

"I need a shower. I appreciate your help. You can go now."

"Okay." The word was a whisper, full of confusion and distress. Crap. He was going to have to tell her.

"I'm sorry." He opened his eyes, about to explain the embarrassing reality, but she was closer to him than he'd expected. If he leaned forward he'd knock her off balance. Her head was tilted up, her chin determined, her eyes wide enough he suspected she was trying not to cry. He couldn't help himself. He put his right palm flat on the back of her shoulder, just to brace her, keep her from falling backward. But even though he swore he didn't pull, she tilted forward, her body brushing his in half a dozen places.

And it hurt. It would have hurt anyway, but with the sweat and the cramping he was even more susceptible. Jolts of electricity flared along his skin. To escape it he instinctively pulled her closer, tighter to him, to eliminate the slight friction between them.

Big mistake. Huge. Lark gasped and pressed her hands to his chest, the pressure just right. The pain dissipated there and along his legs, dragging pleasure behind it so he wanted to crawl inside her. And she knew it. The shock in her eyes darkened to awareness. She licked her lips, and her gaze flicked down to his mouth. He didn't know if it was on purpose, but her back arched to lift her hips against his, and his cock tightened even more. He groaned at the friction, desperately trying not to rub against her, but she drew in an excited breath, and he had no choice. Or no will, anyway. He gave in to the demands of his body and dropped his mouth to hers.

Her lips were hot, and soft, and tasted of her. They met his with hunger and parted with welcome, and she sucked the tongue he plunged into her mouth. No easy, tentative first kiss, this. He *wanted*. Craved. His right hand drove up under her hair, twisting it around his fist so it didn't brush his forearm. His left fell to the small of her back and pulled her even tighter against him.

Lark didn't wrap her arms around his neck, but instead clutched his shirt in both fists, pulling even though they couldn't get any closer together. Jason's body curved around her and he lifted her higher, pressed his cock harder against her. She cried out and threw her head back, flinging one leg up over his hip and surging against him.

That was all it took. The orgasm rushed over him before he could do anything about it, a full-body blowout, like nothing he'd ever felt before. Lark's fingers dug into his shoulders and the throbs there echoed all over his body, most intensely where Lark cradled him between her legs.

He knew in a few seconds he would be more embarrassed than he'd ever been in his life, even the first time he had sex when he hadn't even gotten inside the girl before he came. But right now, with aftershocks still shuddering through him, the embarrassment couldn't take hold.

Lark pulled her head up, her face flushed, eyes shining. She shivered, the movement working up her body and ending in a smirk.

On cue, heat flowed through him. He opened his mouth to apologize, wondering what he could possibly say to make him appear less of a complete asshole. But before he could, Lark leaned up and kissed his mouth, softly.

"Thank you," she said.

And Jason was doomed.

THIRTEEN

For the first time since she'd come to work at Hummingbird, Gabby didn't want to be there.

Once she had secured everything, she logged out of her computer and began locking up to go home. Her urgency to leave was as unsettling as the reasons behind it, and by the time she had the main lab doors locked, she was on the verge of tears. Fighting them distracted her. She barely registered the ding of the elevator and only realized someone was there when footsteps sounded behind her. She whirled, her windpipe closing around a lungful of air.

"Dr. Berwell, I thought you'd be here."

"Nils." She let her breath out with a rush. "You startled me."

He frowned a little and motioned back to the elevator. "You didn't hear it ping?"

"No, I was deep in thought. Um, big staff meeting on Monday." She tried to smile. Then her brain caught up with her adrenaline. "What are you doing here on a Saturday?" Nils was a low-level assistant who did grunt work for her part time, when he wasn't needed in other departments, and was never alone in the lab. He shouldn't have even been able to get downstairs—except that the main desk knew she was here and probably figured she'd asked him to come in.

"I'm working upstairs with Caitlyn. You know Mr.

Madrassa, he's such a workaholic." He giggled and shoved his hands in his back pockets, rocking up on his toes. "Shc said Matthew—I mean, Mr. Madrassa—needs the files on Jason he asked you to put together yesterday?"

Her heart raced so fast she put her hand to her throat, certain he'd see it pulsing in her neck. "He said for me to give it to Jason."

"I know, but Jason's up in his office with him now. They're really busy, so they sent me down."

It was such blatant bullshit Gabby didn't have to think twice about what to do. "All right. Let me get it." She unlocked the lab doors, swiped her card, and let the scanner read her retina. Nils stood by, still rocking back and forth. He started to follow her when she opened the door, but she held up a hand.

"You can stay here. I'll just be a second. It's all on a flash drive."

"Okay."

She hurried into her office and grabbed the erased flash drive out of the pencil holder where she'd left it, then carefully locked back up again and met Nils in the hall, right where she'd left him. She handed it over, hoping her smile didn't tremble.

"Here you go."

"Thanks." He took it and gave her a nod. "Are you leaving, then?"

The last thing she wanted to do was travel with him in the elevator even as far as the main lobby, but she'd obviously been on her way out a moment ago.

"Yes. You? After you take that up, I mean. Or will they be working you all day?"

"Oh, no, this is it." They began walking to the elevator. "I think they'll be here awhile, but they won't need me anymore."

They sure wouldn't. Gabby itched to call Jason. Surely he didn't know Nils was one of the insiders, or he'd have done something about it. She wanted to do something herself—like knock him out and sit on him until someone came. But she couldn't let on that she knew anything.

The elevator ground lower, molasses or something gumming its mechanisms. Was she imagining it, or did the small space smell of nervous sweat? She shifted her weight from one foot to the other and made herself hold still the rest of the way.

Finally, the elevator reached the lobby. "Have a good weekend, Nils!" She glanced back as she stepped out and watched him press, or pretend to press, the button for the top floor. Matthew's office. Then the doors slid closed and she was safe.

Except, of course, she wasn't. The most secure location in which she'd ever found herself had suddenly become as dangerous as a war zone.

Gabby signed out and tried to make small talk with the desk officer, but she knew she sounded inane and distracted. She practically ran to her car once she reached the garage, her head swiveling back and forth until she felt the vertebrae pop. "Victim" was written all over her, but she couldn't help herself.

Finally breathing easy once she was out of the Hummingbird complex and on the main street toward town—with no car behind her—she relaxed her grip on her phone and dialed Jason's number. He didn't answer right away, and her anxiety level rose again.

"Come on, answer, *please*." A click. "Jason?" she said before he could speak. "It's Gabby."

"Are you all right?"

"Yes." She took a deep breath. Of course she was all right. "I need to talk to you."

"Where are you?"

"Just left Hummingbird. But—"

"Where do you live?"

"In Adams Mark."

"Get to a Metro station, park your car, and take the train to the Mall. We'll meet you in front of the Castle."

The jitters returned. "Are you sure? Won't the Metro be more dangerous?"

"Your car is probably tagged. The closest Metro station won't be that crowded right now, and they won't be able to get close without you seeing them. But call me if you see or feel anything unusual or frightening, okay?"

She didn't know how he seemed to understand what was going on without being told, but his take-charge attitude calmed her again more than anything else could. "Okay. I'll be there in half an hour."

"So will we."

Gabby hung up and set the phone on her lap as she pulled up to a stop sign. There were no cars in any direction, and no easy places for anyone to hide. Still, she barely paused before running the intersection. The calm had lasted only until she dropped the phone. If her car was tagged, they didn't need to follow her. They could stay out of sight and follow the signal instead. Jason had to know that and wasn't concerned, but now she wanted to get out of the car as much as she'd wanted to get out of the building a few minutes ago.

How long would it take Nils to discover the flash drive was blank? Who would come after her? He was a pipsqueak and didn't frighten her, not physically, but she doubted he'd be used as muscle. It would be someone else, someone infinitely more able to do her harm.

She screeched the car to a stop in a parking space in the center of town. Only pausing long enough to make sure she had everything, she scrambled out and hurried into Mike's Cab Service. A few minutes later she relaxed, safe in the back of an anonymous cab, heading for the city.

"THAT WAS GABBY?" Lark had been half dressed when Jason's cell phone rang, down the hall. By the time she finished putting on clean clothes after her second shower of the evening, he'd answered and completed the call. She'd caught only the tail end of it.

"Yeah, she's in trouble. We have to go pick her up."

Lark rubbed her hair vigorously with the towel in her hand and watched him reattach a holster to his belt. He was wearing a snug, long-sleeved shirt and jeans similar to what he'd worn before. She had an inkling now of why he was dressed that way in the warmth of summer, but they still needed to talk. As soon as she thanked him earlier, trying to hide her embarrassment at going off from a simple dry hump, he headed for the shower without looking back.

Gabby's timing sucked.

"Let me just grab my shoes," she told him, turning toward her room.

Jason stopped, met her gaze, turned red and looked away. "I think you should stay here."

"No way." Something flared—not quite anger, but intensity. He wasn't leaving her behind. "We're in this entire thing together. And I'm safer with you."

"You're safer here."

Lark didn't bother arguing. She raced down the hall to her room and snatched her sneakers from the floor, reaching the garage door just as Jason started the truck. He hung his head when she jumped in, but when the door had risen he backed out without another attempt to make her stay behind.

"What did Gabby say?" She stuck her left foot into a shoe and wiggled it on without unlacing it.

"Nothing. I wouldn't let her. She parks her car in the main garage—it could be bugged as well as tagged."

"Why do you think she called, then?" A stomp, and the right shoe was on, too. She settled back into her seat.

"Could be anything."

They were silent while Lark considered that. "It could be. But Dad—either drugged, or Not Dad—told her to give the files to you, and she hadn't seen anyone this morning. Maybe she ran into someone after we left her and wanted to let you know who it was."

"That could be it."

"Okay, good, we got that out of the way. Now let's talk about the other thing."

"No."

"I beg your pardon?" It infuriated her that he wouldn't look at her. He was driving, of course, and it was starting to get dark, but he could at least glance her way. She wasn't going to claim to love him, for cripes sake!

"This is not the time to talk about it," Jason said.

Lark huffed. "It's a great time. We're stuck in the car for half an hour, right?"

"It shouldn't be that long. Traffic's light."

Well, Lark didn't need him to talk. She had plenty to say herself. "Fine. You just listen, then." She took a deep breath to avoid launching into speed-babble. Embarrassment was seeping back in. "I apologize for my thoughtlessness earlier. I know you've been holed up for six months and haven't…well, I'm assuming you haven't been with anyone. And that while you were in the hospital…lab…whatever…you weren't usually in the mood to…you know." She made a motion with her fist. *Now* she had Jason's attention.

"What?" He stared at her hand. She flattened it onto her leg, feeling awkward. "Lark, you have no clue—"

"Of course I don't," she quickly agreed. "I've never been through what you have. I'm just saying, I should have figured out a different way to help you. I didn't mean to—" The words choked her and she looked out the side window, not wanting to see his reaction to the next part, even in the dark. "I got carried away, and I'm sorry. I'm not usually—that—responsive," she ended in a near whisper.

Jason blew out a long breath. "Lark—dammit, I didn't want to have this conversation."

"Then don't," she shot back, frustrated. "You don't have to say anything. It was my fault, I take full responsibility, and since I know your next words are some variation of 'I'm too old for you,' please just spare me." Her throat tightened again. Part of her would have been very happy not pushing this conversation, but she couldn't let Jason think she wanted a relationship with him. The attraction, no matter how intense, couldn't offset his health concerns and dangerous job. But that didn't mean she wanted to hear *him* reject *her.*

Jason didn't spare her. He couldn't. There was too much at stake to allow her to believe the wrong thing. Or to avoid the subject—which, he admitted, had been pointless and cowardly.

He didn't like being a coward.

"I probably am too old for you, but it doesn't feel like it." He winced, imagining what Matt would say. "In fact, in a lot of ways, I think you're perfect for me." The admission caused something to swell in his chest, something light and—geez, he couldn't believe he was thinking this way—happy. And the look on Lark's face made him want to slam on the brakes, haul her into his lap, and kiss her for real. The way he should have kissed her back at the house, instead of ravaging her.

"But it's irrelevant, Lark." The pain that chased away her joy pierced his own bubble. "Besides the age difference, and the lifestyle difference, and the fact that I live in DC and travel the world and you live in Boston and travel the world, there's the fact that we're in a dangerous situation that has to take priority over everything else."

"I don't disagree with that last part," she started, but he held up a hand.

"Lark. He's my best mate." He winced at the words and tried to cover. "My best friend. For a decade. He trusts me to protect you—stop laughing!"

"Best mate?" She covered her mouth with her hand

but it didn't stop the unladylike snort. "Have I been wrong all this time about the platonic part? Are you two really soulmates?"

"Stop it. It's a Harry Potter thing," he grumbled, making her laugh all the harder. His entire body blushed.

"You read Harry Potter?"

"I listened to the audiobooks. During all those lonely hours of rehab when no one bothered to come see me, not even your father."

She stopped laughing immediately. "I'm sorry, Jase."

"Forget that. My point is that I will never do anything to hurt that man, and that includes defiling his daughter and if you laugh again I will pull this truck over and leave you on the side of the road."

Instead, he pressed down on the accelerator as if he could speed out of the conversation.

"I think you underestimate my father," Lark said softly, all hint of laughter gone. "I would say I don't care, that I'll be with who I want to be with, but that wasn't how I started this conversation. I don't—I'm not looking for a relationship of any kind." She lifted the bottle of hand sanitizer out of the console and turned it in her hand.

Jason frowned at the bottle she was contemplating with an odd seriousness. He'd appreciated the thoughtfulness when she bought it, but what did it have to do with relationships? Did she think he was too weak? Maybe his cramping episode had scared her off. She thought she'd have to take care of him.

Or maybe it wasn't him at all. Her career was important to her, of course. He was a little irritated at the idea that she thought he'd stand in her way. The work she did was important, finding plant-based medicines to help people like—

Oh.

"Are you thinking about your mother?" he asked softly. That Lark didn't jump or look startled told him she was.

"My father wouldn't trade what they had for anything, even to get rid of the pain of missing her." She dropped the bottle back into the console. "But never having something to miss is different."

Jason could tell she was trying to sound matter-of-fact, but her voice came out tight and shaky. Her father's loss was only an excuse. She'd endured the same pain, and Jason had seen the toll it had taken, watching Kelly battle the simplest of illnesses for years. Even if Jason never got sick, the risk was too high.

It shouldn't hurt this much to be rejected for something he told himself he didn't want.

"Okay, then," he finally said. "We'll just concentrate on getting your father back and neutralizing Kemmerling so you can get back to your normal life." Lark didn't answer. When he glanced over she was facing the window, her elbow on the ledge and her fist pressed to her mouth. "Okay?"

She nodded. "Yeah." He thought she might be crying, but when she turned to face him, her eyes were dry. "On a similar subject, I made some calls while you were running."

That was an easy shift of topic. He hid his faint disgruntlement. "And?"

"My boss blasted me for taking off. The cops want

a statement. I told him I'd go give one Monday, and left a message for the investigator that I would."

"I don't think—"

"That I'll be back by Monday, yeah, thanks for dragging that fear up. The longer it takes us to find Dad, the worse off he'll be. I just felt better with denial."

"Sorry."

"Anyway, there's something weird going on with my ex-boyfriend."

He so didn't want to hear about her ex-boyfriend. But "What?" came out of his mouth anyway.

She shifted in her seat to settle more comfortably against the door. The position had her squarely facing him, trapping him.

"A couple of days before this all started, he got real friendly all of a sudden. We hadn't been going out for a few weeks, but then one evening he came on to me in the elevator. When I put him off, he said he missed *talking* to me."

Jason smirked. "Yeah, something's up."

"Seriously. But there's more. He called me about the BotMed invasion."

"Invasion?" He realized she meant Donald and Isaac. "Oh, that little altercation. Don't worry, it was too small a deal to be on the news or anything. No one—"

"Yeah, I know. So how did he know about it? Plus, he offered to cook me dinner. Take care of me. It was weird. Then he got all commanding when I said I wasn't home. Asking where I was and stuff. Do you think someone got to him?"

"Probably." Jason should have anticipated something like this. "What does he do?"

"What do you mean?"

"Hang on." He navigated the traffic circle and pulled up to the curb in front of the Castle, the administrative building for the Smithsonian. There was no sign of Gabby yet. He put down his window and turned off the ignition, examining the sparsely populated Mall and the path to the Metro entrance before giving Lark his attention again.

"What does Carl do for a living?"

"Investments. Why does that matter?"

"Does he do yours?"

"No. I use the same people Dad does."

There had to be a connection stronger than the boyfriend thing, since they'd broken up. "How do you keep seeing him? What elevator did he come on to you in?"

"He lives in my building."

Of course. "Yeah, I'm sure it was Isaac."

She scowled. "To get to me? But he's got to know I'm not...oh. He thinks he can use Carl to get into my apartment and look for my data."

"It would be much easier than trying to break into the secure building again, especially since he didn't seem to know about the greenhouse. He probably started watching your activities a couple of months ago. As soon as he learned—"

"That you survived," she finished. "That asshole."

Jason didn't ask which one. He looked at his watch, then back toward the Metro. "She should be here by now."

Lark checked her own watch. "Maybe she couldn't get a train right away."

"This time of day there are plenty, even on the weekend. And the station she was going to wouldn't have been crowded. It's near the end of the line." He tried Gabby's phone, but it went right to voice mail.

"Maybe she can't get a signal underground," Lark suggested.

Maybe, but his instincts were screaming. He climbed out of the truck. "Stay here."

He hurried, not wanting to leave Lark alone for long, but the Metro station wasn't far, and there weren't many places to check. When he got back to the truck a few minutes later Lark was in the driver's seat, her fingers tense around the wheel. As soon as he approached she jumped out.

"Well?"

He shook his head. "No sign of her."

Lark backed toward the truck, as if seeking its protection. "That's bad."

Jason couldn't reassure her. It was very bad.

FOURTEEN

THEY WAITED ANOTHER half an hour, but Lark wasn't surprised when Gabby didn't show. They tried her cell phone, office phone and home phone three more times, with no results.

"What do we do?" Lark asked when Jason finally started the truck.

"We take you back to my house and I go looking for her."

"No."

"Lark."

"There's no time, Jason. If there's any chance we can find her…"

He turned the truck off again. "I don't like your vulnerability out here."

"I'm not vulnerable, I'm with you."

He snorted, but she did feel safe. She would have said she proved with Donald that she could hold her own, but if Isaac and his people could get her father, they could get her. So she wouldn't be cocky. But if someone came after her, she was better off with Jason than alone, even in the safety of his house.

Jason didn't answer, but climbed out of the truck and didn't protest when she followed. His jaw line had sharpened, though, and when they paused to let a few cars go by, the small muscles in his temple pulsed.

She vowed to lay low and not give him more reason to be aggravated.

They strode quickly to the Metro station entrance, Jason letting Lark go ahead of him down the escalator, presumably watching her back. The platform was more congested than the Mall above had been. People were heading home after a day of sightseeing and Frisbee-throwing.

"Are we going to take the train?" she asked.

"No, just check the platform." They walked the entire area, even buying fare cards so they could get inside the gates. No sign of Gabby or anyone else they knew.

They hurried back to the truck and headed out of the city.

"We'll try to retrace her steps, figure out how far she got," Jason said.

Lark shivered. "We're going back to Hummingbird?"

"She called right after she left there."

"Is that…a good idea?" She hated that she was afraid of the place her father had built. Goddamn Isaac! She wanted to make him feel this way. Like anywhere he turned there was an enemy. "I mean, will we be targets? We don't know who's…you know. Against us."

Jason shrugged. "We're as safe there as anywhere."

"But you're dead."

"Not anymore." His hands tightened around the steering wheel. "Solving this problem is more important than keeping my survival a secret. I just need to check the logs. It's late on a Saturday night. No one will be there now except active teams."

They sped through the night in silence. Jason parked in front of the building and went inside. Lark waited, her body aching from the tension, and tried to keep an eye on her surroundings, not just stare at the main doors.

Jason was back in less than ten minutes but looked much grimmer.

"What did you find?" she asked as he put the truck in gear.

"That the night desk wasn't surprised to see me."

"What does that mean?"

"Matt didn't keep me as much of a secret as he thought he did. It made it easier to see the logs, at least."

"And?"

"Nils Fredlund was here today."

Lark chewed her bottom lip. She remembered Nils as a scrawny geek type, but that kind of guy, sometimes a little bit of power went to his head. "Do you think he took her?" Or harmed her. "Is that all you got from the log? And where are we going?" They were headed back toward town.

"Nils logged in about half an hour before Gabby did, and he went down to the lab shortly before she logged out. He was probably in the elevator with her after that. She was the only one who swiped to come up to the lobby, but then he went up to the accounting floor before he signed out, immediately after her car left the grounds."

He slowed as they drove into the square. "Shit."

"What?" Lark looked around. She didn't recognize the two people on the sidewalk, and they didn't ring any "sinister conspiracist" bells. Most of the shops were closed and there wasn't much noise coming out of the one bar. The Laundromat looked empty.

Jason parked in an empty spot near a sedan that looked familiar. Gabby's? Lark clambered out to follow him back to the car, but waited on the sidewalk when he waved her away. He inspected the outside of the vehicle, then got on the ground and peered underneath, even though he couldn't fit to slide under.

"It looks clean." He tried the driver's door. Locked.

Lark hurried over and tried the passenger door, but it was locked, too. She cupped her hands around her face and looked inside. No purse, no files, not even any trash on the floor.

When she straightened, Jason was looking behind her. She turned. The car was parked in front of a pet groomer, but next to that was Mike's Cab Service.

"You think she took a cab?" When Lark turned back, Jason was already striding toward Mike's door. "I guess you do."

Lark hurried to follow him through the dirty glass door. "Mike"—whose real name seemed to be Rajendra Fitch—started out surly and uncooperative, but within two minutes was pouring out his life story to Jason. The relevant part was that Gabby had come in and paid for a ride to the Metro station. He dropped her off, and as he was leaving, she was talking to a short redheaded guy and a tall blond one.

Jason thanked the man with a tip and they went back to his truck. He sat with his hand on the key but didn't turn it, then suddenly slammed his fist on the steering wheel.

"Hey, it's not your fault." Lark laid her hand on his arm. He jerked it away. Stung, she opened her mouth to snap at him, but closed it before she did. He was under a lot of pressure and probably hadn't meant it personally.

"She was scared," Jason growled. "I told her the car was tagged. That probably freaked her out and she ditched it. But stopping here to get the cab gave them time to catch up to her. They nabbed her before she could disappear into the Metro system."

"We'll get her back," Lark tried to reassure him.

Jason cranked the engine. "Count on it."

MATTHEW WAS GETTING BORED.

His plan had been to let Isaac take him, confront the guy, learn everything he could about his plans, and foil them. It was kind of hard to do that when Isaac wouldn't show up.

Matthew had spent a lot of his time wondering why the hell Isaac had abducted him in the first place. Since he wasn't here trying to torture information out of Matthew, it had to be to keep him out of the way while Isaac did something else. If that was the case, Matthew was wasting his time here.

He paced the perimeter of the room, testing the softness of the dirt walls and trying to determine which side was at the rear of the building, away from the main entry door. His escape would be short lived if he crawled out right in front of everyone.

The basin and pitcher were solid china, and the only tool he had. He wrapped them in a blanket from the pallet, positioned them for leverage, and stomped hard until they cracked.

Creaking footsteps sounded overhead. Matthew quickly hid the wrapped, broken shards and watched the shadows cross the room above. The steps faltered, as if the person was drunk or carrying something heavy. The lock on the trapdoor scraped, and light flooded the pit as the door creaked open.

"Catch."

Matthew had a split second to either jump back or leap forward. His brain registered subconsciously what they were dropping, and he made the right choice. A body landed in his arms, knocking him to the floor with the woman on top. The trapdoor thudded down, darkening the room again.

He lay flat on the floor, trying to catch his breath. His ribs finished yelling at him for the impact and let his lungs expand, at least as far as they could with the weight on them.

The woman sprawled across him moaned. He shifted, cradling her as he sat to keep her upper body off the dirt floor. His eyes readjusted to the dimness after the flash of light from upstairs. The woman moaned again. He supported her with his right arm and used his left to feel her scalp. She had soft, curly hair and no lumps. She'd probably been drugged, too. Who was she, and why had Isaac nabbed her? It wasn't Ella; her hair was short and straight, and her body not nearly this softly curved. Not that he was noticing.

The woman stirred, then stilled. A moment later she scrambled away from him, moving several feet before she hit the wall and crouched, her hands in front of her.

"What the hell?" Her voice was raspy, the tone groggy. She'd been out a while but had clearly recognized danger almost as soon as she'd regained consciousness. Crossing the floor on hands and knees in the dark wasn't smart, but neither was staying in the arms of a stranger who may have roofied you.

"It's okay," Matthew tried to soothe her. "You're okay. I'm not going to hurt you."

Her shadow stopped cowering and leaned forward. "Matthew?"

"What—?"

She leaped forward, throwing her arms around his neck and slamming into him hard enough to knock him on his ass if he hadn't already been there. Seconds later, he recognized her voice.

"Gabby?"

"Oh, Matthew, we were so worried. You're okay." Her arms tightened across his shoulders, her head turning slightly until her cheek rubbed his. "I can't believe you're okay," she whispered.

His own arms came around her with his first response. Pleasure at her joy, her uninhibited reaction to seeing him—to his body's reaction to feeling her. But then his heart sank.

She was here. In this pit. Besides all the other reasons that was not good, it compromised his plans. He couldn't leave now. Not the way he'd intended to.

Still, he could have this moment. He hugged her and let her cry for a few minutes.

Finally she eased away from him. "Oh, my goodness. I'm sorry." She swiped her hands across her cheeks. "I didn't mean—it's the stress. The last two days...and then the drugs, I'm sure. The relief just overwhelmed me."

"It's okay. What happened?"

She told him about trying to get hold of him this morning about his message—a message he hadn't left—and about Jason meeting with her. She'd gone back to the lab to secure information, and Nils Fredlund had intercepted her.

Matthew wished he could have neutralized Nils before he'd been taken. He couldn't be working alone on the inside, but at least now Matthew could be reasonably certain Gabby wasn't the other one. There was a chance Isaac had dropped her down here to play victim and get whatever he wanted to get out of Matthew, but he didn't think his former employee was that sophisticated.

"I was so stupid, Matthew," she lamented when she came to the end of her story. "I didn't do what Jason told me. They got me at the Metro. I tried to bluff my way out of it but I'm no agent. Nils stuck me while the other guy distracted me by asking about you."

Matthew controlled his surge of anger with difficulty. "Who was the other guy?"

"I don't know."

"Do you know who Isaac Kemmerling is?"

He could sense her shrug. "Everyone knows who he is. I mean, office gossip. But I never met him."

Of course she hadn't. She'd been hired long after Kemmerling left. "Can you describe the other guy?"

"Average height, blond, hazel eyes, good looking in a slick way. He had a mole right here." She raised her hand to her face. "I remember that because I was looking at it when the drugs kicked in." She sighed. "Things tend to fix in your head at the moment you realize you're a complete idiot."

"You're not an idiot," he said automatically. She hadn't been smart, no, but who would expect her to be? She wasn't trained, hadn't been prepared for involvement in something like this. It was significant that Isaac had gone after her himself. Maybe he didn't have much of a team.

"Nils must have checked the flash drive right away and had Isaac ready outside the gate to follow me. I'm sorry, Matthew, I tried."

"You succeeded." He rose and crossed the room, helping her to her feet. "You kept the data away from him. That's all you needed to do."

Gabby looked around. "Where are we?"

"I don't know. Some kind of basement. I was unconscious when I got here."

He was close enough now to see her scowl at him in the dim light. "How could you allow yourself to be taken?"

He didn't tell her "allow" was the operative word. "What did Nils and the blond guy say to you?"

"Um…Nils said it wasn't very smart of me to have played him, and the other guy told Nils to shush. I asked what was wrong, trying to play dumb, which wasn't difficult, actually." She sighed. "Nils grabbed my arm and shoved a needle into it, and that's all I remember. I'm sorry. I've made things worse, haven't I?"

"Remains to be seen. But probably."

"Don't sugarcoat it, I can take the truth."

He chuckled at the wryness in her voice. She was taking this surprisingly well. He'd always thought of her as high-strung and jittery. But maybe that was just because of him. He could hear Jason's voice in his head, saying "Arrogant much?" But the idea generated a kind of excitement deep inside. Something he hadn't felt since Kelly, and had been trying not to feel about Gabby for weeks. Something that needed another time and place.

"So what do we do?" Gabby asked.

Matthew ushered her over to the pile of blankets and eased her down, then settled beside her with his back to the wall, his legs crossed in front of him. "We wait."

LARK DIDN'T LIKE separating from Jason. She could tell he didn't want to leave her, either. But they'd decided they didn't have much choice. Time mattered, and they couldn't examine the flash drive he'd taken from Isaac's office and get Gabby back at the same time.

So Jason took Lark back to his house. She followed him yet again as he searched it and double-checked his security.

"I'm a great big albatross," she muttered.

"You'll be doing something important. That flash drive could have what we need." Jason cleared the guest room, checked the closet, and relaxed. "That's it. No one's here."

"What if I spend hours searching and find nothing more helpful than his grocery list?"

"We still have to look, whether there's anything there or not." He caught her chin in his hand and raised it. "It's important, and so are you." He kissed her forehead, and she rolled her eyes.

"Thanks. That's very patronizing of you."

He smiled, a little less wide than usual, and instead of walloping her in the gut it loosened something in her chest.

"Check in every half hour, okay?" She rested her

palm on his chest for a brief moment. "Or as close as possible."

"I will." He folded his hand around hers. "Don't worry about me."

"I can't help it." She drew a fortifying breath. *Don't do it, it's stupid, don't do it.* But even though she avoided emotional entanglement, she never kept things close to the vest. "About before..."

"No."

"Yes." She grabbed his wrist before he could back away from her. "Despite what I said, I want you to know that I care about you. Come back in one piece, okay?"

His jaw tensed, but he nodded. Maybe it complicated things a little, but Lark felt slightly better for having said it. She watched him go with a sense of foreboding she hoped was simply a product of her own anxiety.

AMAZINGLY, NILS FREDLUND was listed with Directory Assistance.

If Nils were smart, he wouldn't be home. Being listed meant he was easy to find, even by someone without access to Hummingbird's records. But Jason counted on Nils believing no one was aware of his involvement with Isaac. Nils hopefully thought everyone who knew—Gabby and Matt, primarily—was in custody. And this late at night, if Jason was lucky, Nils was off the clock.

His home address was in an old house-turned-apartment building in Silver Spring, Maryland. Jason studied the big house as he strolled up the block toward it. Lights shone through the front windows on both the first and second floors, and from one small window in the rear of the second floor. Besides the hum of nearby traffic, the grass-scented rustle of wind in the neighborhood trees, and the occasional bark of a dog a few houses away, the neighborhood was quiet.

Jason casually climbed the front steps and checked the mailboxes. No names, but Nils's address was 512½, and judging by the placement of the boxes, that was second floor, rear.

The front door's lock had broken long ago, with no apparent attempt to fix or replace it. He stepped into the central hallway and let the door thump quietly closed against his back. The foyer and stairs were dimly lit and covered in threadbare carpet. He leaned forward and craned his neck to look up the stairway, spotting two doors before the light at the top began to spin. Air caught and held in his chest, and his vision tunneled toward darkness.

He backed toward the door and shook his head hard to clear it. Those stairs probably creaked like mad. Better to go around back, anyway. Then he wouldn't alert Nils and send him fleeing into the alley. It had nothing to do with the open, wallpapered, spindle-railed interior stairwell, completely different from the one in which he'd been shot. It was just strategy.

This kind of house should have an outside stairway to the upstairs apartments in the back. He went back outside and circled the building. As he crossed below the side windows, music throbbed through the wall. Good. The hard rock bass might penetrate the floor and make it harder for Nils to hear Jason's approach.

The backyard was dark, the nearest light a security lamp on a telephone pole two houses down. A narrow gravel alley bordered the yard, and two old cars were parked in a gravel indentation in the lawn. The music was louder back here. Jason used it as cover as he jogged up the rickety back steps. The paint was almost completely flaked off, the wood splintery. A couple of steps were broken. The handrail too, in a few places. As he reached the halfway point and negotiated the turn, he looked up to assess his destination. Lights sparked to life in his peripheral vision, and his breathing went harsh in his ears. Wood bit into his left hand, tightly gripping the rail, and the steps under his feet were solid, but his brain told him he was falling backward. He swayed with vertigo, and the lights flashed faster, pinpoints of gold in solid blackness.

He squeezed his eyes closed and bent forward, facing down. He'd been on normal stairs since his accident, Goddammit, why was this happening now?

Because you're working. Just like at Isaac's office. The circumstances weren't similar now, but his physiology was. His thought processes and preparation for a fight had triggered the panic. Now that he knew that, he could fight it. He *would* fight it. He took slow, even breaths, trying to keep aware of his surroundings even as he fought the spinning. He wasn't sure how much time had passed once his head cleared and his heartbeat slowed, but the same song played inside. No cars had appeared at the back of the house. The second floor light still glowed in a patch on the grass.

"He'd so better be there," Jason muttered under his breath. If he'd gone through all this and Nils wasn't in the apartment… He drew in one final deep breath and resumed the climb, this time keeping his face front and only using his eyes to skim ahead of him.

A black-and-white cat hung out on the top step of the upper porch, watching Jason's approach. It opened its mouth in a silent cry as he passed it, and he reached down to scritch the back of its neck. It arched, then turned and dashed through a broken board into the house. Jason went the opposite way, heading to the dark window of the right-side apartment.

The window looked into a tiny, sparse bedroom. A twin bed, a basic computer desk sprouting wires from various pieces of computing equipment, and a tiny TV on an old metal stand were the only pieces of furniture. The open bedroom door showed a kitchenette, the light on over the sink. It appeared to be empty, too.

Jason tried the lockless window, which stuck. Maybe swollen from the day's humidity. He crouched to examine it. Chipping showed thick layers of paint that probably helped hold it shut. The window might have been nailed from the inside, too. He rose again and braced the heels of his hands against the top of the pane. Feet wide, he gathered his strength and shoved.

The window resisted for only a second before it shot up six inches. Now that was cool. He kept forgetting his rehab had actual benefits, not just side effects.

He shifted to the side of the window in case someone had heard the noise, but there was silence from inside. He forced the window up just enough to squeeze through. His boots left muddy prints on the wool blanket covering the bed. He hoped it was Nils's.

He listened for a few minutes to the music downstairs and a few random settling-house-type groans. The odors of old spaghetti sauce and maybe a fruit-scented candle hung in the air, neither fresh. Evidence said Nils wasn't here, but instinct told Jason evidence was wrong. He moved forward, easing around the edge of the doorframe into the kitchen. Still nothing. Then he sensed a presence, someone standing very still outside the kitchenette. He stepped quietly nearer, trying to remember how tall Nils was and where he'd be holding a weapon. Then he lunged around the corner, hands out to grab the bat or gun, or Nils's wrist or throat.

Miscalculating the thought processes of a geek cost him. Every muscle spasmed as a hundred thousand volts slammed through his body, and he crashed to the floor.

FIFTEEN

IT TOOK LARK a while to settle down. The house was so silent that every little sound made her leap to her feet and prowl until she found the source—the air conditioning hissing through the vent above her, the boiler heating the hot water in the basement, creaks of settling walls that she couldn't trace but that made her sweep the house each time.

Finally, after making a cup of tea—and wasting time wondering why Jason had tea in his house, because he sure didn't seem like a tea drinker—she forced herself to sit at the table with his laptop and the flash drive, resigned to reading each and every file.

Most of it was junk, easy to skip through. Maybe important stuff to Isaac, but not relevant to the Hummingbird situation. She waded through three years' worth of security service invoices, but those were the only business-related files. All the rest were lists and random notes. She supposed they could be in code, but it all seemed too straightforward for that.

The information was so boring, she had to keep dragging her wandering mind back to what she was looking at. She wondered if Jason was faring any better. Nils probably wouldn't be that difficult to turn. He was a pipsqueak and no match for Jason, mentally or physically.

She hoped. Jason had winced and hissed a lot when

she touched him, and he'd alluded to undesirable side effects. She hated the idea of the RT-24 causing problems, but few treatments had no downside, and it was still experimental. They could probably modify the formula to mitigate the side effects in future patients. But that didn't do Jason any good.

Then there was the cramping. She cringed, remembering the torment in his face when she'd found him on the treadmill. What if that worsened, and a morning workout stopped being effective? She needed to talk to Gabby about this. Maybe some mineral supplements would help. Or a massage every day. She smiled before she could stop herself, remembering this morning.

Such a thing had never happened to her in her life. An orgasm wasn't that difficult to achieve, when things were done right. But a little more time and some nakedness were usually involved. She flushed, remembering how she'd rubbed herself against him, flung herself around. God, the embarrassment.

Of course, he'd been a little red-faced, himself. Maybe he didn't like being vulnerable, hadn't appreciated needing her help. That was probably why he didn't want to talk about it. It wasn't manly. So when had resistance become desire? She shivered, remembering the kiss, the way he'd fisted his hand in her hair and devoured her mouth. *Something* she'd done had triggered his need.

She wanted to do it again.

The chiming of the grandfather clock in the other room pulled her out of her thoughts. That meant forty-five minutes had passed since Jason left. He was supposed to call her fifteen minutes ago. She eyed her cell phone, then the phone on the wall. Being late might not mean he was in trouble. If she called, she could interrupt him at a bad moment. And getting voice mail, if he'd turned off the phone, wouldn't make her feel any better. She decided to give him another fifteen minutes.

With a sigh, she clicked on another file, this one's header indicating it was a party guest list. She had a hard time imagining Isaac throwing a party. Her eye ran down the list of names, half of which had strike throughs. Maybe those who RSVP'd with a no? Her gaze snagged on something familiar. She studied the name, not recognizing it, but hearing a bell nonetheless. Ella Reinhart. She had an Aunt Ella, and there was a guy at work named Stuart Reinhart. That must be why it looked familiar. She continued reading, but stopped again immediately. The next name on the list was Carl Darron. Below that was Mike Frankel. Her ex-boyfriend Carl's last name was Frankel. She skimmed back up the list, and sure enough, the name before Ella's was Stuart Jones. Stuart. Reinhart. Ella. Darron. Carl. Frankel.

"Holy crap." She'd cracked the code! She grabbed the pad and started writing all the first names on the list. Then she wrote the last names, starting with the second one on the list, and putting it with the first first name. The first last name went with the last first name… She stared. She had no idea what this list was for, but she recognized more than half the names this way.

Her ex-boyfriend. Her boss and two guys from work. A couple of names might be Hummingbird employees, though she wasn't positive. And her mother's sister. Ralph's last name and the other guy's from BotMed were crossed through, but Ella's and Stuart's weren't.

Lark's mind raced through possible explanations. Maybe these were people close to her and to Hummingbird that Isaac thought he could use. But how did the strike throughs factor in? Were they people he'd turned, or not? And was it the first names or the last that mattered? Nils wasn't on the list, of course. That would have been too easy.

She needed Jason. They could figure this out together. Their brains seemed to connect, like network computers accessing more processing power. But he still hadn't checked in, and it had now been an hour and a half. Lark went to the kitchen phone and dialed his cell from memory. It went straight to voice mail, just as she'd expected. She hung up without leaving a message, immediately pacing the kitchen while she figured out what to do.

There were two reasons Jason wouldn't check in. He was hiding and using his phone would alert his quarry, or he was in trouble. If it was the former, going after him would jeopardize his plan, maybe him. But if it was the latter, and she did nothing, she risked losing him as well as her father, not to mention Gabby. That wasn't acceptable.

But dammit, she wasn't a fighter. She braced her arms on the countertop, closing her eyes and swallowing down the bitterness in her throat. She could barely handle a gun, never mind use it, and that made her a liability. Going in after Jason could put him in a worse position.

But it was *Nils*. She'd beaten him in hand-to-hand.

Several years ago, the voice of reason whispered. He could be better now. But maybe not. And she still worked out.

Nils might not be alone. He shouldn't have been a challenge for Jason, not unless he had help, which meant she had even less of a chance of doing any good. She twisted to look at the clock on the wall again, her lungs tightening. She couldn't just sit here all night, worrying.

She had Nils's address. She could just go drive by, see what she could see, gather information to help her decide what to do. She knew how to ride a motorcycle, thanks to an old boyfriend, but she didn't have a license and she had no idea where Jason kept the keys.

She snatched her cell phone off the table and checked the charge. More than half. She switched it to vibrate and stuck it in her front pocket. The gun was trickier. She knew better than to put it in her waistband, especially while riding a motorcycle. Somewhere in this house, Jason had to have a suitable holster.

After a frustrating half hour searching, she found a set of keys she hoped would start the bike and a shoulder holster that wouldn't fit no matter how much she adjusted it. Damn, she'd have to leave the weapon behind. She felt vulnerable, but she'd be no good to anyone with a hole in her butt.

The wind would be cold during the ride, so she shrugged on a zip-up sweatshirt from the front hall closet. The sleeves needed rolling six times, and the hem came halfway to her knees, but it would be warm and add protection on the ride. After double-checking the route to Nils's house on a map and committing all the side roads to memory, she went out to the garage to uncover the bike.

The Suzuki sport bike was different from the little Ducati her ex owned, but the principle would be the same. She hoped. It was a big machine. She was surprised to find the tank full. Her father must have had it gassed and everything when he knew Jason was going to be released.

She swung her leg over. Her toes just touched the ground, but the bike had exquisite balance and wasn't hard to keep up. One of the storage compartments had a garage door opener in it. She hit the button and watched it slowly reveal the driveway and dark, empty street outside. Taking a deep breath, she started the bike, maneuvered out of the garage, and roared off to save Jason.

Or something.

GABBY HUDDLED AGAINST the dirt wall, her legs drawn up on the rough blankets on the floor, and tried to hide her shivering from Matthew. He hadn't said much over the last hour—it was hard to know how much time was passing, sitting here with nothing to do in the dark—and he was probably trying to come up with a plan. She didn't want him to see her as weak and therefore a liability. Getting herself captured had certainly caused him problems.

"Are you cold?" he asked.

"No." She hugged her knees tighter to stop the shuddering, but realized the move just proved her lie. She forced herself to relax and added, "I'm fine."

But then he was beside her, wrapping his arm

around her shoulders, and Gabby no longer cared if he thought her weak as long as he kept touching her.

"I messed things up for you, didn't I?"

"No. Isaac did that." Matthew's tone was light and easy, and it relaxed Gabby even though she knew he was lying.

"I'll do anything you want me to," she told him.

His arm tightened briefly around her shoulders. "Anything?"

She smiled, wishing he meant the double entendre but knowing he couldn't possibly.

"Anything. Well—please don't ask me to shoot someone."

He chuckled. "I won't."

"But I'll play sick, or whack someone over the head with a hammer, or whatever."

"I'll keep it in mind."

He went silent again. They sat that way for a few minutes. His warmth seeped into her, stopping the shivers and then filling her with a level of comfort she shouldn't be feeling, given the circumstances. Gabby wanted to ask Matthew how he'd gotten himself abducted and what he thought Isaac's plan was, but realized there were things she knew that he didn't. Maybe telling him would get him talking and bypass the old-fashioned chivalrous streak that drove him to protect her. The reason was less that she was a woman and more that she wasn't an agent—but it was still misplaced.

"I talked to Jason today. At least," she amended, "I think it was today. When did you disappear?"

"Today." She could hear the smile in his voice.

"Okay, good. Anyway, I saw Lark and Jason this morning after they found out you were captured."

The hand rubbing her arm went still. "What do you mean, after they found out I was captured?"

Gabby opened her mouth, then closed it. She realized they hadn't actually said Matthew was abducted. She'd inferred it and they never corrected her. Maybe she didn't have as much information as she thought she did.

"Someone claiming to be you left me a message to compile all my data on Jason and his treatment and give him the flash drive when he came to see me," she explained. "I couldn't reach you, and then Jason called me and told me to meet him and Lark in town." She described the meeting. "Jason said the call hadn't come from you, or if it had, you'd been coerced. So I guess I assumed you'd been..." How to say it without insulting him? "Taken. I went back to the lab and erased the flash drive, protected all the data, and you know the rest."

Matthew's chest expanded under her as he took a slow, deep inhale. "When did you last talk to them? Is Lark okay?"

"This afternoon. She's fine. Tough."

He let out the breath, just as slowly. "Tell me again what happened this morning."

She repeated everything, adding as much detail as she could. "Was it you who called? Were you drugged?"

"I didn't call. But it's not that hard to fake my voice. It's not distinctive. No accent or special tone."

It was distinctive to her. But then again, maybe not, since she'd been fooled.

"Well?" she prodded.

"Well what?"

She pursed her lips in frustration. That hadn't worked as she'd hoped. "Well, do you have, you know, anything to say about that?"

"It helps fill in some blanks, thank you."

"Matthew!"

He sat, still, his hard chest barely moving under her shoulder. "What are you getting at, Gabby?"

Her breath caught at the sound of her first name in his voice. "I want to know what you know," she managed.

"I don't think that's a good idea."

She sighed. "You think Isaac will torture it out of me or something."

"There are other reasons."

But he didn't deny that he thought she was weak. Blinking back stupid tears of hurt feelings, she pulled away and stood, walking to the center of the room and squinting upward, trying to see between the cracks.

"I'm sure I ruined whatever plans you had. Have you come up with a new one yet?"

"I'm working on it." His voice came from the spot where they'd sat. He hadn't moved, hadn't followed.

"I can help." Her voice broke on the final word, and now she sensed him approach. He wrapped his arms around her from behind, laying them on her own crossed over her stomach. She sighed and twisted her hands to hold on.

"Gabby, I'm sorry," he murmured next to her ear. She gasped at the spear of need that went through her, his body so close, his voice so intimate. It took her a second to refocus and hear his next words.

"They're probably listening," he whispered. He turned her to see the intercom set into the dirt wall. "Cry."

Again, it was several heartbeats before she understood. He wanted her to cover his words with fake weeping. She sniffled and pressed the back of her hand against her mouth to stifle a sob.

"Good. Keep going."

She let out a few whimpers and sniffled again, letting the tears that had welled a moment ago spill over.

"My sister-in-law came to see me after ten years of silence," he breathed. "I knew Isaac had sent her, knew she was going to try something. I let her so I could get close to Isaac."

It didn't seem to have worked, Gabby thought even as she nursed her longing and sense of rejection to feed her crying. And Jason would kill him when he found out. But she only nodded and sobbed a little louder.

"I was going to escape if he didn't show up soon, but now he's got you, and that won't be easy."

So she *had* messed up his plans. Crap. Still, he'd come up with something, she knew he would.

"Why don't you try to sleep," he said louder, lifting his hands to rub her upper arms. Then he whispered, "I need to think."

"Okay. I'll try." She went to the pallet and lay down, but spent the next long, immeasurable stretch of time watching Matthew pace, and letting her mind worry over the problem.

Then she had an idea.

THE PAIN WAS HORRENDOUS.

Jason had never felt anything like it, not before the

accident or since, not even with the unexpected, counter-intuitive results of the nerve regeneration therapy.

Every one of those regrown nerves, plus all the new ones, seemed to be vibrating at once. He couldn't move, couldn't see, couldn't even hear. It was amazing he had any capacity to think.

Slowly, the pain faded from a blaze to a burn to prickles and tingles, and he concentrated on not moving or groaning or giving Nils any idea that he was recovering. He was vulnerable to an enemy in a way he had never been before, and it seriously pissed him off. Why hadn't he thought of a Taser? It was the perfect weapon for someone like Nils, someone without much skill or body mass, facing a bigger, better opponent.

Awareness slowly faded in. He was lying on the floor, probably the wood floor in the hallway, or maybe half in, half out of the room. Moisture on his cheek told him he'd drooled, though he didn't seem to have released any other body fluids, thank God. Nils paced near his feet, talking to someone on the phone.

"He's totally incapacitated. I can handle him."

Jason's right leg spasmed, and his boot thudded on the floor. He squinted in time to see Nils's eyes widen as he stood frozen, staring at Jason's leg.

"Just tell me what you want me to say. Or ask. Or do—do I bring him there, to put in with Matt and the doctor?"

Jason stifled a groan as random zings shot through his extremities and his fingers shook. They'd taken Gabby to wherever they held Matt. That was good, in some ways. It was easier to rescue two people if they were together. Saved time and research. On the other hand, getting two people out of a secure area unnoticed was three times harder than one.

"Okay," Nils said, sounding a little less nervous. "I can do that. No, you don't have to—I can—yes. Yes. I said I can. Okay." Nerves had turned to irritation.

Footsteps signaled Nils's approach, and Jason kept his eyes closed, trying to hold on to any advantage he could. Controlled movement was still beyond his capability. Where was his gun?

Nils came around his right shoulder and hauled on his collar with a grunt. Jason was dead weight, but Nils managed to lift his upper body a little and drag him across the wood. Jason's arms dangled, and his boot heels caught on the grooves between floor planks.

Nope. Not capable of controlled movement yet.

He let his head loll as Nils, panting and grunting, got him into a chair. As soon as he let go, Jason slid to the floor in a heap. He tested his fingers as he went. They wiggled.

"Fucking shitting Goddamned frackle." Nils didn't try the chair again. Instead, he shoved Jason into a sitting position against a ratty old couch, as Jason could see between his slitted eyelids.

"Can you hear me?" Nils yelled next to Jason's ear. Jason scowled and punched Nils in the side of the head. Or he tried to—his arm jerked, but didn't lift more than an inch off the floor.

"I'll take that as a yes." Still huffing and muttering under his breath, Nils tied something around Jason's right wrist, then lifted it into his lap and reached for his left wrist. Jason let his right hand fall back to the floor.

"Goddammit!"

Jason smirked. Nils didn't notice.

Eventually, Nils managed to get Jason's two hands together and looped a clothesline-type rope around them. Jason was gradually regaining full feeling, and as he did he could sense his level of muscular control, but he let Nils think he was still incapacitated. He might get more information out of the guy if Nils believed he had the advantage.

"All right." Wiping sweat off his forehead with his sleeve, Nils collapsed into the chair he'd tried to put Jason in. "Let's talk."

"Okay." Jason wasn't happy with the slurred sound of his voice. He flexed his arms and shifted his legs, but only a little. If he moved too much, Nils might tie his ankles, too. Or shock him again.

"Man, that was fun." Nils's face practically split with a pleased grin. "Big bad agent man, ready to take me down, falling on the floor like a rag doll." He jolted, arms and legs flopping in mockery of Jason. "How did it feel?"

"Joyous. Great fun."

"Yeah, that's what I thought. With all those extra nerves, we figured it would hit you hard."

The confirmation that they knew so much about his treatment didn't sit well. "You knew I was coming here?" That sounded better. Less drunk, anyway.

Nils heaved a sigh. "It wasn't hard to guess. Dr. Berwell talked to you. Then she disappeared. I told Isaac we were better off leaving her alone, with all that protective instinct you guys wallow in, but he wanted her expertise."

"Expertise for what?" Jason's temper rose, fed by

frustration that nothing made sense. “What the hell is Isaac trying to do?”

Nils looked cagey. “You think I’m going to spill the story, like some B-movie villain? I’m smarter than that, Templeton.”

Keep thinking that. “Then I guess the plan isn’t to kill me.”

“Hell, no, you’d be no good to us then.”

“That’s encouraging.” A spasm went through Jason’s back, followed by a smaller one in his left thigh. He gritted his teeth and hissed a breath, worried that the cramping would start again, and kind of surprised it hadn’t already. He was in deep shit if it did.

Neither of them spoke for a few minutes. Jason waited for Nils to get tired of the silence and start bragging or something, but he either had more stamina than Jason had calculated, or more fear. He jerked his arms up a few inches and Nils jumped. More fear, then. So Jason would start.

“Where’s Gabby, Nils?”

“Not tellin’.”

“You have someone you need put back together?”

Nils frowned. “No. Why would you ask that?”

“Because you said you need Gabby’s expertise. She’s a doctor.”

“Oh. Yeah. Well.” He shifted in his seat and fluttered the fingers of one hand. “Expertise with—well, with you.”

“Because she put *me* back together.”

“Yeah.”

“And you want to know how she did that.”

Nils pressed his lips together. Jason could probably

get more by offering more. "Matt thinks Isaac wants to sell the technology."

Nothing.

"Just the RT-24, though?"

Nils's eyes flicked to one side.

"That's what I thought. Not the orthopedic glue or the muscle-tissue compound. Why not?"

Nils stuck the side of his thumb in his mouth and gnawed.

"Not cutting-edge enough? Other people out there are working on it, right?"

Nils's free arm went around his waist and tightened. He gnawed harder on the thumb.

"The RT-24 is brand new," he pressed, cataloging Nils's continued non-verbal responses. "Revolutionary, even. But who would want to buy technology designed to help people?"

Now Jason fell silent. Nils would crack. He just had to wait.

But time ran out. There was a click from the hallway, and the creak of a door hinge. Nils jumped up and spun, his hand going to the Taser stuck in his back pocket. Jason must have been out longer than he realized, if Nils had time to reload the gun. Unless he had two of them.

Didn't matter. Jason took advantage of being out of sight to wiggle his hands out of the rope. Nils wasn't so good at tying knots. He struggled to his feet, swaying and tensing against his legs' desire to give way. He couldn't get the jump on Nils, not like this. He might get close enough to grab him, but he'd get shocked again before he could disable the smaller man. He didn't have the strength to land a good punch.

Nils took a tentative step toward the hall, Taser out. No one appeared in the doorway. A floorboard creaked in the room to their right, probably the kitchen. Nils didn't seem to hear it. He shifted his weight from foot to foot, waiting. Jason, infuriatingly impotent, also waited.

Seconds ticked by. Silence filled the room with its weight. Jason gathered his strength, picturing how he'd leap forward, wrap an arm around Nils's neck, and bear him to the ground, hopefully on top, not under him. He took a deep breath—and a figure flew in from the kitchen, silent and swift.

Nils spun, too late. A cast-iron frying pan came down on his head. He screeched as he fell, his gun hand rising. His finger compressed the trigger, and the Taser leads buried themselves in the plaster ceiling.

Lark dropped the frying pan and stomped her right foot onto Nils's chest.

"Where the hell is my father?"

SIXTEEN

MATTHEW WAS OUT of patience. His best guess put the time at somewhere in the middle of the night. Gabby couldn't stop shivering, not even wrapped in one of the blankets and sharing body heat. Isaac might still be trying to psych Matthew out, making him cool his heels, but he now suspected the kidnapping was more about keeping him out of the picture than trying to get something from him. And Matthew wasn't on board with that.

He explained his plan to Gabby, who didn't hesitate, even when he emphasized the risks. His respect for her, already high, rose even more.

She surprised him by contributing her ideas. Once Matthew was sure they were both in sync, he went to the intercom and pressed the button. A moment later John's voice crackled through the speaker.

"What?"

"We need someone down here. Gabby's sick."

"Sure she is."

Matthew wasn't surprised by John's skepticism. "I know you're too smart to believe me if I were lying, but John, I trained you. Why would I use a ploy you wouldn't fall for?"

After a pause, John asked, "What's wrong with her?"

"Fever. Convulsions. Delirium."

"Why didn't you say something before now?"

"It got bad pretty fast. I thought she was just cold at first." He waited, but John didn't respond. "John?"

"Where is she?"

Satisfaction burned through Matthew. He was biting. "On the pallet."

"You get on the opposite side of the room, against the wall," John ordered. "Sit with your back on the wall, legs out straight. You got it?"

"Yeah. Hurry, though. She's in bad shape. If Isaac wants her because of her knowledge, he's going to be pissed if she's too out of it to share."

A pissed-off boss involved in criminal activities was always a good motivator. In seconds John crossed the floor above. Matthew did as he'd been told and went to sit against the wall. Gabby stayed where she was, moaning and shuddering on the pallet of blankets. When the trapdoor opened and the light hit her face, Matthew was shocked to see how pale and haggard she looked. Maybe he hadn't been completely lying.

The barrel of a semiautomatic rifle appeared in the square hole first, aimed in his direction. He sat still, watching. After a moment John's head slowly appeared, until the man could see Matthew sitting docilely. The big man leaned further into the gap, not enough to make himself a real target, but enough to see inside the entire pit. He eyed Gabby, who lay with her eyes closed, her lips parted as she panted fast, fretful breaths. The barrel of the gun swept around the opening, checking the entire pit, and then disappeared.

"Don't move," John called down.

Matthew didn't move.

A moment later a rope ladder fell into the pit. John

didn't climb down, but jumped to the floor, his weapon aimed unerringly at Matthew.

His satisfaction grew. He'd been right—Isaac had limited manpower. John wouldn't have come down here alone if he had someone else on guard duty with him. Was Isaac's staff that small, or hadn't he pulled everyone into his scheme? Probably the latter. He couldn't be running a legitimate security company without having some employees with integrity. And when someone with no history of criminal bent started down the wrong path, he had to be careful whom to trust.

"Don't move," John said again.

"I won't. I just want her to have help."

John crouched and touched Gabby's head. "She doesn't feel feverish."

"It's cold down here. Skin temperature isn't a good indicator."

"Dr. Berwell, can you hear me?"

Gabby groaned and rolled her head back, but didn't open her eyes. She was doing a good job. It looked real.

"Dr. Berwell?"

Her lids fluttered, but she didn't respond. John cursed and stood. "Come here," he said to Matthew. "Slowly."

He did.

"Pick her up."

"What are you—"

"Just do it."

Matthew already knew John's intentions. He gently lifted Gabby in his arms and cradled her against his chest. A warmth swept through him, nothing physical, but a sense of protectiveness and possessiveness out of proportion to how he thought he felt about this woman. He banished it as soon as it flickered into his mind. He had to concentrate on his plan.

"I'll go up the ladder first," John said. "You carry her up."

"But—"

The gun came up, aimed at his head.

"Okay." Climbing the ladder wouldn't be easy, but he'd known that was what John would make him do. The guard had to keep control at all times, which meant putting the burden on his prisoner.

The big man scaled the swaying ladder quickly, then stood at the top and aimed his weapon into the hole. "Come on."

"Put your arms around my neck," Matthew murmured to Gabby, low enough that John couldn't hear. She didn't move. He jostled her a little, worried that she wasn't faking it any more. "Gabby, put your arms around my neck. I need you to help me." After a few more proddings, she did, shifting her weight closer to his body and taking the burden off. He twisted his arms under her and grabbed a rung of the ladder, balancing her across his arms, and lifted a foot onto the bottom rung. The ladder swayed forward and twisted, tilting him back, and he tightened his grip. He hoped to hell he could do this without dumping Gabby on her head.

He brought his left foot up to join his right, straining to lift Gabby enough to catch hold of the next rung with his right hand. Then his left hand. Right foot one rung higher, now left foot. The climb took forever, Matthew's muscles doing their own vibrating dance by the time he reached the trapdoor. Now was the moment of uncertainty. Would John make himself vulnerable and pull Gabby through? Would he make Matthew come up, or drop him back down in?

"Roll her up here," John said.

"How?" Matthew growled. His forearms and calves screamed and cramped. "I'm barely hanging on."

John reached down with one hand and slapped Gabby's cheek, lightly. "Hey. Dr. Berwell. Little help here."

After a moment Gabby roused. Matthew gritted his teeth. Did she have to play the part so damned well? His hands clamped around the rung, staying put only because the muscles in his fingers had seized up.

"Roll onto the floor, Gabby."

With a distinct lack of coordination, Gabby got herself onto the floor. Free of her weight, Matthew pulled himself high enough to see into the room. It was empty, the walls bare of any kind of decoration, equipment, furniture, or storage cabinets. It looked like an old hunting cabin.

He eyed John, who seemed to be debating his next move. "Let me come up and help you with her," he said in a low voice. John gave him an implacable look with no hint of conscience. "Come on, John. I can't believe you'd be a deliberate party to harm. You can't have known it would come to this."

John hesitated long enough to give Matthew hope, then shook his head. "Back down, sir." Matthew held on, but John poked him in the chest with the gun barrel. "Down. I'll take care of her. But I know you too well."

Matthew had to grin at that. He dropped down to

the dirt floor, landing lightly despite his protesting muscles, and watched as John pulled up the ladder, unhooked it from the metal rings next to the opening, and dropped the door back into place.

The first part of the plan had gone exactly as Matthew had hoped. Now, on to phase two.

NILS IGNORED LARK's demand and yanked at the Taser, trying to pull the leads out of the ceiling. Lark slapped the gun out of his hand. It swung wide, then came back to smack Nils in the side of the head where she'd hit him with the pan.

"Ow! Lark, for God's sake, come on!"

She pressed down harder on his chest. He yelped and grabbed at her foot, trying to push it off. It didn't budge, and she allowed a bit of pride to seep into her fury and fear. Seeing Jason sprawled like that, so vulnerable, had made her decision easy. But now she had to struggle to focus on Nils and not reveal—to either of them—just how much Jason's well-being meant to her.

"Look, Nils, I'm not in the best mood. You tell me right now where Kemmerling has my father and Gabby, or so help me God I'll crack your chest open and crush your heart."

"You think I know?" he shot at her. "Isaac's too smart to tell me where he's got them!" He tried to kick her in the back. She shifted forward, and he missed. Jason chuckled behind her, but Lark didn't spare a glance at him.

"Why does he have them, then?" She leaned forward, her knee bent, and Nils moaned out some air. "What's he going to do with them?"

Nils's fingers pried at her shoe. "I don't know," he wheezed. She pressed harder and reached for his hair.

"All right, all right!" He waved his hands. "I'll tell you. Just—" *gasp,* "—let me up."

Lark knew she should ease back and make him get up slowly, but she didn't have the patience. She fisted his shirt and hauled him up, then shoved him into the chair hard enough to tilt it backward. Her foot caught on the edge of the seat and slammed it back down. Nils paled, eyeing her toes centimeters from his dangly bits.

"Talk."

"Okay. Okay." He took a deep breath and glanced at Jason before giving her his full attention, though he kept his eyes downcast. "What, specifically—"

"Nils!"

"They want to sell the regeneration therapy as a weapon!" he shouted, flinging a hand up in front of his face.

Lark froze, her fist cocked, the building rage arrested by her surprise. "What? How?"

Nils jittered, his gaze flicking back and forth between Jason and Lark's fist. "I don't know. I'm not really a scientist. I just feed Isaac whatever information I can get a hold of. I can go a lot of places inside Hummingbird."

"You learned of the therapy and told Isaac. And he saw that as the way to take down the company?" Lark's mind raced. If Isaac got his hands on proof that Hummingbird had used the untested, unapproved therapy on Jason, he could get what he wanted. But selling it made no sense, especially by calling it a weapon. It wasn't.

Jason's thoughts apparently went in a different direction. "Who's the buyer?" he asked in a low voice.

Nils cringed. "I don't know. I'm low level, man."

"High enough to approach Gabby and stick her with a needle."

Lark heard Jason moving around behind her but didn't take her attention off Nils. A moment later, Jason gently nudged her aside and pulled Nils to his feet, wrapping his wrists with the rope that had been around his own a few minutes ago.

"What are we going to do with him?" she asked.

"I'd like to take him to the police." Jason tightened the rope and Nils yelped. "But they won't have any reason to hold him."

"How about accessory to kidnapping, corporate espionage and assault?" she asked.

"Hey, you attacked me," Nils protested.

She glared at him. "I meant him." She thrust a thumb at Jason.

"Oh."

Now Jason glared at her. Obviously the Taser had hit his ego as hard as his body.

He patted Nils down, something she'd neglected to consider, but found nothing. She watched Jason closely, noting the occasional muscle quiver, but if he was still in pain or weak, he hid it well.

Jason maneuvered Nils to face the hall and marched him in that direction. "There's no evidence, just our word against his. I'm dead, and you're the daughter of his boss, accusing a conveniently disgruntled former employee of serious crimes. He'd be out in hours, if not sooner."

Lark sighed and rubbed her forehead. "Okay, then what?"

"We lock him down." Jason paused at the open door to examine the lock she'd jimmied. "Credit card?"

"Driver's license."

"Clever."

She smiled. "Thanks."

They moved swiftly down the stairs. None of the house's other inhabitants seemed disturbed by the noise. The music downstairs continued to blare, but when they got outside, she noticed the front apartments' lights were all off now.

She almost ran up the back of Jason's leg when he stopped abruptly on the sidewalk.

"That's my bike," he declared.

"Yeah." Lark pulled out the keys.

"My motorcycle," he said as if she hadn't understood.

"Yeah, I know. It's how I got here."

Jason hung his head, his jaw tensing. "You rode my motorcycle."

"Uh, *yeah*. Can we do the macho he-man routine later? I couldn't have saved your ass if I hadn't taken the bike. I assume you prefer to ride it back?" She dangled the keys. "Where's the Rover? I'll haul Nils to the house."

Jason's face darkened as he looked up at the sky and audibly ground his teeth.

"No," he finally grunted. "You take the bike back to the house. I'll follow you with him." He gave Nils a shake. "And then we'll all go."

Lark almost asked "go where?" but swallowed it,

hard. First, he wasn't going to say, not out in the open here. Second…well, he was still a little pissed.

She waited until he and Nils disappeared in the darkness down the unlit street, heading for his truck, before starting the bike. No sense riling him further if she made a mistake or something. In fact, she'd better go ahead so he didn't see the way she drove it. She carefully rode down the street, then kicked it up a notch once she'd turned the corner.

The bike was wiped down and covered by its tarp and Lark stood on the street, waiting, when Jason pulled up. She climbed into the passenger seat and closed her door before he got the vehicle to a complete stop.

"Where are we going?" She pulled on her seat belt and twisted to look for Nils. He wasn't in the backseat, and she couldn't see the floor of the cargo area. "He in the back?"

"A place I know. And yes. And don't talk to me."

Hurt, she turned to face front again. "Okay." After a second, she pulled the hand sanitizer from the console, popped the top, and held it out. Jason hesitated, then gave her his cupped palm. She squirted some sanitizer into it. The tension lightened, even though he still didn't speak.

They drove in sulky silence for about twenty minutes. Jason pulled onto a dirt road or driveway that wound through overgrown grassland and around a copse of trees before it ended in front of a barn. There was no house in sight.

"Ah, the grain silo. Good hiding place. No corners or edges for him to commit suicide on before we can beat the information out of him."

Jason didn't respond to her lame attempt at humor. Lark threw up her hands, then trailed behind as Jason got Nils out of the truck and dragged him to the barn. She half expected him to key a code into a box and open a passage to an underground lair, but he only dropped the sniffling weasel into a horse stall.

"Will that hold him?" Lark examined the metal bars at the top of the door. They lined the gaps between stalls, too, and the wood seemed sturdy enough, with no gaps at floor level, and no window in the outside wall. The hard-packed dirt floor held only a few wisps of straw.

"For now." Jason shoved a huge bolt home and tested the non-existent wiggle of the door. "Come on."

He led her to the other end of the barn, out of earshot of Nils. He moved more naturally now. She assumed he was back to full strength, but his stride was as hard and abrupt as his tone had been.

They went into a room she supposed would normally have been a tack room and office. The dividing wall had been knocked down except for some beams framing the space. White paint covered everything except a scratched wooden desk and a narrow bed with its headboard against one wall. Jason pulled a plastic-wrapped bundle of linens from a trunk and shook sheets and a blanket out of it.

"What's going on?"

"It's the middle of the night. We're going to bed." He started putting a mattress pad over the mattress. Lark went to the other side to help him.

"Should we keep watch on Nils?"

"He can't get out of there. The bolt on the door is too low for him to reach. And even if he can, there's nowhere for him to go. For the drive, I tied him in the back of the truck so he couldn't sit up. He has no idea where we are or what's out there."

The closer they got to the bed being ready, the more tired she was. Whatever emotions and adrenaline had been driving her the last few hours were gone. "This is a pretty small bed," she pointed out.

"I'm exhausted, Lark." Jason yanked a pillowcase over a pillow he pulled out of the trunk and handed it to her. "You have nothing to worry about."

"You might," she said before she could stop herself.

His eyes burned at her for a few seconds before he turned away to get another pillow.

Lark winced, but she'd told the truth. Fatigue had weakened her mental barriers, and every time one of Jason's muscles flexed as he wrestled the mattress into submission, she remembered what had happened earlier that day.

She sighed and shoved her hair back. "Is there a bathroom here?"

"Across the aisle."

Lark found the primitive facilities and did what she could. When she got back, Jason was in bed already, fully clothed. She toed off her shoes, tucked her socks into them, and hung the gigantic sweatshirt on a nail. She hesitated a moment, but it was warm in there and she'd never be able to sleep if she was uncomfortable. She pulled off her T-shirt, removed her bra through the sleeves of her tank top, and unbuttoned her jeans before slipping under the sheet.

"You're killing me," Jason said a moment later, his voice low. He was lying on his left side, facing her.

Lark had faced the same way, keeping her back to him and lying near the edge so they didn't touch.

"It's warm." She looked over her shoulder and spoke softly, so Nils couldn't hear. "Don't you want to take off your shirt? Those long sleeves—"

"No."

She shrugged. "Okay. Good night."

"Lark."

"Don't." She buried her face in her pillow, wishing it was his chest. He smelled incredible, and the heat radiating off him was very different from the stuffiness in the small room. Why couldn't she be as immune to him as every other guy who'd crossed her path? It wasn't just that he treated her like an equal, despite his charge to protect her. Or his body's perfect composition. It wasn't even simple chemistry, hormones driving their mutual attraction.

It was something deeper, something she couldn't even define. Deeper than instinct or the occasional "click" of connection when you met someone you really liked. For the first time, she understood on more than an intellectual level how her father had felt about her mother, and why he wouldn't have changed anything.

She should be glad Jason was resisting as hard as he was, but longing swelled until her fingers ached where she clutched the side of the bed, trying not to roll over to face him.

Jason's hand settled on her hip. She froze, wishing he'd take it away, and equally afraid that he would. Desire crouched, braced, waited. He didn't move. His hand was heavy, strong, belying the vulnerability she kept applying to him. She'd never known anyone so strong.

Don't do it, you'll be sorry, don't do it. The chant slowly faded and Lark rolled to her back, anticipation filling the humid air. She couldn't see Jason in the darkness, but when her lips parted and she breathed him in, she didn't need her eyes. For a moment, the need to trust him, to trust fate, overwhelmed the distance she'd always held on to.

Jason's fingers stroked across her abdomen. "We can't." But even as he spoke he leaned toward her, finding her mouth without error. His mouth was hot, his lips supple, while his hand came up to cup her neck and face. Lark sensed he could hold himself in check for hours, years of discipline keeping him from taking this further. She wanted him to let go, like hours ago in his exercise room. The idea of making him lose control was a potent aphrodisiac. But she knew he wouldn't.

She touched his neck, lightly, to show she wasn't going to push. But instead of continuing the kiss, or easing out of it, Jason jerked away from her hand. Stunned, she automatically turned away, feeling stupid and angry because she didn't know why.

Crap. Jason blew out a breath, annoyed at his uncontrollable reaction. "I'm sorry."

"It's fine." But she couldn't hide that he'd hurt her.

"Let me explain." He waited, but Lark remained tense and said nothing. "It's the regeneration therapy."

It took her a few seconds to respond. She twisted her torso to partly face him. "What do you mean, it's the regeneration therapy?"

He rolled to his back. This would be easier if he wasn't looking at her. "There are additional side effects to all the extra nerves the RT-24 has grown." The bed bounced as Lark flipped completely over to face him. He felt her gaze and swallowed hard. "Light touch causes pain."

Lark gave a soft gasp. "Like I just did on your neck."

"Yes."

"And all those other times I touched your arm or something and you hissed."

He gritted his teeth. "We don't need to run down a list, Lark."

"I'm sorry." He could hear her thinking, remembering his reaction, and probably wondering how he could protect her when he was so easily incapacitated. Or maybe she was reconsidering getting physical with a guy she could break with gentleness.

The first concern was easier to address. "No one's going to try to incapacitate me by stroking my arm," he said. She didn't argue.

"What kind of pain is it?" Her hand, a vague shape in the darkness, hovered over him. He didn't want her to be afraid. That was part of the problem. He caught her fingers and lowered her hand to his chest, pressing it there.

"It's like I have millions of fibers embedded in my skin, and brushing them hurts. Like stingers. As you've seen, it makes this—" he waved his hand between them, "—pretty impossible."

She made a dismissive noise in the back of her throat. "That's why you wear such tight clothing." Her hand moved across his pecs, pressing down, and he fought a groan.

"Yeah, that's why. There's more, though." He had to

tell her the rest before she took him too far. He halted the movement of her hand.

"Is it the same all over your body?" She held still and he relaxed.

"No. Areas that are already sensitive are okay. My hands—the backs are worse than the palms and fingers. My face is okay. Pretty much anything covered by clothing is a problem."

"But if I'm not delicate, it doesn't hurt?" She moved her hand back to his neck and pressed it flat.

"It doesn't hurt. Not that way." She moved it a little, still firm, and pleasure sank into him. "That feels good, actually."

"Really?" She kneaded with her fingers, and this time he did groan.

"Really. That's the other thing. The harder you press, the better it feels." She dug harder, and he didn't think she understood. He realized he'd rolled toward her again, and now his hands were wrapped around her upper arms. He wasn't sure if he was trying to hold her away or pull her closer. "Sexually better, Lark."

She froze. "Oh." A heartbeat. Another. "Ohhh." With a quick movement, she levered herself up and over him, twisting him to his back to straddle his hips. He gave no thought to stopping her, his brain already sluggish.

"So my massage in your weight room…"

"Lit me up." His hands settled on her hips, and she leaned her hands on his chest to hold herself upright. "I've never been so embarrassed in my life."

"You!" She sat back. "I came, fully clothed, *without* RT-24. You were just, um, extra passionate."

He stared, wishing he could see her expression in

the darkness. Didn't she realize what had happened? She ground her hips against his erection, and he didn't have the strength to hold her still. Desire burned through him, intense but not yet overwhelming. He arched a little and grunted against his will.

"I was a little more than extra passionate." His voice came out deeper, rougher. He was losing it, all his normal controls falling apart. "I needed you. Badly enough to take it if you'd tried to resist." The images flashed through his head, taking it but not against her will. His erection grew, need pounding in his chest, his ears, his groin. He savored it even while he tried to fight, only vaguely aware that he should. But it had been so damned long, and Lark—

She shook her head and leaned forward again, further now, her weight bearing down on her hands, nearly blinding him with the pleasure of it.

"No. You wouldn't have. I trust you," she murmured, her mouth an inch away from his. She whispered something else, but he couldn't hear it and then her mouth was on his again, and he lost all ability to think.

Her hair fell forward against his face. It didn't hurt, but wasn't pleasant, either. He brushed it back with his palms and bunched it, holding it to the back of her head.

"Sorry," she said between kisses.

"It's okay." He pulled her down tighter and opened her mouth with his, tasting the inside of her mouth, stroking her tongue. She dug her fingers into his shoulders, making him groan again, and he swallowed it, conscious of Nils in the other room. The walls were thick, the acoustics muffling, but he didn't want to risk the jerk hearing anything going on in here. When his free hand slid up under Lark's tank to cup her breast, he caught her own moan with his mouth and then pulled back enough to say, "Shhh."

She quieted, but still made noises in the back of her throat that inflamed him from the inside. She pushed his shirt up and he levered his upper body to yank it over his head. Then he was lost, as her roaming hands spread pleasure over every inch of his torso. God, she'd learned quickly, the pressure perfect. For his part he kept his mouth on her, his hands on her breasts, tasting and feeling everything he could reach. He was hard enough to burst again, and this time there wasn't a shower handy.

"Lark, sweetheart," he breathed, trying to slow her down. But she bit the side of his neck, and he came up off the bed in blind ecstasy. In seconds he'd flipped her, stripped off his jeans and hers, and positioned himself over her. She opened to him, wet and hot and ready, and it took everything he had, dredged from way down deep, not to plunge into her. "I don't have anything," he grit out, his eyes, jaw, and every muscle clenched tight, trying to hold on to control.

"I don't care." Lark lifted her hips and pulled at his with both hands. "I need you, Jason, now." She said something under her breath again, something he couldn't and probably didn't want to hear, but he realized he shouldn't have started this. Not when it was too dangerous to finish it.

Sanity poked a few holes in the waves of need. "Do you know what your father will do to me if I get you pregnant?"

She laughed softly. "He'll give you a cigar. He's dying for grandchildren, you know."

Jason didn't believe her. Even if she was right, he knew it wouldn't be that easy, for any of them. An image of Lark, pregnant and laughing with her hand on her belly, flashed through his head. Instead of panic it inspired longing of a completely different sort, and he pumped his hips once before jerking back. "I can't, Lark. I can't do that to you. To make that decision now, when we're not thinking clearly."

Lark smoothed her hands down his arms just right, not painfully light, not ecstatically hard. "I know you're right, for so many reasons, but we can't stop. We can make it work. Sex," she hastened to add. "It doesn't have to hurt."

God, right now, it did anything but. A burst of inspiration flared in his brain. "Wait." He jumped off the bed and stood for a second, trying to remember exactly where it had been left. He refused to think about who'd left it and why.

"What are you doing?" Lark asked from the bed.

"Looking for…" He knelt and felt under the bed, all along the side, then around the bottom, careful to avoid the soft brush of the dangling sheet. Nothing. Dammit. He moved around to the other side and encountered a dusty pair of boots and a broken halter. He was nearly to the top of the bed and about to despair when his hand hit the wood box. "Yes!" He pulled it out and flipped up the top, reaching inside and encountering, as he'd hoped, at least a dozen flat, square packets. "We're in business." He grabbed a couple and climbed back onto the bed.

"Where did—"

"Don't ask." He made sure she wouldn't by kissing her again, pressing her back on the bed. She held him more and more tightly, her hands igniting a raging fire. The pressure grew and he rolled on top of her. They touched from chest to toes.

"Please, Jason, now." She arched, her mouth open in a silent cry. "God, I need you."

"Me, too. Hold on, sweetheart." He tore a packet open with his teeth and rolled the condom on one-handed, keeping his body close to hers, letting the knuckles of his hand rub her. She gasped and pressed up against him. For a moment he thought about using his mouth to make her come first, but then she grabbed his cock in her fist, hard, and pleasure shot through him, an orgasm without being a real orgasm. He pressed toward her, letting her use him to spread her moisture and ease his entry. As soon as she let go he pressed deep, hard, as far as he could. She took all of him, then shifted and lifted her knees so she could take even more. Her thighs brushed his hips, the flare of pain making him gasp, and she instantly tightened her legs.

"God, Lark, you feel incredible."

"So do you." She wrapped her arms around his back and lifted her hips. *"Jason."*

"I know." He slid both arms under her and cradled her body to his, then began to thrust. Lark turned her head to let his shoulder muffle her cries. Her entire body tensed as she clutched him tighter. Her heels came around and dug into the backs of his legs, and he was lost.

The explosion went on forever. Colored lights swirled behind his eyes. His brain had disintegrated, and every nerve ending in his body vibrated. He couldn't breathe, but his lungs and sinuses were full of the taste and smell of Lark, and he knew, however physical the stimulation was, he'd never feel this way with any other woman.

SEVENTEEN

GABBY'S NEW SITUATION wasn't any better than her old one. After John had forced Matthew back down into the cellar, he'd carried her through a doorway into another room. Another existence, really. The cellar itself was under a single room of a larger cabin. The space had been dimmer and warmer, furnished in heavy chairs and tables and sharing the space with what appeared, as John sped through, to be a well-built kitchen. But the room John took her to ended up being nearly as cold and damp as the cellar.

The twin-sized bed had a very thin mattress. Each rope that supported it was torture to her aching body. She didn't know if she'd actually become sick or only convinced her body she had, but she hurt all over. Her eyes burned, her head felt fuzzy, and every time she moved, the space around her swirled.

John tried. He covered her with another of the scratchy wool blankets and fed her water and lukewarm soup. He also made her take a couple of tablets he said were ibuprofen, but they weren't helping yet.

"I think you'd better call Isaac," she told John.

"No."

"He's going to—"

"Be here soon. He'll deal with you then."

That was the plan. Despite her trust in Matthew,

though, Gabby shivered in dread. In books and movies, plans never worked out. And if this one didn't, failure could be deadly.

MATTHEW STOOD MOTIONLESS outside the cabin, hidden by a couple of riotous azaleas and listening through the window he'd managed to crack open from the outside. Gabby sounded weak and scared. He wanted to bust in, overpower John and get her out of there.

Immediately after he'd dropped down into the pit, while John was thumping out of the room above, he'd gotten to work. His quick scan of the room above had showed all exterior walls except the side that led into the main building. He'd picked the side opposite the main entry and started digging with the largest shards of the smashed basin. The dirt had been well packed but not hard, and soon he'd dug a sloping hole to the outside, just at the edge of the bottom of the wall. After that, it had been a small matter to reconnoiter the building. Main living room/kitchen in the center, two tiny bedrooms on the other side with a bathroom in between. He'd been positioned outside Gabby's room since, listening.

And thinking, in the long periods when there was nothing to hear. His ability to focus on the job seemed to have departed in the years he'd been mostly out of the field, and his mind kept wandering. Thinking about Kelly, and Gabby, and his relationship with Lark. About how the loneliness after Kelly's death had faded, or seemed to, as he filled his life with his daughter and his business and his friendship. He'd tried dating exactly twice. The company had been engaging but nothing special, and the sex boring. He'd decided he just didn't need it.

Now, though, since Jason's "death" and the crumbling of Hummingbird, at least around the edges, things were different. The loneliness was more acute, his needs more apparent every minute he spent with Gabby.

The sound of wheels on gravel reached him from the other side of the cabin. The sky had lightened enough for Matthew to be able to see the bushes and trees and open ground more clearly, but as the sun began to rise, birdcalls and squirrel chirps also grew in volume. Matthew cursed under his breath. He wouldn't be able to hear as well.

There was a car door slam. Just one. Then a voice calling to John. He couldn't tell for sure if it was Isaac. After that, silence. He turned and lifted himself enough to peer into the bedroom. Gabby was alone on the bed, her eyes on the window. As soon as she saw him, she shook her head. Matthew dropped back to the ground with a smile. She'd read his mind and was telling him not to rescue her yet. He hated leaving her there when he had the perfect opportunity to get her out, but the plan could work. He had to give her a chance.

He slid along the wall to the living room section of the cabin. The early morning cacophony in the woods masked the sound of the voices inside. The ground rose a little higher here. He could stand next to the window and peek inside with less risk of being seen. Two men stood in the center of the room, but the glare of the outside light reflected wrong, and Matthew couldn't see faces. He had to get a better position.

By the time he'd climbed silently to the roof and determined that the chimney perfectly funneled conversation to him, the men had moved Gabby to the living room and were badgering her. The other voice was definitely Isaac's.

"I don't believe for a second that you're sick," he was saying. Measured footsteps paced the wooden floor. "What's Madrassa up to?"

Gabby somehow made her voice sound weak, yet strong enough to carry to Matthew. "I don't know. I was pretty out of it down there."

"Bullshit."

Silence for a minute, then John said, "She's awfully clammy. And pale."

"She's always pale," Isaac snapped, but he didn't sound certain.

"How would you know?" Gabby asked reasonably. "We don't know each other."

Isaac snorted. "I'm sure you know all about me. Or at least as much as Madrassa was willing to reveal. He wouldn't have admitted his role in the fiasco that cost me my job."

Matthew shook his head. Talk about revisionist history.

"What do you want with me?" Gabby asked piteously. "I'm really not feeling well."

"I wasn't amused by your trick with the flash drive."

"So you said. I told you, I must have grabbed the wrong one. But instead of letting me go back to the lab to get it—"

"Shut up." More pacing, then silence. "Where's your ID card?"

There was a moment's hesitation Matthew hoped they didn't notice. "In my purse," Gabby reluctantly said.

"It wasn't there."

"That's where I keep it."

"I said, it wasn't there."

Now Gabby sounded annoyed when she said, "Then I guess you lost it, didn't you?"

Again with the pacing, then, "How much of the RT-24 formula can you remember?"

Gabby laughed. "None. I didn't develop it. I just applied it."

"But you're a research scientist."

"I'm a doctor who tended a patient. Whatever you want to do with that formula, I won't be able to help you."

No, don't say that. Matthew wasn't sure how far Kemmerling would go if he decided Gabby was unnecessary, especially now that she was a witness to a whole series of crimes.

But she wasn't done. "On the other hand, Nils said you wanted information on Jason's condition."

"Why would I want that?" Isaac's voice was tight, as if he wasn't happy with Nils. Matthew held his breath. This might lead Kemmerling to reveal the information they needed—such as what the hell he was trying to do.

"I don't know." Gabby sounded weary. "I'm not supposed to understand your motives."

"Do you have information on Jason's condition? Or are you just trying to buy time?"

"I have a feeling it would be dangerous to lie to you."

"Damned right, it would be."

"I was his doctor. Of course I have information."

"Tell me."

"No."

Matthew had to stifle a chuckle. He'd never seen this side of Gabby. She was reacting to Isaac with strength and confidence she'd never displayed around him.

Then he heard a slap and a muffled cry. Dammit. They'd gambled that Kemmerling wouldn't resort to violence, but they'd gambled wrong. He had to get her out now.

From his vantage point on top of the building, he could see down the drive to the main road, which wasn't that far. But they were still surrounded by woods and probably little civilization, wherever they were. There was only one car parked in the clearing. Isaac must have left John here with no transportation. The car was a newer model, fancy. Hotwiring it probably would take more time than Matthew would have. He'd have to incapacitate Isaac and get his keys, and he didn't think John would stand idly by while he did. This was going to take very tricky timing.

His urgency increased a hundredfold at the next words out of Isaac's mouth.

"Go get Madrassa."

GABBY WAS TRYING, she really was, but she had to admit it. She was a total wuss.

Tears streamed down her stinging cheek, and she tasted blood. The slap hadn't been that hard, she supposed, but it didn't take much to hurt a pansy like her. What tears didn't exit her eyes burned the back of her throat, and nausea climbed up to meet them.

Isaac hadn't bothered to tie her. She should make a run for it, before John discovered that Matthew wasn't in the cellar. There was the door, not even shut tightly. But where would she go? She was so weak, holding her head up took all her energy.

She'd failed.

"I don't understand," she forced out, her words sounding slurred. "You want revenge against Hummingbird, and Matthew, I get that. How will this do it?"

"You want me to reveal my evil plan, huh?" Isaac shrugged. "Let me see..." He tapped his finger against his chin. "No!" He glared out into the empty room. "What's taking so long?"

John didn't answer. Isaac stalked to the doorway. Gabby frantically tried to think of a way to rile Isaac, to make him spit out something he had no intention of saying.

"It must be difficult, being the weaker man. Being outsmarted by those two, and even the daughter. She's got no training, and she bested you."

Isaac narrowed his eyes. "Lark didn't best me. Templeton got the drop on me. I had no idea at the time that he was well enough to travel, never mind fight."

Encouraged, she continued. "But they've all been one step ahead of you this whole time. Matthew knew that woman was up to something. He let you take him."

Isaac froze as he was about to step through into the other room. "What?"

She wasn't sure how happy Matthew would be about her revealing this, but if it kept him from discovering too soon that he was out of the cellar, she didn't care.

"Yeah, he let her stick him. And then he put hints in the message she made him record." He'd finally told her, during their planning, what had happened when he was captured. It had made her feel better that he actually *had* allowed it rather than gotten taken by surprise, though she supposed it would be better to let her hero worship die and just see him as a regular man.

"What hints?" Isaac's voice had tightened again.

"That he'd been taken, that there was a traitor inside Hummingbird, stuff like that."

Isaac cursed and paced in front of the doorway. *Hurry, Matthew.* John had already been gone long enough to discover he was missing. If he didn't make his move soon…

"I don't get why me," she said. "And why Jason?"

Isaac whirled on her, his face mottled. "Jason was the one who put the censure in my permanent file. Who demoted me from lead agent and made sure I got non-essential assignments. He damaged the whole trajectory of my career."

"And now he must pay?"

Isaac's face relaxed and he laughed. "Yeah. He must—"

He never saw it coming. Gabby barely registered the figure flying out of the bedroom and tackling the shorter man to the floor. Matthew grabbed the back of Isaac's head by the hair, knocked his forehead on the floor, and dropped his limp body to the wood planks. Gabby struggled to her feet before Matthew turned to her, his hand held out, his body moving toward the door.

"We didn't get enough," she protested, letting him pull her behind him since her feet weren't cooperating on their own.

"We got enough. He's not going to hit you again." He held his free hand out toward the car as they stumbled down the steps—well, she stumbled—and the headlights flashed with the chirp of the door locks. He helped her into the passenger side and slid across the hood to get into the driver's side.

He scanned the console and dropped the key fob in his hand to jab a finger at a large button behind the steering wheel. Nothing happened. He jammed his foot on the brake and hit the button again. This time lights came on the dash, but the engine didn't turn over.

"What's wrong?" Gabby asked. She leaned over to help, but had no idea what she was looking at. "Why isn't the engine starting?"

"It's a hybrid." Matthew pointed to a diagram on the dash. "Silent engine unless it's drawing gas. But there's something else going on." He bent to look under the steering column and cursed. "He's got a security lock on it. I need—"

But it was too late. Her door opened, and John held his gun against her temple.

"Get out of the car, please."

"Um...no."

Matt's finger hovered over the button again, but he didn't touch it.

"Nice try with the dirt man under the blanket, Mr. Madrassa, but it was a little too small." John pressed the gun tighter against her temple. "Both of you, out of the car."

Matthew's door flew open, and Isaac snagged his collar and dragged him out. Matthew went limp and landed on the ground, where he swept Isaac's legs. Isaac stumbled but didn't fall. It was enough to give Matthew time to get on his feet, and they started fighting. John pulled Gabby out of the car by the upper arm, a little more gently than Isaac had treated Matthew, and waited. Gabby held her breath, watching as the men traded blows, one reeling backward, the other attacking, then both rolling across the needle-strewn ground. Tears dampened her face again, and she tried not to cry out or flinch. Matthew didn't need the distraction, and it could startle the man holding a gun to her head. He seemed more stable than that, but she wasn't taking chances.

After a minute Matthew got the upper hand. He half knelt, half stood over Isaac, the man's shirt bunched in his left fist, his right raised and ready to deliver the final blow.

That was when John fired.

EIGHTEEN

DESPITE HOW LATE she'd fallen asleep and how fitfully she'd dozed, Lark woke early, the light in the barn dim enough to tell her it was barely dawn. Even so, Jason was up already, dressed and making coffee on an ancient coffeemaker in a corner.

"Everything okay?" she asked, her voice gravelly.

Jason turned, smiling, and she knew even though the real answer was *hell, no,* eventually it would be okay.

"Nils is still here."

"That's something, at least." She yawned and sat up, throwing her bare legs over the edge of the bed. She still wore her tank top and had put her underwear back on before they fell asleep. She picked up her bra from the end post of the bed and put it on, replacing her tank with a T-shirt Jason tossed her. "Are we going to talk about last night?"

His smile faded and he handed her a small, chipped mug of coffee. "Not now. After this is all over."

Lark sighed and accepted the mug. "We could just call it a mistake and be done with it."

The silence rang with denial. Lark wasn't sure how much came from him, and how much from her. She'd never deliberately avoided relationships, but had never realized how truly empty and superficial they'd been.

In just a couple of days, she already cared more for Jason than anyone else outside her family.

She should be terrified, and somewhere inside was frantic resistance. But she could barely feel it under the buzz of pleasure and hope.

But judging by the chasm Jason had set between them, he didn't feel the same. Any residual contentment disappeared. She should let it go, at least for now, but her mouth wouldn't stay shut. "Jason, age and my father are not good reasons to avoid a relationship with me."

"Sorry the coffee's black. We don't keep cream or sugar here."

"It's fine." She sipped the coffee and set the mug on the floor to pull on her jeans. "Boston and DC aren't that far apart, either, and—"

"I'm not shallow, Lark." His voice was low, hard. "You're right, those don't matter. This is about far more serious things that we won't talk about until this is over."

She understood, then, what he really meant. While she'd been struggling to overcome fantasies of a future with him so she could sleep, he'd been pondering their present. He thought he wouldn't survive, or that she wouldn't, and he didn't want either of them to make promises. That was the smart way to handle it, except it didn't matter. She knew that it would hurt just as much if he died again, whether he told her he cared about her or not.

But a sudden shaft of sunlight through a high window reminded her that time was a precious commodity. People were in danger, not just them. So she pretended to drop it, to wait until a more appropriate moment. And hoped her deep dread didn't mean there wouldn't be one.

She finished dressing and sat cross-legged on the bed, cradling her coffee. "What is this place?"

"It's an old farm my parents own. They planned to retire here but decided they missed being near the conveniences of the city too much."

"It's stocked."

"They use it as a hideaway from time to time."

"Oh." She tried not to think of the condom he'd found last night, and then wondered if they knew he was alive. "Have you talked to them since you got out of the lab?"

He shook his head and drained his mug. "No time. They're traveling, anyway. Matt's kept them from getting too worried about me." He offered her a refill. She nodded, and he split the remaining coffee between them and then leaned against the wall, well out of touching distance.

"Why did you come after me?" he asked after a moment.

At first, she didn't know what he meant. It seemed so long ago that she'd first gotten on his bike. "You hadn't checked in. Don't argue." She shook her head, tired. "It's done. Did you get anything out of Nils before I got there?"

"Not as much as you did. They want Gabby because of me, and the RT-24 data so they can sell the formula to someone."

"Why did they take my father, then?"

He shook his head. "Nothing ties together, at least not neatly. Abducting Matt doesn't further Isaac's agenda to destroy his reputation. He has to be out there facing the damage in order for it to hurt."

"But his disappearance during a sensitive time does damage."

He grimaced. "We need more information. Did you get anything from the drive?"

"Oh, my God, yes!" She jumped off the bed and dug in her back pocket for her list. "Look!" She handed the crumpled pages to him.

He unfolded the lined paper and scanned the names. "What am I looking at?"

"I found this list—some party list, according to the file name. But when I read them, I found correlations." She explained how the first and last names were one-off, leaning close and pointing to the page. How did he smell so good after everything they'd done over the last twenty-four hours? "I recognized my aunt's name, and that triggered it all. I wrote the original list on the back, with the strike throughs."

Jason flipped it over, then back. His frown deepened. "I recognize some of these from Hummingbird."

"Maybe people Isaac tried to get on his side?" A trace of excitement buzzed through her. This could be their first solid lead. At least, something they could act on.

"Maybe," Jason mused. "Most of the Hummingbird people are crossed off. Your aunt isn't."

"I know, and neither is Carl. But only if you assume the last name is the pertinent strike through."

"Carl's the boyfriend?"

"*Ex* boyfriend." Had he sounded edgy about that? "Are there any employees not crossed off?"

He studied the list again. "One. One of the on-site security team."

Lark pointed to the plus-two next to the name, like a party notation indicating he'd be bringing two other people. "Probably someone else, too, not written on here. I don't know why he'd note it like that, though." She pressed her lips together. Logic said Isaac had only gotten to Nils and the one or two other people whose last names weren't crossed off, rather than all the others. But that meant her aunt and Carl were conspiring against her father.

She sat heavily on the bed again. "Stuart had access to my greenhouse. He probably gave Donald the codes, which allowed him to come after me and the plants." She didn't know why that bothered her so much. She wasn't close to Stuart. Still, they worked together. Had similar goals. What had probably been a shrug-worthy business transaction to Stuart still felt like a betrayal, and it marred what her work life had been. Made her wonder if she could go back to BotMed…assuming she had that choice in the end.

Jason smoothed her hair, and his quiet empathy brought a lump to her throat.

"Let's go talk to Nils," he said.

Lark forced the sadness to convert to anger. It welled, hardening her muscles as well as her emotions. She stood and clenched her fists, stalking to the doorway.

"I'll beat it out of him."

JASON TRAILED LARK into the main barn. He understood the betrayal she had to be feeling, and he'd let her vent it on Nils if she needed to. The guy had earned a little torment. But she'd done good work, figuring out the list. It gave them leads. They'd need them. Nils wasn't as knowledgeable as he pretended, and Jason doubted he had anything else to share.

When he got to the stall, Lark had opened it and stood over Nils. The guy reclined in one corner, trying to look like he wasn't cowering. When Jason appeared, Nils half crawled to the side, away from Lark.

"Hey, JT. I smell coffee. Can I have some?"

Jason didn't answer. He braced his legs wide in the stall doorway and folded his arms.

"Okay, that's the way it's gonna be. I get it." Nils rolled back to sit and rested his arms on top of his updrawn knees, a nonchalant pose belied by the constant darting of his eyes everywhere but at Lark. "I'm not tellin' you nothin'."

"Sure you're not." Lark stepped closer. "Ella Darron."

Nils looked blank. "Who's that?"

"You know who that is. I want to know what she has to do with you and Isaac."

"I never heard of her."

Jason believed him. The guy was far too transparent to lie effectively. Jason was starting to wonder how he'd lasted so long at Hummingbird.

"What about Carl Frankel? Stuart Reinhart?" Lark rattled off one name after another. Nils just kept shaking his head.

"Fine." Lark looked around, then raised her head to scan the barn outside the stall. She spotted something, shoved past Jason, and stalked back in with a pitchfork in her hands. "How about you just tell me what you do know, and I'll stop trying to lead you."

"Whoa, whoa, whoa!" Nils held up his arms to ward off the tines she aimed at his chest. "Come on, now! I told you stuff!"

"Tell us more."

Nils eyed Jason, then Lark, then the pitchfork. She jabbed it at him, poking his arm.

"Ow!" He rubbed it, scowled, heaved a huge sigh. "Fuck. Okay. I told you, Isaac doesn't tell me everything. I don't know anything about those people you said. All I know is that Hummingbird has this nerve regeneration therapy that helped keep Jason alive and stuff, but it makes him hurt."

Jason kept his features schooled when Nils said that. He hated anyone knowing his weaknesses. *Lark knows, and it doesn't bother you anymore.*

"And?" Lark pressed Nils.

"And that's it. I told Isaac, he found a buyer, and he said this was all he needed to take you all down. I swear, that's all I know."

They had a buyer who intended to use a medical breakthrough designed to help people to cause them pain instead. Jason wasn't a scientist, but guessed that adjusting one element of the compound, or adding one minor thing to it, would be enough to turn the pain of regrowth and the irritation of light touch into true agony. He couldn't let that happen if he had the power to stop it.

Lark hovered for a moment. When she feinted with the pitchfork, Nils flinched but didn't say more. Either he was telling the truth and didn't know anything else, or he was afraid enough of Isaac to keep it to himself. They would get no more out of him.

Lark backed out of the stall and Jason secured the

door again. "Like I said last night, we'll lock him down." He led the way back to the office-bedroom. Once they were out of earshot of Nils, he added, "We have a couple of leads. We need to track down Ella Darron." He gathered up saltines and beef jerky from the trunk and a jug of water from a shelf. "Do you know how to get a hold of her?"

"No." She took another jug off the shelf and followed him to the storeroom, where he grabbed a bucket and a roll of toilet paper. "I haven't seen or talked to her in years."

"Okay, tomorrow we'll have Caitlyn check the call logs at the office. If Ella called Matt there, the number was recorded."

She followed him to the stall and waited as he dropped the items in and re-secured the door.

"We'll be back in a couple of days," Jason told Nils, who looked a little panicky. "Or we'll send someone."

"Yeah, someone dangerous," Lark growled through the bars. She looked adorable, but Jason bit back his smirk. He didn't think she'd appreciate it.

"What will we do in the meantime?" she asked when they got back outside.

"We're going to Boston." Jason climbed into the truck and started the ignition. "You have some contacts up there we need to talk to."

MATTHEW AND ISAAC both instinctively froze when the gun went off. Matthew spun, certain he'd see Gabby's lifeless body on the ground, but John still aimed his pistol into the air, one hand locked around Gabby's arm.

Before Matthew could move, before his heart could

even start beating again, Isaac yanked his arms back and snapped cuffs on him.

"Nice try," he gloated, but scowled when his phone rang. He didn't look at the display before barking, "What!" into it. Everyone stood watching him while he listened to the caller, John shifting his handgun back toward Gabby as if to ensure Matthew didn't move.

Isaac said too little to tell Matthew anything, and hung up after only a few seconds. "I have to go back to the city," he told John. "Let's get these two back inside. I'll be back to finish things."

"Problems?" Matthew asked mildly.

"Nothing to do with you," Isaac assured him, glancing at his watch.

"You can go ahead," John said. "I've got these two."

Isaac didn't look convinced.

John waved the pistol near Gabby's ear. "I mean it. He won't risk anything when I've got this."

Isaac opened his mouth, but when his phone chimed again, he made a half impatient, half threatening gesture at John, and stomped off to his car.

Matthew watched him go with regret. That was their way out of here. Or it would have been, if they could get away. He eyed John, calculating ways to overpower him, but even with John gone soft, Matthew didn't think he could beat him with his hands literally tied behind his back. He'd have to wait until they were inside again, and…

John, who'd been watching the taillights of Isaac's car until they disappeared down the lane, holstered his pistol and let go of Gabby. She flinched away, but not far, and looked confused.

Matthew shifted when John walked toward him, trying to keep the man in front of him and position himself between their guard and Gabby. But John held up a key before circling around behind him. A moment later, the cuffs fell away.

"He'll be a couple of hours," John said gruffly. "Stay on guard, though, 'cause it'll take you longer than that to get to civilization."

Matthew didn't state the obvious, but he at least had to ask why. "You don't have a way out of here, either. You can come with us." He sensed Gabby's reaction to that, but had to make the offer.

But John shook his head. "I don't like what Kemmerling's doing. But I can get out without making an enemy of him. He won't want an employee who gets overpowered so easily." He smirked, and Matthew smiled back.

"You really want to do that?"

John nodded stoically and led the way inside. Matthew gestured for Gabby to stay in the yard, and followed his former employee back into the cabin.

"How do you want it?" he asked him, setting his body.

John grimaced. "Don't tell me. And make it convinci—"

Matthew walloped him. And then he made it convincing.

"I TOLD YOU, I don't know what you're talking about."

Half an hour of questions, badgering and threats, and Carl still wouldn't admit he'd had ulterior motives in trying to weasel his way back into her life.

Lark wished she'd brought her pitchfork, though she doubted they would have let her check it on the plane.

"Look, Carl," she began again, but Jason caught her wrist and tugged her away from her ex-boyfriend's desk. They'd had to track him down at work, which wasn't that unusual for a Sunday. "What?" she barked, whirling on him. He looked as implacable as ever, where she was certain she had a wild-eyed, wild-haired look that wouldn't convince anybody to tell her anything.

"He doesn't know anything," Jason said. "We might as well let him get back to work."

"Thank you." Carl picked up a pen and flipped open a file folder. "I just don't know what—"

"I'm sure his name on Isaac's list is meaningless," Jason told her, not looking at Carl at all. "He obviously wouldn't betray you."

"Certainly not." His affront was not only half-hearted, but false enough to be insulting.

"But—" Lark began, not sure what Jason was doing but willing to try to go along with it.

"Isaac had to have his name for some other reason."

"Ohhh." Lark tried not to grin. "Like, targeting him? People he thought I cared about, maybe?"

"What's that now?" Carl looked up. "Target for what?"

"We have no idea," Jason said. He backed toward the door, pulling Lark with him. "If he hasn't approached you, there's a slim possibility he might want to do you harm."

"But he has approached me," Carl blurted. His brow wrinkled. "He wouldn't..." He trailed off and pressed his lips together, his eyes unfocused. He was obviously trying to think through what he knew and what Jason had implied.

Lark waited. When his expression cleared, she pounced. "When did he approach you? Before or after we broke up?"

"After. But it wasn't anything, you know, *wrong.* He had that fellowship with you in Indonesia and said you got some of his papers. He asked me to try to get them for him."

Lark sighed at his stupidity. "Why couldn't he have just asked me for them himself?"

"Well, you know. After things went bad between you—"

Lark laughed, but there was no humor in the sound, only annoyance. "Jesus Christ, Carl, you're a lawyer. Why would you believe that crap? Did he pay you?"

His face reddened. Of course he'd paid him.

"But you didn't tell him we'd broken up and you had no access. You had to try to get back in my good graces, because you're greedy and clueless." If her father suffered because of Carl's stupidity… "What else did he tell you?" she demanded.

"Nothing. I didn't ask for anything else. I understand about women scorned."

Lark snorted. Jason ignored her and moved back to the desk, leaning over it with both us-boys camaraderie and mild intimidation.

Carl responded to both, leaning back but appealing, "C'mon, man, you know how it is."

"I do know how it is." Jason's voice was low. "I know much better than you do how it is. You're in a lot of danger, Carl. You'd better tell me everything Isaac said to you."

"That's all he said." A look of cunning slid over his face. "I did hear a name, though."

Jason straightened. "So? We've got names."

"Not this one, I bet." He leaned back in his seat and braced his hands behind his head. "I only ever talked to Kemmerling on the phone. But one time, someone told him he had another call, and he immediately hung up on me to take it."

Lark rolled her eyes and started toward the door. This trip had been a huge waste of time. They'd questioned her boss, Ralph, who had no idea what they were talking about and had no reason to hide it if he had. Stuart was even more clueless. He claimed he found an envelope with money and a note on his desk asking him to make sure the greenhouse door stayed unlocked. A botanist of the stereotypical absentminded-professor variety, he'd assumed it was work-related and never even considered that it was a bribe.

Lark had expected Carl to be their best source. He'd actively and sneakily tried to steal from her. She'd believed his greed and eagerness would have been enough for Isaac to reveal something, anything, important, but here, too, Carl had just been an idiot.

Behind her, he was trying to negotiate payment in return for the name he claimed to have overheard. Lark barely listened to Jason decline to pay him, but the word that finally echoed in the room made her blood run cold.

"Okay, okay, fine. It was Kolanko."

NINETEEN

"We don't jump to conclusions."

"Okay."

Jason started the engine of the rental car and pulled away from the curb, cutting off a taxi without even a backward glance.

"It could have meant anything."

"I know."

Lark's short, flat responses worried him. The news that Kemmerling had been communicating with Kolanko was cause for concern, but not this extreme shock. He navigated the Sunday-quiet streets for a moment, then tried again to reassure her.

"It might not have been Kolanko on the phone, just someone saying his name."

"Sure."

"Dammit, Lark!" He slammed on the brakes in front of her apartment building and glared at her. "Stop it! You're freaking me the hell out!"

That got her attention. She turned to face him and he was alarmed by the pure lack of color in her skin and the glassiness of her eyes. "Lark, what the hell is wrong with you?"

"I don't—Jason." She drew a deep, shuddering breath and her skin pinkened. "I don't know. There's something..." She looked out the window as if just now becoming aware of where they were. "Let's go upstairs."

"Wait. I have to park." He circled the block twice before a spot opened up, then he slid in ahead of a Cadillac SUV and ignored the driver's cursing. Lark led him up the elevator to her apartment, letting Jason check the alarm and clear the rooms before she went past the foyer.

"It doesn't look like anyone's been here since we left," he said.

"I know. The security guy on duty, Will, told me everything's been fine."

That didn't ensure no one had been here. He went into the kitchen and filled a glass of water from the dispenser in the front of her refrigerator. When he came back into the living room, she was perched on the edge of the sofa, back ramrod straight, staring a hole in the wall on the other side of the room. Jason sat next to her and put the water glass in her hand, wrapping his fingers around hers until he felt her muscles tighten to hold it.

"Come on, sweetheart. Pull it together."

The endearment worked. She snapped her head around, eyes flashing, and Jason couldn't help himself. He kissed her. It was a quick one, not passionate, but he didn't withhold his concern and affection. When he pulled back, Lark had relaxed.

"What's going on in there?" He tapped the side of her head.

She shook it slightly. "I don't know. There's something I should know or realize or figure out. But I can't *get* it." She stood and paced a little, testing the dust on a table near the foyer archway and repositioning a small chair. "Dad said Kolanko didn't blame him. That he was grateful to him—and to you—for saving him and his daughter. Especially from a threat none of them saw coming…" She went stiff again. Jason waited. Her mouth hung slightly open in surprise, and he knew she was close to whatever her subconscious was trying to tell her.

But after a moment she snapped her mouth shut and shook her head harder. "That's it, but not it. Only part of it. A threat none of you saw coming. What can that mean?"

Jason sat back on the soft microfiber sofa. "Looking at the obvious, we were prepared for an attack or infiltration by a business enemy, or an extremist who had a problem with Kolanko's arms dealings."

"Were they illegal?" Lark started pacing again, this time ignoring everything around her. "The arms dealings?"

"No, not as far as the government is concerned. They do business with him, but the official policy is not to buy from or sell to anyone who supplies enemies of the United States."

"But he could still do it without us knowing."

"Unlikely." She shot him a doubting look. He spread his hands. "Look, I'm not in government espionage, but I do work with the Department of Defense and other alphabet agencies. They aren't always on the up and up, that's true, but they for damned sure know who they're dealing with."

Lark pursed her lips. "But it's irrelevant because the attack on Kolanko came from family."

"Yes." Jason got there the same time she did, his

brain clicking as her expression cleared. "Ella is family."

"Of a sort," she agreed. "But—"

"It's a tenuous connection, but it's a lot fewer than six degrees of separation."

Lark sat next to him again, clearly disturbed.

"Her name was on Isaac's list," Jason pointed out.

"I know." She sighed and leaned back against the cushions. "I thought the list meant he wanted to get information from her, or find a way to exploit the connection. Maybe trick her, or threaten her to try to influence Dad. But now..."

"Now you're wondering if she's directly involved."

She nodded miserably. Jason stroked his hand down her hair, and she leaned into him for a second before straightening.

"What do you remember about her? She's your mother's sister, you said. Her only one?"

"They were about two years apart, I think. Ella's older. She was always very driven. One of those aunts who breezes into family events bearing gifts, and leaves before it's time to clean up. Working all the time, disdainful of my mom's traditional path."

"Had they been close before? When they were younger?"

Lark lifted a shoulder. "I don't know. I only remember her from my childhood, and by then she was pretty far along her path of success."

"What happened when your mother died?" Jason's blood sizzled the way it did when he was getting close to an enemy, whether it was someone trying to steal priceless items from a museum or plant a pipe bomb at a business summit. He took Lark's hand, almost unconsciously, as if touching her would connect their brains even more than they already were. He'd only known her for three days, but the way they clicked together gave him a buzz.

Lark rubbed Jason's fingers with her thumb, her brain moving faster, the memories flowing in a slideshow. "Ella visited more often in the last few years, when Mom was in bed a lot, or had difficulty leaving the house without getting sick."

"She probably wanted to spend more time with her sister, if she knew she was—" He cut himself off, and Lark smiled and squeezed his hand.

"It's okay to say dying. I've lived with the reality for ten years. But no, I don't think it was sisterly affection." She let her gaze unfocus, watching the memories flash in and out of her internal vision. Jason sat motionless beside her, quiet while she remembered.

Memories were funny things. Most of the stuff she could dredge up was stupid. Ella shaking the Sweet'N Low packet when she knew it wouldn't open that way, and how her aunt had laughed at her when she said so. She didn't use Sweet'N Low at age nine and her mother had gently explained it was to shake the powder to the bottom of the packet so it didn't spill when she opened it.

Not a helpful memory.

And it wasn't like her mother had had a sickbed, with a long, drawn-out decline. Her respiratory system had been weak, prone to infection, and eventually her body had been unable to battle back to health. At least, that was how she remembered it. Adults never revealed everything to kids, though, not even precocious teenagers. Maybe there had been more to it. Maybe she'd known for years that her time was limited. Ella's visits could have been, as Jason suggested, for her to spend whatever time she could with her.

"Or the will," she murmured, something jolting into her memory. What had it been about the will? When had she heard it? She closed her eyes, trying to visualize where she'd been… In the kitchen. She'd been doing dishes, and her mother and aunt had been at the kitchen table. Not a good place if they didn't want her to hear, but maybe…she started humming the music to Hanson's "MMMBop." Yeah, she'd had headphones on, but between tracks on the CD in her Discman, she'd heard Ella say something about a will. She'd turned the volume down and listened. Hadn't understood what they were talking about, except that it sounded important. But now? She tried harder to call up the words.

"None of those assets have anything to do with Matthew," Ella had argued. "You acquired them before you got married."

Her mother's tinkling laughter, not diminished by her shortness of breath. "I didn't acquire them at all. Grandfather set up an account for me. I've never touched it. It'll pay for Lark's education."

Lark remembered a petulant tone in Ella's response. "Of course, let the child use it. Forget about anyone else."

"Ella, it was Grandfather's wish—"

"That I get screwed. Yes, we've discussed his unequal affection before."

The clock on the mantel chimed, jerking Lark out of her reverie, but she'd remembered enough.

"There was something about some money my great-grandfather left my mother but not Ella, I think," she told Jason. "She had a lot of resentment about that." Enough to make the memory stick in her brain.

"You think she wanted your mother to will it to her?" Jason asked.

"I'm pretty sure. Ella argued that it was Darron family money and should remain in the Darron family. She didn't consider me a Darron, I guess." That should hurt, but curiously didn't. Not as much as the idea that Ella might have directly betrayed Lark's father.

"Where's the money now?"

She shrugged. "I have no idea. Dad paid for my schooling on his own, without using Mom's money. He's told me I have a safety net if I need it, but I don't know what form it's in. Trust fund, probably. I haven't needed it, so I haven't asked."

She watched Jason ponder that while she sank deeper into the sofa and let her head rest on the cushion behind her. She couldn't believe it had only been three days since he rescued her from Don and Isaac. She remembered that first ride to the safe house, when the sparks of attraction had flared, when the danger and urgency weren't so intense. Only three days. Yet she looked at Jason now and it seemed there had never been a time she didn't know him like this. When he wasn't a part of her.

And didn't that just suck? He was like her father, too chivalrous or self-sacrificing or maybe even the opposite, too selfish to share himself with a woman. To share the risks as well as the joy of being with someone you loved. His reluctance to talk about any future for them this morning in the barn was a warning. A precursor to "letting her down easy." Lark didn't know how to convince him he was wrong, especially when part of her still thought he was right.

Jason's gaze sharpened on her face and he frowned. "What's wrong?"

"Nothing." *What would you do if I kissed you right now?* A real kiss, not the distraction he'd applied a few minutes ago. "I guess the next step is to find Aunt Ella."

Jason let go of her hand to glance at his watch. "It's too late to call Caitlyn today. We'll catch her first thing in the morning to get a number and track your aunt down." He looked up at her from under the shock of blond hair that had fallen over his forehead. "Unless you thought of a way to reach her."

Lark shook her head as her hand stretched out and brushed his hair back. "I haven't talked to her since Mom died. We don't even exchange Christmas cards." Her hand lingered on the side of his face, a couple of days' worth of stubble scratching her palm. A heaviness in her chest that she hadn't been completely aware of swelled to bursting. The words, ridiculous words, crowded the back of her throat. It took all her strength to keep her mouth closed, to battle back the emotion threatening to gush out of her.

She didn't need to have felt this way before to understand it. People always said you'd know love when you felt it for real. They were right. But Lark hadn't been prepared for it to be so complicated.

Jason caught her hand against his jaw, then lowered it to the sofa and released it. Lark swallowed hard, annoyed at her disappointment. He wouldn't feel it just because she did. Nothing had changed since this morning.

She stood. "I'm going to get some sleep, then. The guest room—well, you saw where it is. Help yourself to anything you need." She left the room before Jason could protest—or fail to.

ONCE LARK WAS GONE, Jason slumped against the sofa cushion and covered his face with his hands. What was happening here? Whatever it was, it moved him along faster than a freefall from an airplane. He was skilled at reacting to anything that came at him, but those were physical things, concrete realities, not relationships.

His survival was common knowledge by now, at least among a certain crowd. The wrong crowd. Evidence that they'd used experimental technology without sanction could cause Hummingbird many more problems than they already had. He couldn't allow Lark to be dragged into it. She'd sold the compound and hadn't been involved in its development. That meant they could distance her. Unless she was romantically involved with him. Then no one would believe she'd had nothing to do with it.

Jason pressed his fingertips to the pulse pounding in his right temple. Lark wouldn't care what people thought. She'd stick by him no matter what, the same way she stuck by her father. But reputation and legal prosecution were minor compared to the real threat. His already dangerous career had taken a sharp turn. He didn't know if he'd ever stop being a target. He couldn't make Lark one, too. But he suspected any obstacle he threw up would just challenge her. She'd said she wasn't looking for a relationship, but last night contradicted that. And the way she'd looked at him a few minutes ago…

The muscle in his right calf twitched, then tightened. He grimaced and eased to his feet. He'd taken a short run this morning, but hadn't wanted to leave the barn for very long. Combine that with the cramped flight to Boston and driving all over town to talk to Isaac's contacts, and he was heading for a repeat of the weight room yesterday. Lark would do the massage, and the aftermath would be a combination of the weight room and the bed in the barn.

He closed his eyes against the memory, the need that surged through him. He couldn't do that anymore. He'd have to work out the cramps by himself. Luckily, Lark's living room was large enough for long-stride pacing. But long-stride pacing encouraged continued thinking. And he was tired of thinking.

He walked for twenty minutes, counting off the seconds to the rhythm of his stride to clear his mind. The twinges in his calves disappeared, and as he slowed his pace the muscles relaxed. Fatigue crept in. Maybe he should go to bed. But apparently, bed meant Lark now. His brain woke up again—along with other parts of his body.

"You cannot go in there," he told himself, standing in front of the guest room, staring over at Lark's bedroom door. It was closed. She would let him in if he knocked right now. But that would send a message he didn't want to send. Or thought he didn't.

Dammit.

He went into the guest room and got ready for bed, forcing his mind to formulate a plan to find Matt and Gabby tomorrow. Once they'd done that, Matt could take over Lark's protection, and Jason would go after Isaac—and Kolanko, if need be—and he wouldn't need to see Lark again. Ever.

That thought was enough to send him across the hall.

By the time Matthew finished securing John, making absolutely certain Isaac wouldn't know his man had let his prisoners go, the sun had sunk below the trees. They couldn't walk the driveway to the road, just in case Isaac changed his mind and came back sooner than John predicted. He couldn't risk him finding them trudging through the woods.

They walked until they found a shed. In the deep twilight, there was no sign of a larger structure it could belong to. Even though it was too close to Isaac's cabin, too obvious a hiding place, and not big enough for both of them to lie down, it was their best bet to get through the night. The darkness and overgrowth on the forest floor would hinder Isaac just as much as it hindered them, and maybe they'd get lucky and he wouldn't come back until morning.

He and Gabby cleared rusted, nearly empty paint cans and broken gardening tools from the cement floor, spread a smelly canvas tarp across it, and curled up together in the center, spooned, Gabby's head on Matthew's left arm, his head resting on the bunched end of the tarp. They slept fitfully, Matthew half alert for the sound of Isaac searching for them, half listening to Gabby's raspy breathing. Whenever he did drop into real sleep for a few minutes, her restless shifting yanked him back out.

When the sun squeezed through a crack in the wall

and hit Matthew in the eyes, they'd only slept a few hours overall. It hadn't been enough, but it would have to suffice. They couldn't stay here.

"Gabby?" he whispered, rubbing her upper arm. Her skin was hot and dry, but she roused quickly and stifled the groan that came out of her throat when she tried to move.

"Are we okay?" she whispered back.

Matthew eased them to a sitting position. Every muscle in his body let him know how annoyed it was, but he had a clearer head and more strength than he'd had last night.

"We're alone," he told her. He couldn't sense any presence outside, and the morning cacophony was in full force. Unless someone had found them an hour ago and stood frozen outside so the birds and animals ignored him, they were alone.

"I have to go to the bathroom." She didn't show an ounce of embarrassment, and Matthew smiled.

"We'll find you a good tree." He winced as he tried to climb to his feet. The shelf bolted to the wall held as he pulled himself up, then braced and tugged Gabby upright. He made her wait while he checked outside, then emerged first. Since they hadn't been found, Isaac must not have made the drive back last night. Good for them, not so good for John. Matthew had tried not to leave him too uncomfortable, but he wasn't going to be able to get himself free. He should be okay until Isaac found him.

Once Matthew let her come outside, Gabby disappeared behind a thick growth of grapevine and nightshade choking out a wall of autumn olive bushes. Matt moved to the other side of the shed to give her privacy, and studied the patch of flowers he was watering. He hadn't picked up as much from Lark as she'd tried to teach him, but he recognized domesticated plants when he saw them. This had been someone's home at one time. Not the shed, but… He looked around, his eyes picking up the rectangular outline of a building that was no longer there.

Gabby's footsteps crunched dead leaves behind him. He zipped up quickly and motioned with his chin to charred debris about a hundred feet in front of them.

"That's the house we couldn't find last night," he said in a low voice.

"Where?" Gabby squinted, then her eyes widened. "It burned down?"

"A long time ago." The house had burned nearly to the ground, and what walls were left had been overtaken by vegetation. "Let's go." He pointed across the debris. "The road is that way. Let's see if there's a driveway leading out to it. It'll be as overgrown as the house, but probably easier going than through the woods."

They found the driveway easily enough. The owners had actually paved a clearing in front of the house and a few hundred feet out. The hard-packed dirt beyond that had narrowed, but there was still room for them to walk side by side. Matthew instructed Gabby what to do if they heard an engine or voices, but for the ten minutes it took them to get to the road, there was nothing. The main road, too, was empty.

"Which way?" Gabby squinted east into the sun, then west, to their right. "That way?" she asked hopefully.

But Matthew shook his head. "Sorry."

"How do you know?"

He motioned to the left and they started walking. "Haze this way."

Gabby sighed but didn't protest. "Smog."

"Yep."

"Fine." She set out, back straight, stride easy, despite her rough breathing and the sheen of sweat on her forehead. "If we're lucky, there will be a little country store at a crossroads five minutes away."

They weren't that lucky.

TWENTY

"I'VE NEVER HAD so many on-time flights in my life," Lark observed as she and Jason exited the jetway back in DC late the next morning. Caitlyn had been in the office early and found the record of Ella's number in seconds. Lark's aunt had called Matthew's office number with her cell phone, which meant her name was on the log and they didn't need to research a bunch of unlabeled numbers. Jason used a program on his laptop to locate the phone, which was in Virginia, not far from her father's house. They just needed to pick up Jason's truck from short-term parking and get down there.

"I can't believe how smoothly everything is going," Lark said.

Jason held a door for her. "Scary, isn't it?"

"Terrifying."

In truth, not *everything* had gone smoothly. Jason had come into her room last night and, without speaking a word, made love to her even more incredibly than he had the night before. He'd made her lie still without touching him, so he could keep in control and concentrate on her. And concentrate he had. It had been a three-orgasm night for her, a first. He'd taken her to a long, slow peak with his mouth, then a sharper, faster one wrapped tightly in his arms, surrounded by him, filled with him. Then she'd rolled over and come with him buried deeper than she'd ever taken any man, his hands gripping her hips tightly enough to bruise, his teeth lightly clamped on the side of her neck as she held on to the iron headboard with cramped fingers and pressed back against him, wanting him harder and faster. Wanting the impossible.

Wanting him to love her.

He'd stayed in her bed all night, but when she woke he was gone, already showered and packed, with coffee made and stale bagels toasting in her oven. He hadn't said anything about it since, and Lark was determined not to bring it up.

But oh, was she storing ammunition for later.

"What about the property records?" she asked when they'd gotten into his Range Rover. "Why aren't we checking those?"

"When have we had time?" Jason shook his head. "Hummingbird has people who do that kind of research, but we can't trust anyone. And if Isaac owns other property where he'd take your father and Gabby, you know it's not going to be simple to find in the records. He'll have it in a different name, or under a corporation. Not impossible to track, but time-consuming."

Lark opened the laptop once they were outside the airport boundaries and waited for the software to refresh. "The phone hasn't moved."

"Key the coordinates into the GPS, would you?" He headed south and switched on the radar detector he had under the dash.

Lark carefully programmed the navigation system and sat back, watching the screen as it located them, oriented, and started scrolling directions. "Take 495 East when we get to it."

Lark started to think about seeing her aunt again. At the airport, while they'd waited for their flight to board, she'd searched for her online and found her current real estate office in Florida, several articles at travel and relocation sites, and notice of a local award she shared with her partner. Seamus Kemmerling. She probably should have been shocked, but at this point nothing fazed her. In fact, the more connections they found, the better she felt about the whole situation. Not less afraid for her father, but like everything made sense. When things made sense, logical conclusions weren't far behind. It appealed to her scientific bent.

She looked at her watch, anxiety twisting her insides. "It's getting late. She could leave at any moment."

"I'm already doing eighty, Lark." His radar detector beeped and he backed off the accelerator.

"Not anymore."

"Cop." He eyed the patrol car half hidden by trees on the side of the highway. "Being pulled over—"

"Would slow us down, I know. I just have this feeling of dread." She pressed her fist to her stomach, then felt idiotic when Jason put his hand on her knee and the dread eased.

She was not the kind of woman who needed soothing.

It took way too long to get to the coordinates identified by the computer, but it was still not quite nine o'clock when they slowed between a chain hotel on one side and a strip mall on the other.

"Hotel?" Lark eyed the businesses in the strip mall.

The parking lot was almost empty, just a bright green Volkswagen Beetle decorated like a ladybug parked in front of the cleaning service whose name was emblazoned on its side. The take-out chicken restaurant, chiropractor's office, and cross-stitch supply store were all dark. Jason pulled into the hotel lot and parked. Lark leaned forward to study the wide ten-story building. The GPS only gave a general location. "We'll never find her." Her fists tightened again, feeling her father's chances slipping away.

"Of course we will," Jason contradicted. He got out and strode across the parking lot. Lark followed him to a house phone, where he asked for Ella Darron's room. Lark stood close to him, but couldn't make out the voice on the other end of the line when the ringing stopped.

"Ma'am, this is hotel security," Jason said. "We've had word that there's a breach in the perimeter system in your room. Is your window open?" He waited. "Has anything impacted the window from the inside or outside?"

He listened, his mouth quirking a little as her voice rose and became strident enough for Lark to hear, though she still couldn't make out the words.

"We'd better come up and check, ma'am. The safety of our guests is paramount. You're in room three twenty, correct?" The quirk turned into a wide, smug grin as she yelled at him, and he apologized and hung up. "She's in nine-oh-two. Let's go before she decides that was ridiculously transparent and runs."

Lark headed for the elevator, stopping short when Jason went the other way, toward the stairwell. He hadn't told her he had any problems with stairwells, but he'd been full of tension when they left Nils's apartment, and after nearly dying in one, he *had* to have residual anxiety. "Jason..."

"It's faster." He yanked open the door and his jaw practically vibrated, he clenched it so tightly, but he didn't hesitate. Her heart pounding, braced for anything, Lark stayed close behind him as he took the steps two at a time. They burst through the fire door on the ninth floor, panting. Lark wasn't in good enough shape for this, but Jason was. His eyes cleared and his breathing slowed almost immediately.

He checked the number on the first room door. "Other end." He jerked his thumb down the hall and they jogged to room nine-oh-two, reaching it just as the door opened and a woman emerged, pulling a bulging suitcase that was only half zipped. She looked up, wild-eyed, then furious when they pushed her back into the room.

Lark ignored her protests and slammed the bar lock closed on the door. "Hello, Ella." She leveled a cold look at the older woman, watching her furious expression become gaping. She didn't look all that different from Lark's memories. She was just as tanned, carried herself with the same sense of personal focus. Her color-treated dark gold hair hadn't been brushed, and her makeup looked like yesterday's, but her suit was custom tailored, her shoes and the bulging suitcase both designer.

Her aunt collected herself quickly, barking, "What the hell do you think you're doing, Lark Madrassa?" as if Lark were a preteen.

"A better question would be what are *you* doing?" Lark advanced on her aunt, who looked defiant but dropped her suitcase handle and backed toward the bed. "Or maybe why you're here. How you know Isaac Kemmerling?" Her voice rose with the fury and fear that had flash-boiled as soon as she spotted Ella trying to escape. "Maybe you have a story about how you were coerced. Or *maybe*—" she loomed over her aunt, fists at her sides, and roared, "—maybe you can tell me *where the fuck my father is!*"

Ella fell backward onto the bed, catching herself in a half-recline, and Lark stayed in her face, aware that she was acting insane. She backed off. But she'd confused Ella with Nils, because as soon as she had enough space Ella stood, jerked her suit jacket into place, and raised her chin, dignity fully intact. She was going to be a harder nut to crack than the gopher had been.

"I happen to be in town on business that has nothing to do with you. I have no idea where your father is. I haven't spoken to him since your mother's funeral."

"That's a lie." Jason's calm response was a huge contrast to Lark's wild attack, and seemed to disturb Ella more. Her mouth dropped open slightly and her shoulders sagged. She tried to recover, but Lark could see in her eyes that she knew it was too late, that her reaction had limited her options. Lark tried to tap into Jason's calm and hoped that after this, she'd never have to play interrogator again. She really sucked at it.

"We know you called him the other day. And that you went to the house," she added quickly, thinking the call wouldn't be enough to pressure her. "My father runs the best security company in the world. We have you on tape." Of course they didn't. Matthew didn't have cameras on his grounds and definitely not in his house. He'd seen enough invasion of his clients' privacy and didn't want to give anyone the chance to invade his.

"I doubt that," Ella scoffed. "Even if I had gone to his house, he would have changed a great deal to have started filming his life. You forget, child," she added at Lark's disgruntled expression, "I knew your father as an adult long before you did. And your mother confided everything to me."

Anger flared again, this time with hurt. "And you betray her by being party to my father's abduction? Betray me?"

Not a flicker of affection was apparent in Ella's face. "There must be trust for there to be betrayal. I haven't been a part of your life enough to have inspired trust. And your mother never trusted me. Not fully."

"That's why she didn't give you the money you wanted." Lark floundered, no longer certain where to go, but kept talking as Jason moved in her peripheral vision. Since he wasn't chiming in on this conversation, he must have another plan. Lark tried to keep Ella's attention with information she wouldn't know Lark had. "Right? Your grandfather's money? Because of trust."

"You know nothing about that." But Ella sat on the edge of the bed and crossed her legs, draping one arm over her knee in a classically defensive posture.

"I heard you talking about it. She planned to use it for my education. If you had kids, she'd have given you half, right? But you don't, so she didn't. And Dad never touched the money. You can't stand that it's just sitting there unused." She didn't know where all this was coming from. She was just snapping things together, hoping one of the pieces would spark a confession or at least start a conversation. She didn't have her pitchfork and doubted Jason was planning to pull a gun to coerce Ella into talking. "So where does Isaac Kemmerling come into this?"

Ella's gaze stayed fixed on Lark's. Not a good sign.

"Why on earth do you think I'd tell you anything about anything?" she asked, her tone cold.

"Because," Lark said desperately, "you loved my mother. Didn't you? And she loved my father, and me, and he's all I have left." She sensed rather than saw Jason jolt when she said that.

She refocused on Ella, who pressed her lips together and looked away. Lark had touched on something, but it hadn't been enough.

"Come *on,* Ella," she ground out. "Tell me what's going on!"

Jason came up beside Lark then. "Ms. Darron, you drugged your brother-in-law, coerced him to make a recording of lies, and were party to kidnapping, which is a federal offense and could get you jailed for years. You tell us what you know, and we'll make sure you're not implicated when the case goes to trial."

Maybe it was his reasonable tone. Maybe it was the reminder of the severity of her actions. Or maybe she realized Jason had just searched her things right under her nose and found evidence she couldn't explain away. Whatever it was, Ella caved.

And Lark and Jason caught their first break.

JUST A FEW MORE STEPS. Just to that block of shade. Okay, made it. Stop for a second. That's all, keep moving. Get to that big rock.

Gabby had to open and close her eyes in stages, they burned so badly, and sunlight and grit made it worse. The latter coated her glasses when it wasn't infiltrating her eyelashes, and the former refracted weirdly off the dust. The virus that had taken hold of her would have been merely annoying on a normal day, but now it turned every little discomfort into a major obstacle.

They'd been walking for hours. Twice they heard a car and slipped into the woods, but one had been an old farming truck driven by a grizzled gray-haired lady, and one a motorcycle with a guy in a wife-beater and no helmet. There was no sign of Isaac, which struck her as odd. Matthew refused to comment on it.

He refused to comment on much of anything, actually. At first she assumed he was planning, but after a while she realized there wasn't anything *to* plan, not when the only things around them were trees and hot sun and cracked asphalt. Then she decided he was conserving his strength and she should, too. Which meant neither one of them had talked in an immeasurable amount of time.

They reached the boulder that was her next landmark, and she noticed, in the ten seconds she had her eyes open, that it had a nice curve in the top that would be a good place to rest. She considered asking if they could stop, but worried that if they did, she'd never get going again. Plus, her throat had stuck to itself, and she didn't think she could talk.

Matthew suddenly put his hand on her elbow. "Hold on."

Gabby stopped moving and squinted at him. He had a listening posture, so she listened, too. She couldn't hear anything different from the last however-many miles. She would have asked what he'd heard, but he couldn't hear it if she was talking. And then there was that throat thing.

She wondered if she was starting to become delirious.

"Wait here." Matthew led her to the boulder and lowered her into the little seat, making her smile. "I'll just be a few minutes. If a car comes—"

She nodded and waved at the ditch behind the boulder. She could just roll down into it and no one would see her. Matthew hesitated, then disappeared between two trees. Gabby closed her eyes and tried not to sway hard enough to topple over. Maybe Matthew hadn't heard anything. Maybe he just had to go to the bathroom. She didn't. After relieving herself this morning, she hadn't had to go again. With the harsh sun, she'd been sweating like crazy. Of course, they were both dehydrated.

There was no noise to warn her of his return. No leaf rustling or shoe scraping on pavement, no breathing noises or saying her name. Matthew just appeared at her side, took her hand, and led her into the blessed coolness of the woods. She was able to keep her eyes open then, which was good because finding her footing was a challenge.

He must think I'm such a putz. She tripped three times and wanted to cry, except she didn't have the tears. He held her up, gently guiding her around a fallen log and some random animal droppings.

Then she heard it. *Oh, my God.* The words didn't come, her mouth moving silently, but the cheerful splash and gurgle of water over stones filled her with new energy. Her feet lifted higher, her steps became faster, and a few moments later, they were on the banks of a clear, tiny brook. Gabby fell to her knees and dropped her hands down into it, plunging up to her elbows in the icy stream. Her whole body sighed. She cupped her hands and brought them to her mouth, making rude sucking sounds as she drank, but ohhhh, it tasted amazing, cold and soothing on her throat. She thrust her hands back into the water.

"Go slow," Matthew cautioned, but she didn't need the reminder. She was a doctor, a fact she might have forgotten in her misery but that revived along with the rest of her. She drank slowly but deeply, letting her body adjust between handfuls. She splashed it on her face, shoved wet hands through her hair, then pulled off her shoes and stuck her feet into the brook. She sighed and dropped her head back.

"Thank you."

He shook his head and picked up one of her shoes, a dress flat chosen for the thick, padded insole and rubber bottom. The edges of the leather were scuffed and dusty, but they were holding up.

"How are your feet?" Matthew asked, frowning at the shoe.

"Fine." Her voice still croaked. She bent and drank another scoopful of water. "Those are good shoes."

"They are not. And I didn't even notice."

"What could you do? You're not carrying walking shoes in a variety of sizes in your back pocket." She sounded smoother, clearer, the more she talked, but there was still a husky quality to her voice she actually liked. In other circumstances it would be seductive. Circumstances where she wasn't a complete mess. "They're better than pumps, anyway."

"True."

"How about we stay here for a while?" she asked, trying not to sound desperate.

"A short rest."

She couldn't take his tension any longer. The short answers, the lack of eye contact…if there was something worth worrying about, she wanted to know. "What's wrong with you? What's going through your head? We're free. We're out of that cabin, and they aren't—"

"Don't say it."

"Okay." She believed in jinxes, though it surprised her that he did, too. "But what?"

She didn't think he was going to explain. He set her shoe down and examined the other, then swung her legs around to look at her feet.

"I don't have any blisters."

"That's good." He smoothed the water away from her instep. "I have a feeling we're in hunting country, which might mean we won't reach civilization for days."

"Come on, this is Virginia, not Montana." His fingers were making her feet tingle. She pulled them away and put her shoes back on before her feet started to swell. "Even hunters need beer. We'll come across something."

"What if we don't?"

"Matthew." She dropped her foot and leaned to put her hand on his face. "We'll be fine. We'll find a phone or a person driving—we can flag down the next old farm lady we see."

"No one has driven by in hours."

"Then we won't flag someone down. But the road has to go somewhere."

The muscle of his jaw flickered, and his eyes looked hard. "You're sick."

Ah, now she understood. His silence, his abruptness, stemmed from guilt. He was worried about her and couldn't immediately fix everything. If nothing else, Matthew Madrassa was a fixer.

"I've just got a virus." She grabbed his chin and shook it in frustration. "Matthew, I'm a *doctor.* I know my symptoms. I'm not dying, for cripes sake."

He didn't look convinced, and that more than anything gave her the energy to stand up. "Let's go. We won't find a phone sitting here in the woods." She didn't wait, but led him back to the road, pleased when they emerged two feet from her boulder. The sun was high now, and her stomach rumbled. She decided to take it as a good sign and set out down the road again.

"It can't be too much further to a store or something, or even a house. That woman in the truck came from this way. And the kid on the motorcycle wasn't an off-roader. So I'm sure it's just a matter of a mile or two."

Matthew didn't say anything. She stopped chattering, annoyed with herself and exasperated with him. She felt lighter, though, more hopeful, and as they approached a curve in the road, she was certain this was it, what they were looking for.

But she'd only been partly right. Around the bend was a reason to stop walking, but it wasn't what she'd been expecting.

It was the end of the road.

TWENTY-ONE

ONCE ELLA DECIDED to cooperate, things moved fast. She used her laptop and professional access to search property records, looking for some place Isaac owned that could hold Matthew and Gabby.

"I thought everything was localized." Lark watched over Ella's shoulder as she worked, but no screen stayed up long enough for her to catch anything.

"It mostly is, but there are larger databases. Realtors sometimes contact property owners who haven't put their properties on the market but might still be interested in selling. Since we do relocation services, help people transition to other parts of the country, this makes it easier."

"Where does the data come from?"

"Official public records. The owner of the database incorporates the data and charges a subscription fee to those of us who want to use it. Now go away and let me finish this."

Lark joined Jason on the tiny balcony, leaving the door open to watch Ella. He had his laptop propped on the balcony wall and was typing as furiously as Ella was. Lark shoved her hands into her back pockets and tried not to feel superfluous.

"What did you find?" she asked in a low voice.

Jason gave her a cursory glance. "A syringe in her

purse. Prefilled, used. No evidence of medication she would need it for, or even illegal drugs."

"Probably what she used on Dad, then." Lark pulled her hands out of her pockets and folded her arms, trying not to think of her father helpless. "What else?"

He held up a cell phone he'd connected to the laptop. "She called Kemmerling, among other people, but I can't get a fix on all the numbers. Some are in Florida, so probably not related. But there were two calls to landlines in DC. No listings."

"And since they're landlines you can't GPS 'em."

"Right."

"Dammit." She dropped her arms and made a move to pace, but stopped short and eyed the narrow ledge. If she moved, she might knock Jason's laptop to the ground. That would be bad. "What are we going to do with her? We can't just let her go."

"But we can't involve the police yet, either." Jason straightened. "We'll put her under surveillance. I have a team set up. They'll be outside before we leave."

"Who? How can we trust them?" Isaac had gotten to too many people already. They had no idea who else was compromised.

Jason closed the laptop. "I don't know if we can, but they're the people I've worked with the longest, the ones who've had my back dozens of times. For what it's worth, I'd never have picked Nils, even without the ties to Kemmerling."

That would have to be good enough. There was still the possibility Ella would lead them to her father, if nothing panned out here. Lark folded her arms tightly around her body and huddled in the corner of the balcony. It didn't keep her from feeling she was about to fly apart at any second.

"I got something!" Ella called from inside. Lark hurried in, Jason close behind her. Ella scribbled something on a piece of paper.

"Is this it?"

She handed the paper to Jason. "I think so. I can't know if Matthew's there, of course, but—" She stopped when she caught Lark's glare. "Okay, okay. I found nothing under Isaac's name but his apartment in DC and the lease for the security offices. But you're lucky I know Seamus. I know something about their families."

"I didn't think Isaac had any other family."

Ella looked down her nose at them, even from where she sat at the little table. "Perhaps I know my business partner better than you know your enemy."

"Fine. Just tell us!" Lark couldn't stand the delay any more. She snatched the paper from Jason's hand. "How do you know this is what we're looking for?"

"Seamus told me his father and Isaac's used to go hunting together all the time. They owned some land with a hunting cabin on it, a good-sized one. Seamus went with them a few times as a teenager, and said how remote it was. But there was a fire at a nearby house that killed some friends of theirs, and neither brother wanted to go up anymore. So they sold the land. Isaac was furious. He thought they should have kept it for him and Seamus, though Seamus didn't care. The older men, Thomas and Aaron, both died of heart attacks in their early fifties." She nodded at the paper. "That property was sold to a corporation three years ago. The name of the corporation is ISTA. I for Isaac, S for Seamus, T for Thomas, and A for Aaron."

"Pretty tenuous," Jason observed.

Ella gave an elegant shrug. "It's the best I can do. I can keep looking while you go check it out."

"Why don't you go down and plug it into the navigation system," Jason told Lark. "It should accept the coordinates. I'll have Ella print off a map and be down in a minute." He waited until Lark had left the room and gave her time to get to the elevator. Ella watched him the whole time.

"I don't have a printer," she said.

"I know." He didn't need a map. He just didn't want Lark to have to hear painful truths, and maybe Ella would admit them more easily without her niece in the room. "Is the will the reason you hooked up with Isaac to do this?"

Any pleasantness in Ella's expression disappeared, replaced by the ruthlessness and lack of sentimentality that had driven her success. Jason knew she'd answer him. She had no more loyalty to Kemmerling than she had to Matt. She'd always pick her own best interests over anything else, and talking to him now meant he'd leave her alone.

"I didn't 'hook up' with Isaac. He came to me."

"With what?"

"He found out about my connection to Matthew and suspected our relationship wasn't a positive one. He told me his plan and I wasn't unhappy at the idea that Matthew would suffer." She stood, her eyes glittering, and pointed a sharp nail at his chest. "My brother-in-law treated me like crap the entire time he was married to my sister. He poisoned her against me and made sure I got nothing."

"If Lark's right, and he never touched that money, it's still there. Why didn't you just approach him and ask for it when your company was in trouble?"

Her face turned dark red. "We are not in trouble."

"Sure. I bet you didn't want him to know, because your success is all you've ever cared about, right? You wouldn't want him to think he was right about you."

"What do you know about it?" she spat.

"Nothing. But it doesn't take much to understand someone like you."

She snarled, and any beauty or dignity she possessed was gone. "You're just like him. A chauvinistic, self-righteous bastard. I hope Isaac manages to take you both down. In fact, he can kill you for all I care." She reared back and slammed the heels of her hands toward his chest. On a spike of adrenaline, he caught her wrists before she connected with his sternum, but felt a twinge at the movement. Mental, or real?

Two breaths, and the adrenaline ebbed. Everything was fine.

"What are Isaac's plans, Ella?"

She struggled, but he easily held her away from him, blocking her knee when she tried to get him in the only place she thought he was vulnerable. Eventually, she yelled in frustration and went limp in his grip.

"I hope he gets you both arrested for treason," she panted. "And that's all I'll say."

Jason knew he'd get no more out of her and let her go. She lunged at him again. He turned his back, a less vulnerable part of his body. She screamed in rage, but he left the room and headed for the elevator.

It always came down to the same things. Greed and revenge. More than half the threats he'd faced while working for Hummingbird had stemmed from one or the other. This situation was more complex than most, but at its core, it was no different—people failing to take responsibility for whatever results they obtained, blaming others and covering their own inadequacies by seeking to punish, to gain something they had no right to.

He paused in the lobby, amused for a moment at his philosophizing. He sobered when he saw Lark standing next to the Range Rover. Her dark hair blew back in the breeze, and the angle of the sun made her complexion glow. She was beautiful. But at the same time agitated, rocking back and forth next to the passenger door, alternately staring at the hotel's main door and out onto the street.

He hurried over, realizing his keys were in his pocket and she hadn't been able to get into the truck. "I'm sorry, Lark, I didn't think—"

She whirled on him. "Do you know who just drove by?"

"Nnoooo." He hit the button to check the surveillance system, and when it flashed green unlocked the doors. "Who?"

"Nils."

He froze half in, half out of the car. "What?"

"I know!" She yanked open the door and jumped in, immediately leaning toward the navigation system, which wasn't on because Jason hadn't started the truck yet. He slid into his seat and shoved the key into the ignition.

"You're sure it was him?"

"Of course I'm sure. I held him at pitchfork-point." She hit keys on the GPS, then checked the slip of paper. "How did he get out of the stall?"

Jason waited for the system to prep the route. "He's not completely stupid. He probably found a way to reach the bolt, maybe got his hands on a stick or pulled a bar out of rotted wood. The farm is just up the road from town. He didn't have far to hike."

"And what was he doing here? He didn't pull in, so he wasn't coming for Ella." She shook her head and answered before Jason could. "Never mind—it's a main road, blah blah blah. Coincidences do happen, even if no one believes in them."

"Well said." Jason watched her jab at his GPS unit and considered taking over. She probably wouldn't respond well. He reined in his impatience.

"So now Isaac is going to know what we're doing." She hit a wrong button and the unit beeped at her. She made a move to hit the thing, stopped herself, and slammed her hand on the dash instead, letting out a string of curses. Jason let her vent, then gathered her against his chest and held her. He expected her to fall into tears, apologize, and be okay. But even though she let him hold her, even though she wrapped her fingers so tightly around his arm he started to get hard, she didn't lose it. Didn't let go. He didn't know if he should admire her control or worry about how much pain she was harboring.

After less than a minute, she pulled away, took a deep breath, and finished keying the info into the system. It flashed and beeped, then told him to go north on the road in front of them.

"We can't worry about Nils now," Jason said. "Let's

just work on finding Matt and Gabby. This is the closest we've been since he disappeared."

"I know." She pulled her seat belt on and sat back hard against the seat. "You're right. Let's get moving."

Jason hoped he was right, that it was a legitimate lead, and that Ella wasn't sending them on a wild-goose chase, or worse.

And he hoped the thought didn't occur to Lark, either.

THE ROAD DIDN'T peter out, or narrow in underbrush and forest. It just ended, with piles of dirt forming an uneven semicircle around the sharp line of the macadam. Behind the dirt, construction debris lay tumbled among fallen trees and broken brush, and beyond that, thicker forest than what had bordered the road so far.

Gabby had had enough. She was tired of the obstacles, the heat, the pointlessness of everything that had happened the last two days. Adrenaline rushed through her, and she marched up one of the dirt hills. Matthew called her name, but she ignored him. She needed height. Needed to see what was ahead, what was behind, and what they'd missed.

The hill wasn't high enough. It just gave her a better view of the crap on the ground surrounding them. She marched down the other side just as Matthew reached her.

"Gabby, stop." He tried to get in front of her, to catch her arms, but she shrugged him off and kept going. "What are you doing?"

"I'm climbing a tree." She skirted a piece of concrete cylinder and kept going. "We need to see where the hell we're going. Should have done it right away," she muttered. "Haze, my ass."

She got to the edge of the woods and stepped in a hole. Her right ankle snapped sideways and she fell with a cry, rolling with the motion and praying she hadn't done too much damage.

"Gabby!"

"I'm okay." She gasped in air and rolled to her back, waiting for the initial wave of nausea to pass before she could assess the damage. "It wasn't bad, just sudden."

"Lie still." Matthew crouched next to her and lifted her right ankle onto his bent knee. "Did you hurt anything when you fell?"

Gabby brushed dirt off her palms and checked the heels of her hands. "Just a couple of scrapes. I'm okay," she said again, drawing a deep breath and trying to sit. She got as far as her elbows, but Matthew wouldn't let her go any higher. "Let me up. We need to climb a tree and see where we are."

"I'll do it." He gently probed, then rotated, her ankle. She could tell it was already swelling a little, but the pain was minimal, mostly bruiselike when he pressed down. She could walk on it. "Height wouldn't have done any good back near the cabin," he told her. "We were in a valley. But we've been mostly climbing all day." Setting her foot down, he stood and looked for a suitable tree.

Gabby watched him select one and haul himself into the lower branches, then looked back toward the stupid road while she waited. How could the road just end? That truck had come from here, and the motorcycle that passed them went *somewhere*. Unless they missed a turnoff somehow, and that was hard to believe, even in their depleted conditions, considering how slowly they'd been moving. Still, that was the only explanation, wasn't it?

She tilted her head back to see where Matthew was. She forgot which tree he'd climbed into, and searched until a flash of his blue shirt near the top of the tallest evergreen caught her eye. The treetop swayed, then bent, and she held her breath until it eased back upright. The sliver of blue moved higher, then halted for several minutes before it started moving back downward. By the time Matthew hit the ground, Gabby had dragged herself to her feet and tested her ankle.

"Well?" she called before he was halfway back to her.

He shook his head.

"What's that mean? No luck? Too far? What?"

He stayed silent as he made his way through the debris field. When he got to her side, put his hand on her elbow, looked at her ankle, and opened his mouth, she said, "Don't you dare ask how my ankle is before you tell me what you saw."

He looked grim. "We have a choice."

"I take it it's not a good choice," she sighed.

"The haze was smog. Probably DC, though it's too far away to tell. There's a good two miles of thick forest before we get to the next town in that direction."

"And the other way?"

"If we go back the way we came, probably about five miles, to a turnoff we missed, that will take us to a group of buildings that may be the crossroads you were hoping for."

Gabby scowled. "Why the hell isn't there some kind

of bar every three miles around here? Don't hunters drink a lot?" She sighed and tried to buck up. "My ankle is fine if I keep it straight. The uneven ground in the woods will be impossible. But I can handle a few miles of flat road. Let's get moving." She glanced at Matthew, noticing the tears in his dress pants and sweat stains on what was probably an expensive shirt. His "weekend" shoes were sturdy enough to climb trees, apparently, but probably wearing as well as her flats were. As they headed back toward the road, she imagined a giant maze someone had placed them in. One with no exit.

THE REGION OF Virginia to which Ella's information had sent them made navigating difficult. Several times they found themselves on roads the GPS didn't recognize, and they kept having to backtrack and find another way. Jason could almost hear Lark's heart pounding harder with every mile closer to the coordinates. Six dirt roads, two gravel lanes, and a wagon track later, they pulled into a clearing holding a rough-looking cabin and no vehicles. There hadn't been any visual warning that they were close to their destination, and the GPS said they had half a mile to go. But this was the end of the road, and they'd seen no other structures for hours.

"They'll have heard us coming." Lark grabbed the dash as they bounced over a pothole. "We should go in fast."

"No." Jason turned off the engine and removed his seat belt, shifting into mission mode. "You stay here, in the driver's seat. I'll scout the place and go in when I know what I'm getting into. No arguments."

Lark didn't give him any.

The feeling of being close to his target jacked up his senses. When he got out of the truck, he smelled the woods, both fresh and rotting vegetation, and a faint hint of smoke, as if there had been a fire burning, extinguished some time ago. The air was still, thick, and he'd already started to sweat. A drop trickling between his shoulder blades burned, and he rubbed at it before drawing his pistol and easing toward the cabin.

Everything was silent. Birds and animals awaited his next move, and the cabin seemed deserted. He crept up to the nearest side of the building and looked through the window, staying to the left so he could see most of the room without exposing too much of himself. It was a small, sparse bedroom, empty. The room behind it was the same, only it contained a rumpled bed and a chair. On the back of the cabin was a built-on room, completely empty. Jason circled around the back, and found a fresh hole dug from underneath the building. Hope leaped, but he ignored it and continued carefully around the corner.

On the other side he peered into the kitchen and living area, which also looked empty, but he couldn't see everything. Still, it was enough to take a cautious risk and go into the building. The front door opened noiselessly, unexpected in a wooden cabin in this condition.

Jason had no sooner cleared the threshold than a figure bucked where it lay on the plaid couch. Jason whipped his weapon toward him, but the big man faced the back of the couch, his hands fastened with cuffs behind him, feet tied with some kind of fabric—old curtains?—and mouth taped closed with duct tape. Jason swept the room one more time, but there was no one else there. He holstered the pistol and stepped carefully closer.

The guy twisted to look over his shoulder, displaying a blackening eye and dried blood around a swollen nose. Still, Jason recognized him.

"John?" He slowly peeled the tape away from the guy's mouth. "What are you doing here?"

John grunted.

"You work for Isaac?" Jason guessed.

"Did."

"He do this?"

John had to clear his throat before talking, and it came out dry and rough. "Madrassa. Got the jump on me. Before he bolted with the doctor."

"Where is Isaac?"

"What time is it?" When Jason told him, he made a face. "Probably on his way back here."

"How long ago did Matthew leave?"

"Last night, near dark."

Jason stood, thinking. They probably hadn't gotten far when they first took off, and had found someplace to hole up overnight. Still, it had been hours since dawn. They could be anywhere on those roads. They had to get moving, but he hesitated over John, undecided what to do with him.

John knew, though. "Tape me back up," he croaked. "Kemmerling needs to see me like this. He'll fire me. Then I'll be out."

Jason nodded, understanding that Matthew probably hadn't gotten the jump on John without his cooperation.

"What was their condition?" he asked.

"Doc was sick, but mobile."

Jason gave him a drink of water and helped him shift to a slightly more comfortable position before he retaped his mouth and left the cabin. Lark slid over when he got back to the truck. She looked anxious, but held her tongue and gave him a chance to tell her what had happened. Gratitude flitted through her expression as she reached for the handle, and Jason caught her wrist.

"What are you doing?"

She shook her head. "I guess I wanted to thank him. Stupid, huh?"

"No." It was genuine, and something he hadn't done. John had let them go, sure. But he'd held them captive in the first place. For a moment, Jason imagined coming home to Lark and her refreshing perspective. Imagined a balanced life, a reason not to be suspicious or always checking the angles. A sharp craving pierced him, then faded away. His imagination didn't stretch that far.

He turned the truck around and headed back to the main road, stopping at the end to check out both directions.

"To the right," Lark said.

"Why?"

"There's haze that way. Dad would have figured smog, which meant city, which meant suburbs, etc."

He turned right. "You're probably right, but there's a more practical reason to go this way."

"What?"

"We came from the other direction, and didn't see him."

Lark made a face. "That's too easy. Besides, they could have gone down a side road or gotten a ride."

"Could have, probably wouldn't. Plus, if they'd gotten picked up, they'd have called us."

Lark pulled out her cell phone and checked quickly for calls, then shook her head and looked out the window, examining the side of the road.

"I don't see any signs," she said after a few minutes.

"There won't be any."

"But—" She glanced at him and shut up. Jason rested his hand on her knee. He understood. She was excited because they could be close to finding her father, but she also knew enough to fear what condition he would be in when they found him. And the likelihood that they'd find both Matt and Gabby in good condition was slim.

Even so, Jason's heart stopped in his chest when they saw the bodies lying on the side of the road.

TWENTY-TWO

"PULL OVER!" LARK had her door open before Jason stopped the car, and hit the ground running. Well, more stumbling, actually, and unable to regain her balance until she collapsed at her father's side.

"Daddy!" She touched his face, ran her hands down his shoulders, felt his chest for his heartbeat, even though he was sitting up and his eyes were open. She wasn't exactly rational at the moment.

He caught her hands. "Lark, I'm okay."

"Are you hurt?"

"No."

Before he could say more she launched herself at him, wrapping her arms around his neck and weeping in relief at the strength of his hug. He was a mess, dirty and scratched, and his voice was raspy. She had no doubt he was dehydrated, minimum, but he was whole and sane and she'd never been so happy about anything in her entire life.

She pulled back, embarrassed, and wiped her nose on the shoulder of her T-shirt. But the tears kept coming. "I'm so glad we found you."

"I am, too." He held her hand while he turned to Jason, who was checking Gabby over for injuries. "We need to get off the street. Do you have any—"

"Water and food in the truck. Not much, but enough

to tide you over. We're not far from the city, just in a convoluted area."

"We figured that out," Gabby croaked.

Lark gasped. "Oh, Gabby, are you okay?"

Matthew gently pushed Lark back and up. She stood and pulled him to his feet, backing toward the truck while Jason lifted Gabby and carried her to the backseat.

"She's sick," Matthew said, following closely but keeping Lark's hand in his. "Twisted her ankle. Bad sunburn, probably can't tell in the light, but she needs treatment. Probably IV fluids."

"Who's the doctor here?" Gabby patted Jason's cheek with a lethargic hand and let herself be strapped into the seat.

Lark circled the truck and climbed into the back while her father got in next to Jason. She hated letting go of him, but Gabby needed her attention, and her father would want to talk to Jason, exchange intel. She checked Gabby over as best she could, but her father had pretty much cataloged it all. Her right ankle was swollen and slightly purple, her skin very hot and dry to the touch, her mouth parched, her eyes glazed.

"We need a hospital," she murmured over the seat to Jason, who nodded and pulled out, hitting keys on the nav system at the same time. Lark reached over the seat behind her and pulled a six-pack of water bottles onto her lap. "These are warm, but that's probably better, anyway. You're less likely to cramp." She handed two bottles up to her father, experiencing another wave of relief watching him take them from her. He was alive, he was free, and he was going to be okay. She blinked back tears as she opened another bottle and held it to Gabby's mouth.

"I can do it." The doctor took the bottle and tilted it, gulping water for several mouthfuls, then slowing to sips. "God, that tastes good."

"We have food, too." She retrieved the box of snack bars. "Granola, nuts, sugar. You'll have energy back in no time."

"Thank you, Lark."

Lark listened as they drove. Jason brought her father up to speed on what they'd learned, dropping the last bomb as they pulled into the hospital parking lot.

"We have a report that Kolanko is involved."

Matthew stared at Jason for a moment, his hand on the door handle. "That's not possible."

"I'm just telling you what I was told. We didn't look into it yet. Our priority was finding you and Gabby."

The doctor's name seemed to galvanize Matthew, who jumped out of the truck and opened her door to help her out. Lark ran up to the hospital entrance to get a wheelchair.

A few hours later, they gathered in Gabby's room. She'd been admitted overnight for IV fluids and observation. The pale blue, almost white, hospital gown made her red skin blaze. They'd given her pain meds and she dozed fitfully.

Lark had obtained extra chairs and sat in a hard plastic one next to her father, who'd pulled the cushy armchair close to Gabby's bed. He didn't touch her, but he didn't need to, with the way he looked at the woman, and his attentiveness—being ready with water when she licked her lips, boosting or lowering the top of her bed, and fixing her pillows. Their experience had bonded them, obviously. It remained to be seen if he'd be smart enough to take it from there, but Lark hoped he would. He'd been alone and lonely long enough.

Jason had driven to Matthew's house to get him a change of clothes, and the hospital staff had let him use a staff shower—Lark was pretty sure some money had been handed over. He looked normal, except for his own ruddiness and a distinct lack of energy. He needed rest. They all did, now that they were safe.

She knew none of them would get it.

"We need to find Kolanko," Jason said in a low voice. "I know you don't believe he's behind any of this, but he could be the buyer, Matthew."

"Or know him," Matthew admitted. "You're right, whether he's really part of it or not, he's a link."

Jason leaned forward from the edge of his chair. He glanced at Lark out of the corner of his eye, then said in a very low voice, "Ella indicated Isaac wants to get you arrested for treason."

The sudden darkness that descended in the room confused Lark. "Why is that worse than what we thought before?"

Her father didn't answer, only rubbed his face with his palm and then sat, hunched, staring at the floor. She turned to Jason, who took her hand and wove his fingers through hers. She knew it was serious then, because he would never have let on to her father that anything had happened between them.

"Traitors to the United States can be executed, Lark."

"I don't understand why that's worse than destroying his company's reputation and killing him outright."

"It's an extremely difficult charge to fight," Jason explained. "On both sides, actually, but what Isaac is trying to set up will provide the witnesses and proof the government would need to show Matt was 'offering aid and comfort to the enemy.' Selling this kind of technology to an enemy of the United States, if it could be used to hurt people, is an act of war."

"But Kolanko's not an enemy of the United States," she interjected.

"He didn't used to be," Jason said. "I don't know what his status is now, or if there's something else going on the government hasn't found out yet."

"So we won't let it happen." She stared from one to the other, surprised at their postures of defeat. "Come on, you guys, you can't let this stop you."

Her father looked up at her with bleak eyes. "I've been fighting the collapse of my company for six months, watching commercial clients flee in fear. All we have left right now is government work. I've skirted several laws." He waved a hand to indicate Jason. "If Isaac gets enough information to sell the RT-24 and calls it a weapon, and he makes it look like *we* did it, I don't stand a chance. And neither does Jason, frankly. I'm not giving up," he continued when she was about to protest, "but I need some time to process what's happened. And rest."

He was right. He had to be exhausted, and Lark knew neither man was a quitter. They wouldn't sit back and let this happen.

"I'm sorry," she said. "I can't help that I want to get moving on the information right away—but we don't have to talk any more tonight. Let's go home and rest. Everything will look better in the morning."

Her father looked toward Gabby's bed, and Lark caught her breath at the longing that tightened his features. She put her hand on his shoulder.

"She'll be fine, Dad. No one knows she's here, and I don't think Isaac will bother with her now. She's too much trouble."

He didn't respond, but stood and bent over Gabby to kiss her forehead. She murmured something and touched his face, then subsided back into sleep. Whatever she said eased the lines from Matthew's face and lightened the bleakness in his eyes.

Lark's own heart felt lighter as they left the hospital and climbed back into Jason's Range Rover. It seemed her father might be finding love again. And if he was, maybe it would make her relationship with Jason less of an issue.

At least she could hope.

JASON SPENT THE night in Matt's guest room, one he'd slept in dozens of times before, after events or work sessions or before early basketball games. But it was different tonight, with Lark in her room on the other side of the wall. He couldn't stop thinking about her, and wondering if Matthew had sensed what was going on between them. He hoped his friend was too exhausted and had too much on his mind. Jason, himself, had been distracted all day by his attempts to treat Lark normally, not like a woman he'd slept with. A woman he was falling in love with.

He lay in the comfortable bed, staring up at the ceiling, wishing they could make it work. Every obstacle he attacked just led to something even bigger.

Lark being his best friend's daughter seemed manageable now that Jason had seen Matt with Gabby. Being in love made a man look at things differently, and Matt knew him. Trusted him. Who else would he want for his daughter?

The work issue was bigger. Lark had a contract with BotMed, and Jason wouldn't leave Hummingbird or Matt. Boston and DC weren't *that* far apart, but a long-distance relationship was never easy. Making one successful with the kind of work and travel they both did would be near impossible. There was no compromise, either. One of them would have to give up something important.

The memory of Lark standing outside in the sun today, hair blowing, popped into his head. He grinned, thinking about her ferocity when she went at Nils and Ella. Lark had a passionate soul. He wanted that passion directed at him, and not just temporarily.

It suddenly was no longer out of the question for him to leave his job, to find something with no danger component. He could live with desk work if it meant Lark would never have to suffer through losing him violently.

His physical condition was still the biggest issue. He'd blown off Gabby's warnings at first, focused on getting out of the lab and getting Lark to safety. Once this was over, he'd talk to the doctor about precautions. Diet, supplements, air purifiers, whatever he needed to do, he'd do it. The nerve part, well, they'd already proved they could work around that. Some women wouldn't even get through one date of having to think about every touch, or would consider him a wimp. Lark just…handled it. Jason had no difficulty imagining her…handling it for the rest of their lives.

But that was just one small piece of the whole. Lark had implied that she was afraid of watching someone she loved die like her mother. Jason's situation was even worse, because no one knew the long-term effects of his treatments.

And now they had the traitor thing hanging over them.

If Isaac succeeded in labeling Matt a traitor, and the government prosecuted him, it would all be possible only because of Jason's injuries. Matt had broken the law only to save his life. Even if Lark didn't blame him, how could she want to be with him while her father was in jail, or worse? And that was assuming Jason escaped prosecution, himself, which was highly unlikely given his position in Hummingbird. He couldn't make Lark go through that twice.

So stop Isaac before it gets that far.

"That's the plan," he muttered to his subconscious, and rolled over to try to get some sleep.

The next morning, all three of them wound up in the kitchen at about the same time. Together they made fresh-squeezed orange juice, sour cream buttermilk pancakes, and turkey sausage links, avoiding all serious talk until the food was on the table and they'd sat down to eat. Matt had called the hospital early, and Gabby was doing fine. She was being released about ten o'clock. They decided to have a pow-wow about their options before they went to get her.

"We obviously have to go after Kolanko." Lark poured some raspberry syrup on her pancakes and handed the bottle to Jason. "He's the only lead of any value we have left."

"Let's back up and lay out everything we know,"

Matt said. "We're going to need to write it down. Lark, honey, would you get a pad and pen?"

Lark did, but she tossed them at her father. "I'm not your secretary. You write. Your brain will make better connections that way."

Jason laughed, and got the hairy eyeball from Matt.

They spent a good hour and a half laying out all the facts and tidbits they'd collected. Then Matt summarized it.

"Isaac has been nursing a grudge for three years. The Kolanko explosion gave him ammunition, and he infiltrated Hummingbird through at least one person, maybe more. He discovered Jason was alive, and when he continued to survive, gathered intel on his condition and the treatments used to heal him. He devised a plan to sell the RT-24 as a weapon and make it look like we did it. Because getting data from the lab wasn't going to be easy, he went after Lark and her information, which gave him nothing but proof of Jason's status. But Lark had the added advantage of being my daughter, and her abduction would cause me grief. Since it didn't work, he came after me, making me appear to abandon my company in a time of need, which would further damage my reputation. Once he orchestrated the sale he would somehow demonstrate that Hummingbird not only illegally used the compound, but also sold it to an enemy of the state, making me guilty of treason and dooming both Hummingbird and myself, even if the charges don't stick. Kolanko may be the buyer. Maybe his status with the government has changed. Or he may know the buyer, and if he does, it may give us a way to stop Isaac before the plan goes all the way through.

"Did I get it all?"

"Sounds right to me." Lark stood and cleared her place. "I'll be right back, and we can go get Gabby. Then we'll come back here and talk about how to get to Kolanko, right?"

Neither man said anything, but she took it as agreement because she walked out of the room without waiting for their response.

Jason forgot about keeping his head down and watched her a little too long. Matt banged his coffee mug on the table.

"What's going on between you two?"

Jason thought about protesting, for about half a second. No one knew him better, and it would be a pointless insult to lie to him. But he didn't know exactly what to say. *I had hot sex with your daughter about six times and every time she touches me I want to take her up against the wall.* There was, of course, much more to it than that, but that was all Matt would hear. It was all Jason would hear, if Lark were his daughter.

Lark returned to the kitchen, saving him.

"What, you two just sat there? Come on! Put your dishes in the dishwasher and let's go." She waited until the men stood, then headed toward the front door. "I'll start the car and get the A/C on, it's a roaster out there already," she called back.

Jason waited, Matt stared. Finally, Matt said, "I'll let it go for now, but I know there's something going on. Don't make me have to kill you when I just brought you back."

Jason followed Matt to the sink and waited while the older man put his dishes in the dishwasher, as instructed. Matt took Jason's plate and mug from him and dropped them in the racks.

"I don't want this hanging over us while we clear up this situation," Jason said. "I've only known Lark for four days."

"You've known her for ten years."

"Not like this."

Matt squared up with Jason. "Like what, exactly?"

Jason held up his hands, but what defense did he have? "You're my best friend. I could tell you she's a grown woman who makes her own decisions, but you know that. I could tell you I won't touch her, but it's too late." He forced himself not to wince when Matt clenched his fists. "I can't tell you I love her when I don't know for sure, and she deserves to be told first. All I can tell you is that you are my best friend, and I never want to do anything to damage that."

Matt glared at him, then relaxed, rubbing his forehead with a rueful laugh. "You'll understand someday, Jase, what it's like to have a daughter. Instinct tells me to protect her. But I think you'll do a better job of that than I can." He clapped Jason on the shoulder and headed for the front door. "Don't tell Lark we had this conversation. She'll crucify me."

Jason agreed, but knew that wasn't the end of it.

GABBY'S DISCHARGE WAS SLOW, and she wasn't a very patient patient. Lark and Jason were calm enough, sitting next to her bed and trying not to tell her much about what was happening, which didn't help her mood. It was Matthew pacing in the hallway, though, that drove her nuts.

"Matthew, will you settle?" She stood in the doorway to her room, wearing the jeans and soft blue T-shirt Lark had brought for her to wear. Little shocks of pain swept over her whenever anything touched her skin, giving her empathy for what Jason had been dealing with. But her energy level was normal, and the skin on her lips less chapped. They were better off today, at least physically, than they'd been twenty-four hours ago. How could she be anything less than cheerful?

"I'm calm," Matthew tried.

"You are not." She came out and leaned against the wall, snagging his arm to halt his pacing. "Tell me what's going on. I don't think it's just the Isaac stuff."

He stood where she'd stopped him but avoided looking at her. Now that they were out of danger, she expected him to put her off. To tell her she might have gotten the wrong idea, that he was going to fire her to try to keep her safer and hey, have a nice life. But instead, he looked mournfully into the hospital room at Lark and Jason.

"I don't know what to do about them."

Her eyebrows climbed a centimeter before her sun-burned forehead protested. She smoothed her features and tried not to peer around the doorjamb. "What do you mean?"

"They're—involved."

It had been so obvious to Gabby the other day that she hadn't thought to be surprised by it. "So?"

He focused on her, frowning. "What do you mean, so? She's my daughter."

She laughed, part of her marveling at her ability to, when three days ago she'd barely been able to talk to him, never mind make fun of him. "Matthew, do you really think Jason is a worse boyfriend than that Carl guy who sold her out to Isaac? I was listening," she explained. "I was drowsy from the pain meds, but I heard you guys catching each other up last night."

"No, I don't think Jason is worse than Carl. I just—"

"Have a problem thinking of your best friend in bed with your little girl. I understand."

He scowled. "Thanks for the imagery. I was successfully keeping it at bay."

"Sure. Then why are you pacing?"

He pursed his lips, still watching through the doorway, his hands propped on his narrow hips. "He's ten years older than her."

"A nonissue. Ten years is nothing, especially as young as they are."

"As—" He finally focused on her. "How old are you?"

The sunburn was good for one thing, anyway—covering the blush creeping up into her face. She adjusted her scratched glasses. "I'm thirty-nine, which you know very well."

"Actually, I didn't know that."

She scoffed. "You did a thorough background check before hiring me. You knew."

"Well, maybe. If I did, I forgot, since you look and act so much younger."

Gabby folded her arms, both flattered and affronted. "Anyway. It's meaningless with these two. They're in similar places in their lives."

"Okay, then, there's the distance. Lark's in Boston, she has a contract with BotMed, and Jason's…here." He swallowed hard, and Gabby's heart melted.

"Jason won't leave Hummingbird," she said, because to say "leave you" would have made Matthew too vulnerable and sounded too feminine. But it was the truth.

"Maybe that's worse." He rubbed his forehead again and his shoulders slumped. "If something happened to Jason, with this situation or any other in the future, Lark would be hurt. I don't want that."

Gabby took a deep breath and tried not to worry that he was applying the same logic to them. To do that would assume he thought of her that way, and he'd given no real indication that he did. "Anyone can get hurt at any time. There's no way to guard against it. Even keeping your heart locked up, away from everyone, doesn't prevent pain." She pressed her fingertips to his chest, hoping he got the message. "I think Lark would regret doing that, or seeing someone she loved do it. I know I would."

Okay, maybe a little heavy-handed, but even though she had the courage now to face her feelings head-on, Matthew had far too many things to be worrying about to add to them. Romance—either his own or his daughter's—should be low on the totem pole. She dropped her hand and stepped away.

"Don't worry about your daughter. Just worry about the task at hand and deal with that later."

He looked down at her, a smile crinkling the corners of his eyes. "That's good advice."

"Of course it is." Her heart fluttered, and she knew it would show in her eyes. She looked down the hall and found escape. "There's my doctor. Let's get me out of here." She strode down the hall, aiming for determination on the outside but on the inside weeping with longing. An edge came through when she pushed the doctor to sign her release paperwork, which maybe was why he did it so fast. A few minutes later, she was out the door.

She listened to the others planning in the truck on the way back to Matthew's house, and in his office there, and later, during the dinner she'd prepared over protests by the others. She felt fine, except for the tender skin and a residual headache that kept surging. There was no reason she couldn't prepare dinner, especially since she had nothing to contribute to the discussion.

Not that it stopped Lark. Gabby played with her potatoes and admired how Lark just jumped in, despite her lack of training and experience in this area. If she felt uncomfortable sharing her thoughts, or inferior to the experts, it never showed. Gabby wished she could be that way. Even in her own realm, where she *knew* how good she was, she didn't have the confidence to portray herself the way Lark did.

"You okay? Gabby?"

It took her a minute to realize Jason was addressing her. "Yeah, I'm fine. Thanks."

"You're not eating," he pointed out.

She shrugged. It would be silly to say she wasn't hungry after their ordeal, when Matthew sat beside her inhaling the pot roast and mashed potatoes and was on his third helping of asparagus. "The hospital filled me up." Liquid protein wasn't tasty, but it did appease the hunger.

Matthew placed his hand on the back of her shoulder. "Are you sure you're okay?"

"I'm fine." She shoved to her feet and picked up her nearly full plate. "I'm going to go do the dishes."

"No," Lark protested, starting to rise. "You cooked. I'll—"

"You're needed in here." She managed not to say "apparently" or to allow snideness into her tone. It wasn't their fault she was worthless.

A few minutes after she'd entered the kitchen with an armful of dishes, Jason joined her with the rest of them.

"Thanks, Jason." She sorted the items into the sink, dumping the silverware into a tray, and started stacking glasses in the top of the dishwasher. When she turned back to the sink for more, she bumped into Jason, knocking a glass out of his hand. Before it could smash on the tile floor, he caught it with the other hand and a roguish smile.

"What are you doing?" She snatched the glass from him and shoved it into the rack where it would be safe.

"I'm helping." He handed her two more glasses.

"I'm fine out here alone." She placed these with a little more care, trying to ease back her emotions.

"I know. Lark and Matt needed a little father-daughter time."

"Oh." They worked together in silence for a little while, finding an efficient rhythm that filled the machine in a few minutes and settled her riled emotions at the same time. Jason moved to the sink and squirted soap into the roasting pan, then started scrubbing the mashed potato pot.

"You think they're talking about us?" She grimaced and turned away to find a dish towel in a drawer. She'd meant to say "you," not "us," but hey, it was out there, and she had no doubt Jason had always known about her crush on Matthew.

"Me, definitely, though I won't be surprised if Lark brings you up to deflect attention." He handed her the pot and started on the baking pan she'd heated rolls on.

"No one needs this stuff right now," she muttered, setting the dry pot aside. "I mean, life and death trumps crushes."

"I don't think so," Jason said mildly. He handed her the baking pan. "Love makes life and death matter."

Gabby dried in silence, thinking. Stakes were much higher when you loved someone. Keeping them safe from harm, protecting them from pain, sure, but also taking more care with yourself, because getting back to that person was just as important, if not more, than the job you were doing.

Or something like that.

"Do you think I have a chance?" Jason asked.

Gabby laughed. She'd been about to ask the same question. "I think Lark is a strong-willed woman who will get what she wants. Assuming it's what you want, too."

His mouth quirked, but he concentrated on scrubbing the roasting pan. Gabby put the other pans away and watched him. "What about me?" He took a deep breath before answering. She saw it, even though he tried to hide it by scrubbing the bottom of the pan extra hard. "Never mind. I don't want to hear it."

"No, you do. Have a chance, I mean." He turned on the water to rinse the pan. "I didn't think so before, but things have changed. A lot of things have changed. It's just—Gabby, if he's going to be charged with treason, he'll want you far, far away from him."

Which meant tonight might be her last chance, she realized. Enough with the flittery mouse. She was going after what she wanted, what she needed—what she *deserved.* Tonight.

Jason sneezed.

"Oh, my God!" She dropped the towel on the floor and lunged at him. "Oh, no. No. I can't believe I was so *stupid!*"

"Wha—?" Jason backed away from the hand she flung at his forehead, laughing. "What are you doing?"

"I *exposed* you, Jason! Don't you remember, I told you when I released you from the lab—"

"It's not a lab," he corrected, still laughing.

"Shut *up!* I told you how compromised your immune system is. That you need to be careful."

"I have been, Gabby, don't worry. It was just a sneeze."

"There's no such thing as just a sneeze. We were in the same car together, with whatever I had. You carried me!" They hadn't determined how sick she'd really been, if her symptoms were reactionary or viral. The fever had disappeared with the IV hydration, so she'd assumed the former. But she should never have taken a chance with Jason's health, *never.* Even if she hadn't made him sick, he'd been at the hospital with her. He could have been exposed to anything there.

"Let me feel your skin!"

Jason finally stood still, chuckling. "You're feistier than I ever gave you credit for." He let her press her hand to his forehead, then the back of his neck. His temperature seemed normal.

"Have you been stuffy? Sniffling? Coughing? Eyes burning, trouble breathing, anything?"

"No!" He turned back to the pan. "I'm as healthy as I was when you discharged me. From the lab," he teased, but she wasn't in the mood. She snatched the roaster from him and rubbed the towel vigorously over it.

"It's not funny, Jason. Pay attention. If you have any more symptoms, tell me. Immediately."

"Yes, Mom. Seriously," he added when she glowered at his teasing. "I won't mess around. I know it's important."

Gabby headed upstairs to the guest room, appeased but abandoning her plans to seduce Matthew tonight. Because maybe she could overcome all his fears and protectiveness and caution. But one thing was certain.

She'd never have a chance with him if she killed his best friend.

TWENTY-THREE

"I KNOW JASON's job is just as dangerous as yours. For God's sake, I've been living it for a week. *It doesn't matter!*"

"Of course it matters."

Lark took a deep breath, ignoring his repeated list of reasons why it wasn't a good idea for her to be involved with Jason, and why—though he didn't say it—he wouldn't admit to his feelings for Gabby. She'd watched him since they left the hospital. Her father never did or said anything that anyone else would pick up on. But he'd been discreetly attentive, and the look on his face—well, she'd seen a similar look on Jason's.

And she didn't want to give it up.

She sat on the ottoman in front of her father and took his hands in hers. "Think back to when you first met Mom. First fell in love with her. What would have kept you apart?"

"Nothing." It was an automatic response, and she could see he regretted it immediately.

"Exactly." She squeezed his fingers. "You guys had me when you were twenty."

"I know, but—"

"You knew, right? You knew it was going to last, no matter what. And it did."

"It was different." He tried to pull his hands away, but she held on.

"Why? Because your job wasn't dangerous yet?"

Something shifted across his face, something she'd seen before but had nothing to connect it to. She felt him withdraw, even though this time he didn't move.

"No, that's not why. My life was infinitely more dangerous than yours has been, Lark. I never wanted anything that I've seen to touch you."

She let go and leaned away from him. "So you think I can't handle adversity."

"No!" He thrust a hand through his hair. "Dammit, Lark, stop twisting everything I say."

"Look." She took a deep breath. "The day of Jason's funeral, you tried to convince me the loss was worth it. That having someone in your life was an acceptable emotional risk."

"I meant some regular guy," he argued. "There are degrees of risk."

"I love Jason, Daddy." The words came out much softer, more plaintive than she'd intended. But her father softened and reached for her. She stayed back, not done. "I know it seems sudden and that relationships borne of adversity don't last, yada yada, but I *know*." She pressed a fist to her chest, unsurprised at the pain building there. Deep inside, the old Lark was screaming a protest, struggling to pull a cloak of disinterest around the mass of raw, desperate, expanding emotion. But she wanted her father to be happy. Wanted them *all* to be happy. "I don't care what the risks are." *Liar!* the inner Lark screeched. She ignored it, the truth ringing through her words as she really got what he'd been trying to say then. "I want to be with him. I want to make it work somehow. And nothing that happens in the next few days will change that, or hurt less if something happens to him. Please, Dad, stop fighting it. Embrace it."

He stood and pulled her into his arms, blinking back tears he hadn't produced since Kelly died. "I'm happy for you then, honey." He released her and gripped her shoulders, his eyebrows folding together again. He couldn't stop seeing all the potential pitfalls. "Are you sure he feels the same way?"

She grinned. "I'm going to go find out." Her kiss landed hard on his cheek, and she tossed "Good night" over her shoulder as she dashed through the doorway into the kitchen hall.

"Good night."

He stood alone in the living room for a few minutes, absorbing all the things a father felt at such moments. Fear for his child, acceptance that she was an independent woman and he couldn't put a protective bubble around her, and pride and happiness for her choice.

The subtext of what she'd said—that her words applied to his situation as well—wasn't lost on him. *Stop fighting it. Embrace it.* His own decade of loneliness added to the message. Too much protection could just mean lost time. Wasted time. And now that he was older, he had less to lose.

He turned off the lights, checked the alarm system, and headed upstairs. Doing it properly would be smart, he knew. He had champagne in the back of the refrigerator and fresh strawberries from a grocery store run during a break in their brainstorming. But for now, he didn't think they needed trappings.

The upstairs hall was silent. Gabby was in the guest room next to Matthew's bedroom, which was closest to the stairs. Jason was probably in Lark's room, at the far end of the hall. He grimaced and shook the thought out of his head. Luckily, the thick carpeting and solidly built walls muffled any sound from that distance.

He crossed to Gabby's door and knocked softly. He wasn't sure when she'd come upstairs and hoped she wasn't sleeping. But he'd barely had time to drop his hand to his side before the door opened.

For several long seconds, Matthew couldn't find his voice. Gabby had been getting ready for bed. Her hair was piled haphazardly on top of her head, and she wore a pale green silk robe that ended well above the knee and plunged in a deep V from where it draped around her neck. She made no move to cover herself or tighten the robe's belt, and Matthew's throat relaxed. She wasn't going to send him away.

"Do you have everything you need?" He winced at the impersonal question.

"Yes, I'm fine. I picked up some toiletries at the store earlier, and Lark loaned me some more clothes." She brushed a curl away from her face and touched the side of her glasses. "Thank you, Matthew, for everything."

"No. I did nothing but bring you trouble." He stopped himself. "But that's not what I want to talk about. Can I come in?"

She backed up and motioned into the bedroom, and he stepped inside.

Her skin seemed to glow in the soft light from the bedside lamp. Her eyes definitely did. His already rapid heart rate kicked into a higher gear, anticipation rising, making his whole body buzz slightly.

"What did you want to talk about?" She continued

stepping back as he approached her, so he stopped moving. "Tomorrow's plan?"

"No." He stepped forward again, slowly. "I want to talk about you."

"Me?" A finger pointed at her chest and her eyebrows went up. "You're going to fire me after all, aren't you? I was hoping you'd wait until we could get back into the office, so I could…well, I can still show you. Jason's data is inaccessible. I'll have to show you how to get into it, and I'm sure Tompkins will do a great job overseeing the next stage of research. It would be nice if you could give me a letter of recommendation—"

"Gabby." Matthew took one long stride forward and slid his hands around her face, cradling her jaw and the back of her skull. "I'm not firing you."

"Oh." The sound came out on a puff of air. Matthew tilted toward her, and her breath shuddered into her lungs, her whole body tensing even as it eased closer to his.

"Can I kiss you?" he murmured, his eyes already latched on to her mouth. Suddenly, he couldn't remember a time when he didn't want to taste her. She jerked a tiny nod, and he slowly dropped his head, savoring the warmth of her skin under his palms, the anticipation of her soft body under his hands, the heat of her mouth around his tongue.

The reality was infinitely better than the anticipation. Gabby opened to him immediately, coming up against him and wrapping her arms around his back. Matthew sank into her, losing awareness of himself and his surroundings in a way he hadn't in forever. His hands roamed over her body, taut yet womanly, shaped perfectly to mold against him. He maintained enough presence of mind to be careful with her sunburn, but as the kiss went on he got hungrier and hungrier, fueled by her near-frantic response to him.

He slowed the kiss, gentling by degrees, and when he lifted his head he was shocked to see tears trembling on her lashes. "I'm sorry," he said automatically, lifting a finger to brush them away.

"Don't say that, please. Ever." She blinked hard but didn't let go of him. "Matthew, please don't pull away from me. I've—I—"

"I won't." He gripped her waist with his hands so they wouldn't tremble, and stole another kiss. "I want you, Abigail."

"Now?"

The word could have meant a lot of things, but Matthew understood. "Now, and for as long as you'll have me."

Gabby threw herself against him, and Matthew couldn't have explained why he'd resisted this for so long.

WHEN LARK WENT into Jason's room, he tried to pretend she was there to talk about tomorrow. She rolled over that discussion, but he hid in the bathroom, putting away new toiletries, while she waited patiently on his bed. Her conversation with her father had cemented everything for her. Maybe Jason's relationship with her father—and, hell, *her* relationship with her father—and their jobs would doom them. Maybe one of them would die, if not in the next few days, on some other mission or circumstance. But none of that was any different from the obstacles in any other relationship, and Lark couldn't believe how differently the world looked to her now. Instead of her mother's slow decline, she remembered the way her parents had been together. How could she have witnessed that, and not wanted it for herself? There had to be joy to balance the pain.

So she was going for it. All the way. To hell with the consequences. She crushed a spurt of fear as she stood, went into the bathroom, and dragged Jason back out, mouths locked. He had no chance to protest or spout his tired argument. She knew exactly how and where to touch him to make him lose it. And then she played dirty.

Jason loomed over her on the bed, his gorgeous body touching hers from shoulder to ankle. Moans echoed in the room as she stroked him into a frenzy, accompanied by the gasps and cries she couldn't hold back every time he dipped his fingers deeper or pulled a bit of her skin between his teeth. He reached for one of the condoms he'd bought on the grocery run and rolled it on. Lark lifted her hips, knees bent, ready to take him in.

That's when she said, "I love you, Jason."

He convulsed, as if wanting to pull back, but she dug her fingers into his shoulders. He groaned, closed his eyes and thrust deep into her. Sparks shot through her vision, pleasure flooding her body, her heart. She sobbed his name. His face buried in her neck, Jason moved in the rhythm they'd perfected, and Lark lost control, blinded by the sheer ecstasy of the climb. Part of her was aware he hadn't responded, but she hadn't been looking for a response. She'd said what she felt, at what she'd *thought* was the peak of emotion.

She'd been wrong. God, she ached. She pushed her hips up against him, wanting him deeper, wanting to crawl inside his skin. Her right hand gripped his hair, while her left pulled at his hip, his lower back, his ass, trying to get closer, harder. "Oh, God, Jason, I love you." She repeated the words, not sure she was even coherent, and Jason reared back with a shout he tried to muffle. He shuddered and burst, and then pumped into her with short, fast strokes that sent her soaring, shattering into pieces that would never go back together the same.

Neither of them spoke for a long time. Lark held him to her when he tried to roll off, firmly stroking his hair and his back and shoulders, just feeling. She held as tightly to her joy and despair as she held on to him.

Eventually, as they cooled and the air conditioning brought goose bumps up on Lark's skin, Jason maneuvered the covers over them, somehow doing it without letting go of her or moving his face away from her neck and shoulder. She'd just about given up and was about to allow herself to drift into sleep when his hands tightened on her waist and tugged her even closer to his chest before he murmured, "I'm sorry, but I love you, too."

GABBY LAY DRAPED on Matthew's chest, listening to his heart beat and watching the numbers flip on the old alarm clock next to the bed. Matthew's hand stroked her arm, and she rubbed her thigh on top of his.

She'd never been happier in her life. Even if he opened his mouth and said it couldn't happen again. Even if he was taking what was available because he was overwhelmed and lonely, and he didn't really care about her. She didn't care. Nothing could spoil what they'd just shared.

And he didn't say it couldn't happen again. He didn't apologize, or ask if she was okay. He just lay underneath her, holding her close, and breathed.

"Thank you for not starting out with caveats," she finally said when her brain couldn't take it anymore and forced her to speak.

"Hmmm?"

She lifted her head a little. His eyes were closed, but his hand was still moving. "Are you awake?"

His lids lifted slowly, lazily, and he looked so satisfied her heart skipped. "Barely. What did you say?"

"I said thank you for not starting out with caveats." She put her head back down on his chest, this time at a steeper angle so she could breathe him in, taste his skin. "About how you don't know what will happen tomorrow, and the last thing you want is to hurt me, and if I don't want this I can say no, and—"

"I get the picture." He lifted his shoulders off the bed and rolled them both over so she was on her back, looking up at him. His blue eyes burned with emotion, and her tears welled up again.

"It's been a very long time for me, Gabby." He traced his finger down the side of her face and across her mouth. "Both the sex and the emotion." His mouth curved briefly. "One longer than the other. I haven't opened myself to anyone since Kelly died."

"I know," she whispered. "I'm—"

"You're not grateful." There was bite in his tone. "You're deserving. I've been fighting this for a long time, and tonight it just didn't seem worth fighting anymore." He relaxed a little, settling onto his side next to her, propping his head with his arm under the pillow. "I don't know if you realize it, but I avoided coming to the lab as much because of you as because I was ashamed to face Jason."

"Oh, Matthew." Sorrow swirled with happiness she didn't dare allow. She rolled to face him and touched his cheek. "Why?"

"I told myself it was because I didn't want to lead you on, but it was really because I sensed what we could have, and it scared me." His face puckered in a slight frown. "I don't admit to fear well."

"I know." She snuggled closer and braced herself. He'd overcome that fear tonight, but that didn't mean anything for the future. "I want to go with you guys tomorrow."

"You will."

"I will?" She raised her head to stare at him. "No argument? No, 'you're safer here, let the professionals do the hard work'?"

"You're not safer here. Even without knowing who the other people on Isaac's list are, Hummingbird is more secure than my house, and leaving you alone is not an option."

"Thank goodness." She settled back onto the pillow. "I was prepared to stow away in Jason's Range Rover, but I was afraid you'd take the Town Car instead."

Matthew chuckled, his fingers toying with her curls. "We also need you. I want to pull all the RT-24 development data and prepare it to send to the government. If we can get it established before Isaac's plan is complete, we might have ammunition against treason charges. And I want to destroy all the data on Jason."

The doctor in her rebelled at that. "Even if we can't

use it for research purposes, Matthew, I can't destroy his medical file. He's unique. He'll need special treatment for the rest of his life."

"One file, yours, as secure as possible. You'll be his doctor. As well as an attendant at his wedding, I imagine." He grumbled more than stated the latter.

Gabby laughed. "I hope you come around before the wedding," she teased him. "Is he really about to propose?"

He sighed and shifted under the sheet. "No. But if he doesn't soon, Lark will. I don't want to talk about that."

"Okay." Gabby let the subject go. If Matthew was relenting about his daughter, maybe his whole perspective was shifting, and she didn't have to guard against a reversal. "Let's talk about the plan some more, then. I didn't think you'd include me, so I didn't pay full attention before," she admitted.

He kissed her. "From now on," he said, "you're in on everything."

TWENTY-FOUR

LARK DRAGGED HERSELF down to the kitchen at six in the morning, after a quiet but not completely restful night of snuggling, whispering and dozing.

Jason had gotten up and showered before she had, so she wasn't surprised to see him in the kitchen, a mug of coffee ready to hand to her. She *was* surprised to see her father and Gabby giggling over the omelet pan.

"What the—?" She raised her eyebrows at the other couple as she sipped the coffee, then hummed in approval. "Thank you."

"I figured you'd need it. I don't know, they were doing this when I got down here."

Matthew said something in Gabby's ear, his arm around her back. Bubbles rose inside Lark, as if she'd been carbonated. Her father had apparently taken her words to heart. Okay, she didn't want to think about how he and Gabby had spent their night, but he actually looked relaxed and happy, which was exactly what she wanted for him. And now, maybe he'd relax and be happy for her, too.

Still. Did they have to act so gooey? She shuddered and asked, loudly, "When do we leave?"

Her father looked up and grinned. Almost beamed. "About an hour. I reached Kolanko on his cell. He's actually in DC right now and agreed to meet us at the office."

She snitched a piece of bacon from a plate next to the stove. "What did you tell him?"

"Just that I wanted to meet with him, had some things to discuss. He agreed right away."

They'd debated for a long time about where to arrange the meeting. They had no idea how many other staff members had been compromised. Jason had made sure Nils was locked out of the system, but there hadn't been time to notify every employee. But they needed to access the lab, and Matthew and Jason could secure their own domain far better than anyplace else. So Hummingbird it was.

"Was Kolanko suspicious?" Jason asked.

"No. He's been supportive since the explosion. He's grateful for his daughter's life and told me months ago to call him for anything we needed."

"We're all going, right?" Jason moved to the far counter to pour himself another cup of coffee.

"Yes. I need you with Kolanko, and then Gabby can get us into the lab and collect or destroy the data."

It went unsaid—though it hadn't the night before—that Isaac might come after them harder after their escape.

But he wasn't stupid enough to target Hummingbird itself.

"What time is the meeting?" she asked her father.

"Eight o'clock."

"And the strategy?"

"Jason and I will talk to him," Matthew responded. "You and Gabby will sit quietly in my office and not worry your pretty little heads."

He was clearly joking, and laughed when Gabby slugged him in the chest, but Lark couldn't laugh. She hated that Jason would be away from her, that Kolanko could be as much a threat as anyone else. She leaned against the counter and watched everyone else eat, her appetite gone. She realized then that Jason wasn't eating, either, but that he'd downed two glasses of orange juice. She met him at the refrigerator when he pulled out the jug for another refill.

"You okay?"

"Yeah, fine. Why?" He poured only half a glass this time.

"You seem unusually thirsty."

"Nah. It's healthy. Vitamin C will help with the cramps. You know."

She wasn't sure she believed him. She checked her watch and sighed. The sooner they got to Hummingbird, the sooner they could solve the problem and get on with the rest of their lives.

THEY ARRIVED AT Hummingbird half an hour before the meeting time. Matthew went to secure the conference room, while Jason took Lark and Gabby to his office.

"Don't talk to anyone," he cautioned. "Don't go anywhere with anyone or use the phones." He unlocked a cabinet and pulled out four small handheld units that he quickly coded. "Just hit this button in an emergency." He indicated a small red button on the side, and handed one to each of the women. "They're low range, so *stay here,*" he re-stressed. "Once you hit the stairs or elevator, you'll be too far away." Hummingbird had better equipment than this, but it was locked away on another floor, where they set up ops.

There was no time to get to it, and accessing it could tip someone off.

"We'll be fine. We've got Caitlyn out there as our first line of defense." Lark stepped closer and leaned up to kiss his cheek. "Go get this over with. And good luck."

Jason kissed her and gave Gabby's shoulder a reassuring squeeze, then hurried to join Matt in the conference room. Kolanko arrived a few minutes later.

"Mr. Templeton," he boomed in his heavy European accent once the soundproof door closed behind them. "It is a true miracle to see you standing here." He took Jason's hand in both of his and pumped his arm sharply three times. "Welcome back to the living. I owe you so much."

"Thank you, sir. Please, call me Jason. How is Adrina?"

"She is getting better. She had some nightmares, unfortunately. She didn't understand what was happening, but remembers the fear as we ran, and that you fell."

"She saw me?" The possibility hadn't occurred to him. He'd thought they'd been long downstairs by the time he went over the rail, and was horrified that he was causing a child nightmares.

"Not exactly. She heard the noise and looked up, and then others talked about what happened in her hearing. She has had some anxiety, but is overcoming it now. Do not worry, Jason, it is not your fault, and that she lives is due to your skill and dedication. Now, Matthew, let us get to business. I know you are a busy man."

"As are you. We appreciate you meeting with us."

The men sat at the conference table, Matt at one end, Kolanko by the door, Jason at Matt's left hand. They weren't sitting next to each other in a confrontational posture, and all could see each other's faces. It was the best way to indirectly put Kolanko at ease.

"I am happy to be of service in any way I can."

"We're glad to hear that." Matt leaned forward, his arms on the table, his hands folded. "We understand you're working with Isaac Kemmerling."

"But of course. You know this, yes? He is your representative."

That was so not what Jason was expecting to hear, and in his shock, he couldn't help exchanging a glance with Matt. Both faced Kolanko immediately, but the motion had been obvious. The big man sat back, his expression hardening. "What am I missing?"

"Isaac doesn't represent us," Matt explained. "He's a former employee who resigned after censure and has been searching for an opportunity to take revenge on us for three years. The incident at your hotel gave him that opportunity."

Jason listened while Matthew sketched the recent events, just skimming the surface so Kolanko understood what was at stake. The room twisted around him for a second. He blinked hard and waited for a wave of dizziness to pass. He swallowed, and his dry throat caught on itself. He should have brought a bottle of water into the conference room with him. There was a small refrigerator in the corner. He stood and went around the table to it, glad to find a collection of small bottles. He waited until Matt paused, then offered water to the others. Matt declined, but Kolanko accepted graciously, making Jason's actions seem hospitable. But Matt eyed him for a second too long before continuing the recitation.

The water glided down Jason's throat, cold and soothing. Everything seemed to sharpen instantly. There. That was all that was wrong. He needed something to drink. Maybe all the chemicals used on his body put him in greater need of hydration, something the techs hadn't been aware of because he'd been well hydrated in the lab.

He screwed the lid onto his empty bottle and set it aside, refocusing on the conversation.

"We're asking you to tell us everything you can about your dealings with Isaac," Matt was saying. "Anything you can give us to block his intent and, if necessary, testify to the government or in court."

The evenness of Matt's tone revealed the importance of what he was asking, which gave power to Kolanko. Maybe he didn't hear it. After all, Jason had spent a decade learning to read his boss. But the big man looked down at his hands flat on the table, his face in a slight frown, and Jason's heart sank.

He wasn't going to help them.

HER FATHER OWNED an exceptionally high-quality desk chair.

Lark spun in a circle, letting her vision relax to fuzz as the office whirled around her, oriented by a flash of white—Gabby in her lab coat, freshly laundered armor. The doctor sat in a soft armchair on the far side of the office, perusing a law enforcement magazine. Lark, however, was bored. Bored, bored, bored.

Which was really a superficial mask for anxiety. She hated not knowing what was happening, what they'd do after the meeting, how to stop Isaac or keep her father from facing the death penalty.

When her cell phone buzzed in her pocket, she leapt to check it. She needed a distraction, any distraction. The display said "Ralph." Lark wrinkled her nose. Maybe not that much of a distraction.

Feeling guilty for not calling in for so long, and telling herself Jason had meant don't use the *office* phones, she answered.

"Lark Madrassa! Where the hell are you?"

"Ralph."

"Of course it's Ralph! You were supposed to be at work two days ago!"

"I came in Sunday. We talked. You know I had some personal issues to deal with."

"'Had' being the operative term. You missed your appointment at the police station, too. You promised to be here to do inventory and haven't even called in. I've left you six messages at home and on your cell." He ranted on and Lark let him, because she deserved it. But she found she couldn't care. Even his threat to fire her if she didn't show up tomorrow was meaningless in the face of everything else.

Movement outside the office caught her attention, and she watched Caitlyn through the glass. The assistant had looked over her shoulder into the office, Lark was certain of it. Now Caitlyn paused with her hand on the phone, her body still, as if listening hard. After a moment, she picked it up and dialed.

"Gotta go, Ralph." Lark hung up her cell and waved Gabby over as she picked up her father's extension. She hit a few buttons to conference herself in and angled the receiver for Gabby to listen, too. The line was ringing, and they could hear Caitlyn's breathing while she waited.

Gabby nudged Lark until the computer monitor hid their posture, then snatched a piece of paper and wrote, "Can she hear us?"

Lark nodded and cupped her hand over the receiver without touching it. Gabby held still, her mouth pressed together as if to keep herself from talking.

"Hello?"

Lark and Gabby exchanged knowing looks. It was Nils.

"Hi, it's me," Caitlyn said.

"What," Nils barked, not even making it a question.

"They're here."

His response was a little less rude this time. "Who, they?"

"All of them. Matt and JT are meeting with Kolanko." Nils swore, but Caitlyn continued, "Lark and the doctor are in his office."

Gabby straightened just as Caitlyn turned. She pretended to study something on the monitor, then looked up at Caitlyn and smiled. The assistant returned it with a tiny curve of her mouth and turned back around. Gabby immediately crouched to listen again.

"Hang on," Nils said, and the phone rasped and rumbled. He probably held it against his stomach. They could make out a few words, but nothing they could put together. Caitlyn heaved a big sigh.

"Okay." Nils came back on the line. "Keep them all there. Madrassa and Templeton are in the soundproof conference room?"

"Yes."

"How long?"

"It's only been about ten minutes. I expect it to be a while longer."

"Isaac and I will be right there. Let us in. We'll make Berwell take us to the lab and get the data we need."

Caitlyn agreed and hung up. Lark waited until the receiver was down before hanging up herself. Panic fluttered around disbelief in the pit of her stomach. Caitlyn had worked for her father for years. She'd been so wonderful at the funeral. How could she do this?

"What do we do?" Gabby looked stricken, but shifted so Caitlyn couldn't see her face if she turned around again. "We should tell Matthew and Jason."

"No." Lark forced herself not to stand up and pace, alerting Caitlyn. She tried to think like Jason and her father. Isaac was actually coming here, himself. They could catch him in the act, the most effective way to stop him from achieving what he wanted to do. "We can't do anything to let Caitlyn and Isaac know we know," she said. "The phone lines are probably compromised, so we can't call into the conference room."

"Use your cell phone," Gabby said.

She tried, but her father's line didn't even ring. She didn't know if the soundproofing interfered with his signal, if he'd turned off the phone, or if someone—like maybe Kolanko—was jamming it.

Gabby pulled the handheld unit Jason had given her out of her lab coat pocket. "We can just do this."

Lark chewed her lip. She was getting nauseous with the desperation to act and trying hard to appear normal. "They'll come running, and it could ruin everything with Kolanko." She checked her watch. "Maybe they'll be done before Isaac and Nils get here. We'll save that as a last res—put it away," she hissed in a whisper as Caitlyn rose from her desk and crossed on her fancy high heels to the office door, the glossy drape of her dress swaying gracefully. Lark hated everything about her. She couldn't even see the efficient, caring assistant anymore.

"Can I get you girls anything?" she asked, leaning through the doorway. "Something to drink or eat?"

You'd probably poison it. "No, thanks," Lark told her. "We ate."

"Okay. Holler if you need anything. Oh, I have today's paper out here if you want to read it."

"Sure."

Lark waited impatiently while the assistant returned to her desk, gathered the loose sections of the *Washington Post,* and came back to the office. Gabby accepted the paper and carried it to the sitting area where she'd been before. Lark checked her watch, her heart sinking.

They were running out of time.

MATTHEW WATCHED JASON'S eyes close for a three-second count. It was at least the fourth time that had happened, and he'd gotten a second water bottle for himself though Kolanko hadn't finished half his first.

"When did Isaac first contact you, sir?" Jason asked, sounding mostly normal except for a slight rasp no one else would notice.

"A month ago. He claimed to be working for Hummingbird, and told me about your amazing recovery. He said you were seeking a buyer for the RT-24 regenerative compound."

"Did he say why we wanted a buyer?" Matthew

didn't get it. Kolanko was a smart man. He should have been suspicious of such a sale.

"He said FDA requirements were too much of a hindrance and it would be unprofitable for you to develop it in this country."

"Did he tell you it could be used to hurt people?" Jason asked.

"No!" Kolanko looked surprised, then thoughtful. "Of course, it makes sense. There are complications, no?" He didn't wait for confirmation. "If the formula could be intensified to increase those complications, make them the intended outcome…yes, now I understand."

"Understand what?" Matthew's spine stiffened.

"Mr. Kemmerling has at least four other potential buyers. He would not reveal their names, or who they represented, but I like to know against whom I am bidding. I learned two of the identities, but they were not who I would have guessed. Now I understand why."

Matthew folded his hands together and pressed them to his mouth. Isaac had no intention of selling to Kolanko, he was pretty certain of that. His inclusion in the buyer list was just another bit of explosive being primed to take down Hummingbird. Kolanko had been the company's biggest supporter after the incident. If he was revealed to be a potential buyer for something that could be used in acts against the United States, his credibility would be toast, and Hummingbird would crumble a little more.

Jason laid out their requests, for Kolanko to go to the FBI and tell them about Isaac's plan, and to testify if need be, but the man shook his head.

"I cannot see a good end for any of us, my friends.

Going to the FBI will only incriminate myself, and thus far I have an unblemished relationship with your government. Why do you not go to them yourselves?"

"We have no solid evidence," Matthew admitted. "Not to mention the questionable circumstances of Jason's survival."

"This isn't just about us." Jason's rasp had deepened, and he cleared his throat. "Lark and Dr. Berwell have a lot to lose, as well. If Matthew is found guilty—"

"I understand, Mr. Templeton. But your daughter," he addressed Matthew, "is a grown woman who has suffered tragedy in the past. She has, how is it described, coping skills? I have my Adrina to consider. She is a small child, who has suffered much at the hands of her own mother. I could not allow her to face the trials of a father under suspicion." He stood and squared his shoulders.

"I'm sorry, my friends. I wish you well. But my answer must be no."

TWENTY-FIVE

"IS THERE A way to get out of here without Caitlyn knowing?" Gabby flipped a page of the Local section of the *Post* while Lark paced in the three square feet that were out of Caitlyn's sight.

"Not directly."

Gabby waited, but Lark didn't say anything else. With a deep breath, Gabby finished the pep talk she'd been giving herself for the last five minutes. *You've been growing a spine for days. Now is the time to use it.*

"Okay, here's the plan."

Lark stopped on the spot. "Shoot."

The younger woman's eager acceptance took Gabby aback, but she rallied. "We pretend we have to use the bathroom. You're going to show me where it is because I've never used the one up here. That will get us by Caitlyn. We'll sneak to the conference room and tell them you're sick, so one of them will come out. Then we can tell them what's going on."

"What if we can't get in?" Lark asked.

Gabby was ready. "Then we go down to the lab to get rid of all the data before Isaac gets here."

Lark winced. "Destroy it? All of it?"

"All but Jason's most crucial medical file. He'll need that, especially because of the immunity issues."

Lark gasped. Gabby stopped speaking.

"Oh, no," Lark moaned. "I can't believe— I wasn't paying attention."

"What?" Gabby's heart leaped into her throat. Had he lied to her the night before? Or just been unaware, maybe. But he *knew* the risks. The danger. "What is it?"

"Nothing." Lark dropped her hand from her head to her hip and shook her head hard, a classic posture of denial. "He drank a lot of juice this morning, but I'm sure that's nothing. Now, what about destroying the records?"

Gabby wavered, but she couldn't get to Jason right this second. He'd be okay for a short while longer. They'd get through the next hour, then she'd treat him. She had everything she needed downstairs.

"If the data is all gone there's nothing to sell and nothing for the prosecution to use as evidence," she explained.

"What about continuing the research?"

For a moment Gabby hesitated, mourning the potential loss of everything they'd gained. But it wasn't the end. They would just have to start over, and if they did it once, they could do it again, this time following proper procedure. But Lark looked heartbroken. Gabby moved to her side. "I'm sorry. I know how important it is to you, finding these treatments. But—"

"I know." Lark patted her hand where it rested on her shoulder. "Destroying lives isn't worth those it might save." She didn't appear to completely believe that, but she took a deep breath and nodded. "Okay. One problem. We don't have a key to the lab."

Gabby held up her ID card. Lark raised her eyebrows.

"I keep it in a buttoned pocket when I'm not in the building. Nils took my purse when they accosted me at the station, obviously assuming that's where I kept my card. They didn't search me well, I guess. Isaac demanded the card, but didn't argue when I told him it had been in my purse. I've kept it with me since we got away."

"Incompetents," Lark snorted. "Let's go."

They headed out into the reception area, breezing by Caitlyn's desk.

"Where are you going?" the woman asked, jumping up.

"Bathroom," Lark said. "Gabby needs it, I'm showing her where it is."

"Too much coffee this morning." Gabby gave the frazzled, nervous grin-and-dip that was part of her usual demeanor, and Caitlyn bought it. She sank back down onto her chair.

They moved at a normal pace down the hall, though Gabby wanted to run. She jerked the lapels of her lab coat, feeling better when it settled into place.

"How did you know how to do the phone thing, anyway?" she asked Lark.

"Figured it out somehow, years ago. Hi, Ted," she greeted an agent they passed. Gabby smiled at another, a woman she'd never met. Every person they encountered was a possible threat, a potential obstacle, even a non-Isaac one. Isaac had gotten to Matthew's most trusted staff person, Caitlyn. That meant he could have gotten to anyone.

"I used to listen when I knew Dad was talking to a teacher or something. He had a hard time getting to conferences at school, so he did them over the phone."

"Thank God he did," Gabby said, slowing her pace. She'd started to hurry too much.

They passed a large room full of cubicles, all the visible agents with their heads bent over paperwork or talking on the phone. It was weird that normal work continued, that most of these employees had no idea what had been happening over the last few days.

They made it to the bathroom and Lark sagged against the door in relief. "Step one done. Now the conference room."

"Wait." Gabby swung all the stall doors inward, making sure they were empty. "I'd better go to the bathroom for real. I did have too much coffee."

"Hurry. I'll keep watch." Lark cracked the door to peer out into the hallway. Gabby took thirty seconds, plus a few more to wash her hands, and hurried to the door. Lark flung it open.

And found Caitlyn blocking their way.

MATTHEW ARGUED WITH Kolanko for several minutes, Jason backing him up. They told him he'd be a good role model for his beloved daughter, doing the right thing and standing up for his principles. That Adrina would be well taken care of, because he was a smart man with contingency plans. That he was an ethical man and couldn't live with himself if Matthew got the death penalty and he could have prevented it.

Nothing changed his mind.

"You know," he said peevishly, "when your assistant contacted me to arrange that first meeting with Isaac—"

"What?" Matthew and Jason said together.

"My assistant?" Matthew added, the sting of betrayal overpowering even his growing desperation.

"Yes. She called my secretary."

"What was her name?" Matthew wouldn't jump to conclusions. Someone could have pretended to be his assistant.

But Kolanko dashed that hope immediately. "Caitlyn. I recognized her voice—she has a lovely, smooth voice, not easily mimicked," he said, obviously understanding what Matthew was looking for. "And my software identified the number as a direct call from Hummingbird, your office. We track these things as carefully as you do."

"Caitlyn's the missing plus one," Matthew said to Jason as he surged to his feet. "The one on the list. The girls are with her."

"Don't let them hear you call them girls." But he already had the door open. They raced down the hall, Kolanko huffing behind them. Matthew, lighter than Jason, passed him on a curve and knocked into an agent coming the other way.

"Sorry!" he yelled back. He had no idea who the person was. All his focus was on the reception area ahead of him. The empty reception area. Caitlyn wasn't there. He didn't stop, wrenching open the door to his office even though he could clearly see it was empty. Jason came in behind him, and Matthew turned in a circle, his hands thrusting into his hair as if to hold his head on. He locked on to Jason, who was as wild-eyed and frantic-looking as Matthew felt.

"We lost them."

"Ow. Stop it." Gabby tried to wrench her arm out of Caitlyn's grip, but the woman only pinched tighter. She dragged Gabby out of the elevator, not looking back to see if Lark followed. Of course, Lark did. Gabby didn't have to look, either, to know it. The detonator in Caitlyn's hand, the one with the button mashed down by her thumb, ensured it. She'd told them there was a small block of plastic explosive molded to the conference room table, just enough to blow the entire room to smithereens. All three men would also be in bits and pieces, and maybe a couple of innocent agents on the other side of the wall, the bitch had told them with glee.

"My father would have checked," Lark had said, trying to call her bluff, but Caitlyn only grinned.

"I did it after he cleared the room, when I stocked the fridge. He has no reason to doubt me."

So here they were, in the hallway outside the deserted lab. Gabby lamented giving everyone the day off so they wouldn't be around when she came to destroy the data. If there had been techs down here as normal, that would have put a crimp in Caitlyn and Isaac's plans. But, she immediately reconsidered, at least now there weren't more people in danger.

"Stay right there." Caitlyn swung Gabby around to slam her back against the wall. Gabby let her, trying to act the way she would have acted a week ago when confronted by this situation. It was her one advantage.

While she acted meek and frightened, Lark lunged and backhanded Caitlyn on the cheek. The woman staggered, then flung up the hand holding the detonator.

"Are you crazy?" she screeched. "Do you want your father blown up?"

"You're out of range," Lark scoffed, advancing on

the taller woman. "That kind of detonator has to be within a hundred yards of the receiver."

"Unless you boost the signal with this, you stupid bitch." Caitlyn turned the detonator to show a small box on the back. Lark froze. "Now stand over there next to your smart friend while I make a call." She sidestepped to the in-house phone on the wall next to the lab door. She didn't take her eyes off the two women while she dialed a three-digit extension.

"Hi, sweetie, it's me. How are you?" She simpered and giggled while exchanging endearments and promises with whoever was on the other line. It was a marked contrast to the glittering malice in her eyes and her threatening posture. "Listen, baby, Isaac Kemmerling and Nils Fredlund are on their way. Let them in, would you? I'll take the west elevator up to meet them. Oh, and baby? Tonight, I'll let you do that thing you've been wanting to do to me." She laughed far back in her throat, and Gabby had no doubt what it was doing to the guy on the other end of the line.

She sighed and leaned against the wall, disgusted that her fate was in the hands of a horny moron.

JASON PRETENDED HE didn't notice that Matt was at a complete loss, uselessly turning in the center of his office. He clamped down on his own fear. One of them had to keep his head. He grabbed the phone on Matt's desk and started to dial security downstairs, but hesitated, then hit the button for the call log. His eyebrows lifted when he saw the code for conferencing in to Caitlyn's extension.

The line downstairs buzzed twice.

"Front desk," an unfamiliar voice answered the phone.

"This is Jason Templeton. Have you seen Lark Madrassa or Dr. Berwell in the last half hour?"

"Yes, sir, they just left."

"Did they sign out? Were they alone?"

"It was just the two of them, yes sir, and they did sign out." But there was a catch in the guy's voice. Jason didn't believe him. He motioned for Matt to check Caitlyn's phone. "They didn't say where they were going, sir."

Jason hit the mouse to turn off the screensaver on Matt's computer. The officer had offered information he wasn't asked for, and his voice had gone high. "Has anyone else come in?" He opened the security program and found the log for the front door.

"No, sir, just employees."

The guard's voice was still high, and the system showed the front door had been opened from inside. The electronic sign-out register showed no one leaving, least of all Lark or Gabby. The guard must have let someone in. Dammit.

Jason thanked him and hung up. He went out to Caitlyn's desk.

"She made a call to an unregistered number," Matt told him. "I dialed it. Nils."

"I think they might still be here. The guard lied to me, and someone came in a few minutes ago."

Matt looked torn. "One of us needs to go secure the guard."

Jason nodded. They couldn't leave the entire building's security compromised. But Lark's safety, and Gabby's, were paramount.

"The other can go to the lab," Matt continued. "It's the logical place. The data is down there, and they need Gabby to access it." He gripped Jason's forearm for a moment, then froze, his gaze flying to Jason's face. "You're hot."

"Thanks, but you're not my type."

"No, I mean you're feverish." He released him and cursed. "You need treatment. Fuck! Why didn't you say something? The simplest—"

"Matt." Jason put a hand on his friend's chest, halting him when he would have shoved Jason out the door, intent on locking him in a sterile chamber. "We don't have time for this. We need to get to Gabby and Lark."

Matt swore again, pacing away from Jason and then back. "All right. Let's get this done fast. I'm not letting you die again."

"I don't plan to try. Let's go."

They parted in the main hall after a fast round of rock-paper-scissors, leaving Kolanko standing at the reception desk, looking lost.

LARK WOULD GIVE anything to know if Caitlyn was bluffing about the detonator. She watched the betraying bitch carefully, but her thumb never let up on the button. She had to have a cramp by now, but never shifted her grip or switched hands. She was in complete—and smug—control, standing with no excess movement, her eyes alertly watching both Lark and Gabby, not letting them get too far apart and split her attention.

"Who did you call? Front desk?" Lark asked, figuring keeping her talking would at least pass the time and help keep herself from going crazy.

Caitlyn's heavily lipsticked mouth curved into an even more smug smile, and her thick lashes fluttered a little. "We've been having sex on his break, at lunch, and occasionally at night. It's amazing what you can get a guy to do when you're willing to…experiment."

"Ew." Lark made a face. "We don't need details, thanks." She wasn't sure how to interpret Caitlyn's easy offering of information. Was she just bragging because she was stupid? Or did she think Lark and Gabby wouldn't be a threat later?

Caitlyn shrugged. "It doesn't hurt that he's married. Doesn't want the stupid cow to know. He'd have to pay alimony and child support, since she's a stay-at-home mom." The phone next to her buzzed and she lifted it immediately. "Yes? Great. We'll be right there." She hung up the phone and waved the detonator like a gun, toward the elevator. "Back up. We're getting the guys."

Lark wished she meant Jason and Matthew. A lot of stuff her father had taught her over the years—like, amazingly, the range of certain electronics—seemed to be surfacing from the recesses of her brain, now that she needed it. But her father and Jason were better equipped to overpower the stupid assistant. Plus, if they were here, they wouldn't be in the rigged conference room, and *she* could overpower the stupid assistant.

But of course, when the elevator doors opened to the lobby, Isaac and Nils crowded inside. Caitlyn made Gabby swipe her card again, and back down they went.

Isaac didn't speak to any of them, but Nils apparently couldn't resist lording his superior position over Lark.

"Hey there, sweetheart. Bet you're surprised to see me."

"Not really," she said in as bored a voice as she could muster, watching the numbers light up overhead so he couldn't see the hatred burning in her eyes. "I saw you drive by Ella's hotel yesterday." She cast a quick glance his way, satisfied to see his face fall.

"Well, I bet you wanna know how I got out of that barn," he rallied.

"No."

"Shut up, Nils," Caitlyn said. "You're pathetic."

"Hey, I'm the right hand here, precious. You're just the assistant."

"Both of you, get a grip." Isaac stepped out of the elevator and raked disgusted looks down both of his henchpeople. "I can't believe you were the best I could come up with."

Caitlyn's cheek flickered with the clenching of her jaw. Isaac did have the best. Caitlyn had access to all Matthew's logs, schedules, information and possibly his computer. Nils was a blender, floating from department to department without notice. Isaac had chosen his infiltrators well. Lark wondered if praising him for it would get her anywhere.

They filed into the lab at Isaac's instruction. Lark cast around for something to do, some means of reversing their situation, but had no idea how to take back the advantage. Resignation settled over her. Cooperation seemed the best way to keep them all from harm, at least for now.

Isaac pointed to Lark, then to a chair at a long, low

table in the middle of the room. “Sit there. Wait.” He pinned Nils with a glare. “Can you handle her?”

“Of course.” He lifted his hand and clicked the trigger of a contact-model Taser, which arced with blue electricity. Lark rolled her eyes but sat as directed, hoping Gabby was up to whatever came next.

Sure enough, Isaac addressed the doctor. “I want the data on the RT-24 and Templeton’s condition. Can you access it out here?”

“No. Only in my office.”

Good job, Gabby. She was dividing the enemy. Lark didn’t think Isaac would want to crowd them all into that tiny room. And while Gabby’s voice had quivered the tiniest bit, and she vibrated with pure nervousness, Lark saw steel in her eyes and in the straightness of her spine.

“Let’s go.” Isaac nudged Gabby toward her office. “Caitlyn, put that ridiculous thing down and go watch the elevator. Let me know if someone starts to come down.”

Caitlyn smirked and dropped the apparently fake detonator into a metal trash can. Lark flinched at the clang.

“Should have trusted your instincts, chippie.” Caitlyn sashayed out the door, pausing to block it open with the trash can. Lark squeezed her fists and half rose to go after her, but the distinctive click of a hammer cocking made her freeze.

Isaac smirked and pointed a pistol at Gabby’s head. Lark sank back down, furious.

“Well, now.” Nils pulled a chair on wheels over next to Lark. “Just the two of us. How fun.”

Lark, who was sitting in a stationary chair, kicked

the seat of Nils's wheeled one. Nils flailed, knocking a tray of flasks to the floor and hitting two other chairs before he managed to stop. He scowled as he pulled his chair back, halting out of her reach. "Don't do that again."

"Wouldn't dream of it." Lark slumped, folding her arms and scowling toward Gabby and Isaac. They'd left the door open, and she could hear the argument between them.

"I want it now, Abigail!"

"You can threaten me all you want, Kemmerling, but I can't make it happen any faster. It's all encrypted. I can give you the compressed, encrypted file if you want."

"No." Lark could practically hear his teeth grind from here. "The encrypted file does me no good, as it will self-destruct when I try to unencrypt it. I'm not stupid, you know."

"Then you have to wait."

"How long?"

Gabby typed on the keyboard. When she kept going and didn't answer, Isaac gripped her shoulder, squeezing until she cried out. "How long?"

"I'm trying to figure that out. Have some patience!"

"Yeah, right," Lark muttered.

"Shut up." Nils sparked the Taser at her a second time. Lark snorted but didn't speak again.

They sat that way for several minutes. Nils got fidgety, playing with tools and supplies on the table, shifting his feet, then rolling his chair around and around the room, feinting at Lark as if to keep her on edge.

She couldn't have been less intimidated. Isaac

scared her because he was losing, which meant he'd be desperate. Nils was still just doing a job.

"I'm bored," Nils called, shoving his chair backward until he came even with Lark again. "We don't need this one, right? She's superfluous. Can I kill her?"

"No." Isaac responded without looking away from the computer screen or keyboard. Gabby sat, watching something on the screen, her hands poised over the keys. "We need her for insurance in case Madrassa catches wind of our presence."

Nils groaned. "But I'm boooorrred. Can I have some fun with her, then?"

"Be my guest."

He grinned and lunged at Lark, but she swung her arm to block and direct his away. Then she thrust the heel of her hand into his chin, just hard enough to knock him back onto his chair.

His face darkened with rage. "You'll pay for that." This time he went for her leg, managing to get half a zap on her. It wasn't a full charge, but still made her leg jerk. She slid, limp, to the floor. Furious, she struggled to get up. Nils grabbed the back of her collar and dragged her to a closet in the corner.

"I'll be in here," he called out. "Don't interrupt if you need me!" His voice was gleeful with anticipation, and Lark gritted her teeth. No frickin' way this idiot was going to take advantage of her.

She waited until he latched the door behind him, then came up swinging. Her right leg shook, so she balanced on her left and threw two quick punches. One sent the Taser flying. The other connected with Nils's eye.

He screeched and lashed out, connecting with her upper arm and rib cage. The pain was no match for the adrenaline racing through her bloodstream, though. She ripped a clump of hair from his head and grabbed him by the nostrils, and he went down squealing. She kicked him with her jiggly foot and he dropped the rest of the way to the floor, unconscious.

Lark stood panting a moment, getting her bearings. Her entire focus had been on Nils and this tiny space, but now she heard a commotion outside. Her suddenly shaky fingers fumbled the door lock. A sob of frustration and fear escaped her before she got it open. She burst out of the room and halted, the rush of blood in her ears keeping her off balance.

Caitlyn stood by the office door, looking frightened. Isaac yelled something at her, but she didn't move. Gabby pounded at the keyboard, the screen flashing so fast Lark had no idea what was going by.

And Jason, beautiful, furious Jason, roared across the room toward Isaac.

The rest happened fast. Caitlyn screamed and reached for something to throw. Lark ran over and backhanded her across the face again, this time hard. The woman crashed against the counter, hit her head on the cabinets above it, and fell to the floor. A gun went off, and Gabby cried out. Lark cringed and spun in time to see Jason leap at Isaac. The weapon flashed again, the report not registering in Lark's ringing ears. Jason wrested the gun from Isaac's hand but gasped for air before he went down to one knee next to Gabby, who clutched her left arm just above the elbow.

Lark opened her mouth to scream.

TWENTY-SIX

MATTHEW FOUND EXACTLY what he'd expected at the front desk. The officer was sweating before he got there, and hastily wiped his forehead with his sleeve when he saw his boss coming.

"Good morning, sir." He stood and nodded at Matthew. "I just spoke to Mr. Templeton, sir. Did you want to see the register?" He reached for the signature unit, but Matthew shook his head.

"I've seen it. I want you to tell me what's going on. What did Caitlyn tell you to do?"

"I don't know what you mean, sir." He started to lift his arm, spotted the stained sleeve, and reconsidered wiping more sweat with it. A drop coalesced and dripped down the side of his face as he stuck his thumbs into his waistband and thrust out his chest.

"Drop the act. I know you've been having sex with Caitlyn. I let it go because as stupid as it was, I didn't think it had anything to do with me. I was wrong, wasn't I?"

The officer's bravado faded. "Uh, sorry, sir, yes, I'm...involved with her. But—"

"And what did she tell you to do?"

A light flashed on the console, accompanied by an urgent beep. The officer lunged for it, cursing. Matthew cursed harder and pushed through the swinging door into the circular station. The light indicated a gun had been fired somewhere in the building.

The officer typed frantically at the computer, backing up when he'd brought up the security camera image that corresponded to the alert. It was the lab.

"Oh, God, oh, God, I didn't know, I didn't mean it, I just…oh, God."

"Tell me what is going on," Matthew ground out. There was no one on the screen, but scattered tools and broken glass indicated *something* had gone down.

The guard couldn't tear his eyes from the screen. He babbled frantically, "I let Kemmerling and Fredlund in. They met Caitlyn at the elevator. Dr. Berwell and Ms. Madrassa, I think, were in the elevator with her. They must have—oh, God."

"Shut up." Cold from his brain to his gut, Matthew picked up the phone and hit a button. He pulled cuffs from the officer's belt and secured his right wrist, and started speaking as soon as an agent picked up.

"Allison, I need an officer at the front desk immediately. Two of them. One to staff the desk, the other to take someone into custody. And call the police. Tell them there's been a gun fired on the premises, they're to enter the main lobby and wait for me." He hung up, pulled the officer's belt off him, and flung it across the lobby floor after removing the pistol from the holster. Then he dragged him to a pillar, wrapped his arms around it, and secured the other cuff. "Wait here."

Then he took off for the lab.

"OHMYGODOHMYGODOHMYGOD." LARK HAD controlled her scream but couldn't stop saying "ohmyGod" as she stumbled across the floor to Jason and Gabby, barely noticing Isaac run out into the hallway. She went to Jason first. He was on one knee, the opposite hand wrapped around the gun he'd wrested from Isaac and braced against the floor while he tried to get his breath. Lark tried to pull him upright, looking for blood on his chest or arms or legs or anywhere and not finding any.

"Gabby," he wheezed. "Gabby's been shot."

"It's okay." But the doctor's voice was weak. "My monitor got it worse."

Sure enough, the computer monitor's glass was shattered and faint smoke curled up from the unit. Lark dismissed it and tried to check Gabby's arm without looking away from Jason. Panic still struggled to choke her, numbing her hands and fuzzing her brain.

"What's wrong, Jase? Please, tell me."

"He's sick," Gabby whispered. "I knew it. I thought so yesterday. But he denied it."

"I'm okay," Jason muttered. "Just ran down all the stairs. Not in shape."

Everyone in the room knew that was a lie. Lark touched his forehead. It practically scorched her fingers. He jerked away and dragged himself to his feet.

"You need—" Gabby started.

"I need to go after Isaac."

"He's trapped," Lark said, shifting to Gabby's side when Jason didn't keel over. "He doesn't have a card. He can't operate the elevator or get to the stairs."

"I know. But he's smart. If I don't go after him, he could get into the ventilation system or the wiring shafts and work his way into a less secure area. Take care of Gabby," he told Lark. "The sooner I find him, the sooner you can take care of me." He disappeared into the hallway.

Lark stood, torn, while Gabby bled at her feet and Jason staggered after a healthy opponent. Then Gabby let out a small moan, and she crouched next to her.

"How bad is it?" Lark made her lie down on the floor and raise her arm in the air. She grabbed a cushion off a chair and an extremely thick book—the *Physicians' Desk Reference,* it said on the front—and propped Gabby's feet on them.

"I don't think the bullet went through," Gabby said, sounding a little stronger. "It hit me at a weird angle."

"Okay." Lark pulled the belt from Gabby's lab coat. "Can I wrap this around it?"

The doctor nodded. "That should work." She let go of the wound, which oozed blood at a much slower rate than Lark had expected. She relaxed a little and quickly wrapped the belt around the wound, folding the lab coat's sleeve over it as a bandage to absorb the blood and help provide pressure.

"Jason's sick, Lark."

"I know." She stood and grabbed the phone, dialing for an outside line, then 9-1-1.

"I mean really sick. He has immunity issues."

"I know, my father told me." She wanted to cover Gabby's mouth, because every time she talked the voice in the back of Lark's head got louder. The one crying that this was just like her mother, killed by a flu that would have been nothing to most other people.

"Hello," she said to the dispatcher who answered. She shoved the voice as far back as she could, and relayed her request for an ambulance. "She's in an inaccessible area, so if we're not in the lobby, just wait. I'll get her up to you."

"We've already dispatched police to that address, ma'am. Are you in immediate danger?"

"I'm not, but other people are. Send more." She hung up and stepped over Gabby, starting to crouch to figure out how to get her upstairs.

"No!"

Lark recoiled at Gabby's shout. "I need—"

"You *need* to go after Jason," she insisted, feeding Lark's rising urgency. "He's sick, weak, and facing a strong, healthy enemy. Don't you get it, Lark? He needs help. He probably can't handle Isaac himself, and if he's not treated immediately, he'll die!"

JASON STALKED DOWN the hallway, listening hard to the dead silence. At least, to what silence he could hear over the ringing in his ears, residual effect of the gunshots. The fluorescent lighting flickered overhead, making his vision blur. He blinked and squinted. His arms holding his pistol up vibrated slightly, and a new full-body ache had joined the party.

Great time to admit he was really sick.

Think, Templeton. Isaac had never been down here before, as far as they all knew. Even if he'd somehow obtained access to the building plans, he still had to figure out what was where. Every door down here was kept locked, except the bathrooms.

Jason headed toward that end of the hall, listening hard. Every door he passed was latched tight, which didn't mean Isaac wasn't in there but cut the odds a little. Now the question was which bathroom should he check first? Habit would send most people to the bathroom they're used to going into. Was Isaac good enough to override that, on the run, and go into the ladies' room?

Jason bet he was and eased carefully through that door, which he held until it silently met the jamb. A faucet dripped, and the lights hummed. There was otherwise no other sound, and no quality of waiting that he could detect. Still, he checked all the stalls and the janitorial closet before leaving the room. The ceiling was solid, not acoustical tiles. Isaac hadn't gone up there.

The men's room was different. Isaac had either not overcome habit, or anticipated Jason's expectations. This time there was no humming or dripping, but the air was too still. He could feel Isaac holding his breath.

No sooner had Jason detected his presence than Isaac burst through the first stall door. It didn't slam into him, but did catch his gun hand and send the weapon clattering across the floor.

He recovered, blocking Isaac's first punch and ducking the second, but the other man landed a blow on the side of his head. His vision blurred again, the ringing in his ears almost unbearable, but he couldn't succumb. Lark and Gabby were out there, vulnerable, and everyone's future hinged on Jason capturing Isaac *now.* He swung and his fist connected with something cloth-covered. Isaac grunted but landed another hit. Furious at his weakness, Jason tapped his rage. Where was his bionic strength now?

He grabbed Isaac by the back of the neck and swung him toward the sink, intending to smack his head on it. Isaac slipped and landed on the floor, immediately sweeping Jason's feet. Jason hit the ground flat on his back. The air whooshed out of his lungs and sparkly, colorful dots filled his vision. The door banged open and Isaac's footsteps went out into the hall.

It took far too many seconds for Jason to drag air in through his nose, roll over and push to his feet. He found his weapon and staggered to the door, bracing himself as he opened it.

But he wasn't prepared enough. As he swung around the doorjamb into the hall, he registered a red blur and pure, malicious glee on Isaac's face as he drove the end of a fire extinguisher into Jason's chest.

LARK WASTED PRECIOUS seconds arguing with Gabby, not wanting to leave her with Nils and Caitlyn, no matter how unconscious they were. Gabby insisted she'd be fine—she could hide in her office and they'd think everyone had left. Lark hesitated, watching blood stain the white fabric of the lab coat.

But the heat of determination in Gabby's eyes convinced her. She went around the table and grabbed Nils's Taser before she raced out into the empty hallway. She stopped again, listening. They could be anywhere. But muffled thumps and what could be grunts came from the end of the hall. She headed that way, startled when the men's room door opened and Isaac emerged, alone. Lark ducked into the intersecting hallway.

"Stupid," she muttered under her breath. He'd seen her. She expected him to come right after her. But he didn't. There was silence again, eerie and taut in the too-bright hallway. Lark took a deep breath, made sure the Taser was ready, and whirled around the corner. Isaac stood in the hall, holding a fire extinguisher. Lark hesitated, confused—there was no sign of flames, and he wasn't moving. Then the bathroom door opened again and she understood. She started running, breath filling her lungs to yell a warning, but too late. Jason emerged, gun first, but far too close to Isaac. He drove the end of the extinguisher into Jason's chest. Jason went down, worse than being Tasered, his entire body limp.

Lark screamed. Isaac spun, but instead of attacking her, he ran to the end of the hall and hammered the extinguisher against the stairwell door, trying to open it. Lark skidded to the floor next to Jason, her breath sobbing now, not sure what to do, what to check first. She ripped open his shirt. His chest looked odd, a curved purple bruise already forming but also a spot of concavity, as if…she touched it gently, not wanting to press.

"Oh, God, no." Gabby appeared, collapsing beside Lark. She was pale and holding her wounded arm. "He got hit in the chest?"

"Fire extinguisher." Lark spread her hand across the center of his chest. "What do I do?"

"Does he have a pulse?"

Lark pressed her fingers to his neck while Gabby pressed the fingers of her good hand to his wrist. They shook their heads in unison. Lark rose up on her knees, automatically getting in position to do CPR, but Gabby pulled her back.

"We can't do CPR if his sternum is fractured. Get the AED. Other end of the hall."

Lark jumped up and sped to the other end. The defibrillator hung in a box next to the elevator. She wrenched at it fruitlessly until she realized it lifted off its bracket. The run back seemed endless, her legs heavy as if she were running through water. At the far end of the hall, Isaac still worked to get away, apparently not considering Gabby and Lark a threat since Jason was incapacitated. And dammit, he was right.

"Here." Lark finally reached Jason and Gabby and dropped to the floor again.

"You have to do it. Open the cover."

Lark pressed the button and flipped off the plastic cover. Underneath were flat adhesive pads connected to a cable. She automatically checked that the cable was plugged in, and pressed the "on" button. A computerized voice told her to place the pads as illustrated.

For a moment nothing made sense to Lark. Panic made it impossible for her to act. The realization that Jason was dying should have galvanized her, but instead it paralyzed. She stared at the diagram, helpless.

She was going to be alone.

Then Gabby slapped her.

Everything snapped into place, and a deep calm descended over her. Later, she'd be embarrassed and filled with self-loathing. Right now, she was going to save the man she loved.

"God, I hope." She quickly peeled the backing off the negative pad and pressed it to the upper right side of Jason's chest, and put the positive pad on the lower left side. "The ambulance and paramedics should be upstairs," she told Gabby. "Go get them."

The doctor was smarter than Lark had been. She went without a word. The uneven click of her shoes on the linoleum told Lark of her slow progress, and she had to fight the urge to go instead. Gabby had only one arm—she couldn't help Jason by herself.

Lark pressed the "analyze" button and waited, ignoring the continued bangs and curses coming from Isaac's end of the hall. "Come on, come on." She was about to scream with frustration when the display flashed "shock" and she hit the button, tears running down her face at the effect on Jason's body.

"Administer CPR," the machine told her, and Lark actually wrung her hands. She couldn't compress a broken chest, probably shouldn't have used the AED on him, since the inside of the cover had a warning label with the line, "Do Not Use On Trauma Patients" screaming up at her in red letters. Uncertain what else to do, she pressed the "analyze" button again. It came back "no shock." She pressed her fingers to Jason's neck. He had a pulse. But he didn't seem to be breathing. She adjusted his head, pinched his nose, and lifted his jaw to begin rescue breathing.

She wasn't sure how long she'd been doing that, lost in the rhythm and desperation, when all hell broke loose. The elevator dinged, shouting voices and rumbling wheels coming toward her. At the same time the stairwell door burst open. Lark jerked upright in time to see her father come roaring out of the stairwell, the most foolhardy move she'd ever seen him make. He had no weapon, no position, no awareness of his enemy's position—and he paid for it. Isaac made some kind of martial arts move and her father crumpled.

Urgent hands dragged her away from Jason. She was surrounded by navy blue uniforms, but they were all rescue personnel. No cops. Jason lay at her feet, her father ten yards away. And Isaac was escaping.

No, he's not! Lark retrieved the Taser and followed him. She was ending this.

Now.

TWENTY-SEVEN

ISAAC HAD A discouraging head start. By the time Lark got through the stairwell door—adding a precious few seconds hesitating over her father's inert body—the asshole's footsteps echoed two or three floors ahead of her. Lark didn't allow herself to think of the difference as insurmountable. She told herself Isaac was lazy, that he was heavier and slower. And that his motivation was no match for hers.

Tight turns. Fast feet. Use your arms. She coached herself up three flights, hauling against the metal rail, staying on the inside, landing on her toes and immediately pushing harder. Isaac couldn't get out of the stairwell without a keycard on any level but the main lobby.

She was pushing herself so hard she didn't realize at first that the footsteps had stopped. Her subconscious made her stumble on the last steps to the lobby landing, so Isaac's grab for her gave him mostly air. He cursed and whirled for the door. Lark lunged and hit the button on the Taser when he was halfway through. Isaac's momentum carried him out onto the shining tile floor, and into chaos.

The lobby teemed with Hummingbird agents and cops. Voices and radio static echoed against the ceiling and walls, a bombardment of movement and noise. Lark took in the big picture for only a few seconds before it disoriented her and almost sent her sprawling after Isaac. She managed to grab on to the crash bar of the stairwell's fire door.

Isaac belly-crawled a few feet away. Lark didn't know what he thought he was going to do. She took three steps forward and hit the Taser again, this time on the back of his shoulder, and holding the button until the safety shut off the stream.

"Hey!" Two uniformed cops lumbered over, one with his hand on his weapon, the other with his already drawn.

Lark dropped the Taser and threw her hands in the air. "I'm Lark Madrassa, the owner's daughter!" she shouted. "My father and other people are downstairs, hurt, and this man is responsible!"

The officers didn't hesitate. One cuffed Isaac while his partner ordered Lark down to her knees and did the same to her. She didn't fight or protest, knowing they were just doing their jobs, but it about killed her to go along, to let herself be dragged out to a patrol vehicle without knowing her father's or Jason's condition.

They let her stand outside, at least, while a female officer patted her down and started questioning her. Lark answered as patiently as she could, but when uncountable minutes had passed, she couldn't help herself.

"What's going on in there? That's my father. My… friends. Please at least tell me the paramedics are working on them."

Just then the front doors opened and two gurneys were wheeled out, followed by her father walking under his own power but holding an ice pack to his head. As soon as he saw Lark he strode over, gathering her into his arms despite the cuffs holding her arms behind her back.

"Is he alive?" she choked out, her gaze locked on Jason's pale, still face.

"He is. You saved him."

This time, a voice said. It was inevitable that there would be a next time. Lark knew this. She knew if she stayed with Jason, something—either another enemy or a simple virus—would take him down again. He had great strength, but also great vulnerability. But it didn't matter.

It was already too late.

TWENTY-EIGHT

THE FIRST THINGS Jason became aware of were the comforting beep of a heart monitor and the alarming swish of a respirator. He didn't know why he had those reactions to them. He felt floaty, but couldn't open his eyes to see why.

I'm back in the tank. But that couldn't be right. His body was heavy, only his mind floated. A couple of voices murmured nearby, but there was something in his throat. He couldn't ask them what was going on.

Lark.

Then he went back to the black.

When he awoke again, the respirator was gone. His mind was much clearer, already telling him that the steady beeping was receiving signals from the clip on his finger, and his raw throat was a welcome sensation because it meant he was breathing on his own. But halfway through a full indrawn breath, he stopped, registering, finally, the pain.

He groaned and opened his eyes, the brightness of the room hurting almost as much as his chest. But after he'd blinked a few times, he realized it wasn't that bright at all. The overhead lights were off and the curtains at the window pulled, only a soft yellow glow from behind him lighting the room.

Wait a minute. Curtains? The lab didn't have curtains.

Jason turned to the right and found Gabby grinning at him. Her arm was in a sling and she didn't have a lab coat on, but she propped a clipboard against her hip with her free hand and skimmed it through new glasses before beaming at him again.

"Well, mister, I hope you realize you've now used your quota of miracles and three other people's."

"What happened?" he croaked.

Gabby winced and held a small pitcher of water so he could drink through the bent straw. "Sorry about the throat. You were on the respirator for only two days, but it'll take a while for that to ease."

"I remember." Jason shifted in the bed. Nothing seemed to hurt but his torso. "I got hit in the chest."

"Yeah, exactly what I told you *not* to do." Gabby sat in a plastic chair at the side of his bed. "You also got sick. We've been pumping you with antibiotics and fluids, but we didn't want to use anti-inflammatories because the fever is supposed to help your body fight the infection. It seems to have worked." She held her hand to his forehead, even though he knew the monitor above his head told her his temperature as well as pulse and heart rate.

"So my sternum broke, huh?" He shifted again and tightened his mouth around a moan. Sonofabitch, that hurt.

"Yes, and your heart stopped. Lark saved you."

Jason relaxed against the pillows, and he hadn't even been aware of how tense he was, fearing that Gabby was avoiding mentioning Lark because something had happened to her. Her tone was normal, though, so he was free to ask, "Is she okay?"

"Oh, yes. After she saved your life and Matthew

was clocked in the head with that same fire extinguisher—he had a concussion, but he'll be okay—she went after Isaac. You'll have to ask her what went down." She held the pitcher out for him again, and he drank, savoring the coolness against his throat.

The door opened and Matt came in. He smiled when he saw that Jason was awake but stopped to kiss Gabby before settling gingerly in the chair.

"I'll be outside." Gabby wrapped her arm around him and held his head to her chest for a moment, her eyes closed while she pressed her face to his hair. "Don't forget to tell him our news," she murmured before leaving.

"What news?" Jason asked, but Matt shook his head. Slowly. "I hear you got clocked pretty good. You okay?"

"Yeah, I'll live. Man, JT, you have got to stop doing this."

Jason couldn't help smiling. "I know. Everyone's okay?"

"Yeah. Isaac is in custody. He had some big story but no one believes him, there are too many conflicting reports from other people."

"Who?"

"Kolanko." Matt leaned forward and propped his elbows on his knees. The lines on his face seemed deeper, the skin sagging just a little, and Jason had a feeling he knew what was coming at the end of this catch-up session.

"He agreed to come forward, then?"

"Yeah, after we raced off and the cops and stretcher came in, he realized it was more than words on paper. He'll testify if he has to. Nils and Caitlyn are talking, too. They're not willing to go down silently for Kemmerling."

"I don't get that." Jason tried not to frown because his head had started to ache sometime in the last few minutes. "Nils makes sense. He's one of those guys who will do anything if he gets the right kind of attention. But Caitlyn's been your assistant for seven years. What could Kemmerling offer her that would turn her against you?"

Matt shrugged and looked even more desolate. "I don't know. Power, money, love?"

"None of those seem enough."

"Whatever Isaac promised her was, but if she revealed it, no one told me." He leaned back and rubbed his hands up and down his thighs.

Here it comes. Jason braced himself.

"I'm closing Hummingbird."

Whoa. That wasn't what he'd expected, and the words knocked him off his moorings.

"What about the lab?" It wasn't the right question, but Matt understood, anyway.

"All the data is gone. Gabby wasn't trying to unencrypt it for Isaac, she was destroying it. She even did your medical file. You didn't need surgery, so the docs here don't know what happened to you. You know, before. But we did fake your death, so there will be some repercussions for that."

Jason wasn't worried. They could connect it to everything that had happened over the last week, and without proof, no one could act on whatever accusations Isaac made. "What's happening to Kemmerling?"

If Matt realized—and he surely did—that Jason was ignoring his pronouncement, he allowed it. "The charges are complicated, but abduction is in there, as is conspiracy, slander, fraud—enough to put him away for a long time. They're telling me he'll plead guilty—he won't have much choice, with John and Kolanko and Ella added to the witness list."

"They'll all testify?"

Matt nodded and sighed. "Jason."

"I heard you. I'm trying to decide whether or not I should argue." If there was any point.

"It's too big. Too much damage, no matter how we come out of this." Matt sighed and rubbed his hand across his forehead. "I'm going to do private consulting, no government work."

Jason nodded, his throat raw again, but the water pitcher out of his reach. "I think that's a good idea."

"I want you to join me. Be my partner."

It was something Jason had always wanted, something they'd had in reality if not officially. And he was ready for smaller, too. But as much as he yearned to say yes, he wanted something else more.

"I'll think about it," he told his boss, his best friend. "But I don't think I can. As soon as I'm out of here, I'm moving to Boston."

Matt gave him a funny kind of smirk. "We'll talk about it later. There's no rush." He stood and made a move to leave.

Jason couldn't let him, not without putting it all out on the table. "I love her, Matt."

Matt stopped, looked down at him. Gave nothing away.

Jason swallowed and winced at the drag on his

damaged throat. "Now that this is all over, there's nothing—well, there's only you standing in our way." He hoped. Maybe Lark wasn't here because she couldn't handle this. She might be getting a cool brush-off ready. Jason didn't care. He'd do anything to convince her being together was worth the risk.

"Nope, you were right the first time." Matt smiled. "There's nothing standing in your way."

Intense relief swept away the pain. Well, half of it, anyway. "Thanks." He lifted his hand, and Matt clasped it tightly before he turned and started for the door. Now all he needed was Lark. But then he remembered.

"Hey," he called. "What's the news Gabby mentioned?"

"Oh, yeah." Matt came back to the bed and looked down at Jason again, his mouth twitching. "Will you be my best man?"

Jason's wide grin intensified the throbbing in his head as he reached to shake his friend's hand again. "Damn. Good for you, man. I can't believe you did it."

"I'm not rushing into anything. We set a date for six months from now. I told Gabby I want her to have time to change her mind once she gets to know the day-to-day me. The one who's not struggling to save his best friend and his business or rescuing her from an evil mastermind." But the lines that Jason had noticed just moments ago had faded. There was a sparkle in his eyes that hadn't been there since his wife died. Only one thing would make Jason happier than his friend being in love.

And then she was there. Lark peered through a two-inch crack she'd made with the door. Barely enough space for Jason to see through, never mind identify the person on the other side, but he knew it was her, and he craved her with every damaged and repaired fiber of his being.

"Your turn." Matt gave him a light tap on the shoulder and headed out, holding the door for his daughter and giving her a one-armed hug as he passed. "We'll talk later."

"Yeah," Jason agreed, but his attention was all on Lark, the only one of them who seemed unharmed. "You okay?"

"Fine." She looked sheepish as she took her turn in the ugly chair. "Not a scratch."

"But Gabby said you went after Isaac."

"I did." She tucked a piece of hair behind her ear and slipped her other hand through the bedrail to touch his. "He tripped. I Tasered him with Nils's Taser and it was all over. Well, except for convincing the police to arrest him for trespassing and assault. But it was easy." She drew in a breath and blew it out, her hand tightening around his fingers. "Seeing you go down? Not so easy."

Jason suspected she was glossing over the details, but let it go for now. Not important. "Gabby says you saved me." He tightened his fingers in hers, emotion swamping him as he considered what it had to be like, watching him almost die.

She shrugged. "It was a team effort. How are you feeling?"

"Horrible," he admitted.

She chuckled. "Sorry. Stupid question."

"It's okay. I'll be fine. Gabby says, and she's the best."

"Yeah." Her face lit up. "Did they tell you?"

He nodded. "You okay with that?"

She laughed. "It seems so long ago I hated even the idea of her having a crush on him. Now I'm maid of honor in their wedding." She sobered. "Did Dad also ask you about the partnership?"

"Yes, but I told him no."

She looked shocked and started to pull away. "No!"

He held on. "I want to move to Boston, Lark. I'm changing my priorities."

She glowered. "Well, that would be a stupid way to do it."

Jason had thought a cracked sternum hurt. The pain of her rejection kept him from speaking for a moment. He almost nodded, almost accepted it. Even if he took heroic precautions to keep from getting sick or injured again, the specter would always loom over them. She'd had to wait two days to be sure he wasn't going to die like her mother had. The danger wasn't past, never would be. He'd always be at risk, even if he didn't partner with her father.

But if he didn't have Lark, he couldn't work with Matt. A long, lonely life without his best friend or the woman he loved loomed ahead of him.

Fuck that. Maybe he'd never be able to convince her, but he had to try. He loved her, and that made all the risks acceptable.

Assuming she loved him back. He finally managed, "Did I misinterpret what you said the other night?"

"No. Oh, no, honey." She stroked his arm, and the pain eased. "No, I meant—well, I got fired. I never reported for work."

Jason cursed, but Lark shook her head. "I think I want to do something else." She was quiet for a moment, her thoughts turned inward. Jason watched her, unable to keep the fear from growing. Every muscle tensed, doubling his pain, but he didn't push her, didn't want to rush the letdown that seemed more inevitable with every throbbing second that passed.

Lark visibly pulled herself back to the present and straightened. Her soft gaze landed on his face, and her lips curved. "I've already got some résumés in around town. You wouldn't be happy working for someone else, and I'd feel much better if my father had your back. And vice versa."

Everything clicked into place, and Jason could breathe again. He let go of her hand and reached for her. "Come here."

"I'll hurt you," she protested, but didn't move away.

He caught the back of her neck and tugged her toward him. "Just don't support yourself on my chest."

"I love you," Lark whispered, grabbing the rail to hold herself up as he drew her in for a kiss.

"I love you, too." He kissed her for a long time, trying to convey his gratitude and appreciation and happiness when he couldn't move anything but his mouth without his body screaming at him. But she got it. Oh, yeah, she got it. He could see it mirrored in her eyes when she finally pulled away.

"How does a double wedding sound?" he asked.

Lark shook her head, but kissed him again, reassuringly. "We don't have to rush this," she told him, staying close. "Let's just live together and find our own time, okay?"

Jason nodded and lay back, sighing. A week ago he

had thought he was starting a new life, reborn from the broken remains of the old one.

Now, he finally was.

* * * * *